ALSO BY HARUKI MURAKAMI

FICTION

IQ84

After Dark

After the Quake

Blind Willow, Sleeping Woman

Colorless Tsukuru Tazaki and His Years of Pilgrimage

Dance Dance Dance

The Elephant Vanishes

First Person Singular

Hard-Boiled Wonderland and the End of the World

Kafka on the Shore

Killing Commendatore

Norwegian Wood

South of the Border, West of the Sun

Sputnik Sweetheart

The Strange Library

A Wild Sheep Chase

Wind/Pinball

The Wind-Up Bird Chronicle

NONFICTION

Absolutely on Music (with Seiji Ozawa)

Novelist as a Vocation

Underground: The Tokyo Gas Attack and the Japanese Psyche

What I Talk About When I Talk About Running: A Memoir

Murakami T

THE CITY AND ITS

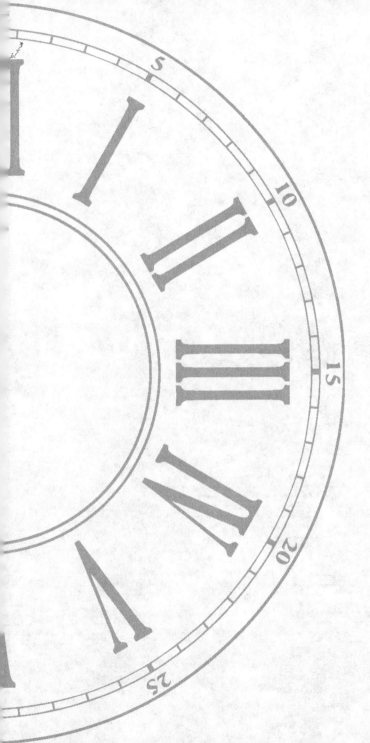

UNCERTAIN WALLS

HARUKI

THE CITY
AND ITS

MURAKAMI

Translated from the Japanese
by Philip Gabriel

UNCERTAIN WALLS

Alfred A. Knopf ⊐Γ New York 2024

THIS IS A BORZOI BOOK
PUBLISHED BY ALFRED A. KNOPF

www.aaknopf.com

Knopf, Borzoi Books, and the
colophon are registered trademarks
of Penguin Random House LLC.

Library of Congress Cataloging-in-Publication Data
Names: Murakami, Haruki, [date] author. |
Gabriel, Philip, [date] translator.
Title: The city and its uncertain walls / Haruki Murakami ;
translated from the Japanese by Philip Gabriel.
Other titles: Machi to sono futashika na kabe. English
Description: First edition. | New York :
Alfred A. Knopf, 2024. | "This is a Borzoi
book published by Alfred A. Knopf." |
Identifiers: LCCN 2024017338 |
ISBN 9780593801970 (hardcover) |
ISBN 9780593687840 (trade paperback) |
ISBN 9780593801987 (ebook)
Subjects: LCGFT: Novels.
Classification: LCC PL856.U673 M3313 2024 |
DDC 895.63/5—dc23/eng/20240531
LC record available at https://lccn.loc.gov/2024017338

Jacket art direction and design by Chip Kidd
Jacket and interior illustration by Eric Baker

Manufactured in the United States of America
First United States Edition

Where Alph, the sacred river, ran
Through caverns measureless to man
Down to a sunless sea.
—Samuel Taylor Coleridge,
Kubla Khan

PART ONE

PART ONE

YOU WERE THE ONE who told me about the town.

On that summer evening we were heading up the river, the sweet fragrance of grass wafting over us. We passed over several little weirs that held back the flowing sand, stopping from time to time to gaze at the delicate silvery fish wriggling in the pools. We had both been barefoot for a while. The cold water washed over our ankles, while the fine sand at the bottom of the river enveloped our feet like the soft clouds in a dream. I was seventeen, and you were a year younger.

You'd stuck your flat red sandals in your yellow plastic shoulder bag and were walking from one sandbank to the next, just ahead of me. Blades of grass were pasted to your wet calves, wonderful green punctuation marks. I was carrying my worn-out white sneakers, one in each hand.

Perhaps tired of walking, you plunked yourself down on the summer grass, wordlessly gazing up at the sky. With a screech a pair of small birds flashed across the sky. In the silence that followed, a hint of bluish twilight began to entwine itself around us. As I sat down beside you, I had an odd feeling, as if thousands of invisible threads were finely tying your body to my heart. The minute movement of your eyelids and the slight flutter of your lips were enough to stir my heart.

At that time neither you nor I had names. The radiant feelings of a seventeen-year-old and a sixteen-year-old on the grass of a riverbank, in the summer twilight, were the only things that mattered. Stars would soon be twinkling above us, and they had no names either. The two of us sat there, side by side, on the riverbank of a nameless world.

"There's a high wall surrounding the whole town," you began, drawing out the words from the deep silence, like a diver scouring the seabed for pearls. "It's not that big a town, but it's not small enough to absorb in a single glance either."

This was the second time you'd talked about the town. And now the town had a high wall around it.

As you spoke, the town revealed a single lovely river and three stone bridges (the East Bridge, Old Bridge, and West Bridge), a library and a watchtower, an abandoned foundry and communal housing. In the faint light as twilight drew near, we sat shoulder to shoulder, gazing at that town. At times we were on a far-off hill, our eyes narrowed; at other times, the town was so close that we could reach out and touch it, with our eyes wide open.

"The *real* me lives there, in that town surrounded by a wall," you said.

"So the you that is sitting here next to me isn't the real you?" I had to ask.

"That's right. The me here with you now isn't the real me. It's only a stand-in. Like a wandering shadow."

I thought it over. *A wandering shadow?* But I kept my opinions to myself.

"Okay, so in that town what is the *real* you doing?"

"Working in a library," you replied in a quiet voice. "I work from around five in the evening until around ten at night."

"Around?"

"All time there is *approximate*. There's a tall clock tower in the square, but the clock doesn't have any hands."

I pictured a clock tower without hands. "So can anyone come into that library?"

"No. Not everyone can enter. You need special qualifications to do that. But *you* can. Since you have those."

"What do you mean by . . . *special qualifications?*"

You smiled gently but didn't answer the question.

"So as long as I go there, I can meet the *real* you?"

"As long as you can find that town. And as long as—"

You fell silent, your cheeks reddening a bit. But I could understand the words that you didn't say.

As long as you really are seeking the real *me.* These were the words you didn't venture to say.

I gently wrapped an arm around you. You had on a light green sleeveless dress. Your cheek rested against my shoulder. But on that twilit summer evening, the you I held wasn't the real you. As you said, it was a mere stand-in, a shadow.

The real you was in a town surrounded by a high wall. In a town with willows on lovely sandbanks, with a few small hills, and quiet beasts each with a single horn. People lived in old communal housing, living plain but perfectly adequate lives. The beasts ate the leaves and nuts from the trees, though most of them passed away in the long, snowy winters, the cold and hunger overcoming them.

How I longed to go into the town. Longed to meet the *real* you.

"The town is surrounded by a high wall so it's very hard to enter," you said. "And going out is even harder."

"So how can you go inside?"

"You just need to wish your way in. But truly wishing for something, from the heart, isn't that simple. It might take time. In the meanwhile, you might have to give up all sorts of things. Things that you treasure. But don't give up, no matter how long it takes. The town isn't going anywhere."

I imagined meeting the real you in that town. I pictured it all: the beautiful expanse of apple trees outside the town, the three stone bridges spanning the river, the cries of the invisible night birds. The small old library where the *real* you worked.

"There's always a place ready for you there," you said.

"A place for me?"

"Yes. There's only one position open in the town. And you are to fill it."

What position could that be?

"You'll become a *Dream Reader*," you say in a low voice. As if revealing a crucial secret.

I couldn't help but laugh. "You know, I can't even remember my own dreams. It would be hard for someone like that to become a Dream Reader."

"No, a Dream Reader doesn't need to have his own dreams. All you need to do is read all the old dreams collected on the shelves of the library."

"Do you think I can?"

You nod. "Yes, you can do it. You have the qualifications. And the *me that's there* will help you do the work. I'll be right beside you, every night."

"So I'd be a Dream Reader, and every night I'd read old dreams on the shelves of the library. And you would always be with me. The *real* you," I said, repeating aloud the facts given me.

Your bare, slender shoulders under the straps of the green dress trembled under my arm. And then stiffened.

"That's right. But there's one thing I want you to remember. That even if I do meet you in that town, I won't remember anything about you."

Why?

"You really don't know why?"

I know. The person whose shoulder my arm is gently around here is a mere stand-in. The *real* you lives in that town. That mysterious, far-off town surrounded by a high wall.

Your shoulder under my arm was so soft and warm that it was hard to think of it as anything other than that of the *real* you.

IN THIS REAL WORLD, you and I lived not so far from each other. Not far away, but not so close that we could drop by whenever we wanted. To get to your place took me an hour and a half, changing trains twice along the way. Neither of the towns we lived in was surrounded by a high wall, so of course we could come and go freely.

I lived in a quiet residential area near the sea, while you lived downtown in a much larger, livelier city. That summer I was in my third and final year of high school, and you were in your second year. I went to a local public high school, and you attended a private girls' school in your city. For various reasons, we couldn't see each other more than once or twice a month. We'd take turns—I'd visit your town, then next time, you would come to the town where I lived. We'd walk to a small park near your home, or to a public botanical garden. The botanical garden charged an admissions fee, but next to the greenhouses was a nice little café that was never crowded and it became our favorite spot. We'd order coffee and apple tarts (a bit of a luxury for us) and lose ourselves in quiet conversation.

Whenever you came to my town, we'd walk along the riverside or the sea. There was no river near the downtown area where you lived, and no sea either, of course, and when you came to my town, it was the first thing you wanted to see. You were drawn to all that natural water.

"Somehow seeing water always soothes me," you said. "I love the sound it makes."

I'd met you the previous fall, and we had been going out for eight months. Whenever we saw each other, we'd find some out-of-the-way place to hug and kiss. We never went beyond that, though. We didn't have enough time to spare, first of all, nor a private place to take our relationship to the next level. But more than that, we were so wrapped up in talking that we were reluctant to take any time away from our conversations. Neither of us had ever met anyone we could talk to so freely about our feelings, our thoughts. It was close to a miracle to run across someone like that. So once or twice a month, we'd talk on and on, oblivious of the time. We never ran out of things to say, and when we said good-bye at the station, I always felt there was something else, something vital, that we'd forgotten to discuss.

I'm not saying I didn't have any physical desire for you. Take a healthy seventeen-year-old boy being with a sixteen-year-old girl whose chest was swelling out beautifully, and put his arms around her lithe young body—how could sexual desire not be part of the mix? But instinctively I knew it was better to put those feelings on hold. What I needed now was to see you once or twice a month, take long walks together, and open up to each other about all kinds of things. An intimate exchange of information, getting to know each other more deeply. Then, in the shade of a tree, hugging and kissing—this was so wonderful that I didn't want to rush into anything else. If we did, something crucial about our relationship might be lost forever, something we might never regain. The physical could come later, down the road. That's what I thought. Or maybe intuition told me.

So what did we talk about, huddled together? I can't remember now. We spoke of so many things that I can no longer recall each one. But I do know this—once you began talking about that odd town surrounded by a high wall, it became our main topic of conversation.

Mainly you talked about how the town was laid out. I would ask practical questions and you would answer them, and as we did, the details of the town began to form and were transcribed. You were the one who created the town. Or maybe it was there, inside you, already. But when it came to putting the pieces together so you could visualize it, so you could describe it in words, I do think I played a role as well. You talked about it, and I wrote it all down. Like ancient philosophers and religious figures who had a faithful, meticulous scribe, or disciples, perhaps, at their side taking down their every word. I noted it all down in a special little notebook just for that purpose, the ever-competent secretary, or faithful disciple. That summer, the two of us were completely engrossed in this collaborative project of ours.

IN AUTUMN, in anticipation of the oncoming cold season, the beasts' bodies were covered with a shiny, golden coat of fur. The single horns in their foreheads were sharp and white. They washed their hooves in the waters of the icy river, gently lifting their heads to enjoy the red nuts on the trees, and chew on the leaves of the Scotch broom.

That was a lovely time of year.

Standing on the watchtower built alongside the wall, I waited for the instrument—fashioned from a unicorn horn—to blow at twilight. Moments before the sun set the horn would sound— one long note, followed by three short ones. That was the rule. In the gathering dusk, the gentle sound of the horn slipped over the cobbled road, seemingly unchanged for over hundreds of years (or maybe even longer). And that sound had seeped into the gaps in the stone walls around the houses, and into the stone statues along the hedge in the plaza.

When the horn sounded out in the town, the beasts lifted their heads up toward ancient memories. Some stopped chewing leaves, some stopped pawing the road with their hooves, others awoke from naps in the last sunny spots of the day, all of them with heads raised at the same angle.

For a moment they all were frozen, like statues. Only their soft golden fur swayed in the breeze. But what were they gazing at? Their heads tilted in one direction, their eyes stared into space, but the beasts remained motionless, listening intently to the sounding of the horn.

When the final blow of the horn had faded away into the air, some scrambled to their feet, lining up their front legs, while others stretched and straightened up, and they all began walking at nearly the same moment. It was as if they had been released from a spell. Soon, the streets of the town clattered with the hooves of the beasts.

The line of beasts continued down the winding cobblestone street, with no obvious leader, with no one guiding them along.

Eyes downcast, shoulders swaying slightly, they continued down to the silent river. Despite the silence, each beast was obviously connected by an undeniable bond.

As I watched this scene many times, I came to understand how precisely they kept to the same path and speed. Picking up other beasts along the way, they continued over the arched Old Bridge, to the plaza with its sharp steeple (where the clock in the clock tower, as you had said, was missing both hands). A small group that had gone down to the sandbank by the river to eat green grass now joined them. They continued upstream on the path beside the river, through the factory district alongside the dried-up canal that stretched out toward the north, and added another group that had been in the woods in search of nuts on trees. They next turned to the west, along the covered passageway of the foundry, climbing the long staircase traversing a hill on the north.

There was but one gate in the wall surrounding the town. Opening and closing it was the job of the Gatekeeper. The gate, heavy and solid, was reinforced with thick iron slabs nailed vertically and horizontally to it. Despite the gate's formidable appearance, the Gatekeeper was able to easily open and close it. No one else was allowed to lay a finger on it.

The Gatekeeper was a large, sturdy man, devoted to his work. His pointy head was shaved clean, as was his face. Every morning he'd boil water in a large cauldron and carefully shave his head and face with a large, sharp razor. His age was unclear. He was also responsible for blowing the horn every morning and evening to assemble the beasts. He would climb up a six-and-a-half-foot-tall tower in front of his Gatekeeper's cabin, aim the horn at the sky, and blow. How could such a crude, coarse-looking man produce such a soft, charming sound? I found this strange every time I heard it.

At twilight, once he'd shepherded every last beast outside the wall, he would close the heavy gate and lock it with a huge padlock. It clanged shut with a cold, metallic sound.

There was a place for the beasts just outside the north gate. There they would sleep, mate, give birth. This place had a forest and thickets, and a stream, and all of this, too, was walled in. It was a low wall, just a little over three feet, but for some reason the beasts couldn't get over it. Or they didn't try.

On either side of the gate, the wall had six watchtowers, with old, spiral wooden staircases that anyone could climb. From the top, you could see everything that the beasts were doing. But usually no one climbed the stairs. The residents of the town seemed to have little interest in the lives of the beasts.

For one week in the beginning of spring, though, people would climb the watchtowers to see the beasts do battle. Then the beasts were unimaginably aggressive and wild, with the males forgoing food in a desperate fight to win over the females. They'd bellow, and aim their sharp, single horns at their opponents' neck and stomach.

It was only during that one-week mating season that the beasts did not enter the town, since the Gatekeeper kept the gate tightly locked then to protect the townspeople from danger. (And consequently, no horn sounded in the morning and night.) More than a few of the beasts were gravely wounded in the fights, some even dying from their injuries. And from the red blood that flowed onto the ground sprung a new order and new life. Like new buds that appear all at once on green willow branches in spring.

The beasts lived in a special cycle and order unknowable to us. Everything they did repeated in an orderly way, an order atoned for with their very blood. Once that violent week came to an end, when the gentle April rains washed away the blood, the beasts became tranquil, gentle creatures once more.

I've never witnessed that scene with my own eyes, however. I just heard about it from you.

The beasts in autumn squatted down here and there, their golden fur glistening in the evening sun, silently awaiting the echoes of the horn to be absorbed into the air. There were probably at least a thousand beasts.

And so another day in the town drew to a close. The days passed, the seasons changed. Yet days and seasons are but temporary things. The real time of the town is found elsewhere.

YOU AND I NEVER VISITED each other's homes. We never met each other's families, never introduced our friends. We didn't want anyone in this world to bother us. We were satisfied with a world for just the two of us and didn't want anyone else to be a part of our relationship. Practically speaking, too, we also had no time to spare. As I mentioned before, we had so many things to talk about, and only limited time to do so.

You said almost nothing about your own family. All I knew were a few small details. Your father had worked as a local public servant, but when you were eleven, through some misconduct on his part he was forced to resign and now worked in the office of a private cram school. What this *misconduct* was all about, I had no idea, but it seemed like something you didn't want to talk about. Your birth mother had died of cancer when you were three, and you had almost no memories of her. You couldn't even recall what she looked like. When you were five your father remarried, and the next year your little sister was born. So your present mother was actually your stepmother, though once you happened to say something that suggested you felt a bit closer to your stepmother than to your father. A throwaway comment in tiny print in the corner of a book's page. Regarding your half sister, who was six years younger, you said little, only, "She's allergic to cat fur, so we don't have any cats." That's all.

When you were a child, the only person you truly felt close to was your maternal grandmother. Whenever you had a chance, you'd take the train by yourself to your grandmother's house in the neighboring ward. On school holidays you'd even stay over for a few days. Your grandmother loved you unconditionally and would even buy you little presents from her meager income. But every time you went to visit your grandmother, the expression on your stepmother's face made it clear how dissatisfied she was, and though she never came out and said anything, you visited your grandmother less and less. And several years ago, your grand-mother suddenly passed away from heart disease.

You explained these things to me in bits and pieces. Like find-ing a ragged item in an old coat pocket.

One other thing I remember clearly even now is that whenever you spoke about your family you stared, for some reason, at your palms. As if in order to follow the thread of the story, you needed to carefully decipher something written there.

As for me, there was very little I felt I needed to tell you about my family. My parents were just your average, everyday kind of parents. My father worked in a pharmaceutical company, and my mother was a full-time housewife. They did things like ordinary, run-of-the-mill parents, and talked like ordinary, run-of-the-mill parents. We had a pet, an elderly black cat. There wasn't anything notable about my life at school, either. My grades weren't so bad, though not good enough that anyone would notice. The one place at school I could really feel relaxed in was the school library. I loved to read books there and to spend time daydreaming. Most of the books I wanted to read could be found there.

I clearly recall the day I first met you. There was an awards cer-emony for a high school essay contest. The top five recipients were invited to the ceremony. I was in third place and you were in fourth, so we were seated beside each other. It was in the fall. I was in my second year of high school and you were in your first. The ceremony was completely boring, so during the lulls, the two of us exchanged a few words in low voices. You wore a navy-blue blazer and a matching navy-blue pleated skirt. A white blouse with a ribbon, white socks, and black slip-on shoes. Your socks were pure white, your shiny shoes perfectly polished, like seven kindly dwarves had neatly buffed them at dawn.

I wasn't a great writer. I'd loved reading since I was a kid and would pick up a book whenever I had a spare moment, but I don't think I had any literary talent. But all of us in Japanese class were forced to write an essay for the contest. And mine was chosen from all of these, sent to the selection committee, made it to the finals, and unexpectedly was awarded one of the top prizes. Honestly, I couldn't fathom what was so good about what I'd written. When I reread it, it struck me as worthless, mediocre. But some of the judges thought it was worth a prize so it must have had something going for it. My teacher, a woman, was ecstatic that I got a prize. This was the first time in my life that any teacher had been so pleased with anything I'd done. So I kept my opinions to myself and gratefully accepted the prize.

The essay contest was held every fall, district-wide, and each year they assigned a different theme. The theme that year was "My Friend." We had to write five pages by hand, and sadly I didn't have a single friend I could write that much about, so I wrote about our family cat. I tried to convey how that old female cat and I got along, our life together, how we expressed our feelings to each other—though there were limits to this, of course. My cat was clever, with her own personality, and I had a lot of things to say about it. I guess there must have been a few cat lovers among the judges. People who love cats naturally like other cat lovers.

You wrote about your maternal grandmother. About the reciprocal feelings between a lonely elderly woman and a lonely young girl. And about the subtle, true values that arose from this relationship. The essay was charming and moving. A hundred times better than the one I wrote. I couldn't understand why mine got third place, while yours got fourth. And I told you that honestly. You grinned and said you thought the opposite. What you wrote, you said, was so much better than mine. Really, you added. No lie.

"Your family's cat seems wonderful."

"Yep, she is very clever," I said.

You smiled at that.

"Do you have a cat?" I asked.

You shook your head. "My younger sister's allergic to cat fur."

That was the first tidbit of personal information I got about you. *Her younger sister is allergic to cat fur.*

You were a beautiful young girl. To my eyes, at least. Petite, with a sort of roundish face and slim, lovely fingers. Your hair was short, with neatly trimmed black bangs on your forehead. Like careful, scrupulously drawn shading. Your nose was straight and small, your eyes quite large. By most standards, the balance between the size of your nose and your eyes was off-kilter, but for some reason that imbalance attracted me. Your light pink lips were small and thin, always properly closed. As if some vital secrets were hidden deep inside.

The five of us award recipients climbed up onstage in order and were ceremoniously presented with certificates and commemorative medals. The tall girl who won first prize gave a short speech. We were also presented with fountain pens. (The fountain pen company sponsored the contest. The pen remained my favorite for years.)

Just before the tedious, boring ceremony ended, I jotted down my name and address in my memo pad, ripped out the page, and surreptitiously passed it to you.

"I was hoping maybe you could write me a letter sometime?" I whispered, my voice dry.

Normally I'd never be so bold. I was basically a shy person (and timid, too, of course). But the thought that we'd say good-bye there and never see each other again felt like a huge mistake, totally unfair. So I gathered my courage and plunged ahead.

Looking a bit surprised, you took the piece of paper, folded it twice, and stowed it away in the breast pocket of your blazer. On top of the gentle, mysterious slope of your chest. You brought a hand to your bangs and blushed slightly.

"I'd like to read more of what you write," I said, sounding like someone giving an awkward excuse, after opening the wrong door.

"I'd like to read the letters you write, too," you said, nodding a few times. As if encouraging me.

Your letter arrived a week later. It was amazing. I must have read it at least twenty times. Then I sat down at my desk and, using the pen I'd received as a prize, wrote a long reply. This is how we began writing to each other, and how our friendship began.

Were we boyfriend and girlfriend? Was it okay to easily label us that? I don't know. But at least during that period, for nearly a year, our hearts were purely one, unsullied by anything beyond. And we went on to create and share a special, secret world of our own—a strange town surrounded by a high wall.

I FIRST OPENED THE DOOR to that building three days after I came to the town, in the evening.

The building was undistinguished, made from old stone. If you walked toward the east for a while, along the road that ran parallel to the river, past the central plaza that faced the Old Bridge, there it was. There was no sign at the entrance that identified it as the library. There was just a brass plate with the number 16 engraved on it, somewhat carelessly attached. The plate was discolored and hard to read.

The heavy wooden door creaked as it opened inward, where there was a dimly lit square room. No one was in sight. The ceiling was high, the lamps on the wall shone only a faint light, and the air gave off an odor like someone's dried sweat. The dimness made everything seem a bit hazy, as though it had broken down into molecules and were about to be sucked away somewhere. The worn-down cedar floorboards creaked sharply here and there as I walked. There were two vertical windows, and not a single item of furniture.

At the far end of the room was a door. A simple wooden door, with a small, frosted glass window at eye level. The number 16 was written there, too, in old-fashioned, decorative script. There was a faint light that came through the glass. I knocked twice, lightly, on the door and waited, but there was no response, no sound of footsteps. I waited a beat, calmed my breathing, then turned the discolored brass knob and softly pushed the door open. The door squeaked, as if warning that someone had come.

Inside was another squarish room, about sixteen feet per side. The ceiling wasn't as high as the first room. And no one was there, either. There were no windows, just plaster walls. No paintings or photographs or posters or calendars, and, of course, no clock, just blank, smooth walls. There was one rough wooden bench, two small chairs, a table, and a wooden coatrack. With no coats hanging from it. In the middle of the room was a rusty old-fashioned woodstove, a fire burning inside, and a large black kettle sat on top puffing out steam. In the rear of the room was what looked like a library checkout counter, with an open ledger. As if some urgent matter had called whoever it was away in the middle of work. No doubt before long that person (a library staff member, undoubtedly) would return.

Behind the counter was a dark-colored door that must have led to the stacks. Which meant that, indeed, this was a *library*. Not a single book in sight, yet the overall appearance was very much that of a library. Big or small, old or new, libraries around the world all had that specific look.

I took off my heavy coat, hung it on the coatrack, sat down on the hard wooden bench, and warmed my hands at the stove, waiting for someone to make an appearance. There was no sound whatever, only a silence, like being at the bottom of the sea. I tried clearing my throat once, but it didn't sound like a throat clearing.

It was about fifteen minutes later that you opened the door from the stacks and emerged. (Probably about that long. There wasn't a clock, so I wasn't sure of the exact time.) You looked over at me on the bench and stiffened for a second, taken aback, your eyes wide. You took a long, slow breath and then said, "Sorry to have kept you waiting. I had no idea that anyone had come."

I didn't know how to respond, so I kept quiet and just nodded a couple of times. Your voice didn't sound like your voice. It was different from what I remembered. Or maybe every sound and voice in this room took on a different tone.

The lid of the kettle suddenly began rattling and trembled slightly, like an animal just waking up.

"And—how may I help you?" you asked.

What I'm after is old dreams.

"Old dreams, is it?" you said, your small, thin lips pressed in a straight line as you gazed at me. Naturally, you didn't remember me.

"As you know, though," you said, "only a Dream Reader is allowed to touch old dreams."

I silently removed my thick green glasses, pushed up my eyelids, and showed you my eyes. Unmistakably the eyes of a Dream Reader. I couldn't go outside in the bright light during the day.

"Alright. You are qualified," you said, and glanced down. My eyes probably disturbed you. But that's the way it was. To enter the town, I had to have my eyes altered.

"Will you start work today?" you asked.

I nodded. "I don't know how well I'm able to read dreams, but I have to slowly get used to it."

Still there was not a sound in the room. The kettle, too, remained silent. You excused yourself and went back to writing in the ledger, and quickly finished up. I sat on the bench, watching you. Outwardly you hadn't changed. You looked the same as you did back in that summer twilit evening. I remembered the bright red sandals you wore then. And the grasshopper that had suddenly buzzed from a nearby clump of grass.

"Haven't I seen you before somewhere?" I had to ask, knowing it was pointless.

You looked up from the ledger and gazed at me for a while, your pencil in your left hand. (That's true—you're left-handed. In this town, and in a town that isn't this one.) You shook your head.

"No, I don't believe I've ever met you before," you answered. I think you spoke so politely because, though you were still sixteen, I was no longer seventeen. For you I was now a grown man, far older than you. It couldn't be helped, yet the passage of time pained me.

You finished recording your work in the ledger, shut it, stowed it away on the shelf behind you, and began to make some herbal tea especially for me. You picked up the kettle on the stove and carefully mixed the hot water and the crushed herbs, making thick, greenish tea. You poured this into a largish ceramic cup and placed it before me. This was a special drink made for a Dream Reader, and preparing it was one of your tasks.

I slowly sipped the herbal tea. It had a thick, distinctively bitter taste and wasn't easy to get down. But the nutrients in it would heal my wounded eyes and calm me. A special drink for those purposes. You watched me from behind your desk. You must have been concerned whether I'd like the herbal tea you'd made for me. I looked at you and gave a small nod of approval. To say, *It's fine.* And a smile of relief came over you. I'd missed that smile so very much. I hadn't seen it in a long while.

The room was warm and still. Even without a clock, time soundlessly passed. Like a slender cat stealthily making its way along the top of a wall.

WE DIDN'T EXCHANGE LETTERS all that often. About once every two weeks or so. Yet each one was lengthy. The letters you wrote were generally longer than mine. Not that the length mattered.

I still have every letter you wrote, but I didn't make copies of the ones I sent, so I can't recall exactly what I wrote. Nothing earth-shattering, I'm sure. Just daily life and little things that took place. I wrote about books I'd read, music I'd listened to, movies I'd seen. I wrote about things that took place at school, too. I was on the swim team (circumstances beyond my control made me join, and I wasn't at all what you would call an eager member), and I think I wrote about our practices. When I knew you were the one reading it, the words just flowed. It was strange how natural it felt to open up about my thoughts, my feelings. It was the first time in my life I could write like that, the words gushing out. As I said, I'd always thought that writing wasn't my forte. You're the one who drew out that hidden ability in me. You always enjoyed the scraps of humor in my writing. That's what was missing most from my life, you told me.

"Like a vitamin or something?" I asked.

"Like a vitamin or something," you said, nodding hard.

I was so taken by you, I thought of nothing else when awake. You haunted my dreams, as well. In my letters, though, I tried to keep that in check, not opening up about my feelings. I confined myself to actual, tangible things. Back then I wanted to cling to a tangible world, things I could actually touch—with a bit of humor thrown in, if I could. If I wrote about the inner workings of my heart—about affection or love—I felt like I'd be driven into a dead end.

Your letters took the opposite approach and were less about actual things around you and more about your inner life. Or dreams you had, or short fictional pieces. What's stayed with me most were several dreams you described. You often had long, involved dreams, and could clearly recall the details, as if remembering actual events. I found this incredible. I hardly ever dreamed, and even when I did, the content eluded me, my dreams falling to pieces, scattering the moment I woke up. Even if a particularly vivid dream made me bolt awake in the middle of the night (not that this happened much), I'd fall asleep again right away and, come morning, couldn't remember a thing.

When I told you this you said, "I keep a notebook and pencil at my bedside, and as soon as I wake up, I write down my dreams. Even when I'm busy and pressed for time. When I have really intense dreams in the middle of the night and wake up, I fight the urge to fall asleep and instead I write them down in as much detail as I can. Since most of those are really important dreams and teach me a lot of important things."

"A lot of important things?" I asked.

"About the me I don't know about," you replied.

For you, dreams were almost on the same level as events in the real world, not something that you'd easily forget or something that would vanish so easily. Dreams were like a crucial water source nurturing your heart, conveying something vital.

"It takes practice. If you put in the effort, you should be able to recall your dreams, too, down to the details. You should give it a try. I really want to know what kind of dreams you have."

Okay, I said. I'll give it a go.

Despite my efforts (though I didn't go so far as keeping a pencil and notebook next to my bed), I couldn't work up any interest in my dreams. They were all so vague and incoherent, too hard to fathom. The words spoken there were unclear, the scenes incoherent. And sometimes the content was ominous, nothing I could tell anyone else. I much preferred hearing about your long, colorful dreams.

You said I sometimes appeared in your dreams. That made me happy, to think I could be a part of your inner world. And it seemed to please you, too, that I'd be in your dreams. Most of the time, though, I didn't play a major role, but was more like a supporting character in a drama.

Did you ever have the kind of explicit dreams I did? Ones you'd find hard to talk about in front of me, the kind I often had (where I'd wind up soiling my underwear)? Were you totally open and honest with me about your dreams? As I listened to you talk about them, I wondered.

You seemed to always talk very openly about all kinds of things. But no one knows for sure, actually. I think everyone in the world has secrets. They're necessary for people to survive in *this world*.

Wouldn't you agree?

"IF THERE'S ANYTHING PERFECT in this world, it would be this wall. No one can climb over it. And no one can destroy it," the Gatekeeper declared.

At first glance the wall just looked like some old brick structure that could easily topple over in the next strong storm or earthquake. Perfect? How can you say that? When I voiced my concern, the Gatekeeper reacted like I'd just insulted his family. He grabbed me by the elbow and dragged me over to the wall.

"Look at it up close. There are no joints between the bricks. And each brick is shaped slightly differently from the others. Yet they fit together so perfectly, you couldn't get a single hair between them."

And he was right.

"Try scratching a brick with this knife." The Gatekeeper took out a work knife from his coat pocket, snapped open the blade with a click, and passed it to me. The knife looked old, but the blade had been meticulously sharpened. "You won't be able to scratch it at all."

And he was right. The tip of the knife made a dry scratching sound, but didn't make a single white line on the brick.

"You see? Storms and earthquakes and cannons—nothing can wreck this wall. Or even damage it. Nothing has up until now, and nothing ever will."

As if posing for a commemorative photo, he rested a palm against the wall, tucked his chin in, and gazed proudly at me.

No, I said silently to myself, there's nothing in this world that's perfect. If it has shape and form, it's got to have a weak point, a blind spot. But I didn't say this out loud.

"Who made this wall?" I asked.

"Nobody made it," said the Gatekeeper, with unshakable conviction. "It was always here, from the very beginning."

At the end of the first week, I picked up several of the old dreams you'd selected and tried reading them. But I couldn't decipher a single intelligible thing. All I heard was an uncertain murmuring. And all I saw were a few unfocused, fragmentary images, like snippets of tape or film randomly spliced together and played backward.

Instead of books, the stacks in the library were full of countless old dreams. Covered with a thin layer of white dust, none of them seemed to have been touched for ages. The old dreams were egg shaped, in all different sizes and colors, like eggs laid by a variety of animals. Not exactly egg shaped, actually. When I took them in my hand and examined them closely, I saw that the bottom half swelled out more than the top half. The balance, too, was off. But because of this imbalance, they could sit on the shelves without toppling over.

The surface was hard as marble, and quite smooth. Yet it wasn't heavy. I had no idea what material it was made out of, or how strong it was. If one fell to the floor, would it break? At any rate, they had to be treated delicately, like the eggs of some rare creature.

There wasn't a single book in the library—not a single volume. In the past there must have been books everywhere, along with people who came to learn and enjoy them. Just as you'd find in any ordinary town library. There was still a faint scent of that atmosphere lingering over the place. Yet at some point all the books on the shelves had been removed, replaced by old dreams.

There didn't seem to be any Dream Readers other than myself. At least at the present, I appeared to be the only one in town. Had there been another Dream Reader before me? Perhaps. Given all the detailed rules and procedures they had in place, and how diligently they were followed, I imagine I wasn't the first.

Your duties at the library included protecting the old dreams lined up there and managing them. You chose the dreams that should be read and noted them down in the ledger after reading. Just before evening, you opened the door to the library, lit the lamps, and, in the cold season, lit a fire in the stove. To do so, you had to make sure you didn't run out of canola oil for the lamps or firewood for the stove. And you made a thick green herbal tea for the Dream Reader—for me, in other words. A calming tea that would help heal my eyes and soothe me.

Using a large white cloth, you would carefully wipe away the white dust that had accumulated on an old dream, and then place it on the desk in front of me. I would remove my green-tinted glasses and rest both hands on the surface of the old dream. I'd enclose it in my hands, and, in about five minutes, the old dream would awaken from its deep slumber and its surface would glow faintly. And a natural, pleasant warmth would seep into both my palms. Then the dreams would begin to spin their way into me, hesitantly, at first, like a silkworm emitting a thread, then with more enthusiasm. They had something they needed to relate. I imagined how they'd been patiently waiting on their shelves for the time when they would emerge from their shells.

But the voice they spoke in was so subdued that I couldn't catch many words. The outlines of the images they projected were incomplete, and would grow dim and fade away, sucked up into the air. This was probably not their fault, but mine—perhaps my new eyes were not functioning properly. My ability to understand was still a work in progress.

And then the time would come to close the library. There was no clock anywhere, but you always knew when the time was drawing near.

"How was it? Did your work go well?"

"Not bad," I replied. "But it's so tiring to read even one dream. Maybe I'm doing it wrong."

"No need to worry," you said, turning off the air vent on the stove. You had blown out the lamps one by one and were seated across the table from me, looking straight at me. (Your gaze made my heart pound.) "There's no need to rush things. Here we take as much time as we need."

You followed each step precisely as you closed the library. A serious look in your eyes, unhurried, composed. The order of those steps never varied. As I watched you work, I wondered if it was really necessary to be so strict about locking up the library. In this quiet, calm town, who in the world was going to break into the library in the middle of the night to steal or destroy old dreams?

"Do you mind if I see you home?" I ventured to ask, on the night of the third day, as we emerged from the building.

You turned around and looked at me, your dark eyes wide, reflecting a single white star in the sky. You looked unsure what my offer meant. Why do I need you to see me home? you seemed to be wondering.

"I've just arrived in town, and you're the only one I can talk to," I explained. "If I can, I'd like to walk with someone, and talk with them. And I want to know more about you."

You gave this some thought, blushing slightly.

"But I live in the opposite direction from your home."

"I don't mind. I enjoy walking."

"But what is it you want to know about me?" you asked.

"For instance, where do you live in this town? And with whom? And how did you come to work at the library?"

You were quiet for a while, then said, "My home isn't so far away." That's all. And that was a fact.

You were wearing a blue coat made from a rough material like an Army blanket, a frayed crewneck sweater, and a gray skirt a size too big. All of which looked like hand-me-downs. Yet even in those shabby clothes, you were beautiful. Walking with you down the nighttime street, my chest tightened. So much so I felt as if I couldn't breathe. Just like on that summer twilit evening when I was seventeen.

"You mentioned you'd just come to this town, so where, if I may ask, did you come from?"

"From a town far to the east," I answered vaguely. "A large town very far away."

"I don't know anyplace other than this town. I was born here and have never been outside the wall."

Your voice was soft and gentle. The words you spoke were rigorously protected by that solid, twenty-six-foot-high wall.

"Why did you come all the way here? You're the first person I've met who's come from elsewhere."

"I wonder why myself," I answered evasively.

I came here to see you—but I wasn't able to confess this to you. It was still too early. Before I did that, I needed to learn much more about the town.

We walked along the road beside the river, toward the east, the streetlamps few and far between, and only faintly illuminating the night. Just as when I'd walked with you in the past, we walked side by side. The water flowing in the river sounded tranquil. Night birds called out, in short, clear calls, from the woods beyond the river.

You seemed to want to know more about the "faraway town to the east" that I came from. That curiosity brought me a little closer to you.

"What sort of town was it?"

What kind of town was it, indeed, where I'd lived until recently? All kinds of words were exchanged there, the place overflowing with excess subtext produced by these words.

But if I explained it like that, how much of it would you understand? You were born and raised in this town where so little happened, where words were so few. A self-contained place, simple and serene. With no electricity or gas, a clock tower without hands, a library without a single book. A place where the words people used only had their literal meaning, where everything had its rightful place, fixed, unwavering, in a place you could see.

"In that town you lived in, what sort of lives did people have?"

I couldn't give a good answer to your question. Hmm—what kind of lives *did* we live there?

You asked, "That town is very different from this one, isn't it? The size, how it came to be, the way people live. What is the biggest difference, I wonder?"

I inhaled the night air deeply, searching for the right words, the appropriate expression. And finally I said, "People there all have shadows with them."

THAT'S RIGHT—people there all had shadows with them. Me, and you—we each had a shadow.

I remember your shadow very well. We were on a deserted street in the beginning of summer and you were stepping on my shadow and me on yours. It was like a game of Shadow Tag I used to play as a kid. I'm not sure how it started, but we began to play. On the early-summer street, our shadows were dark, dense, and alive. It was so intense that we could feel physical pain if our shadow was stepped on. It was, of course, just an innocent game, but we took it seriously. As if stepping on the other person's shadow would have major consequences.

Afterward we sat down next to each other in the shade on an embankment and kissed for the first time. Neither of us took the lead, and it wasn't planned. No clear resolve from either of us to do it—it just happened. Our lips came together, and we merely followed where our feelings led. You closed your eyes and the tips of our tongues lightly, hesitantly, touched. I remember that afterward, neither of us could say anything. I think you and I both felt that if we said the wrong thing, we'd lose that precious feeling still tingling on our lips. So we stayed silent for a long while. Then we both burst out with something at the same exact moment, our words jumbling together. We laughed and kissed again.

I have a handkerchief of yours. A simple handkerchief of soft white gauzy material, with a single lily of the valley embroidered in a corner. You lent it to me one time for some reason. I planned to wash it and give it back, but never did. Actually, I didn't give it back on purpose. (If you had asked for it back, of course I would have returned it right away, pretending to have forgotten.) I'd often take the handkerchief out and, for a long time, quietly enjoy the soft material in my hands. That softness and you were one and the same. I'd close my eyes, lost in memories of my arms around you, our lips together. This was true when you were still with me, and even after you vanished *somewhere*.

I remember very well a dream you wrote about in a letter to me (or more precisely one *part* of a dream). It was a long letter that took up eight pages of stationery. Your letters were written using the fountain pen you won at the essay contest, always in turquoise-blue ink. When we wrote each other we both used the fountain pens we received as a prize. A kind of unspoken agreement. Those fountain pens weren't high quality, but for us they were precious mementos. Treasures, bonds between us. I always used black ink. *True black*, the same color as your jet-black hair.

"Here's a dream I had last night. And you were in it, a little," you wrote at the beginning of your letter.

Here's a dream I had last night. And you were in it, a little. Sorry it wasn't a major role, but what can you do? It's a dream. I don't create my dreams—they're given to me, by someone else from somewhere. I can't change dreams the way I want to (probably), and besides, supporting characters are really important in any play or movie, right? The supporting actors can make or break a play or movie. So even if you didn't have the lead role, be content with that, okay? And aim to win the Academy Award for Best Supporting Actor.

All that aside, when I woke up my heart was racing. [This was underlined, with a thick line, later on with a pencil.] 'Cause I still felt you right beside me even when I came back to reality. Though if you had really been there it would have even more fun . . . but I'm joking, of course.

And like I always do, I picked up the notebook and stubby pencil I keep next to my bed and wrote down everything about that dream, as exhaustively as I could (I'm never sure how to spell that word). That's the first thing I do when I wake up. Whether it's morning or the middle of the night, or if I'm still half awake or in a hurry, I write it all down in my notebook in as much detail as I can recall. I don't keep a diary (I've tried many times but never kept at it even a week), but with writing down dreams I've never missed a day. Diligently recording my dreams instead of keeping a diary must seem like a declaration—that for me, what happens in my dreams is more important than real life.

But actually, I don't think that's it. Obviously, my daily life and the events in my dreams are far apart—as different as a subway and a balloon. And just like everybody else, I'm captive to everyday life, clinging to the humble surface of the earth. Even the most powerful person, or the richest, can't escape that gravity.

It's just that, once I've snuggled into bed and fallen asleep, the *world of dreams* that arises there is so very vivid to me, the same as reality—or often (for some reason I like the word *often*) my dreams seem even *more* real. And what takes place in my dreams is, for the most part, totally unexpected. So sometimes I can't tell which is which. Like I wonder, "Wait a sec—did I really experience that, or did I dream it?" Have you ever had that feeling? Like I can't draw a line between dream and reality . . . I think that my tendency is much stronger than it is for other people. (The needle's off the charts.) Something must have made me that way. Something innate.

I first noticed this quality around the time I started elementary school. But when I talked about my dreams with my friends, no one seemed interested. Nobody cared about the dreams I had, or thought they were as important as I did. And the dreams they did care about were drab, unexciting, unappealing. I don't know why, though . . . So, I soon stopped talking about dreams with my classmates. I never talked about dreams with my family (and honestly talked to them as little as possible, no matter what the topic). Instead, I began keeping a little notebook and pencil beside my bed when I went to sleep. Ever since, that notebook has been my indispensable friend, my trusty confidante. Maybe this doesn't matter, but for me, writing down dreams with a stubby little pencil is best. Nothing longer than about three inches. Every night I'd sharpen a few of them with a knife so they'd be ready to go. Long brand-new pencils are a no-go! Why, I wonder? Why can't I write down my dreams unless it's with a stubby little pencil? Weird, if you think about it.

Saying that notebook is my one friend makes it sound like *The Diary of Anne Frank* or something. I'm not in hiding, of course, or surrounded by Nazi troops. At least the people around me don't have swastika armbands on their sleeves, but still.

Anyway, then there was that essay contest, and then I met you at the awards ceremony. That was the most beautiful thing that ever happened to me. Not the contest, but meeting you! You were interested in hearing about my dreams, and you listened so intently. This was the greatest thing. It was almost the first time in my life I could talk as much as I wanted, about what I wanted to talk about, to someone who was genuinely interested.

By the way, do I use the word *almost* too much? It feels that way. I use some words too frequently (another word I have trouble remembering how to spell). I've got to be careful. Actually, I need to reread what I write and do a revision (another word I misspell), but when I reread my writing, it makes me want to rip it to shreds. For real.

Ah, right—I was talking about the dream I had. That's what I need to write about. I always go off on some other topic and can't get back to the main point. Another one of my flaws. By the way, what's the difference between a *flaw* and a *defect*? Is *flaw* correct here? But I'm getting off track again, right? They're *almost* the same thing. [This was underlined again in pencil.] Anyway, back to the topic at hand. The dream I had last night.

In the dream, I was naked. Stark naked. There's the expression *without a stitch*, right? I always thought it was strange, kind of an exaggeration, but I looked at myself and saw I really was without a stitch. I mean, there might have been a piece of thread on my back where I couldn't see it, not that it mattered. I was in a long, narrow bathtub, a white, classic Western-style bathtub. The kind that might have cute claw feet. But there was no water in the tub. I was lying, naked, in an empty bathtub.

And when I looked closer, I saw it wasn't my body. The breasts were too big for me. Normally I think it would be nice to have bigger breasts, but now that I did it felt unnatural, uncomfortable. A really weird sensation, like I wasn't the real me. They were heavy, and I couldn't see below them very well. The nipples seemed too big, as well. I was thinking that big breasts like these would swing back and forth when you ran, getting in the way. Maybe my smaller ones were better after all.

And I noticed, too, that my stomach was swollen. But not because I was fat. Every other part of my body was slim. My stomach alone was like a balloon. I realized I must be pregnant. From the size of my belly, I'd say I was seven or eight months along.

And what thought do you think popped into my head then?

Clothes. With breasts this big, a stomach this swollen, what could I possibly wear? I was wondering if there were clothes somewhere that would fit me. I mean, I was completely naked and had to put on *something*. The thought made me uneasy. If I have to go out on the streets like this, then what?

I stretched my neck up like a crane and gazed all around the room but didn't spot any clothes. No bathrobe, either. Not even a towel. I literally couldn't find a stitch.

And then I heard a knock. Two heavy, short thuds on the door. That threw me. I couldn't let anybody see me like this. As I lay there, confused over how to react, the person at the door swung it open and came inside.

This room was a bathroom, but huge. As big as a regular-sized living room, and there was even a sofa. The ceiling was really high. There were lots of windows, too, and sunshine shone in brilliantly through them. From the light I figured it must be late morning.

Who was this? I couldn't find out, to the very end, because I couldn't see the person's face. As the person opened the door, the sunlight shining through the windows suddenly became more intense, forming a halation, and I couldn't see a thing. Just a dark, large shadowy figure standing in the doorway. From the silhouette, though, I figured it was a man. A very large man.

I had to cover myself. Since I was *without a stitch*. And a man I didn't know was there. But like I said, even if I had wanted to cover myself there wasn't anything I could use. No towel, no basin, no brush, nothing. With no other choice, I tried to hide the important part—is that the right way to put it?—below my belly with my hand. But my hand just wouldn't reach. Since my breasts and stomach were too big, and for some reason my arms were much shorter than normal.

Yet the man was coming closer toward me. I had to *do* something. Just then the baby in my belly—at least I think it was a baby—started acting up, wildly. Like three unhappy moles deep down a dark hole, staging a revolt.

I suddenly realized this wasn't a bathroom anymore. As I said, the room was the size of a living room, and now it really was one, and I was lying, naked on a sofa. And for some strange reason I had an eye at the center of each of my palms. Eyes with eyelashes, blinking. And dark black pupils. They were staring at me. But I didn't feel frightened. Both eyes had a whitish scar. And were crying. Terribly silent, sad tears.

This is where the story reaches a crazy climax, and that's where you appear in a minor role—but unfortunately I have to go out. I have something to do, so I have to leave my desk. Meaning I'll break off the letter at this point, put what I've written already into an envelope, paste on a stamp, and dispatch it (is that the spelling? And why don't I look things up in a dictionary?) into the mailbox in front of the station. I'll write the rest of that dream next time. Look forward to it, okay? And write to me, too—*please*—a letter almost too long to finish reading.

    ■   ■   ■

In the end I never heard what happened in the rest of that dream. The next letter she wrote me was about something completely different (I think she forgot about writing the rest of the dream). So I never did learn what kind of supporting role I played in it. And I probably never will.

IT'S TRUE THAT people there all have shadows with them.

In this town, people lack shadows. Once you get rid of your shadow, you really understand, for the first time, that shadows have their own weight. In the same way that you don't ordinarily feel Earth's gravity.

Getting rid of a shadow, of course, isn't so easy. It's disturbing to part with someone, no matter who it is, especially when you've spent so many years together with them and grown so close. When I came to this town, I had to leave my shadow with the Gatekeeper at the entrance.

"You can't step inside the wall with a shadow," the Gatekeeper informed me. "You either leave him here or give up on going inside. One or the other."

I got rid of my shadow.

The Gatekeeper had me stand in a sunny warm spot and then he grabbed my shadow. My shadow trembled in fear.

The Gatekeeper turned to my shadow and gruffly said, "It's alright. Don't be afraid. I'm not going to rip out your fingernails or anything. It won't hurt, and it'll be over soon."

Even so, the shadow struggled a bit, but he was no match for the powerful Gatekeeper and he was soon ripped apart from me, and he wilted and slumped down on a nearby wooden bench. Once separated from my body, my shadow looked much shabbier than I'd imagined. Like a pair of discarded old boots.

The Gatekeeper said, "Once you're apart from each other it looks really strange, doesn't it. Hard to believe you had a thing like that stuck to you, huh?"

I gave a vague reply. It still hadn't hit me that I'd lost my shadow.

"Shadows, you know, are useless," the Gatekeeper continued. "Do you ever remember your shadow doing anything very important for you?"

I didn't. At least, I couldn't come up with anything on the spot.

"Am I right?" the Gatekeeper said proudly. "And yet he has quite the big mouth on him. *I don't like that, this one's okay, though—* always quibbling, even though he can't do a thing on his own."

"What's going to happen to my shadow?"

"I'll treat him well, like a guest. I have a room and a bed ready for him, and though I don't provide gourmet fare, he'll get three square meals a day. And I'll ask him to do some work here occasionally."

"Work?" I asked. "What kind of work?"

"Odd jobs. Mostly outside the wall, but nothing major. Picking apples, helping out with the beasts, and so on . . . It depends on the season."

"What if I want to get my shadow back?"

The Gatekeeper narrowed his eyes, gazing steadily at me. Like he was looking through a gap in a curtain, surveying a deserted room. And then he spoke.

"I've been doing this job for a long time, but I've never run across anyone who asked to get their shadow back."

My shadow crouched down there quietly, looking at me, as if asking for something.

"No need to worry," the Gatekeeper said, encouragingly. "You'll get used to a life without a shadow. Before long you'll forget you even had one. Like—did I really have one of those?"

The shadow crouched there, listening to the Gatekeeper's words. I did feel a little guilty. Unavoidable, I suppose, since I was getting rid of my alter ego.

"This gate is the sole entrance to the town," the Gatekeeper said, pointing a plump finger at the gate. "Once a person passes through and goes inside, they can't ever go outside again. *The wall doesn't allow it.* That's the rule. We don't make you sign a pledge or seal it in blood, nothing extreme like that, but it's an unmistakable contract. You understand that, right?"

I understand, I said.

"One more thing. Since you're going to be the Dream Reader, you'll be given the appropriate eyes. This is a rule, too. It might be a bit inconvenient until your eyes heal. You understand that too?"

Then I passed through the town gate. Abandoning my shadow, accepting the wounded eyes of a Dream Reader, signing the unspoken contract that I would never again go through this gate.

In that other town (the town I used to live in), I explained to you, everyone drags their shadow along with them. In the light, your shadow moves along with your body, while in the darkness, your shadow hides. And when it's completely dark, your body and your shadow can rest together. But a person and his shadow are never pulled apart. Shadows are always there, whether you can see them or not.

"Does the shadow help the person in some way?" you asked.

"I don't know," I said.

"Then why doesn't everyone get rid of them?"

"They don't know how to. But even if they did, I doubt anyone would discard their shadow."

"How come?"

"Because people are used to them. Whether they serve any purpose or not."

Naturally you couldn't comprehend what that meant.

In the sandbank there was a scattering of riverside willows. Tied to the trunk of one tree with a rope was an old wooden boat, the flow of the water gently lapping around it.

"Since before we can remember, our shadows have been torn away from us. Like a baby's umbilical cord being cut, or baby teeth falling out. And the shadows cut away from us are forced outside the wall."

"And the shadows live on their own in the world outside?"

"They're mostly sent away to the outside. It's not like they're abandoned in the middle of the wilderness."

"I wonder what happened to your shadow?"

"Who knows. But I'm sure he died long ago. Shadows separated from the body are like plants without roots. They don't live long."

"And you've never met that shadow?"

"My shadow?"

"Yes."

You looked at me with a strange expression. And then you said,

"The dark heart is sent somewhere far away, and finally it loses its life."

You and I were walking together on a path beside the river. Occasionally the wind rose up and rippled the surface of the river, and you gathered together the collar of your coat with both hands.

"Your shadow will pass away before long. When the shadow dies, dark thoughts vanish, too, leaving behind a stillness."

When you said it, *stillness* sounded like an eternal quietude.

"And the wall will protect this, right?"

She looked straight at me. "That's why you came to this town. From somewhere far away."

The Workers' District was a desolate area spread out northeast of the Old Bridge. The canal, which had once been full of clean, clear water, was now dried up and filled with thick, gray mud. Still, a memory of moist air lingered.

Just past the dark, deserted factory district, there was an area dedicated to communal housing for workers, with old wooden two-story structures that looked on the verge of collapse. People who lived there were known as *workers*, though none of them actually worked in factories. It was just a convenient label that didn't really mean anything anymore. The factories closed down long ago and the tall chimneys no longer belched smoke.

A narrow, paved road wound its way through the buildings like a maze, its flagstones imbued with the smells and sounds of the lives of countless generations of people. As we walked along the worn stones, the soles of our shoes didn't make a sound. At one point in this maze, you came to a sudden halt, and turned and spoke.

"Thank you for walking me home. Do you know how to get back to your place?"

"I think so. Once I get out on the canal it should be easy."

You rewound your scarf and gave me a short nod. Then you turned around, quickly walked over to one of the doors of a dark wooden residence—all of which looked the same—and vanished inside.

I walked slowly home, vacillating between two towering emotions. I felt that I was no longer all alone in this town, while simultaneously I felt that I would always be alone. My heart felt torn in half. The branches of the river willows made a quiet sound as they swayed.

I WAS PROVIDED WITH a small home in the area called the Officials' District.

The house was equipped with only basic furniture and household goods. A single bed, a round wooden dining table, four chairs, a few built-in shelves, and a small wood-burning stove. That was it. There was also a small closet and bathroom. But no desk to work at, no sofa to relax on. Nothing decorative inside. No vases, no paintings, no ornaments, not a single book, and, of course, no clock.

I could prepare simple meals in the kitchen. I could use the small woodstove if I wanted to cook something, but there was no electricity or gas. The plates and chairs were simple and mismatched, as if they'd been hastily assembled from various places where they'd been used before. There were slatted shutters at the window. I closed them during the day to keep out the sunlight (a necessary accommodation for my weakened eyes). There was no lock on the door. People in this town didn't lock their doors.

In the past, this area must have been a quite elegant part of town. With little children playing out on the street, a piano ringing out from somewhere, dogs barking, and, in the evening, the inviting smell of a hot dinner wafting from open windows. Gardens in front of the houses must have been filled with lovely seasonal flowers. A sense of that still lingered in the district. And as the name indicated, most of the people must have been government employees in local official offices. Or military officers.

I woke just before noon and made a simple meal with the food provided, the only real meal I had each day. People in the town didn't seem to have to eat very much. One simple meal a day seemed to suffice. And my body adjusted surprisingly quickly to this lifestyle. After eating, I took care of the plates, closed the shutter, and stayed put in the darkened room, spending the day resting my eyes, which were not yet healed completely. Time gently flowed by.

I sat in the chair and untangled my consciousness from the cage of my physical self, so that I could run freely in a broad meadow of thoughts, like a romping dog off his leash. I lay down on the grassy field, my mind blank, and stared vacantly at the white clouds passing in the sky. (A metaphor, of course. I wasn't actually looking up at the sky.) Time passed by as I basically did nothing. Only when necessary would I whistle to call it back (this, too, a metaphorical expression. I wasn't really whistling).

As the sun began to set and it grew darker, around the time when the Gatekeeper prepared to blow his horn, I would "whistle" and call my consciousness back to my body and set out from my house and walk to the library. I'd wind my way down a hill and then upstream along the river. The library was just beyond the plaza. In the plaza, in front of the Old Bridge, loomed the clock tower, with its clock without hands, like some sort of symbol.

No one else ever visited the library other than me. So it was always just you and me.

Yet I didn't see any improvement in my skill at Dream Reading. My doubts and anxiety only increased. Was it a mistake appointing me Dream Reader? Maybe I didn't have what it took to do the job? Maybe I was doing the wrong thing, in the wrong place? One time, during a break in work, I told you my doubts.

"Don't worry," you said. You were seated across the table from me, gazing into my eyes. "It will take a little time. Just go on working as you are. You're in the right place, doing the right thing."

Your voice was gentle and calm, but also full of confidence. Sturdy and unshakable, like the bricks that made up the high wall in the town.

In the intervals between reading dreams, I drank the thick green herbal tea you prepared for me. You took your time, your sober expression like a scientist conducting an experiment as you painstakingly prepared the tea, using a small mortar and pestle, a pot, and a cloth strainer. In the narrow garden behind the library, there was a small vegetable garden with all kinds of herbs, and one of your duties was taking care of these. I asked you the names of the herbs, but you didn't know either. Like so many other things in this town, these herbs might never have had a name.

After I finished work for the day, and we had closed up the library, I walked with you on the road along the river, going upstream, seeing you back to the communal housing in the Workers' District. This became a daily routine.

The autumn rain looked like it would never cease, a light drizzle without beginning or end. There was no moon that night, no stars, no wind. And no cries of night birds. The only sound was the drops of water plopping down from the tips of the thin branches of the river willows on the sandbank.

As we walked down this nighttime road, side by side, we mostly stayed silent. But I never found this silence hard to bear. In fact, I might have welcomed it, since silence activated memories. You didn't mind silence either. Just as most people in the town didn't need to eat much, likewise they didn't need to say much.

When it rained you wore a thick, stiff yellow raincoat and a green rain hat. I took an old, heavy umbrella with me, something I found at my house. The raincoat you had on was about two sizes too big for you and rustled like you were balling up wrapping paper in your hands. For some reason it was a sound I had missed. I wanted so much to put an arm around your shoulders (like I did in the past), but here I couldn't.

You came to a halt in front of the communal housing in the Workers' District and, in the poor lighting, gazed at me for a time. Small frown lines formed between your brows, as if you were starting to remember something important. But in the end, you couldn't remember a thing. The possibility never materialized— it was sucked away and vanished.

"See you tomorrow," I said.

You nodded silently.

Even after you disappeared and all sound had faded, I remained standing there, silently savoring your lingering presence. Then I walked away, in the still-falling drizzle, toward the western hill where I lived.

"There's nothing to worry about. It just takes time," you said.

But I wasn't so sure. Could I really trust time that much—or what we understood as time in that town? After this seemingly endless autumn, what would come next?

I TOOK A TRAIN to visit you in the city where you lived. It was a Sunday morning in May, the sky clear and fresh, the single white cloud floating in the sky shaped like a smooth fish.

When I left, I told my parents I was going to the library. But I was going to see you. In my nylon backpack were sandwiches for lunch (my mother had made them and wrapped them tightly in plastic wrap) and my school books, though I wasn't planning to do any studying. There was less than a year left until the university entrance exams, but I tried to put that out of my mind.

On a Sunday morning there weren't many passengers in the train. I settled down on a seat and batted the word *permanent* around in my mind. Not a simple task for a seventeen-year-old high school boy who had only just become a senior, since the breadth of what he could imagine as permanence was pretty limited. The only thing that came to mind was a scene of rain falling on the sea.

Every time I see rain falling on the sea a certain emotion washes over me. Probably because the sea eternally—or at least for a period of time that's nearly eternal—never changes. Seawater evaporates and forms clouds, and the clouds rain, in an endless cycle. In that way the water in the sea is replaced again and again. Yet the sea as a whole doesn't change. The sea is always the same sea. An actual substance you can touch, yet at the same time a pure, absolute concept. What I might feel when I watch rain falling on the sea is (probably) that sort of solemnity.

Which is why whenever I thought about wanting to make the emotional bond I had with you stronger, to make it more *permanent*, what came to mind was that scene of rain quietly falling on the sea. I picture us sitting on the beach, watching that sea and rain. We're seated close together under a single umbrella. Your head rests gently on my shoulder.

The sea is so calm. There's barely a breath of wind, and without a sound, tiny waves lap at regular intervals at the shore. Like a bedsheet fluttering in the wind. We could sit there forever.

Though no image came to me of where we would head after this, where we should go. Since the two of us sitting together on the shore, under an umbrella, was already perfect. When something is perfect, where are you supposed to head to then?

This might be one of the issues with eternity—not knowing where you should go next. But how much value was there in a love that didn't seek the eternal?

I gave up thinking about the eternal and started thinking about your body. About the swell of your breasts, about what lay underneath your skirt. Imagining what was there. I'd fumble with the buttons on your white blouse one by one. I'd fumble, too, trying to undo the hook of the white bra I pictured you wearing. My fingers would slowly reach out under your skirt. I'd touch your soft inner thighs and then . . . No, I don't want to think about that. I *really* don't. But I can't help it. It's a whole lot easier to imagine than the eternal.

But as I was imagining all this, I suddenly realized that a part of my body was totally stiff. Like some indecent marble ornament. Inside my tight jeans my erect penis was terribly uncomfortable. If it didn't simmer down, I doubted I could stand up.

I tried thinking again about falling rain and the sea. The *stillness* of that scene might calm my teenage sex drive. I closed my eyes and focused. Try as I might, though, I couldn't conjure up the image of the shore. My will and my sexual desire, each with a different map in hand, were heading in opposite directions.

We always met in a small park near the subway. A place we'd met many times before. The park had playground equipment for little kids to play on, water fountains, and a bench under a wisteria arbor. I would sit on the bench and wait for you. But this time, at the appointed hour, there was no sign of you. That was unusual. You'd never been late before. Actually, you always arrived earlier than I did. Even if I arrived a half hour earlier than the time we set, you'd already be there, waiting for me.

"Do you always come this early?" I asked.

"More than anything, I enjoy waiting here by myself for you to come," you told me.

"Enjoy waiting?"

"That's right."

"More than actually seeing me?"

You grinned but didn't respond. All you said was this: "I mean, when I'm waiting like this, there are endless possibilities, not knowing what's ahead, what we're going to do. Right?"

Maybe you were right. Once we actually met, those unlimited possibilities inevitably were replaced by a single reality. And this must have been hard for you. I could understand what you were trying to say, though I didn't think that way myself. Possibilities are just that, possibilities and nothing else. For me, *actually* being beside you, feeling the warmth of your body, holding your hand, and sneaking in some kisses, away from prying eyes, was far better.

Thirty minutes passed, and you still did not appear. I kept anxiously glancing at the hands of my watch. Had something happened to you? My heart pounded with a dry, ominous beat. Did you suddenly fall ill? Or were you in a traffic accident? I pictured you being rushed to the hospital in an ambulance, straining to catch the wail of the siren.

Or had you somehow—how, I didn't know—sensed the sexual fantasies I'd had on the train that morning and had they disgusted you, so that you never wanted to see me again? These thoughts made me embarrassed, and my earlobes grew hot. But those kind of things can't be helped. In my mind, I tried my best to explain it to you, and to defend myself. It's like some large black dog. Once it starts to move in a certain direction there's nothing you can do. No matter how hard you yank at its leash—

You showed up forty minutes late. You sat down, without a word, on the bench next to me. Not a word of apology for being late. And I didn't say a thing either. We sat there, side by side, without speaking. Two little girls were playing on the swings, vying to see who could swing higher. Your breathing was still ragged, a faint sheen of sweat on your brow. You must have run all the way there. Your chest rose and fell with each breath.

You had on a white blouse with a round collar. A simple white blouse nearly the same as the one I'd imagined in the train. With the same kind of little buttons I'd (in my imagination) undone. And you wore a navy-blue skirt. A slightly different shade of blue from what I'd pictured, but basically the same skirt. That you were dressed very close to what I'd been imagining—fantasizing about—took me by surprise, left me speechless. I couldn't help but feel sort of *unsettled*, and tried hard not to imagine anything beyond that. At any rate, dressed in your white blouse and plain navy-blue skirt, seated on a park bench on a Sunday, you looked stunning.

Yet something was different about you. I couldn't put my finger on what it was. All I knew, at a glance, was that *something was different*.

"Are you okay?" I finally managed to say. "Did something happen?"

You wordlessly shook your head. But something *had* happened. I could pick up on it, the delicate sound of wings beating at a decibel beyond a human's audible range. You rested your hands in your lap, and I gently covered them with mine. It would be summer soon, yet your tiny hands were cold. I tried to warm them, even a little. We stayed that way for a long while. You were silent the whole time. Not the momentary silence of someone searching for the right words, but silence for its own sake. An introspective silence, complete in and of itself.

The little girls were still playing on the swings. I could hear the regular, rhythmic creaking of the metal. How wonderful it would be, I thought, if what lay before us was the vast sea instead, with rain falling on it. If we were looking at the sea, then this silence would be much more intimate, much more natural. But this was fine too, the way it was. I didn't dare ask for anything more.

Finally you took your hands away and stood up without a word, as if you'd just remembered something important you had to do. I hurriedly followed and got to my feet. And, still without a word, you began walking, with me following. We left the park and walked down the street. We went from a wide street to a narrow one, then back onto a wide one. You didn't say anything about where you were going, or what you were going to do. Which also was unlike you. Whenever we met you burst out with all kinds of things, like you couldn't wait. As if your head was forever packed full of things you had to tell me. But today, after we saw each other, you had yet to utter a single word.

Before long it dawned on me—you had no set destination. You were merely walking because you didn't want to stop in one place. To keep on moving itself was the goal. I walked beside you, following your pace. And I kept silent as well. My silence, however, was that of a person unable to find the right words.

How should I act? You were the first girlfriend I'd ever had, the first person I was so close to that I could call my sweetheart. Which is why, being with you, facing this *unusual circumstance*, I couldn't decide what I should do. The world was filled with things I'd not yet experienced. My knowledge of female psychology, especially, was like a blank notebook, nothing written in it. So I was flustered, unsure what to do in the face of this you-I'd-never-seen-before. For the time being, though, I needed to stay calm. I was a man, and a year older than you. Though that probably didn't make much of a difference. It might have meant nothing. But sometimes—especially when there's nothing else to rely on—a silly token *position* like that might be helpful. Who knew?

At any rate, I couldn't panic and at least had to appear calm. So I swallowed any words and continued to walk alongside you, at your pace, as if this were nothing out of the ordinary.

How long did we keep on walking? Every once in a while we'd stop at an intersection, waiting for the light to change. I wanted to hold your hand then, but you kept your hands tucked in your skirt pockets, your eyes fixed straight ahead.

Had I done something to make you angry? Did I mess up somehow? I didn't think so. We'd talked on the phone only two days earlier, in the evening. And you were in a good mood then, cheerful. I'm really looking forward to seeing you the day after tomorrow, you said. We didn't talk after that. There was no reason for you to be angry with me.

Stay calm, I told myself. I'd done nothing to upset you. Whatever troubled you was, most likely, something personal, unrelated to me. As I waited at each intersection I took a few deep breaths.

We must have walked for about thirty minutes. Or maybe a little longer. I looked around and saw we were back in the little park. Our bewildering hike through the city had brought us back to where we'd started. You headed straight for the bench at the wisteria arbor and sat down without a word. And I sat down beside you. Just like before, we sat side by side, not talking, on that wooden bench with its peeling paint. With your chin tucked, you stared at the space straight ahead, barely blinking.

The two girls on the swings were gone. The two swings hung there, motionless in the May sunshine. The empty, unmoving swings looked introspective, somehow.

You rested your head lightly on my shoulder, as if suddenly remembering that I was there. I rested my hand on top of yours. The size of our hands was so very different. I was always surprised at how small yours were, impressed that such tiny hands could do so much. Twisting open bottle tops, for instance, or peeling tangerines.

And then you began to cry. Voicelessly, your shoulders trembled faintly. Maybe all that fast, ceaseless walking had been meant to keep you from bursting into tears. I gently put my arm around you. Your tears fell, audibly, onto my jeans. Sometimes you made a choking sound and a short sob. But you spoke no words that I could make out.

I kept silent too. I was just there, taking in your sadness—what I took to be your sadness—as it came. I'd never experienced this before. To react to, and accept, the sadness of someone other than myself, and have them fully trust me.

If only I were stronger, I thought. If only I could hold you more tightly and say more encouraging words—the most apt, right words that would break the spell. But I was not yet prepared. And this fact left me sad.

I SPENT MY FREE TIME, apart from when I was at the library, drawing a map of the town. I'd use time on cloudy afternoons, and though at first it was more like a diversion, I ended up completely absorbed in the task.

The work began as I tried to grasp the outlines of the town, to understand the shape of the wall surrounding it. According to the simple map you had drawn in pencil in my notebook, it was shaped like a human kidney facing sideways (with an indented part at the bottom). But was that the real shape? I wanted to make sure on my own.

It turned out to be a harder task than I'd thought. No one around me grasped the accurate shape—or even an approximate one. Not you, nor the Gatekeeper, nor the old folk in my neighborhood (I got to know several of them and we'd exchange a word or two from time to time) had reliable knowledge of what shape the town was, and they didn't seem to care to know. *It's kind of like this*, they'd say, and sketch out a shape, but these were all vastly different. Some were close to an equilateral triangle, some nearly elliptical, and to others the shape looked like a snake swallowing some large prey.

"Why do you want to know that kind of thing?" the Gatekeeper asked, looking suspicious. "How does knowing the shape of the town serve any purpose?"

I'm simply curious, I explained. I just want to know about it, not because it's useful or anything . . . But *simply curious* seemed a concept beyond the Gatekeeper's comprehension. He looked at me, dubious, with an expression that said *This guy must be up to no good*. So I gave up on asking him anything more.

"What I'd like to say to you is this," the Gatekeeper said. "When you have a plate on top of your head it's best not to look up at the sky."

I didn't quite get what he was getting at, though I did understand that this wasn't some philosophical reflection, but more of a warning.

Other people's reactions to my question—yours included—were much the same as the Gatekeeper's. The residents of the town seemed to have no interest in the size of the place where they lived, or its shape. And they couldn't grasp the fact that anyone would care. I found this odd. Wasn't it only natural for people to want to know more about the place they were born, and lived in?

Perhaps curiosity didn't exist there. And even if it did, it might be rare, its scope quite limited. But that might stand to reason. If a person who lived in the town became curious about all sorts of things, like the world outside the wall, he (or she) might want to see what lay beyond. And if they began to think that way, it wouldn't be good for the town, since the town had to remain perfectly sealed off inside its wall.

I concluded that if I wanted to know the layout of the town, I had to walk it myself. I wasn't averse to walking, and I could do with the exercise. But with the handicap of my poor vision, the work proceeded at a sluggish pace. Long walks outside were limited to cloudy days and twilight. Bright sunlight hurt my eyes and made me tear up for a while. But thankfully (I guess I should say that) I could spare as much time as I liked for the task. And as I mentioned, that autumn the weather continued to be overcast.

With my green-tinted glasses, a couple of scraps of paper, and a short little pencil in hand, I'd walk along the inner wall, noting down its shape as I went. I made some simple sketches as well. I didn't have a ruler or compass (neither existed in the town) but could make out general directions from the position of the sun faintly hidden behind the clouds, and could measure out distances from the number of paces I took. I started from the Gatekeeper's shack at the north gate and walked counterclockwise, just inside the wall.

The road alongside the wall was in bad shape. There were many places where it disappeared altogether. There was little evidence of people using it. It did seem to have been used a lot in the past (I spied signs of this in places), but now it looked like no one walked along it. Generally, the road ran close to the wall, but occasionally it made a wide detour away from it in another direction, and in some places bushes blocked the way, so that I had to force my way through. I made sure to wear thick gloves.

The land that ran along the wall appeared to have long been abandoned and neglected. Now no one at all resided around the wall area. Occasionally I'd see what looked like a house, but all of these were deserted. The elements had made most of the roofs cave in, the windows were cracked, and walls had collapsed. All that remained for some of the houses was a trace of the stone foundation. A few were still standing, but the outer walls were choked with a vigorous growth of green ivy. But even these ruined homes were not empty inside. When I got closer and peered in, I saw an overturned table, rusty utensils, and what looked like a cracked bucket. All were covered with a thick layer of dust. They had absorbed the dampness and were half falling apart.

It seemed as though, in the past, many more people had lived in this town. And lived ordinary lives here. Yet at a certain point *something* had happened, and most of the residents had abandoned the town, leaving behind their furniture and household goods.

So what in the world had happened?

A war? An epidemic? Or some huge political upheaval? Had people moved elsewhere on their own initiative? Or were they forcibly deported?

At any rate, *something* had taken place once and most of the residents had, without delay, moved elsewhere. Those who remained had gathered along the central plain next to the river, or on the western hills, and lived together, shoulder to shoulder, a quiet life, seldom speaking. The rest of the land had been abandoned and left to the wild.

The remaining residents didn't talk about that *something* that had happened. It wasn't that they refused to, but more like it had been erased from their collective memory. Maybe that memory had been completely lost, like the shadows they had given up. Just as the people of the town had no horizontal curiosity about geography, they lacked any vertical curiosity about history.

The only creatures who inhabited this area after the people had left were the unicorns. They wandered in small groups in the woods near the wall. As I walked along the path, the beasts would hear my footsteps and turn their heads to look at me, but then show no more interest. They'd go back to searching for leaves and nuts. Sometimes the wind would blow through the woods, and the branches would rustle like a clatter of old bones. As I walked through this abandoned, deserted land, I took notes on the shape of the wall.

The wall didn't seem to care about my *curiosity*. If it had wanted to, the wall should have been able to put a stop to my exploration. By cutting off the path, for instance, with a fallen tree, or with a barrier of thickets, or by making me lose sight of the path. The power of the wall should have easily been able to do that. Seeing the wall up close day after day I'd gotten the strong impression that *this wall has that much power.* No, less an impression than a certainty. And for its part the wall watched over every move I made. I could sense its gaze on my skin.

Yet it never put up any of those obstructions in my way. So I was able to make my way along the path by the wall unimpeded, noting down every detail of the wall's shape. The wall seemed not to worry about my little experiment—or maybe it actually found it of interest. **If you want to do that, go right ahead. Because it's not going to serve any purpose.**

My topographical survey/investigation of the wall ended after about two weeks. One night when I came home from the library, I came down with a high fever and had to stay in bed. Was this the wall's doing? Or did something else cause it? I had no idea.

My fever continued for about a week. The fever left my body covered with watery pustules, and my sleep was filled with long, dark dreams. Waves of nausea would well up periodically, but it just made me feel ill and I never actually vomited. My gums ached dully, and it felt like I had lost the strength to chew. So much so I feared that if the fever continued, all my teeth would fall out.

I dreamed of the wall, too. In the dreams the wall was alive and moving, as if it were the inner wall of some gigantic internal organ. No matter how accurately I might note its shape on paper, or sketch it, soon the wall changed shape, making all my effort meaningless. I'd revise my writing and drawings only for the wall to change once again. In my dreams I was puzzled about how a wall made of such solid bricks could change shape so pliably, yet it was constantly transforming before my eyes, laughing scornfully at my pitiful efforts. In the face of such a formidable presence, all my days of effort were pointless—the wall was flaunting this in front of me.

"What I'd like to say to you is this," the Gatekeeper said, emphatically advising me. Or perhaps warning me. "When you have a plate on top of your head it's best not to look up at the sky."

While I was feverish, it was one old man who lived nearby who stayed with me and took care of me. The town must have chosen him and sent him to help out. It's not like anyone told people I was sick, yet the town was aware that I was laid up with a fever. Or perhaps this was a fever that was *expected*, one that all newcomers to the town experienced. And the town had made preparations ahead of time.

At any rate, the old man showed up one morning without warning, and without saying hello marched right on in. (As I said before, no one there locked their doors.) He soaked a towel in cold water, placed it on my forehead, changed it every few hours, wiped the sweat from my body with a practiced hand, and occasionally gave me a word or two of encouragement. After my symptoms improved somewhat, he fed me hot porridge from a portable container he brought, one spoonful at a time. He gave me drinks, too. The fever left me drowsy and only half awake and at first I couldn't make him out well—to me, he appeared to be something out of a dream—but I remember him tenderly, patiently nursing me. White hair clung like weeds to the top of his egg-shaped head. He was small and thin, but stood very straight, with never a wasted movement. When he walked, he dragged his left leg a little, his steps making a distinctive, unbalanced sound.

One rainy afternoon, when I was finally starting to regain full awareness, the old man sat down on a chair by the window, and as he sipped an ersatz coffee made from dandelions, he told me some stories of his past. Like most of the residents of the town, he remembered little (or perhaps tried hard not to recall past events), though he did remember a few personal facts, disconnected yet clear memories. Probably parts of the past that weren't inconvenient to the town. You couldn't completely wipe out people's memories or a person wouldn't be able to live. Naturally there was no proof that these memories hadn't been conveniently rewritten or fabricated. Yet the stories the old man told sounded to me— or at least to my ears, with a mind still a bit fuzzy from the fever— as though they had likely occurred.

"I used to be a soldier," he told me. "An officer. Back when I was much younger, before I came to this town. So this is a story about another place. There everyone had their own shadow. There was a war then. I can't rightly recall who was fighting whom. Guess that doesn't matter anymore. Over *there* somebody was always fighting somebody else.

"Once I hid in a trench and a shell exploded and a fragment hit the back of my left thigh and I was transported to the rear. Back then we couldn't easily get anesthetics and my leg hurt like crazy, but at least it was better than dying. Fortunately, they treated me early enough and didn't have to amputate. I was sent to a small hot springs town in the mountains, where I stayed in an inn while my wound healed. The inn had been taken over by the military as a sanatorium for wounded officers. I'd soak every day for a long time in the hot springs to help heal my leg, and the nurses would take care of me. The inn was an old, traditional one, and my room had a veranda with a glass door. From the veranda you could see a beautiful river valley right below. It was on that veranda that I saw the ghost of a young woman."

A ghost? I was about to ask but couldn't get the words out. But still the old man's large, antenna-shaped ears seemed to pick up on my question.

"Yep, it was definitely a ghost. I woke up suddenly at one a.m. and found that woman seated on a chair on the veranda. Lit up by the light of the white moon. I knew at a glance it was a ghost. No woman that beautiful existed in the real world. She was that lovely precisely because she was not of this world. I was speechless, frozen. And I thought then that I would give up anything for this woman. A leg, an arm, or even my life. I can't express that beauty in words. That woman embodied all the dreams I ever had, all the beauty I'd ever pursued."

Here the old man became quiet and stared fixedly out of the window. It was gloomy outside so the slatted shutters were wide open. The smell of wet flagstones crept in coldly through a gap around the window. After a while he emerged from his reverie and resumed his tale.

"The woman appeared to me every night after that. Always at the same time, seated on a wicker chair on the veranda, staring outside. Her perfect profile facing toward me. But I couldn't do a thing. In her presence, words wouldn't come and I couldn't even move the muscles of my mouth. It was like I was paralyzed and could only stare. And after some time had passed, she would vanish, before I was even conscious of it.

"I tried sounding out the owner of the inn about this. Was there, I asked, some tragic backstory related to the room I was staying in? But the owner said he'd never heard of any. And it didn't sound like he was lying or trying to hide something. So I was the only one who'd seen that ghost, or apparition, of a woman in that room. But why? Why me?

"My wound eventually healed, and though I still limped a bit, I was able to live a normal life again. Because of my injury I was released from the army and allowed to go back home. But even back home I couldn't shake the woman's face from my memory. No matter how attractive the other women I slept with, no matter how good-natured the ones I met, it was always that woman's face that I saw. Seeing her felt like I was walking on top of a cloud. My soul was possessed by that woman, by that ghost."

My mind was still fuzzy as I listened to the old man's tale. Rain and gusts of wind lashed the window, like an urgent warning.

"One day, though, it came to me—I had only seen one side of her. She always had the left side of her face toward me, and never moved. Her only movements came when she blinked, or occasionally tilted her head, ever so slightly. Just like those of us living on the earth always see only one side of the moon, I only saw one side of her face."

The old man vigorously rubbed his left cheek. His cheeks were covered with a white beard he'd trimmed with scissors.

"I could barely think straight, and I just had to see the right side of that woman's face. It even felt like, if I didn't, my life would be meaningless. The urge was uncontrollable, and I abandoned everything and headed off toward that hot springs town. The war still continued—it was a long, drawn-out conflict—and it wasn't easy to get there, but I used my army connections and got a special pass and could stay at that inn. I asked the innkeeper I'd gotten to know and was able to spend one night only in the same room. That room with a glass door to the veranda. And I settled in, waiting, with bated breath, for night to come. The woman appeared at the same hour, in the same place. As if she had been waiting for me to return."

Again the old man fell silent, and took a sip of his now cold ersatz coffee. A long silence ensued.

So, did you see it? The right side of that woman's face? I asked, almost inaudibly.

"That I did," the old man replied. "With all my might I broke free of the paralysis and got up from the bed. It wasn't easy, believe me, but I was determined. I slid open the glass door, stepped out onto the veranda, and walked around the woman on the wicker chair so I could see her right side. And I gazed at the right side of her face, lit up in the moonlight . . . Though I wish I never had."

What was there?

"What was there? Well, if only I could explain it," the old man said. And he sighed, his sigh as deep as an old well.

"I searched for a long time to find the words to explain to myself what I saw there. I perused all sorts of books, asked all sorts of wise men, but could never find the words I was seeking. And not being able to find the right words, the appropriate wording, made my suffering deeper by the day. Distress was a constant companion. Like a person in a desert dying for water."

With a hard clatter the old man returned his coffee cup to the ceramic saucer.

"The one thing I can say—is that what was there was a scene from a world a person should never, ever lay eyes on. Yet at the same time it's a world that everyone has inside us. It's inside me, and inside you, too. And yet it's something you should never see. Which is why most of us live our lives with eyes closed."

The old man cleared his throat.

"Do you get it? Once you see it, a person can never go back to where he was. After you've seen it . . . So you'd better be careful. Very, very careful. Take care to never get anywhere near that kind of thing. If you get close, you'll want to gaze inside, guaranteed. The temptation is too hard to resist."

The old man held up his index finger, pointing straight toward me. And he repeated himself firmly.

"So you'd better be careful. Very, very careful."

Is that why he abandoned his shadow and came to this town? I wanted to ask the old man. But I couldn't get the words out.

The old man seemed not to have heard my wordless question. Or maybe he did hear but didn't intend to answer. The hard sound of rain lashed against the window, filling in the silence.

"I GET THIS WAY SOMETIMES," you said, wiping away the tears with a white handkerchief. Though by then the tears had nearly stopped (the supply of tears had run out?). We were still seated, side by side, on the bench in the park beneath the wisteria arbor. These were the first words out of your mouth that morning.

"My heart goes rigid."

I stayed silent. What should I say? And how?

You went on. "When that happens, there's nothing I can do. All I can do is hold on to something and let time pass."

I did my best to understand, even a little, of what you were trying to get across.

My heart goes rigid?

I couldn't picture what that meant, specifically. The body stiffening I could understand. It had to be like being paralyzed. But the heart? How did that go *rigid*?

"But this time, you were somehow able to *get through*?" For the time being I probed no further.

You nodded faintly.

"Probably, for now," you said. "There might still be aftershocks."

We sat there for five or ten minutes, wordlessly waiting for these *aftershocks*. Like people hanging on to the thickest pillar in their house, waiting for the aftershocks of an earthquake to subside. Under my arm your shoulders slowly rose and fell. But *that* didn't seem about to return. Most likely.

"What should we do now?" I asked you, a little later.

The day had just begun. The sky was blue and clear. We could go anywhere and do whatever we liked. We had no set plans. There were some slight practical limits (like neither of us having enough money), but otherwise we were basically free.

"Can we stay like this for a little longer? Until I calm down," you said. You wiped away the last traces of tears, folded the handkerchief into a small square, and placed it in your lap, on your skirt.

"Sure," I said. "Let's stay here for a while."

The tension finally drained away from your body, like the tide steadily receding from the shore. Looking at your clothes (your white blouse), I could sense the physical change, and it made me happy. I felt like I'd helped, if only a little.

"So you get that way sometimes?" I asked.

"Not so often, but sometimes."

"When that happens do you always walk around, like you did just now?"

You shook your head. "Not always. Mostly I just stay in my room. Shut in, not talking to anybody in my family. I don't go to school, and I don't eat anything. I just sit on the floor, not doing anything. When it's bad it might last for days."

"You don't eat for days?" I couldn't imagine it.

She nodded. "I drink water sometimes, but that's all."

"Is there a reason you get like that? Like something bad happened and you get depressed?"

You shook your head. "No particular reason, no. I just *simply* get that way. A huge wave rolls over me, without a sound, I'm swallowed up, and my heart gets rigid. I can't tell when it will come, and how long it'll last."

"Sounds pretty inconvenient," I said.

You smiled. Like a tiny ray of sunlight breaking through the clouds. "You're right. It might be *inconvenient*. I never thought of it like that, but now that you mention it, I'm sure it is."

"Your heart gets rigid?"

You thought about this. "It feels like there's a string deep in my heart that's snarled and tangled and I can't unravel it. The more I try to untie it, the more tangled and balled up it gets. So *tight* I can't deal with it. You've never had that happen to you?"

I don't think I've ever experienced that. When I said this, you turned your head toward me a little.

"That's the part I like about you."

"That my head doesn't get all twisted up inside?"

"Not that. I like that you just listen to me without trying to analyze things or give advice."

The only reason I didn't say anything more was that I had no idea how to interpret this *rigid heart* condition of yours, what advice or opinion I should give. But if you were alright with me sitting here, not saying anything, my arm around your shoulder, I was okay with that. In fact, I was thankful for it. Still, I felt I should ask something, no matter how minimal.

"So . . . when did that wave-like thing come on today?"

"This morning, when I woke up," you replied. "When the sky was gradually getting lighter. And I thought I wouldn't be able to see you today. I don't know how to describe it, but my body just wouldn't move. I couldn't move my fingers, or even button up my shirt. I knew I couldn't see you when I was like that."

I was silent, just listening.

"I stayed in bed, the covers up over my head. I wanted to disappear without a trace. But when the time came I was supposed to meet you, I knew I couldn't leave you sitting there, waiting for me in the park. I used every bit of strength I had to stand up, button up my blouse, and run all the way to the park. All the while I was afraid that maybe you'd already left . . . I didn't even have time to comb my hair. I must look pretty awful."

"No, you look wonderful. The same as always," I said. And I wasn't lying. From top to bottom you were lovely. The same as always. No—you were lovelier than usual.

"No—you're lovelier than usual," I added.

That's a lie, you said.

No, it isn't, I said.

You were silent for a while.

"Ever since I was little," you finally said, "I've had this irritating kind of personality. No one's ever liked me, or accepted me. Other than my late grandmother, *not a one*. But Grandmother is dead, and there's no way to tell what she really thought. Maybe she had the wrong idea about me."

"Well—*I* really like you."

"Thank you," you said. "I'm so happy you said that. But I think it's because you don't really know me. Because if you did—"

"Even if that's true, I want to know more about you. All kinds of things. Everything."

"There might be some things you're better off not knowing."

"But when you like a person a lot, you want to know everything about them. It's only natural."

"And you'll accept *that*?"

"Yes, I will."

"Really?"

"Of course."

Seventeen, and in love, on a beautiful Sunday in May, of course I didn't have any doubts.

You picked up the small white handkerchief from your lap and dabbed again at your eyes. I saw fresh tears rolling down your cheeks. I caught a faint scent of tears. So tears actually have a scent, I thought. That smell touched me. Gentle, enchanting, and a little sad.

"You know," you said.

I waited for you to go on.

"I want to be yours," you said, almost whispering it. "Completely, totally yours."

I choked up. Deep inside me, someone was knocking on a door. They were on some urgent mission, pounding on the door over and over. That sound rang out, hard and loud, in an empty room. I felt my heart in my throat. I took a deep breath, trying to somehow push it back where it belonged.

"I want to be yours," you continued, "in every way there is. Yours from top to bottom. I want to be one with you. I mean it."

I pulled your shoulder closer. Someone was using the swings again. That regular, metallic creak, less an actual sound than a metaphorical signal trying to tell me about another way things could be.

"But don't rush things, okay? My heart and my body are apart from each other. In slightly different places. So I'd like you to wait a while. Until I'm ready. Does that make sense?"

"I think so," I said, my voice hoarse.

"A lot of things take time."

I gave some thought to the passage of time, the creak of the swings in the background.

"Sometimes I feel like I'm the shadow of something, of someone," you said, as if revealing a vital secret. "My real self isn't here.

It's somewhere else. The me that's here looks like me, but is nothing more than a shadow projected onto the ground and walls . . . I can't help thinking that way."

The May sunlight was strong, and we were sitting in the cool shade beneath the wisteria arbor. *My real self is somewhere else?* What was *that* supposed to mean?

"You've never felt that way?" you asked.

"That I'm just somebody's shadow?"

"Right."

"I don't think I've ever thought that."

"Mm, maybe something's wrong with me. But I can't help thinking that."

"If that's true, that you're nothing more than someone's shadow, then where is your real self?"

"My real self—the real me—is in a town far away, living a completely different life. A town surrounded by a high wall that doesn't have a name. There's only one gate, which a strong Gatekeeper guards. The me that lives there doesn't have dreams, and doesn't weep."

This was the first time you spoke about that town. Naturally, I couldn't understand what you were talking about. A town without a name? A Gatekeeper? Confused, I asked, "Can I go to that place? To that town without a name where the real you lives?"

You tilted your head and gazed at me from up close. "You can if that's what you *really* want."

"I want to hear more about the town. What kind of place is it?"

"The next time we see each other," you said. "I still don't want to talk about it today. I want to talk about something else."

"No problem. Let's take our time. I'll wait."

You grabbed my hand with your tiny hand. Like the sign of a promise.

MY FEVER HAD ABATED, I was finally able to walk outside, and for the first time in a long while, I pushed open the door to the library. Inside, the air seemed more stagnant than before. It was a humid, cloudy evening. No sign of anyone in the inner room, and the fire in the stove had gone out. No light was on, the faint, hazy twilight filtering into the room through invisible cracks.

"Is anyone here?" I called out. I didn't get a response, and the silence only deepened. My voice was hard and dry, with no reverberation. It didn't sound like my own voice. I touched the kettle on top of the stove. It was completely cold. The fire in the stove seemed to have been out a long time. I looked around and called out, even louder, "Is anyone here?" But again no answer. The room seemed unchanged, everything the same as the last time I'd come. Though everything looked colder than before, tinged with a bleak, desolate color.

I sat on the bench, waiting for you to come. Or for someone else to come. I waited, but no one appeared. No one seemed about to, either. I found a match and lit the small lamp on top of the checkout counter. The room grew a little brighter. I was thinking of lighting the stove, too (which was ready to go, with firewood inside), but I wasn't sure if that was permitted, and besides, the room wasn't that cold. So I decided not to. I pulled the collar of my coat tighter, redid the scarf, stuck my hands in my pockets, and passed the time for quite a while.

Still not a sound in the room.

Had something unusual happened while I was laid up with a fever? Or had there been some change in the system regarding how the library was operated? Had it become clear that I was unsuited to be a Dream Reader and now I wouldn't be able to see you anymore? Several ominous possibilities flitted through my mind. But I couldn't settle on an answer. Every time I tried to figure something out, my mind became a heavy cloth sack, sunk in a bottomless deep.

Perhaps I still had a little residual fever. Seated on the bench, I leaned back against the wall and before I knew it I had fallen asleep. How long I slept, I don't know. Despite the uncomfortable position, I slept deeply. Some sound woke me, and there you were, right in front of me. You had on the same sweater you'd worn when we first met, with your arms crossed in front of your chest as you worriedly looked at me. You must have lit the stove while I was asleep since I could see red flames wavering inside it. White steam puffed out of the kettle (proof that I'd slept a surprisingly long time). The lamp, too, had been changed for a larger, brighter one. With that warmth and light, and with you there, the library was back to the way I'd known it. The desolate chill from before had vanished somewhere, which was a relief.

"I had a fever for a long time and wasn't able to come here. I couldn't get out of bed."

You gave a few short nods but didn't express any opinion. Or words of consolation. Maybe you'd already heard about my high fever from someone, or perhaps you hadn't. I couldn't tell from your expression. *It's not so strange if that happened* is what your face might have been telling me.

"But you no longer have a fever?"

"My joints are still a little stiff, but I'm okay and can get back to work."

"Hot, thick herbal tea should get rid of any lingering fever."

I took my time finishing the hot herbal tea, which warmed me and cleared my mind. I sat down at the old wooden table in the middle of the stacks. How long had it been used here for dream reading, I wondered? The residue of countless old dreams had seeped into it, and my fingertips felt the presence of that history in the worn-down grain of the wood.

Old dreams were lined up on the shelves of the stacks, too many to count. The stacks rose to the ceiling, and you had to use a wooden stepladder to retrieve them. Your legs showing from under your long skirt were youthful, pale, and slim. Despite myself, your beautifully formed calves held me in thrall.

It was your task that day to select the dreams to be read and line them up on the table. Ledger in one hand, you checked the numbers as you picked the dreams from the shelves, then laid them down in front of me—ever so carefully and gently. Sometimes I could read through three dreams in a night, and sometimes only two. Some dreams took a long time to read, while others just a relatively short time. Overall, the larger ones took more time. But up until then I'd never made it through more than three in a night. That was the limit of my ability. Once the dreams had been read, they weren't returned to their original shelves, and you carried them to a room farther back. I don't know what happened to them once they'd been read.

By my rough calculations, even if I got through three dreams a day, it would take at least ten years to get through the old dreams lined up on the shelves of the stacks. And there was no guarantee that the ones here were all the old dreams that were "in stock." No guarantee that other old dreams weren't added to the inventory each day. (By the amount of dust on the ones you chose, I knew they must have been quite old.) But thinking about this wasn't going to get me anywhere. All I could do was read, one by one, the dreams laid out before me every day—all the while not understanding the reasons and goals involved.

Had my predecessors—the other Dream Readers who'd come before me—done the same thing, intently making their way through old dreams, without any explanation being given to them as to why, not grasping the meaning behind these activities? Had they done a reasonable job of it? And what became of them?

Whenever I finished reading a dream, I needed to take a break. I would put my elbows on the table, cover my face with my hands, rest my eyes in that darkness, and recover from my fatigue. As always, I couldn't catch the words spoken by the dreams all that well but could surmise that it was some sort of message. They were trying to convey something—to me, or to someone else. But what was said there was speech I couldn't follow, spoken in a language I wasn't familiar with. Yet even so, each individual dream had its own joy, sadness, or anger inside, sucked in from somewhere—all of which passed through my body.

Reading dreams, I could feel, quite intensely, the sensation of them *passing through me*. And I also came to think that what they desired was not understanding in the usual sense of the word. Sometimes as they passed through me they stimulated me internally, from an unexpected direction, summoning up long-forgotten feelings of excitement. Like ancient dust at the bottom of a bottle swirling up when someone breathes on it.

You brought over a hot drink for me when I took breaks. You made more than just herbal tea, sometimes a coffee substitute, or a cocoa-like drink (but not cocoa). Most of the food and drink in the town was plain, most of it substitutes, not the real thing. The taste, though, wasn't bad. They had a—how to put it?—kind of friendly, nostalgic taste to them. The people's lives were simple, full of all kinds of workarounds.

"You seem to be used to dream reading now," you said, encouragingly, from across the table.

"Slowly but surely," I said. "But reading a dream leaves me exhausted. Like all my strength is gone."

"You still have a bit of fever left, I would think. But you'll get over the tiredness. The fever is something that always appears. After you have it, things settle down."

Having a temporary fever like that must be a rite of passage for a new Dream Reader, something they had to go through. That's how I would be accepted, little by little, as a part of this town, and assimilate into the system. I guess I should have been happy about that. Because you were happy.

The long, damp fall was finally over, and the harsh winter had arrived. Several of the beasts had already passed away. The morning of the first heavy snowfall, a few of them lay on the ground in their area, in the two inches or so of snow that had accumulated, their golden fur taking on a more whitish hue for the winter. The first to expire were older beasts, the ones who were physically weak, and the young beasts who had been abandoned for some reason by their parents. The season mercilessly weeded them out.

I climbed up the lookout tower and gazed down on the corpses of the beasts. A melancholy, yet captivating scene. The morning sun shone dully behind the snow, while below hung a layer of the beasts' white breath in the air, like morning mist.

Soon after dawn the horn sounded, and the Gatekeeper swung open the gate as always, leading the beasts inside. After the living beasts passed through, the corpses of the deceased lay there outside the wall, like lumps that had swelled from the earth. I kept watching, entranced by the scene, until my eyes could no longer take the morning light.

Despite the cloudy skies, the light made my eyes sting more than I'd expected. Back home, the tears spilled out when I closed my eyelids, and trickled down my cheeks. I lowered the slatted shutters and protected my eyes in the darkened room, gazing at all the shapes that rose up and dissipated in the darkness.

The old man came, as always. He placed a cold towel on my eyes and gave me hot soup to eat. There were vegetables and a kind of pseudo bacon in the soup, and it warmed me.

"On snowy mornings," the old man said, "even if it's cloudy, the light is far more intense than you think. Your eyes have yet to fully heal. Why'd you go out, anyway?"

"I went to see the beasts. Several had died."

"Ah, because winter's come. A lot more will die from now on."

"Why do the beasts die so quickly like that?"

"They're weak, from the cold and hunger. It's always been that way. It hasn't changed."

"Will they all die?"

The old man shook his head. "They've managed to hang on like that since long ago. And I imagine they'll continue. Many lose their lives in the winter, but then spring and the mating season comes, and babies are born in the summer. New lives push out the old."

"What happens to the beasts' bodies?"

"They're burned. By the Gatekeeper." The old man warmed his hands in front of the stove. "They're tossed in a hole, oil is poured over them and lit, and by afternoon you can see the smoke from anywhere in town. They're burned most every day."

As the old man had announced, smoke rose in the sky every day. About the same time every afternoon, perhaps around three thirty, from the angle of the sun. Winter grew deeper by the day, the harsh north wind and occasional snow assaulting the elegant, single-horned beasts like a persistent hunter.

On the afternoon of a day when the snow had stopped and it was overcast, I visited the Gatekeeper's cabin for the first time in a long while. The Gatekeeper had taken off his long boots and was warming his massive legs in front of the fire. Steam from the kettle on top of the stove mixed with the purplish smoke from his cheap pipe, turning the air in the room heavy and stagnant. On top of his broad worktable lay a line of hatchets and adzes, of all types and sizes.

"Hey there. How're the eyes? Still bothering you?" the Gatekeeper asked.

"They're a lot better, but still hurt sometimes."

"Just hang in there. As you get used to living here, the pain will fade."

I nodded.

"So, are you worried about having given up your shadow?"

Now that he said it, I realized I'd hardly thought about my shadow for some time. I only went out at twilight or on cloudy days and had little chance to consider my shadow, or to think about being bereft of one. I couldn't help but feel guilty about it. We'd been a single being for such a long time, how could I forget him so easily?

"Your shadow's doing okay," the Gatekeeper said, rubbing his rugged hands in front of the stove. "I let him go out an hour a day and get exercise, and he has a good appetite. Would you like to see him?"

I would, I replied.

The place where the shadow lived was between the town and the world outside. I couldn't go to the world outside, and the shadow couldn't enter the town. This *shadow enclosure* was the only spot where people who had lost their shadows and shadows who had lost their people could see each other. To get there, you passed through a wooden door in the backyard of the Gatekeeper's cabin. The enclosure was a rectangle roughly the size of a basketball court. At the end of it stood the brick walls of a building, while on the right was the wall that surrounded the town. The other two sides were tall board fences. In one corner was a single elm tree, and my shadow was seated on a bench beneath it. He was dressed in an oversized crewneck sweater and a worn leather coat, and was gazing up at the cloudy sky through the branches, his eyes listless.

"There's a room he stays in over there," the Gatekeeper said, pointing to the building at the end of the enclosure. "Not as nice as a hotel, but a decent, clean room. We change the sheets once a week. Would you like to check it out?"

"No, we can just talk here, that'd be fine," I said.

"No problem. You can talk about all the things you've been saving up. But I will tell you this—don't try to get attached again. Ripping him away again wouldn't be a picnic."

The Gatekeeper sat down on a round wooden seat next to the back gate, lit a match, and got his pipe going. He'd no doubt keep an eye on us from there. I slowly made my way over to the shadow.

"Hey," I said.

"Hello," the shadow answered weakly, looking at me. My shadow looked one size smaller than the last time I'd seen him.

"Are you doing okay?" I asked.

"Yes, thanks for asking." I detected a slight tone of sarcasm.

I thought of sitting down next to him but was afraid that something might lead us to be reattached, so I stood. As the Gatekeeper said, ripping away a shadow was no easy task.

"Are you in this enclosure all day?"

"No, sometimes I go outside the wall."

"To get exercise?"

"Exercise, right . . ." My shadow frowned. He motioned toward the Gatekeeper with his chin. "The only exercise is helping *that* guy burn the beasts. I dig holes in the ground with a shovel. I guess that's a form of exercise."

"From my window I can clearly see the smoke from burning the beasts."

"The poor things. They keep on dying every day. Dropping like flies," he said. "We drag the corpses and toss them into a hole, then pour in canola oil to burn them."

"Sounds awful."

"I wouldn't call it enjoyable. The only saving grace is there's hardly any smell when we burn them."

"Are there other shadows here? Other than yourself?"

"No, no other shadows. It's only been me, since I got here."

I didn't say anything.

"I don't know how long I can stay like this," my shadow said in a low voice. "Shadows forcibly ripped apart from the body don't live very long. All the shadows who preceded me in the enclosure passed away, one after the other. Just like the beasts in the winter."

With my hands stuck in my coat pockets, I gazed down at my shadow. Occasionally a burst of north wind would blow through the elm branches, making a sharp sound above us.

My shadow said, "It's up to you to decide what you're looking for in your life. It's your life, after all. I'm a mere appendage. I don't have any great wisdom, nor any real role to play. Yet if I totally vanish, it will cause some inconvenience. I don't want to sound conceited, but I haven't been with you all this time for no reason."

"But I couldn't help doing this," I said. "I gave it a lot of thought."

Did I really? I suddenly wondered. Had I really *given it a lot of thought?* Or wasn't I like some powerless piece of driftwood, washed up here on the tide?

My shadow gave a small shrug. "I can't say anything—that's something for you to decide. But if you do want to return to the world you came from, if you do still feel that way, you'd better make up your mind soon. There's still time, but after I die, it'll be too late. Just remember that."

"I will."

"How about you? Are you getting along okay?"

I tilted my head. "Still hard to say for sure. There are a lot of things I need to learn. It's a completely different place from the world outside."

My shadow was silent for a time. Finally he raised his head and looked at me. "Were you . . . able to meet the person you were hoping to see?"

I nodded silently.

"I'm glad to hear it," my shadow said.

The wind noisily blew through the elm branches.

"At any rate, thank you for coming to see me. I'm really glad we could see each other." He raised a hand, in a thick glove, ever so slightly, in farewell.

The Gatekeeper and I went through the back gate toward his cabin.

"We should have some more snow tonight," the Gatekeeper said as we walked along. "My palm never fails to itch before it snows. The way it itches now I'd guess we'll have about this much snow." He opened his fingers about four inches apart. "And lots of beasts will die."

Back in the cabin, the Gatekeeper picked up one of the hatchets and, eyes narrowed, examined the sharpness of the blade. He took a whetstone, and with practiced hands began honing the blade. A sharp scraping sound rang out, menacingly, in the room.

"Some say the body is the temple of the soul," the Gatekeeper said. "And it could well be. But for someone like me who deals with the corpses of those poor beasts day after day, the body is no temple, but a mere dirty hovel. And I'm finding I believe less and less in the soul, crammed into that pathetic vessel. Sometimes I think it'd be best to douse it with oil, too, like the body and burn it all up. I mean, it's just a worthless thing whose only role is to live and suffer. So tell me, is my way of thinking wrong?"

How should I respond to that? Asking about the body and the soul only left me confused. Especially in this town.

"Anyhow, you'd best not take seriously anything your shadow tells you," the Gatekeeper said, picking up another hatchet. "I don't know what he told you, but those guys are pretty glib. They only want to save themselves, so they'll give you every reason they can think of. Best to keep your guard up."

I left the Gatekeeper's cabin, climbed up the western hill, and returned to my house. I turned around and saw that the sky in the north was covered with thick dark clouds filled with snow. As the Gatekeeper predicted, it looked like it would start snowing in the dead of night. And even more beasts would take their last breaths, in the midst of the snow. They would lose their souls, become nothing but pathetic empty shells, be tossed into a hole dug by my shadow, have oil poured on them, and be burned to ashes.

THAT ENTIRE SUMMER—the summer I was seventeen and you were sixteen—every time we met, you talked enthusiastically about that town. What a wonderful summer. I was in love with you, and you were in love with me (I think). Whenever we met, we'd hold hands and, away from people's eyes, we'd kiss, then huddle together, talking endlessly about that town.

The town was surrounded by a well-built wall about twenty-six feet high. The wall had been there since long ago, painstakingly constructed of uncommonly hard bricks so that even now not a single one was chipped.

A single river wound its way through the town in gentle curves, dividing it almost equally into north and south. Three beautiful stone bridges spanned the river. Near the Old Bridge, an ornately decorated stone construction, was a large sandbank lined with tall river willows, their supple branches hanging down toward the surface of the water.

On the north side of the wall was a gate. There had been another similar gate on the eastern wall but it was painted over now, and tightly filled in. The north gate—the only way into or out of the town—was guarded by the brawny Gatekeeper. The gate was only opened twice a day, in the morning and evening, to allow the beasts to pass through. The taciturn, yellowish beasts with their single sharp horns would form an orderly line every morning to enter the town, then, at night, sleep together in their grounds just outside the wall. These legendary beasts could exist only in these environs, since the only thing they ate were the nuts and leaves of a special kind of tree that grew throughout the town. The beasts were beautiful to look at but lacked vitality. Their horns were razor sharp, yet they never injured any of the townspeople.

The people who lived within the wall could not go outside the wall, and people outside the wall could not enter. That was the rule. To enter the town, a person could not have a shadow; but in order to leave, a shadow was necessary for survival. The Gatekeeper was a resident of the town, so he did not have a shadow, but when his duties required, he was allowed outside of the wall. So he was able to pick apples from the apple forest outside and eat as many as he liked. If there were any left over, he generously shared them with others. They were delicious apples, and many people were very grateful to him. The beasts chronically lacked food, and though they were always hungry, they never ate the apples. Which was unfortunate, since their grounds outside the wall were near many apple trees.

The population of the town wasn't clear—perhaps no one cared to know—but it wasn't very large. The majority of the residents lived in the northeast in the Workers' District along a desiccated canal, or on the gentle slopes of the western hill, in the Officials' District. People who lived in the Officials' District never visited the Workers' District, and vice versa.

Naturally I had many questions about the town, what it was like.

"So there's no electricity there?" I asked.

"No, no electricity," you replied, without hesitation. "No electricity or gas. The people light lamps, and cook, using canola oil. The stoves are wood burning."

"What about running water?"

"Water flows in pipes from a spring on the western hill. Turn a tap, and drinking water will flow out. There are lots of wells, too, and a lovely, clean river. So even in a bad summer drought, the town never lacks for water. The water supply system and sewage system made long ago still operate, and there are flush toilets."

"What about food?"

"Most people get by on food they grow themselves. And the townspeople eat very sparingly. They've adjusted to the environment they're in and their bodies no longer require much."

"They've evolved," I said.

"Probably," you replied.

"Do some people make things?"

"No one specializes in making dishes, tools, and clothes, so people get by with homemade essential items. They exchange tools as needed and borrow things and lend them out. And they repair and take good care of things that have been around a long time. There are lots of things in the town left over from the past. Things that people who left the town couldn't take with them. When something is really necessary, occasionally it might be brought in from the world outside. There must be a simple exchange of goods going on somewhere."

"So canola oil is an important source of fuel, right?"

"Right, and there's no lack of it. There are plenty of canola fields, and lots of oil can be easily extracted. And the people conserve and do their best to live frugally."

"Is there a kind of town hall there? An organization that decides different policies and the roles people play?"

"It's not such a big place, so probably people decide things among themselves, talking things over, and create simple rules that way. But I don't really know about that. I was a very young child when I was in that town."

"Besides those beautiful beasts with single horns, are there any other animals there? Like dogs or cats, cows or horses?"

You shook your head. "I never once saw any. There probably aren't any other animals in town besides the unicorns. No dogs or cats or domestic animals—which means there's no butter, milk, cheese, or meat, other than alternative foods. Birds, of course, are an exception. They can freely fly over any wall, no matter how high."

"Do the unicorns have shadows?"

"They do. And everything else has shadows too. Only humans don't."

"And the you that's not you—the *real* you—is still living in that walled-in town, is that right?"

"Yeah, the *real* me is living there. As I said before, I'm working in the library."

I wrote it all down in a special notebook—everything you said about the town, how it was constructed, all the sights. That's how I obtained all sorts of knowledge about the town and how it became palpably real to me.

"What good will it do for you to take notes?" you asked, looking curious. You didn't see the need to write down each and every thing.

"I do it so I don't forget, that's why. I want to write everything down and record it precisely. So there's no mistake. Because this town is something that just the two of us—you and I—share."

If I go to that town I'll be able to have the *real* you. And you will probably give me *everything*. Having you in that town is all I could want. There your heart and your body were one, and beneath the faint light of an oil lamp, I could hold you tight. That's what I was seeking.

In the fall the letters from you stopped coming. A new school year began, and your last letter arrived in the middle of September. After that, not a single one. I kept writing you long letters, but got no reply. Why? Had your heart, as you put it, *gone rigid*, but for a long time, making it impossible to write?

"I want to be yours," you'd said on the park bench. "Completely, totally yours."

Those words kept echoing in my head. I knew they weren't a lie, an exaggeration, a passing whim. You never said something that wasn't truly from your heart. Whatever you said was a promise that I could count on, written down in special ink on special paper.

So I wasn't so worried. I had to be patient. As I waited for a letter from you, I kept up my usual pace of letter writing. I wrote down everyday things that happened to me, thoughts that popped into my head. I'd add questions that had occurred to me about the town behind the wall. Always with the same stationery, the same fountain pen, the same ink. But after more than a month had passed with no letter from you, I decided I'd just go ahead and call your house. I'd never called you before. You'd said something to the effect that you didn't want me to call you there. A round-about way of putting it, but I got the message. Something about your situation (what that was, I have no idea) made you dislike the idea of a phone call from me. But I couldn't just continue to wait for a letter from you. I just couldn't.

I tried you six times, but no one ever picked up. All I heard was the sound of the phone ringing, in vain, its ring in time with the beating of my heart. Maybe no one was at home. The seventh time I called (it was past nine thirty at night), a middle-aged man answered, in a low, sullen voice. I told him my name, apologized for calling so late, and said I wanted to talk with you. But the man said nothing in reply and simply hung up, like slamming a door shut in my face.

October came and went, I turned eighteen, and November arrived. Autumn deepened. My high school life would soon draw to a close. I grew more worried. Had something happened to you? Had you just vanished into thin air, like smoke? Or had you, by chance, forgotten all about me?

No, you wouldn't forget me that easily. Like I wouldn't forget you. Again and again, I tried to convince myself. But how much did I know about the psychology and physiology of women anyway? No, forget about generalizations—how much did I know about *you*?

I realized I knew next to nothing about you. I had almost no concrete information or objective facts, nothing I could state with certainty was *for sure*—all I had to go on was what you yourself had told me. You told me these as facts, but I had no way of knowing if indeed they really were the truth. It might all have been made up. As a possibility—and just as a possibility—it wasn't impossible.

The only certain thing I knew, the only palpable fact, was the "town surrounded by a wall" that you told me about over the course of a summer. All the details were in my notebook. That was the secret town whose existence only the two of us knew about. If I went there, I could meet you—the *real* you. When I grew tired of waiting for a letter from you, when I felt glum, I would often close my eyes and imagine the sandbank on the river, lined with river willows. The lush green branches swaying in the gentle breeze. I could smell the fragrance of the Scotch broom leaves that the unicorns were so eagerly eating. I could feel, with my fingertips, the hard, cold surface of the bricks of the wall.

Autumn was over and winter came on. The calendar reached its last page, people bundled up in coats, with Christmas carols, as always, playing throughout the city. All my classmates could think of were the college entrance exams. Not that I cared. Whether I was at home, in the classroom, riding the train, or walking down a street, all I thought about was you. And the details of that nameless town you and I had created together. I added more details on my own, more color to the picture.

"For me, lots of things take time," you'd said. I kept repeating those words to myself, silently, like some spell. And I watched, patiently, as time passed. I glanced at my watch all the time, checking the calendar on the wall I don't know how many times, sometimes even opening up a historical chronology chart. Time passed slowly, though, never once reversing course. One minute took one minute, one hour took exactly one hour. Time passes ever so slowly, yet it doesn't rewind. That's the lesson that period of life taught me. Obvious, of course, but sometimes it's the obvious things that have the most significance.

And then finally, one day, a letter from you arrived. A thick envelope, with a long letter inside.

WATER FLOWED DOWN from the ridges, beneath the wall next to the east gate—now heavily boarded up and painted over, then down through the middle of the town. Just as the human brain is divided into right and left, the river divided the town into two halves, north and south.

Past the West Bridge, the river turned to the left, inscribing a gentle curve as it flowed by the hillocks and then reached the south wall. At the wall it came to a stop, forming a deep pool, where at the bottom it was swallowed up by limestone caves. Outside the south gate lay a vast stretch of rugged limestone wasteland, as far as the eye could see. It was wild, odd-looking scenery. And beneath that wasteland lay countless channels, like veins. A dark labyrinth.

Occasionally weird-looking fish would swim up through that dark river and wash ashore. Most of them had no eyes (or not fully developed ones). Once exposed to the sun, they'd give off a truly hideous smell. Not to imply that I'd ever actually seen them. I'd just heard stories.

Apart from that ominous detail, the river was entirely graceful and refreshing. There were all kinds of seasonal flowers blossoming on its banks, the pleasant sound of running water as you passed by, and it provided fresh drinking water for the beasts. The river was nameless. It was simply called "the river." Just as the town was without a name.

As I heard all kinds of intriguing stories about the pool next to the south wall, I began to want to see it with my own eyes. But I didn't know enough yet about the topography of the town to walk there on my own. To get to the pool you needed to cross some steep hills, apparently, and the path there was mostly in ruins. So I asked you to lead me there. On some cloudy afternoon, I asked, would you be able to go with me to see the southern pool?

You thought it over for a time, your thin lips set in a tight line.

"It's best not to get close to the pool, you know," you said. (You'd

grown used to me now and felt comfortable speaking informally.)
"It's a very dangerous place. A few people have fallen in and were
sucked underground and never seen again. And there are other
frightening stories about the place. Townspeople try to avoid it."

"I just want to look at it from a distance," I explained to you.
"See what it's like. If we don't get near the water, we'll be okay, I
imagine."

You shook your head a fraction. "No, no matter how careful
you are, the water there still calls to you. The pool has the power
to do that."

I had my doubts. Wasn't that just a rumor intentionally spread
to keep people from going near there? All sorts of scary stories
about the world outside the town were whispered among the people, most of them completely baseless. The stories about the pool
(ominous traditions handed down) might be the same kind of
threatening tales. For the pool connected with the world outside
the wall, and if the goal was to keep townspeople from going outside, it was possible you'd construct a psychological mechanism to
make them avoid it. For me, these frightening tales about the pool
only sparked a greater curiosity. But in the end my persistence
won you over and you agreed to go on a short hike (or maybe a
long walk) to the pool.

"Can you promise me you'll never get close to the water's edge?"

"I won't go near it. I'll just look at it from a distance. I promise."

"The road's going to be pretty rough, I think. It might be falling apart. Hardly anyone ever goes there, and the last time I went
was ages ago."

"If you'd rather not go, that's okay. I can go by myself."

You shook you head emphatically. "No. If you go, then so will I."

On a cloudy afternoon we met up at the Old Bridge and headed
south. You had on gloves and carried a bag made from rough cloth
on your shoulders. Inside was a water bottle, bread, and a blanket,
like you were going on a holiday picnic. I couldn't help remembering the time, in the world outside the wall, when I went on dates
with you—or your twin "other self." There I'd been seventeen,
and you sixteen. You had on a sleeveless green dress. A pale green

that was perfect for summer—like the cool shade beneath a tree. But that was a different world, a different time. And a different season as well.

The road climbed uphill, the rocky places even steeper, and we could catch glimpses of the river meandering below. But more often the dense trees blocked the view of the river. Leaden clouds hung low in the sky, and rain or snow seemed imminent, but you had earlier declared we needn't worry about that. So we hadn't brought along umbrellas or rainwear. For some reason everyone in this town had their own strong convictions when it came to predicting the weather. And as far as I knew, these predictions were never off.

The frozen snow from three days before crunched under our shoes. We passed several beasts along the way. They were trudging along the road, their thin necks listlessly swinging from side to side, white breath coming from their half-open mouths. With blank eyes, as if in a dream, they were searching for the remaining leaves on the trees. As winter deepened, their golden fur turned a bleached white, making them one with the snow.

Once we'd climbed the steep slope and passed the southern hills, we no longer saw any beasts. They never set foot any farther than that, you told me. The beasts inside the wall followed several strict rules. Rules made just for *them*. No one knew, though, when or how those rules had been established. It was hard to understand the reason for many of them, or the meaning behind them.

We walked downhill for a time, and the clear-cut road petered out, replaced by an indistinct, overgrown footpath. The river had vanished, as had the sound of the water. Carefully, we wandered through a deserted, dried-up field, passing a couple of dilapidated, abandoned houses along the way. There'd apparently been a small village here at one time, but now, only fragments remained. You walked ahead of me, and I followed. Even on the slopes that rendered me breathless, you walked on casually, your steps calm and even, with your healthy young legs and heart, and it was all I could do to keep up. Before long, there came a strange sound I'd never heard before. At times it was low and thick, at times suddenly higher pitched. Then it would stop altogether.

"What's that sound?"

"The sound of the water in the pool," you said, without looking back at me.

But it didn't sound like water. To my ears it sounded like the wheezing of a giant, diseased respiratory organ.

"It sounds like it's saying something to us."

"It's calling out to us," you said.

"The pool has its own will?"

"Long ago people believed there was a dragon that lived at the bottom of the pool."

Pushing aside the grasses with your thickly gloved hands, you silently made your way forward. The grasses became progressively higher, making it even harder to stay on the path.

"The path's much worse than when I last came here," you said.

We headed toward that strange water sound, trampling down the grasses and making our way through a thicket for about ten minutes, when all of a sudden, the view cleared. Before us lay a gentle, lovely grassy plain. The river beyond, though, wasn't the same river I saw in the town. Here that graceful flow, with its soothing sound, was no more. At the final curve, the river reached its end, its color suddenly transforming into a deep green, swelling up for all the world like some snake swallowing down its prey, and creating a huge pool.

"Don't go near it," you cautioned, grabbing my arm. "There are no ripples on the surface so it looks quite placid, but once it sucks you down, you'll never surface again."

"How deep is it?"

"Nobody knows. No one's ever dived to the bottom and returned. According to tales, in olden times heretics and prisoners of war were thrown in. This was before the wall."

"If you're thrown in, you never resurface?"

"At the bottom of the pool are caves, and people who fall in the water are sucked inside. And they drown at the bottom, in the pitch dark." You shivered, as if you'd felt a chill.

The breathing sound emitted by the pool was oppressive. That breathing was low, then suddenly higher, then it broke apart, like it was coughing. And then an eerie silence came on. This cycle repeated. Perhaps this was the sound of the caves sucking in massive amounts of water. In the grass you found a slice of wood about the thickness of a sheep's leg bone and tossed it into the pool. The wood floated silently on the surface for about five seconds, then shuddered a few times, stood up vertically like a finger in the surface of the water, then disappeared below, as if something had pulled it down. And it never resurfaced again. All that remained was the pool's deep breathing.

"You see that? At the bottom is a powerful whirlpool that drags everything down to the darkness."

Keeping a safe distance from the pool, we spread out the blanket we'd brought on top of the grass and sat down. We drank water from the canteen, and quietly chewed on the bread you'd brought in your bag. Viewed from a distance, the scenery around us looked perfectly peaceful. The grassy plain stood before us, dotted with leftover lumps of white snow, and at its center stood a pool, smooth and tranquil, without a single ripple disturbing its surface. Beyond the plain lay rough limestone rocks on a rocky mountain, on top of which loomed the southern wall. Except for the intermittent, irregular breathing of the pool, it was quiet all around. I didn't see any birds. Maybe even the birds, able to freely travel back and forth over the wall, avoided flying over the pool.

Beyond this pool lay the outside world. I imagined myself leaping in, being sucked down by the current, and swimming under the wall to emerge into the world outside. But what lay beyond this was a darkness, a wasteland below the limestone rocks that exist in the world outside, after passing under the wall. And if you believed the stories the townspeople told, you'd never come out on the surface of the earth alive again.

"It's true," you said, as if reading my thoughts. "It's a frightening world down there, in the bowels of the earth, without any light. The only things living there are fish with no eyes."

The old man with the limp who'd nursed me back to health when I'd had a high fever—the former officer who'd seen the ghost of a beautiful woman in a hot springs inn—came to update me on my shadow. He doesn't seem to be doing very well, he reported.

"I had to stop by the Gatekeeper's cabin, and he said your shadow has no appetite and throws up almost everything he puts in his mouth. The last three days he hasn't been able to go out to work. He apparently wants to see you."

That afternoon, after I saw the smoke rising from the burning beasts, I visited the Gatekeeper's cabin. As I'd thought, the Gatekeeper wasn't there, but outside the wall. Burning the beasts took time. I went inside the cabin and came out the exit in back to the shadow enclosure.

My shadow was lying face up on his bed in his room. The room had a woodstove, but it wasn't lit. The air was cold, and it had that stuffy smell of rooms with sick people. At the top of the wall was a skylight window that faced the square. The lamp wasn't lit, and the room was dim.

I sat down on the small chair beside the bed. My shadow stared up at the ceiling, his breathing slow. His lips were dry, probably due to the fever, and scabby in spots. With each breath came a small, hoarse sound from the back of his throat. I felt bad for him. Until a short time before he'd been, unquestionably, a part of me.

"I heard you aren't feeling well."

"I'm not," my shadow said weakly. "I don't think I can hang on much longer."

"Where does it hurt?"

"It's not like that. It's a question of longevity. As I told you, shadows on their own don't last long. A shadow separated from the body is a fleeting thing."

I had no idea what to say.

"I will probably die here, like this. And then I'll be burned in a hole along with the beasts. Oil poured over me. But unlike the beasts, no smoke will rise up from my body."

"Do you want me to light the stove?" I asked.

My shadow shook his head slightly. "No, I'm not cold. All sorts of sensations are fading away. I can't taste food anymore, either."

"Is there something I can do?"

"Lend me your ears."

I crouched down and brought my ear closer to my shadow. In a small, hoarse voice, almost a whisper, he said, "You see the knots in that wall there?"

I looked over at the wall across from the bed and did see three or four black knots. The wall was made of cheap boards.

"They've been keeping watch on me."

I looked at the knots for a while, but they never looked like anything other than old knots in a board wall.

"Keeping watch?"

"They move around at night to different spots," my shadow said. "In the morning they're in different places. It's true."

I walked over to the wall and inspected each knot closely. Nothing seemed unusual. They were just dried-up knotholes on rough-hewn wood.

"During the day they stay put. But at night they move around. And they blink sometimes. Like people's eyes."

I traced one of the knotholes with my finger. It just felt like rough wood. *Blink?*

"When I'm not looking, they'll quickly blink. But I know what they're doing. They're secretly blinking."

"And they're watching you."

"Right. Waiting for me to breathe my last."

I went back to where I'd been and sat down on the chair.

"Make up your mind within a week," my shadow said. "If it's a week or less, you and I can become one again and get out of this town. And I'll recover. There's still time if we act now."

"But I'm not allowed to leave here. I made an agreement when I came into the town."

"I know. According to the agreement you can't go out this gate again. Which leaves only one other exit—the pool in the south. The entrance to the east of the river is blocked by an iron grate, so it's impossible to go out from there. The pool's the only possibility."

"But there's a powerful whirlpool at the bottom of the pool and you'll be sucked down into a channel in the depths of the earth. I actually saw it the other day. It's impossible to get out alive that way."

"That's bogus. They just made up that scary story to threaten people. I think if you go into the pool and under the wall, you'll soon be breathing the air outside. While I've been here, I've been looking into things in the town, trying to figure them out. People stop by this cabin from time to time, and the Gatekeeper's more talkative than you'd expect, so I've heard a lot. A dark channel in the depths of the earth has got to be a made-up story. This town is full of made-up stories. From its origins and on so many other topics, it's full of contradictions."

I nodded. He could be right. As my shadow said, the town might be full of made-up stories, the origins of the town itself rife with contradictions. Since this was nothing but an imaginary town you and I had dreamed up over the course of a summer. Nevertheless, the town might actually be able to snatch away a person's life, since it was already out of our hands and had grown on its own. Once it was set in motion, I couldn't control that power or alter it. *Nobody could.*

"But if what they say *is* true?"

"Then we both might drown."

I was silent.

"But I'm certain of it," my shadow said. "Certain that the story is nonsense. I can't prove it, though. You can only trust my intuition. This might sound like bragging, but shadows have a certain amount of ability in that area."

"Yet you can't prove it."

"That's right. Unfortunately, I have no real proof."

"If possible, I'd like to not drown in the darkness."

"Neither would I, of course. But let me say one thing. You think what's in the outside world is the girl's shadow and the real girl is here in this town. But is that true? It might be the opposite. Maybe what's in the world outside is the real girl, and what's here is merely a shadow. If that's true, then what's the point of remaining in this world of made-up stories and contradictions? Are you certain about this—that the girl in this town is the *real* her?"

I mulled over what my shadow had said. But the more I thought about it, the more confused I became.

"But is that possible? For a real person and their shadow to change places? To mistake which is real and which is the shadow?"

"*You* wouldn't do that. And neither would I. The true person is just that, the shadow a shadow. Yet something might happen to reverse things. Maybe things can be deliberately replaced."

I stayed silent.

"I think you and I should become one again and return to the world outside the wall. I'm not just saying this because I don't want to die here. It's for your sake, too. I mean it. Listen. In my eyes the world out there is the real world. People struggle there, grow old, grow weak, and die. Not so wonderful maybe, but isn't that what the world's really like? You're supposed to accept that. And, as best I can, I join you in that. You can't stop time, and when you die, you're dead forever. Things that disappear are gone for good. You have to accept that that's the way things are."

The room was steadily growing darker. The Gatekeeper might soon be back.

"Don't you find this place like a theme park?" my shadow asked, and laughed listlessly. "The gates open in the morning, and close at night. And there's scenery, like a stage backdrop, all over the place. There are even unicorns roaming around."

"Can you let me think about it?" I asked. "I need time to think."

"Why do you think the beasts die so easily here?"

I don't know, I said.

"They take on all kinds of things, and quietly pass away. Probably as a sacrifice for the people here. To create the town, to keep the system going, someone has to take on that role. And those poor creatures are the scapegoats."

The room had grown considerably colder. I shivered and drew my coat collar closer.

"Understood. You need time to think," my shadow said. "This town has as much time as you need. But sadly I don't have much time. Please, within a week, decide one way or the other."

I nodded. I left my shadow, and the Gatekeeper's cabin, and headed to the library. I passed by a group of four beasts going the other way. Even after they disappeared from view, I could still hear the clatter of their hooves on the cobblestones.

I DIDN'T OPEN THE LETTER that came from you, but placed it, still sealed, in a drawer for half a day. I wanted to read it as soon as I could, of course, but I had a premonition (a fear, perhaps) that I'd better not. So I waited, my heart trembling all the while.

It was past ten p.m. when I took the letter out of the drawer and carefully opened it with scissors. Inside was a letter on six pages of thin stationery. Finely written words in fountain pen, in the familiar turquoise-blue ink. At my desk I closed my eyes, calmed my breathing, unfolded the pages, and began to read.

> Hello. How are you? The season has changed. Everything around me seems different, even the air. I may have changed a bit as well. But how, I can't say. I can't see myself, how I am. It would be nice if my heart could be clearly reflected in a mirror.
>
> I haven't written you a letter for a long time. I started to write many times, but always failed. I'd write a couple of lines and then run into a wall. One sentence just wouldn't connect up with another. Words didn't want to connect with each other and scattered in all directions. And then they'd be gone for good.
>
> I've almost never experienced that before. What I mean is even if all kinds of other things weren't going well, writing always saved me. One sentence led to another, all of them expressing what was in my heart (of course—*of course*—only up to a point). But I don't think I can anymore, and it makes me terribly disappointed. No—not disappointed. More like a feeling of despair, like all the doors in the house are closed and locked tightly from the outside. A deep sense of helplessness . . . a heavy lead box sunk at the bottom of the sea, that can never be opened. I mean, if I can't write letters, I won't

be able to share my feelings with you anymore.
And that would be like not being able to breathe.

I haven't spoken a word to anyone for over a week.
None of the words I say (or will say from now on)
express what I intend them to, none of them make any
sense. So I've kept silent all this time. Not that silence
is the goal, but if I were to speak words that aren't real
[a thick line was drawn under these words with a pencil]
I feel like I would crumble to pieces and end up like a
discarded piece of trash.

Somehow today, as you can see, I was able to pick
up my pen and write. I don't know why, but I can write
now, like a ray of sunlight had shone through a gap in
thick clouds. For the first time in ages . . . Weird, isn't
it? Maybe this is a fragment of a miracle or something.
So I'm writing this quickly while I still have hold of that
fragment. Like a race against time (imagine a telegraph
operator in the communications room of a ship,
desperately tapping out a message as his ship is sinking).

So my writing here is pretty rough, the meaning
unclear in places, I'm sure. But anyway, I'm trying to
get down, in one fell swoop (is that the right spelling?),
what's on my mind. Because I have no idea when I'll
be able to write a letter next. Maybe tomorrow (or ten
minutes from now) I won't be able to even get out a
single line again. My words will scatter in directions I
never intended. Turn a corner and the world might very
well have vanished.

So—what am I?

That's a huge issue.

I think I said this before, but the me who's here is
just a substitute for the *real* me. Nothing more than the
shadow of the real me. An actual shadow. And a shadow
separated from their body won't live long. It's pretty rare
to survive this long, like I've done. It's not normal. When
I was three, I was forced to leave my body—driven
outside the wall of the town where I lived and raised by

temporary parents. My late mother and my father, who's still alive, think (or thought) I'm their real daughter, but of course that's an illusion. I am just somebody's shadow, nothing more, blown in by the wind from a far-off town. They don't (didn't) know this and believed I was their real child. *Someone* led them to believe this. In other words, their memories had been completely changed. So they can't imagine how much I've suffered as a result (being nothing but someone's shadow).

Honestly, until I met you, I never revealed this to anyone, that I'm a mere shadow. I thought no one would understand. They'd think I'm insane. Which is why meeting you like this had been so special for me. I never imagined a miracle would happen to me, and truthfully, I still don't totally believe it. *Yet it actually occurred.* Like a windless morning when something beautiful flutters down from a clear sky.

I haven't gone to school for a long time. It's painful for me to go outside. I tried many times to go but couldn't even turn two corners. Rounding the first corner was excruciating, and I couldn't bring myself to round the second. I was terrified. No, that's not it . . . The reason I couldn't round that corner was because I knew what lay beyond.

At any rate, I just couldn't face you, couldn't let you see me like this. My vitality (or *something like* vitality) is draining away, like air escaping from a balloon. I can't keep it from deflating. I only have but two hands, ten fingers, and can't stop it. I don't know what to do. So what *should* I do?

But please believe me. What I told you before on the park bench is all the truth.

I am yours. If you wanted it, I think I want to give you all of me. Everything. It's just that right now I can't. Please understand this.

I told you then that things take me time. I forget the

exact words, but I recall saying something like that to you. Do you remember? But I might not have much time left. Which is why I'm pounding desperately at the telegraph key, tapping out my SOS. Pounding and pounding . . . Yet I might not get the final message out. The sea might break down the door at any minute and rush in. Icy, malicious, salty—the deadly sea.

Farewell.
    I hope the day will come when I will be better, when the sunlight breaks through the clouds and I can write a nice long letter in ink to you with my good old fountain pen. I really do hope so. (I really do. Truly . . . from deep, deep down in my heart.)

December **

** [Your name]

    But that sunlight never seemed to shine through. For that was the last letter I ever received from you.

DAY AFTER DAY I read old dreams in the back of the library. Other than the week I was laid up with a high fever, I didn't take a day off. And you too were there every day (the town had no days of the week, and therefore no such thing as a weekend), helping me with my work. You wore faded, mended clothes, though they always seemed quite clean. Those plain, unadorned outfits highlighted your beauty and youth more than any other clothing could. Your skin was lustrous and taut and gave off a fresh glow under the light of the oil lamps. As if it had only just now come into being.

One night I had a strange dream. No, not a dream, but a scene from one of the old dreams I'd read in the stacks. Or perhaps one of the reminiscences the old man, the former soldier, had told me when I'd been sick, and my mind was hazy. Maybe it had been etched so strongly in my memory that my mind re-created it.

In that dream (or dream-like experience), I was a soldier. A war was on, and I wore an officer's uniform and was leading a patrol. I had six soldiers under me, including a seasoned NCO. We were on a recon mission in the mountains where the war was taking place. I don't know what season it was, but it wasn't hot or cold.

Early in the morning we saw a group of people, all dressed in white, near the top of the mountain. There must have been about thirty of them. My patrol immediately took up combat positions, but we soon realized that wasn't necessary. The people weren't armed, and among them were elderly people, and women and children. We could have stopped them and questioned them about who they were and what they were doing, but since they wouldn't have understood our language, I gave up on the idea. (We were fighting in a land far away from our homeland.)

The men and women were all dressed in the same white clothes. They wore rough, simple white outfits, as though they'd wrapped a sheet around themselves and fastened it with rope. No one had on shoes or sandals. They looked like some religious group. Or patients who'd escaped from a hospital. They didn't look likely to harm anyone, but to play it safe, we followed them.

The people in white were climbing up a steep slope, utterly silent. A tall, thin old man was in the lead. He had long white hair down to his shoulders. The rest silently followed. They finally reached the peak. On the right-hand side was a sheer cliff, and they headed toward it. The white-haired old man jumped. Without a word, without any hesitation, like it was the most natural thing in the world, he held his arms slightly apart and leaped off the cliff. And the others followed suit, one after another, no indecision whatsoever. Like a flock of birds taking flight, they spread their white-clothed arms, and lightly leaped into the air. Women, children, not a single one left, all without expression. It almost made me think they might really be able to fly.

But of course they couldn't fly. We rushed over to the edge of the cliff and gazed down below, fearful of what we'd see. The floor of the ravine was littered with dead bodies. The white clothes were spread wide like flags and dyed with splattered blood and brain matter. A rocky area at the bottom of the ravine stuck up like sharp fangs and had shattered the people's heads to pieces. I'd seen many miserable dead bodies in battle, but something in this horrific, bloody scene made me want to avert my eyes. But what shook us most was their silence and expressionless faces as they leaped to their deaths. No matter what awful circumstances they were facing, could someone really face their death so calmly, so numbly?

"Why?" I asked the sergeant next to me. "Who *were* these people? And why would they have to do that?"

The sergeant shook his head. "Probably they wanted to obliterate their minds," he said dryly. He wiped his mouth with the back of his hand. "Sometimes that's the easiest thing to do."

"My shadow seems to be dying," I confessed to you one night at the library.

We were in front of the stove, seated across from each other at the table. That night with the herbal tea you'd also brought out a sweet apple dish sprinkled with white powder. Here this was a precious food. The Gatekeeper had most likely given you some apples and you'd made it specially for me.

"He won't last very long," I said. "Since he's so weak."

When you heard this, your face grew a bit cloudy. "I feel sorry for him," you said, "but there's nothing that can be done. A dark heart will, sooner or later, die and perish. You have to accept that."

"Do you remember your shadow?"

You rubbed a slim finger on your forehead, as if tracing the plot of a story.

"As I said, my shadow was ripped away when I was very young and I haven't met her since. So I don't know what it means to have a shadow. Does not having one . . . cause problems?"

"I don't really know. I haven't had any particular problems since he was ripped away. But if my shadow is lost forever, I get the feeling that something else very important will be lost too."

You gazed into my eyes. "What would that very important thing be?"

"I can't really say. I can't grasp what it is to lose your shadow forever."

You opened the little door to the stove and added a few sticks of firewood, then used the bellows to stir up the fire.

"So your shadow wants something from you?"

"He wants to be together with me again. Then he will regain his vitality."

"But if you and your shadow are together again, you can't stay in this town."

"Exactly."

You can't look up at the sky with a plate on your head, the Gatekeeper had told me.

"If that's the case, then you have to give up on your shadow," you said quietly. "I feel sorry for him, but you'll get used to life in this town without one. After a while you'll probably forget about him. Just like everyone does."

I took a bite of the sweet apple dish and enjoyed the flavor.

The sweet-sour taste spread through me. *What delicious apples*, I thought. I realized this was the first time since I'd come to the town that I thought anything tasted *delicious*.

Your eyes reflected the light from the stove. No, it wasn't reflected light, but light that dwelled within you.

"There's nothing to worry about," you said. "Since you've come here you've done an excellent job. Everyone's impressed. I'm sure things will continue to go well."

I nodded.

Everyone's impressed.

THAT WAS THE LAST LETTER I ever received from you.

I read it, over and over, so many times I memorized every detail. And I pictured you on a sinking ship—I always imagined a huge passenger ship like the *Titanic*—in the telegraph room, desperately tapping out a message. Sending out a final message to me. As the icy seawater might at any moment break down the door and inundate the room.

I prayed that a miracle would happen and the seawater wouldn't flood inside. That the ship would right itself and barely avoid a catastrophe. I could imagine the heartwarming scene on deck as the crew and passengers, having narrowly escaped danger, hugged each other, shed tears of gratitude, and thanked God or whomever for their good fortune.

Most likely, though, things didn't go that well. No miracle happened, no good fortune visited them, no hugs of joy. Since after that I never heard from you again.

I wrote and sent many more letters to you but never got a reply. None were returned as undeliverable, address unknown. And no phone calls came. I went ahead and called your home. But no matter how many times I dialed, all I heard was a recording telling me *This number is not in service at this time.* The phone was of no help to me. If you wanted to tell me something you would call me.

So there was no word from you at all, and I couldn't meet you or talk with you. A new year came, with college entrance exams in February, and I was slated to attend a private university in Tokyo. I could have gone to a local university, of course, and I'd originally been planning to (so I could be even a little closer to you), but in the end, I chose to go to Tokyo, to put physical distance between you and me. If I had remained at home, I would have spent my life waiting for you to get in touch. And a *life spent waiting* would mean I couldn't think of anything other than you. Of course, I wouldn't mind. Since you were what I wanted in this world, more than anything.

At the same time, I had a kind of premonition that if I continued my life as it was, I couldn't hold myself together, and would lose something crucial inside. I had to put an end to it. And I knew that for our relationship, physical distance was nowhere near as important as emotional distance. If you really wanted me, really needed me, physical distance would be no obstacle. So I made the decision to leave the city I had grown up in and move to Tokyo.

In Tokyo I continued to write you letters, though I never got a reply. What fate awaited the stack of letters I wrote you? Did you ever read them? Or did someone toss them, unopened, in the trash? It's an eternal mystery. Still, I went on writing, using the same fountain pen, the same stationery, the same black ink. Writing letters was all I could do.

In the letters I wrote about my daily life in Tokyo. About things at my university. About how most classes at university were unimaginably boring, about how I wasn't really interested in the people around me. About the tiny record shop in Shinjuku where I had a part-time job at night. About the lively, noisy city. About how futile my life was without you. About what we could do if we were together, about all kinds of exciting plans for us. But again, no replies. It felt like standing on the edge of a deep hole, talking to the darkness at the bottom. Yet I knew you were there. I couldn't see you. Or hear your voice. But you were there. That much I knew.

All that was left was the bundle of thick letters you'd written me in turquoise-blue ink, and the white gauze handkerchief I'd never returned. I read and reread those letters over and over, treasuring them. And held that handkerchief tight in my hand.

Life in Tokyo was very lonely. It was as if now that I'd lost contact with you (though I was unsure if that loss was temporary or permanent), I couldn't get along with other people. I always had that tendency, but now it became all the stronger. I couldn't see the point of being with anyone other than you. At university I didn't belong to any clubs or groups, and never found anyone I could call a friend. My mind was focused solely on you. No—more like I was focused on the memories you'd left inside me.

I stayed holed up in my apartment, reading lots of books,

watching double features at second-run movie theaters, taking long swims at the city swimming pool from time to time. I'd go on long, aimless walks until my legs gave out. Tokyo is a huge city, and I could walk endlessly and still never run out of streets. Did I do anything else besides that? Maybe. I can't remember.

Summer break came, and with it a long-awaited return home, but things only got worse. I went to the part of town where you lived almost every other day. I sat on the park bench where we used to sit, under the wisteria arbor, and I thought about you. Retracing memories of the time we'd spent together. All the while holding on to a sliver of hope that you might show up. But it never happened.

Using your address and a map, I tried visiting your home. At that address stood a small two-story house. No garden or garage, just an old house with a narrow entrance. But the nameplate at the front door showed somebody else's last name. Your family seemed to have moved. So had the letters I sent you been forwarded? If I went to the local post office, would they tell me your new address? I doubted it. And even if they did, I knew it wouldn't help. I knew, once more, that if you had had something you had to tell me, you would have gotten in touch, no matter what it took.

And so I lost all clues that might have helped me find you. You had, seemingly, disappeared from my world, without a trace, or a word of explanation. And I had no idea if this withdrawal was something you wanted, or whether it was some irresistible power (like cold seawater crashing down the door and rushing in). All that remained was a deep silence, vivid memories, and an unfulfilled promise.

It was a sad, lonely summer. I kept descending dark stairs that went on forever. So deep it felt like they would take me to the center of the earth. I didn't care, though, and continued descending. I could tell that gravity and the density of the air around me were slowly changing. But so what? It was just air. Just gravity.

And I grew all the more isolated and alone.

THAT AFTERNOON, after I saw the gray smoke from the burning beasts rising outside the wall, I hurried to the Gatekeeper's cabin. There was no wind, and the smoke rose straight up, sucked into the thick clouds. As I'd expected, the Gatekeeper was away again, outside the wall, burning the beasts' bodies. I went out the back door of the Gatekeeper's cabin like before, cut across the shadow enclosure, and saw my shadow again, lying there. He was still gaunt and pale, coughing painfully at times.

"So, have you decided?" my shadow asked, hoarsely, as if waiting.

"I'm sorry, but it's hard to make up my mind."

"Is something bothering you?"

Unsure how to reply, I looked away and gazed out the window. How should I explain it to him?

My shadow sighed. "I don't know what happened, but I think the town is trying to stop you. Using all kinds of methods to do so."

"Am I that important to the town? That it would go to such lengths to stop me?"

"Of course it would. I mean, it's like you're the one who created this town."

"I didn't do it on my own," I said. "I just lent a hand, a long time ago."

"But without your enthusiasm, all these detailed structures would never have come about. You supported this town for a long time, nourishing it with the power of your imagination."

"It's true this town came out of *our* imagination, but over time the town's taken on a will of its own and has its own goals."

"It's beyond your control? Is that what you mean?"

I nodded. "This town is like a living being that moves on its own. A pliable, clever living being that changes shape as needed. I've sensed this ever since I came here."

"But if it can freely change shape, it's more like a cell than a living being."

"Maybe so."

A cell that thinks, protects itself, and attacks.

We were silent for a time, and I glanced out the window again. Smoke was still rising outside the wall. Many beasts must have lost their lives.

"So what are all these old dreams I keep on reading every night at the library?" I asked my shadow. "What meaning do they have for the town?"

My shadow laughed weakly. "You got me there. I mean, you're the one who reads them every night, right? Why ask *me* about this?"

"Well, you're here, and I thought you might have heard something. From the Gatekeeper, or people who stop by."

My shadow quietly shook his head. "Old dreams are collected in the library, and the Dream Reader—you, in other words—reads them every day. Everyone knows that. And everyone knows that every night when you're done, you walk her home . . . It's a small town, you know. But as for what role your dream reading plays for the town, I honestly don't think anybody knows. I get that feeling."

My shadow coughed dryly, then seemed lost in thought. I took my hands out of my pockets and rubbed them together on my lap. The room had grown colder.

My shadow spoke. "I've said this before, but can't you consider that maybe here, she's only a shadow, and that the girl outside the wall is the real person? It's bothered me for a long time. I've asked people who come here, and I've gathered bits and pieces of information and given it some thought. Here's my hypothesis: Isn't this a land of shadows, where shadows gather, huddle together in this isolated town, and live quiet lives?"

"Okay, but if this *is* a land of shadows, why was I, the real me, allowed to enter this town and why are you, a shadow, confined here and dying? I could understand if it were the opposite."

"I think that the people here don't know they're shadows. They think they're real people, and that their shadows have been ripped apart from them and driven away to the world beyond the wall. But maybe it's the other way around. Maybe those driven outside the wall are the real people, and those who remain here are the shadows. That's my conjecture."

I considered this. "And the real people banished outside the wall are convinced they're shadows. Is that what you mean?"

"That's right. That they exist on false memories."

I kept rubbing my hands together as I tried to follow the logic. But halfway through I lost the thread.

"But that's just your hypothesis."

"That's right," my shadow admitted. "It's all just a hypothesis I came up with. I can't prove it. But the more I think about it, the more convinced of it I am. I've examined every detail, from every angle. Anyhow, I've got lots of time to think here."

"So according to your theory, what role does my dream reading at the library play?"

"That's just an extension of the theory."

"I don't care—I'd like to hear it."

My shadow paused for a moment, caught his breath, and then spoke.

"I think old dreams are like echoes of the minds left behind by real people, people who've been banished from the town in order for it to exist. Real people are driven out, but it's never completely perfect, there's always something left behind. Those remnants of the mind are gathered together and tightly locked away in special receptacles called old dreams."

"Echoes of the mind?"

"While people are still young here, the body and the shadow are ripped apart. And then the body is exiled outside the wall as something superfluous, something harmful. So the shadows can live peacefully. But even if the body is banished, its influence doesn't totally disappear. The tiniest parts of the mind that can't be removed, like seeds, remain, and quietly grow inside the shadows. So the town finds them, collects them, and seals them inside special containers."

"Seeds of the mind?"

"That's right. Human emotions. Sadness, confusion, jealousy, fear, distress, despair, doubt, hatred, bewilderment, anguish, skepticism, self-pity . . . and dreams, and love. In this town, feelings are not just useless but harmful. Like *seeds* of an epidemic."

"*Seeds* of an epidemic," I said, repeating my shadow's words.

"Yes. That's why they're completely scraped away and sealed in airtight containers, then stored deep inside the library. And ordinary people are forbidden to get near them."

"So my role is—?"

"Is to take those souls—or echoes of the heart—calm them, and eliminate them. It's not a job that shadows can do. Only real people, with real emotions, have empathy."

"But why do they have to be calmed? They're sealed away in airtight containers, content to be asleep, so you could just leave them be."

"You can seal them away as tightly as you'd like, but the very fact of their existence is a threat. The town might think that somehow, the dreams will acquire the power to break free and escape. If that happened, the town would be destroyed. So they need someone to lessen that power, and dissolve it, if but a little. If someone listens to the voices of the old dreams, and dreams along with them, then maybe it will keep the dreams calm. That's probably what they're hoping for. And right now, the only one who can do that is you."

I was stuck between two thoughts.

The happiness of seeing you every day at the library, of sharing dream reading with you under the light of the oil lamps. Talking with you across the rough-hewn table, enjoying the herbal tea you brewed for me. Walking you home every night after work. How much of that was real, and how much was fiction? I couldn't say. But all the same, the town gave me that joy, that stirring of the heart.

But then there were the times I had with you in the world outside the wall, the undeniable memories left to me. The little park where we met, the rhythmic creaking of the swings where little girls played. The sound of the ocean waves I heard with you, the thick sheaf of letters, the single gauze handkerchief. Secret kisses. These undeniably took place in reality. And no one can steal them away from me.

Which world should I belong to? I couldn't decide.

A GIRL DISAPPEARS from your life without a trace. You're seventeen then, a vigorous young man. And she's the first person you ever kissed. A wonderful, lovely girl you're attracted to more than anyone else. And she said she likes you too. When the time comes, she said, she wants to be yours. And then that person—unannounced, without a word of good-bye, or anything resembling an explanation—leaves you. Disappears. Literally, like smoke vanishing.

What could have happened to her?

Had some urgent turn of events forced her to move away, to another town? (But whatever the situation, she should have been able to tell you.) Or was she walking down the street when something fell from the sky, striking her in the head, and as a result, she lost her memory? Or was she no longer alive (killed in a traffic accident; murdered by some random, passing attacker; or dead from some fast-acting, rare disease, or by suicide?). Or was she kidnapped and locked away somewhere? (But by whom? And for what purpose?) Or had she suddenly stopped liking you— hating to even see your face or even hear your name? (Had you said something wrong, or done something you shouldn't have?) Or was there a tiny black hole on a street corner somewhere that secretly opened up and sucked her inside as she passed by, like a leaf sucked down a drain? Or, perhaps . . . in this world every possibility is quietly awaiting a person. Danger lurks around every corner. But you have no way of knowing what actually happened to her.

Can you possibly imagine how painful it is to suddenly have the one you love leave for no reason, how much it hurt your heart, how deeply it ripped you apart, how much you bled inside?

What hurt most of all was the feeling that the whole world had abandoned you. That you were now a person without a shred of value. A meaningless scrap of paper, or simply invisible. You hold your palm up, gazing at it until you can gradually see through to the other side—it's no lie, it's real.

You search for a reasonable, convincing explanation. You need that more than anything. But nobody has one. Nobody tells you where to go now. No one consoles you or encourages you. (It wouldn't help even if they did.) You're left utterly alone in a desolate land. Not a single tree or blade of grass to be seen. A strong wind is already blowing in one direction there—a wind that stings the skin like tiny needles. You've been mercilessly excluded from a world of warmth. Isolated. With thoughts that have no outlet, lying heavy, like a lump of lead, inside you.

There should be some word from her. With that in mind you wait, patiently. But maybe there's nothing else you can do. But although you continue to wait, no word comes. The phone doesn't ring, no thick envelopes arrive in the mail. No knocks at the door. Only silence, and nothingness. Silence and nothingness become your friends. Things you wish would not be your friends. But no others will stay with you. You cling to a thread of hope, of course you do. But in the face of the blunt instruments of silence and nothingness, the shadow of hope grows ever fainter.

And so I reached my eighteenth birthday, and then another year passed after I received that final letter. Time passed heavily, yet somehow briskly. A milestone would appear, only to fade away. And then another would come.

I couldn't comprehend how I was supposed to be as a person. Why was I here, doing what I was doing? And does such a strong wind always blow like this? I asked myself this so many times.

An answer never came.

ON MY WAY to the library it began to snow. A dry snow, with small flakes, the kind that doesn't melt easily. I couldn't tell, though, if much would accumulate.

When I arrived at the library, the woodstove was blazing away as always. A large black kettle sat on top, puffing out steam. With a small mortar and pestle you were mashing herbs you'd picked in the garden. A time-consuming task. I could hear the rhythmic crunch as you patiently went about the task. You stopped as I entered, looked up, and sent a small smile in my direction.

"Has it started snowing?" you asked.

"Just a little," I said. I took off my heavy coat and hung it on the coatrack next to the wall.

"It shouldn't snow that much tonight. It won't pile up," you said. And you were probably right. Like always.

You brushed off the dust from an old dream, placed it on the desk, and I began to read. I embraced it in my palms, warming it, activating it. Before long the old dream awoke and began relaying its message in words I couldn't hear.

Old dreams—were they, as my shadow had speculated, the vestiges of people's hearts that had been scraped away and put into storage? I had no way of knowing if that theory was right or wrong. From my perspective it was just "microcosmic chaos." Are our hearts really that unclear and inconsistent? Maybe these old dreams could only emit bits and pieces of confused messages because they were nothing more than remnants of an old mind comingled together?

The old sergeant who appeared in my dreams had said to me, his voice cold, "Sometimes obliterating the mind is the easiest thing to do."

"I might be leaving this town," I confessed to you. I couldn't just leave without saying anything—even if the town was, somehow, listening to our conversation.

"When?" you asked. You didn't seem particularly surprised.

We were walking side by side along the path by the river. I was escorting you back to your home—just like every other night. It had stopped snowing. The clouds had opened up in one spot, and through that gap I could see a few stars. Like grains of ice, the stars shone a pale, cold light onto the earth.

"Soon, before my shadow passes away."

"You've decided this?"

"I think so," I said. Though I was still wavering inside. "But there's something I want to tell you before that happens."

"What is it?"

"A long time ago I met you in the world outside the wall."

You halted and wrapped your green scarf tighter around your neck. And then looked at me. "You met me?"

"Another you—the you outside the wall."

"Was that my shadow?"

"I think it might have been."

"My shadow died a long time ago," you said in the same flat tone with which you announced that the snow wouldn't accumulate.

Your shadow died a long time ago. I repeated these words in my mind. Like an echo from deep inside a cave.

I asked, "What happens when shadows die?"

You shook your head. "I don't know. I was given a job at the library, and I just do what I'm supposed to do. Open the doors, light the stove when it's cold out, make tea with the herbs I picked . . . that's how I help you in your work."

As we were parting you said, "You might not come to the library anymore. But how can you get out of this town? You can't get out from the gate, right? When you entered the town, you agreed to that."

I stayed silent. I couldn't put it into words here. Somebody might be eavesdropping.

"When I met you outside," I said, "I fell in love with you—with her. In the blink of an eye. I was sixteen then, and you were fifteen. About the same age you are now."

"Fifteen?"

"Yes, in the way the outside world counts things, *she* was fifteen."

We came to a halt in front of your residence for what might be our last conversation together. The snow had stopped, but it was still freezing cold.

"In the world outside the wall, you loved my shadow. And she was fifteen," you told yourself. As if confirming the impossibility of this statement.

"I wanted her so much, and hoped she would want me just as badly. But a year later she suddenly vanished. Without warning, with no explanation."

You redid the green scarf around your slim neck. And then nodded. "It couldn't be helped. Shadows are going to eventually die."

"I came to this town wanting to see her one more time. I thought if I came here, I could see her. But at the same time I wanted to see *you too*. That's one reason I came inside the wall."

"To see me?" You looked dubious. "But why? Why did you want to see me? I'm not the fifteen-year-old girl you were in love with. We might have been one originally, but my shadow was cut away from me when I was little, and we were separated. We became separate beings."

I gazed into her eyes. Like searching the depths of a clear mountain spring. And I said, "You're not her. I know that. The you who lives here doesn't dream, and doesn't love anyone."

And she disappeared into the entrance of the communal housing. That might have been an eternal farewell. But for you it was a good-bye like always. Because here, everything is eternal.

AROUND THE TIME I turned twenty, somehow I managed to make it past the nonsensical period of my life. Looking back on it now, I'm amazed that I made it through those days safely—though not entirely unscathed.

I had no interest in college or my studies and seldom went to class. Made no friends, either. I read books alone and worked sometimes at a part-time job. I met a few men and women where I worked, went out drinking with them sometimes, but didn't get to know them any better than that. But no matter what I did I never felt at peace. Nothing interested me. My days were rambling and vague, as if I were walking in a daze through thick clouds. All because I'd lost you. Because the strong desire I had had been left unfulfilled.

But one day I woke up. What sparked this awakening, I really can't recall now. Something trivial and trite, no doubt. The smell of a freshly boiled egg, for instance, a fragment of a long-forgotten melody, the feel of a freshly ironed shirt . . . whatever it was must have triggered a special part of my mind, bringing me back to my senses. And I thought this: *I can't go on like this.*

If I go on living like this, my body and mind will fall apart and if, someday, you were to come back to me, I wouldn't be able to accept you anymore. I knew I had to avoid this at all costs.

I forced myself back on the right track. I'd missed too many classes, and my grades, no surprise, were atrocious, so I had to repeat the year. But I didn't mind. That was the price I had to pay. I turned over a new leaf—attending all my classes, seriously taking notes (no matter how boring the class might be). In my free time I swam at the college pool to keep fit, bought brand-new clothes, cut back on drinking, and began to eat better.

As I lived this kind of life, I did make a few friends, men and women. I was interested in them and liked them, and they recip-rocated. Not such a bad thing, overall. As I continued to wait patiently for you, at a different level I learned how to live a regular life like everybody else.

And I had a girlfriend. A girl in my college a year younger than me who was taking the same class. A cheerful girl, who was fun to talk with. Smart, with charming looks. She helped so much with my return to life, and I was grateful to her. But inside I always held back a part of me, keeping a piece of my heart in reserve just for you.

But is that possible? To reserve a secret part of your heart for someone, while another part of you loves someone else? To some extent, but it can't go on forever. So I wound up hurting my girl-friend, and that ended up hurting me. And I became all the more isolated and alone.

It took me five years to graduate from college, and then I got a job with a book distribution company. I didn't go back to my hometown. My job covered a lot of areas and there was much I needed to learn. I'd wanted to get a job with a book publisher and become an editor, but I was shot down in the interviews. Must have been because of my mediocre grades in college. But a book distribution company of course dealt with books, so even though it wasn't what I was originally hoping for, it was a worthwhile job. My days as an adult in the world became, for the most part, fulfilling. I got used to the job and was gradually given more responsibility.

My relations with women, however, remained about the same. I went out with a few more, even seriously considered getting married. I wasn't going out with them just for fun. But in the end, I could never build a genuine relationship built on trust with any woman I dated. Something would always happen, and, by the end, I always screwed things up. *Screwed up* really describes it.

There were two reasons. One is that I already had you. Your existence, your words, what you looked like—all of this was part of my heart. I was always, at some deep level, thinking about you. That had to be the number one reason.

But at the same time, there was a constant fear inside me. The fear that even if I managed to unconditionally love someone, there would come a day when the person I loved would suddenly vanish, without explanation, and I would end up rejected for a reason I could never fathom. That woman could one day vanish like smoke, leaving me behind, alone. With a hollow and empty heart.

I never wanted to go through that again. It would be better to live quietly, all alone.

I cooked my meals for myself, worked out at the gym, kept everything nice and neat around me, and when I had free time, I read. Regularity is key to a single life—even if at times it was hard to draw a line between regularity and tedium.

To others my life might have looked free and easy, and it's true that I was thankful for the freedom and quiet. This was the kind of lifestyle a person like me could accept, but I suppose others would find it unbearable. Far too tedious, too quiet, and, more than anything, lonely.

But when I hit forty, the realities of this life were unfulfilling. Was I going to spend the rest of my life like this, all alone, with no one else beside me? I'd grow even older, even more alone. I'd be in the final stretch of life, my physical abilities fading. Things I could do easily, without thinking, would be beyond me. I couldn't exactly picture my future self, but it was easy to imagine how unpleasant that life would be.

Forty . . . when I think of it, I'd been waiting for you ever since I was seventeen, so for some twenty-three years. In the interim not a word from you, nothing. Silence and nothingness, as always, were my constant companions. I was quite used to them by now, since they'd become a part of me. Silence and nothingness . . . take them away and there'd be nothing else to say about my life.

So my fortieth birthday came and went, unremarked (no one celebrated it). Work was going well. And I'd reached a pretty good position in the company, with pay that was far more than adequate (not that there was anything I was dying to acquire). My elderly parents back in my hometown were still praying I'd get married and have children. But sadly, that wasn't an option.

My thoughts were still of you. I'd enter a small room deep in my heart and reach back into my memories. The bundle of letters you wrote to me, the handkerchief, the notebook where I had written down the details of the town surrounded by a wall. In that little room I'd pick these up, fondle them without end, gaze at them (just like a seventeen-year-old boy). Every one of my secrets were kept in that room, secrets no one else knew. You alone could unravel the riddles there.

But you weren't there. Where you were, I had no way of knowing.

My forty-fifth birthday came, and not long after this none-too-happy milepost, I once again fell into a hole. Suddenly, without warning. Just like I'd lost my footing before, back in those awful days when I was about twenty. But this time it wasn't a metaphorical hole I fell into, but an actual hole dug in the ground. I can't remember when or how I fell. It was probably pretty simple— I took a step and found no ground below my feet.

When I regained consciousness (which must have meant I'd been unconscious), I found myself lying at the bottom of that hole. Nothing hurt, so maybe I hadn't fallen. Maybe I was chosen and *placed* there. But by whom? I had no clue. At any rate, my body had been moved far away from the world I'd known. To a place far, far, far, far away from reality.

It was night. Up above the hole I could make out a rectangular patch of sky. Myriad stars twinkled in the sky. The hole didn't seem too deep. I should have been able to climb out to ground level. Knowing that, I felt relieved. But I was exhausted, totally worn out. I couldn't even get up from the ground. Couldn't lift a hand, and even opening my eyes was a struggle. My body felt like it would fall to pieces. I was so tired that I closed my eyes and again lost consciousness, sinking into a deep sea of the unconscious.

How much time passed after this? When I opened my eyes, the sky was completely light. Small white clouds scudded across the sky in the wind, and I could hear birds calling out. Morning, it seemed. A pleasant, sunny morning. And someone was leaning over the edge of the hole, looking down at me. A big man with a smoothly shaved head. Wearing some layered, strange, messy-looking clothes, with what looked like a shovel in his hands.

"Hey! You there!" he called out in a deep voice. "Why are you down there?"

It took some time for me to figure out if this was real or a dream. It was neither hot nor cold out, the smell of new grass in the air.

"Why am I down here?" I said, repeating the man's words.

"That's right. I'm asking you that."

"I don't know," I replied. My voice didn't sound like mine. "Where *is* this place?"

"You mean where you're lying?" the man said cheerfully. "I don't know where you came from, but a little friendly advice—you'd better get out of there as soon as you can, guy. That's the hole I throw the beasts into, and then pour oil on 'em and burn 'em up."

IN THE AFTERNOON it started to snow. Countless white snowflakes fell to the earth from a windless sky. It wasn't the light kind of snow that swirls in the air. Each snowflake had its own solid weight and fell straight to the ground like a stone.

I left my home, went down the western hill, and hurried toward the gate. Fragments of snow were frozen to the backs of the beasts I passed on the street, but they kept their eyes down, resigned to it, breathing out white breath as they sluggishly trod their way forward. The past few days the cold had gotten worse, and the nuts and leaves that served as their food were scarcer. Even more beasts would expire, starting with the weakest.

A pillar of gray smoke rose outside the north wall, thicker than ever, billowing into the sky. The Gatekeeper was keeping busy today, too, gathering the corpses of the beasts and burning them. The smoke rose straight up into the sky, sucked into the heavy clouds like a thick twisting rope. I felt sorry for the beasts, but the more corpses there were, the busier the Gatekeeper became, gaining me more time.

The Gatekeeper wasn't in his cabin. The stove was burning brightly, though, warming up the room. Hatchets and adzes were neatly lined up on his worktable. The blades looked newly honed, threateningly seductive, glistening, glaring wordlessly in my direction. I walked through the Gatekeeper's cabin, cut across the shadow enclosure, and went into the room where my shadow lay.

The smell was heavier than before, with a premonition of death hanging over the room. As I entered the room some of the dark knotholes in the wooden walls looked at me, as if sending out a warning. As if telling me, *I know what you're thinking.* My shadow was wrapped in a quilt, sleeping like the dead. I put a finger under his nose to check if he was breathing and saw he hadn't died yet. My shadow finally woke up and listlessly writhed.

"Have you made up your mind, then?" my shadow asked weakly.

"Yes. Let's get of here now, together."

"Right now?"

"Right now."

"I was sure you wouldn't come back," my shadow said, slightly turning his head in my direction. "I must look terrible."

I helped my shadow's gaunt body sit up, and we went outside, with me basically supporting him. And then I put him on my back. The Gatekeeper had warned me never to touch him, but I didn't care anymore. My shadow hardly weighed a thing, so it wasn't hard to carry him. As my shadow adhered more to me, he should get strength from my body and slowly regain strength. Like a plant in the desert desperately absorbing water. I wasn't very confident, though, how much strength I could give my shadow at this point.

"Bring me that horn over there, if you would," my shadow said from my back as we cut through the Gatekeeper's cabin.

"Horn?"

"Right. If we have that it'll be hard for the Gatekeeper to chase us."

"He'll be really angry," I said as I eyed the glistening hatchets and adzes.

"It's necessary. If this town wants to, it can become very dangerous. We have to be ready for that."

Without understanding why, I did as told, and took down the horn from where it was hanging on the wall and put it in my coat pocket. The old horn had turned amber colored from years of use. Made from one of the beasts' single horns, it had fine engraved carving on it.

"We don't have much time," my shadow said. "Let's hurry. I'm sorry I can't run by myself."

"If we cross town with you on my back, a lot of people will see us."

"They'll find out soon enough that we're escaping. Anyway, we have to get to the south wall as quickly as we can."

Lugging my shadow on my back, I left the Gatekeeper's cabin. No going back now. We reached the river, and crossed the bridge, heading south. Snowflakes melted in my eyes, and I couldn't see in front of me. I kept bumping into beasts. Every time I did, they cried out in strange little voices.

Probably because of the falling snow, there weren't many people out on the streets, but still, there were a few who saw us. They just came to a halt and stood there, silently looking at us. It was pretty rare in this town to see anyone running. Would they report us somewhere? Report that the Dream Reader was with his shadow again and running away from the town? Or maybe this didn't mean anything to them?

Since coming to the town, I'd done no real exercise, and light though my shadow was, running with him on my back wasn't easy. I kept puffing out heavy white breaths into the air. The air I inhaled, mixed in with all the snow, was freezing. My lungs stung like they were being pricked with needles. We finally arrived at the foot of the southern hill and I took a break, catching my breath, and turned to look behind me.

"This can't be good," my shadow said. "Take a look. There's not as much smoke now from burning the beasts."

My shadow was right. Through the ceaseless snow, I could see that the smoke beyond the north wall was thinning out.

"The snow must be making the fire go out," my shadow said. "If so, the Gatekeeper will go back to his cabin to get more oil. And he'll see I'm not in the enclosure anymore. He's a fast runner. Then we'll be in big trouble."

It wasn't easy to clamber up the steep slope of the southern hill with the shadow on my back. But I'd made up my mind. Giving up halfway wasn't an option. And like my shadow said, *If this town wants to, it can become very dangerous.* I kept on climbing, sweating under my coat. I somehow made it to the top, my legs as stiff as rocks, my calves cramping up.

"Sorry, I've got to take a break," I said, crouching down, out of breath. I knew we were in a race against time, but my legs could barely move.

"Okay, rest here for a while. I'm sorry I can't run, but don't worry about it. Would you mind handing me that horn?"

"The horn? What're you going to do with it?"

"Don't worry, just give it to me."

Not knowing what was going on, I took the stolen horn from my coat pocket and handed it to my shadow. He held it to his lips, took a big breath, and blew it as hard as he could. He aimed it at the town down below, blowing one long note, followed by three short ones. The usual sound of the horn. I was surprised that he could play it so well. It sounded almost exactly like when the Gatekeeper blew it. I wondered when he'd learned that skill. Did he learn just by watching?

"What are you *doing*?"

"Blowing the horn, as you can see. This will buy us some time." The shadow then hung it on a nearby tree trunk, so it'd be easy to spot. "This way the Gatekeeper will be able to find it and take it back. Because he'll be after us for sure. If he gets back the horn, maybe he won't be quite so angry."

"How does this buy us time?"

"If we blow the horn," my shadow explained, "the beasts will all head toward the gate. And then the Gatekeeper will have to open it and let them outside. And once they're all out he'll close the gate. In his job, he must follow those rules. It takes time for all the beasts to go out. And it'll buy us that much time."

Impressed, I looked at my shadow. "That's very smart of you."

"Listen. This town is not perfect. Even the wall isn't perfect. Nothing's perfect in this world. Everything has its weak point, and one of the weak points of this town is those beasts. The town maintains an equilibrium letting the beasts in and out in the morning and evening. And we just wrecked that balance."

"I bet the town will be angry."

"Most likely," my shadow said. "If the town possesses something like emotions."

As I massaged my tight calves, my legs finally loosened up. "Okay, let's head out," I said, then stood up and hitched him up on my back again.

It was all downhill now, and I could, for the time being, make it on my rested legs. There was the occasional uphill slope along the way, but it was almost all downhill. I had to watch my step, but I was no longer out of breath. The road petered out, replaced by a trampled-down path that was easy to miss. We passed by a small, decaying village. The snow kept on falling. Then snow clung to my hair, forming hard lumps. I regretted not having worn a hat. The thick clouds covering the sky seemed to have an inexhaustible supply of snow. And as we walked, that weird, choking sound from the pool reached me intermittently, fading in and out.

"If we've made it this far, I think we're good," my shadow said from my back. "Once we cut through those bushes we'll be at the pool. The Gatekeeper won't be able to catch us."

I was relieved to hear that and took a break. We seemed to have made it through okay.

But right when I thought that, at that very moment, the wall loomed up in front of us.

Without warning the wall suddenly stood before us, blocking our way. The same high, solid town wall. I halted and gulped. Why was there a wall *here*? When I came down this path before, there hadn't been one. Without a word I stared up at that twenty-six-foot-high barrier.

You shouldn't be surprised, the wall told me in a deep voice. **That map you made is utterly worthless. It's just lines scribbled on a scrap of paper**.

I suddenly knew: The wall was able to freely change its shape and location. It could move anywhere it wanted to. And the wall had decided *not to let us get out*.

"Don't listen to it," my shadow whispered from my back. "And don't look at it. It's just an illusion. The town is showing us an illusion. So close your eyes and go through it. If you don't believe what it says, and aren't afraid, the wall doesn't exist."

I did what my shadow said, just shut my eyes tight and kept on walking.

The wall spoke. **No way you guys can get through the wall. Even if you did get through one, another wall would be waiting for you. It'll be the same, whatever you do.**

"Don't listen to it," my shadow said. "You can't be afraid. Just run on ahead. Get rid of any doubts and trust your heart."

Yes, go ahead and run, the wall said. And it laughed loudly. **Run as far away as you'd like. I will always be there.**

The wall's laughter rang in my ears, as I kept my head down and ran straight ahead, heading right toward where the wall should be. At this point I could only trust what my shadow said. *Don't be afraid.* I gathered my strength, got rid of any doubts, and trusted my heart. And my shadow and I passed through what should have been a thick brick wall, like we were swimming through it. Like passing through a soft layer of jelly. An uncanny, incomparable feeling. That layer seemed made of something between the material and the immaterial. Time and distance didn't exist there, and there was a unique sense of resistance to it, like grains of different sizes mixed together. With my eyes closed, I cut through this slimy obstacle.

"Like I told you, right?" my shadow said in my ear. "It's all just an illusion."

My heart made a dry, hard sound as it beat inside the cage of my ribs. In my ears I could still hear the wall's loud laughter.

Run as far away as you'd like, the wall had told me. **I will always be there**.

I SCRAMBLED THROUGH the final clump of bushes and emerged into a meadow from which the pool was visible. When I got to the pool, I let my shadow down from my back. He was still a bit unsteady on his feet but had recovered enough to walk on his own. Some color had returned to his gaunt face. We'd adhered to each other for quite a while, yet my shadow and I were still separate beings. Maybe he still didn't have enough energy to unite with me.

"While you carried me, I could get the nourishment I needed," my shadow said. "It's not quite enough but should be sufficient. Let's take a breather and then make our escape."

I stood there, catching my breath as I looked carefully around me. The pool looked the same as before. Beautiful, clear blue water, a calm surface without a single ripple, the occasional choked, bubbling sound of water rising up from the depths, with an ominous gasping mixed in. The sound made by massive amounts of water sucked into the caves far below. Other than that, there was no noise. Not a breath of wind, no birds flying. Around us pure white snow continued to silently fall. What a beautiful scene, I thought. It moved me, in a way. I was sure every detail would remain in my memory, until the moment came when I took my last breath.

In my head, there was a battle going on between reality and unreality. At this moment I was standing right in the interstice between this world and the other world. There was a fierce split between the conscious and the unconscious, and I had to choose where I should belong.

"You're sure we can escape okay from here?" I asked my shadow, pointing to the pool.

My shadow said, "This pool connects directly to the world outside the wall. As long as you get into the caves at the bottom and swim underneath the wall, you'll come out in the outside world."

"But people say the pool connects with a limestone channel at the very bottom and that everybody sucked into that cave drowns there, in the dark."

"That's a lie the town made up to scare people. There's no maze at the bottom."

"Instead of going to all that trouble, wouldn't it be easier to surround the pool with a high fence or railing? Instead of making up some elaborate lie?"

My shadow shook his head. "That's where their wisdom helps. The town has set up a psychological enclosure of fear around the pool. Which is far more effective than a fence or railing. Once fear takes root in your heart it's not easy to overcome."

"So how can you be so confident?"

My shadow said, "I said this before, but this town is full of contradictions. And in order to keep the town in existence these contradictions have to be eliminated. Which is why certain measures are taken, and there's a system in place to deal with them. It's a very elaborate system."

My shadow's breath was white as he rubbed his hands together.

"One measure is those poor beasts. Letting the beasts in and out of the town every day, and letting them breed in a certain season and weeding out others, occurs only to rid the town of its latent energy. The dream reading you have done at the library is another measure. The fragments of the mind accumulated in those old dreams are sublimated through that process and vanish into the air. What I'm trying to say is that this town is a very technically clever, artificial place. The balance of everything that exists is carefully sustained, with elaborate measures that work to maintain the entire system."

It took a while for me to digest this.

"And the town uses fear as one method to maintain that balance?"

"Exactly. The town has convinced people that the southern pool is a dangerous place. The reason is that the pool is the only means for the town's residents to go outside the wall. The Gatekeeper keeps a sharp watch over the north gate, the east gate has been filled in, and the spot where the river enters the town is blocked off by a strong iron grate. I don't think there are many people here who want to go outside the wall, but still the town is blocking any possibility of escape."

"But we have no reason to be afraid of that."

My shadow nodded. "There's no need to be afraid. Fortunately, your soul hasn't yet been taken from you. So here we can reunite, go through the pool, and return to the outside world."

In my ears the voice of the wall rang out. **Even if you did get through one, another wall would be waiting for you.** And that raucous laugh.

"Aren't you scared?" I asked my shadow. "Of drowning in the darkness underground?"

"I'm scared out of my wits. It's frightening just to think about it. But we've already decided. Aren't you the one who created this town in the first place? You have that much power. Just a while ago you were able to push through that hard wall right in front of you. Am I right? What's important is conquering fear. And aren't you really good at swimming? And you can hold your breath a long time too."

"But what about *you*? Can you swim?"

My shadow laughed weakly. He spread his hands wide.

"Man alive! Look, I'm your shadow. If you can swim, I can swim too, right next to you. At the same pace and the same distance. Of course I can swim."

He was right. We could swim the same way, side by side. I looked up at the sky, the cold snow falling on my face.

"What you're saying is pretty convincing," I said.

My shadow smiled weakly. "I'm honored by the compliment. But in a sense, this is all something you thought of, things you're saying to yourself. Because I am, bottom line, your shadow."

"It does make sense, what you're saying."

"Then it's about time to leap in. Though it's not exactly swimming season."

I stood there, silent. I looked up again at the sky covered with thick, snow-filled clouds, then looked my shadow straight in the face. I made up my mind and went ahead and said it.

"Okay, but I can't leave this town. I'm sorry, but you go on by yourself."

MY SHADOW STARED at me for a long while. I tried to say something several times but swallowed back the words each time. Like giving up on some food that is hard to chew and instead sending it down your throat. The right words just weren't there. My shadow looked down, tracing a small shape with the tip of his boot on the cold ground. Only to rub it out with the sole.

"You've given it a lot of thought, right?" he said. "This isn't something you decided just now because you're afraid of leaping into the water?"

I shook my head. "No, I'm not scared anymore. I did feel fear until a while ago, but now I don't. What you said rings true. If we want to, I think we can safely get through the wall."

"But you're still going to stay?"

I nodded.

"But why?"

"First of all, I don't see a reason to return to the world I came from. In that world I'll only get more and more lonely. And come face-to-face with an even greater darkness. There's no way I can be happy there. We can't say this town is a perfect place. As you pointed out, it's rife with contradictions. And to eliminate those contradictions, there are all sorts of processes at work. And eternity is a long time. During that time my consciousness, as a separate being, will gradually fade. The town will eventually swallow me. But even if that happens, I don't care. As long as I'm here, I won't be lonely. Because in this town I know what I should do, what I ought to do."

"Reading old dreams."

"Someone has to read them. Someone has to release those countless old, dusty dreams, locked up inside those shells. I can do that, and *they* want me to."

"And somewhere on the shelves of the library you might find the old dream *she* left behind."

I nodded. "Maybe so. If my hypothesis is correct."

"And that's one of the things your heart desires."

I stayed silent.

My shadow sighed deeply.

"If I leave you behind here, and I get outside the wall, I'll probably die in the not-too-distant future. You and I are a real body and shadow. Separate us, and I won't live long. Not that I mind. I'm just an accessory, after all."

"But you might survive in the outside world and be my substitute. As far as I can see, you have the qualifications, and the wisdom, to do that. After a while, you won't be able to tell the real person from the shadow."

My shadow thought this over, and then shook his head slightly.

"We're just piling up one hypothesis on top of another. Soon we won't be able to tell what's hypothetical and what's real."

"Maybe. But we need *something*. Some pillar we can lean on if we're going to do anything."

"Your mind's set?"

I nodded.

"But still you came all this way with me, to the very end."

"Honestly, I didn't know until the last minute which way I'd go," I said. "Until I actually stood in front of this pool. But I've made up my mind. And I'm not changing it—I'm going to stay in the town by myself. And you're going to leave."

My shadow and I gazed at each other. "As your longtime companion," he said, "it's hard for me to agree to this, but I can see you're determined. I'm not going to argue anymore. I pray you'll be happy staying here. So pray for me, too, leaving here. As hard as you can."

"Of course, I'll pray for you, as much as I can. Pray that things go well for you."

My shadow held out his right hand. And I clutched it. Shaking hands with my own shadow—what a strange thing. It was strange, too, how my shadow's handshake and warmth were the same as anyone else's.

Was he really my shadow? Was I the real me? As he'd said,

it was getting hard to distinguish the hypothetical from the real.

Like an insect shedding its shell, my shadow shed his wet, heavy coat, and pulled his boots off his feet.

"Apologize for me to the Gatekeeper, if you would," he said, smiling faintly. "For stealing the horn from his cabin and setting the beasts in motion. I had no choice, but he's still going to be angry about it."

My shadow stood there alone in the falling snow, gazing for a time at the surface of the pool. Then he took a deep breath. He breathed out, his exhaled breath hard and white. And without looking back he leaped headfirst into the pool. He was so thin but still made a huge splash, sending out a ring of high ripples after him. I watched as these ripples formed concentric circles and then gradually moved away. They finally disappeared, leaving the same placid surface as before. All I could hear was the ominous burbling as the caves down below sucked in water. No matter how long I waited, my shadow never resurfaced.

For a long time after, I gazed at the undisturbed surface of the water. Maybe something completely unexpected would happen. But nothing did. Only countless snowflakes fell, and then melted away, on the surface.

I finally turned around and headed back down the path we'd taken. I never looked back. I made my way down the path with its high grasses, passed by the dilapidated houses, climbed up the steep hill, and then descended. I didn't see a single soul until I crossed the Old Bridge and arrived back at the official residence I lived in. The townspeople weren't about to go out when it was snowing this hard. And the beasts were already outside the wall, lured there by the fake signal from the horn.

The first thing I did when I got home was to carefully dry my hard, wet hair. I used a brush to wipe away the snow frozen to my overcoat, and a spatula to scrap the heavy mud from my shoes. There were blades of grass struck all over my pants, like small fragments of old memories. I slumped down in my chair, shut my eyes tight, my mind swirling with random thoughts. How long I stayed that way I don't know.

When the soundless darkness began creeping over the room, I pushed my hat down low on my head, raised my collar, and headed down the path along the river toward the library. It was still snowing, but I didn't use an umbrella. At least for now I had a place I needed to go.

PART TWO

PART TWO

THE FLOW OF THE RIVER became an elaborate maze, and, just as it traveled deep underground, our reality, too, seemed to proceed inside us, branching out down several paths. Different versions of reality mixed together, different choices became intertwined, out of which a composite reality—or, what we come to understand as reality—took shape.

Of course, this was just my interpretation, my own personal feelings. If I'd been told, "This is the only reality. There are no others," I might have accepted it. Like the crew of a sinking sailboat clinging to the mast, maybe we are only capable of clinging, desperately, to one reality. Whether we like it or not.

But how much do we know about the secret, dark labyrinth of a river that flows underneath us, below the solid ground we stand on? How many have actually seen it and, having seen it, could make it back to the other side?

On long, dark nights I stare forever at my dark shadow stretching out to the wall. That shadow doesn't say a word anymore. I talk to him, ask him questions, yet he never responds. My shadow has gone back to the way he was originally—flat, silent. Yet still I talk to him, since I need his wisdom, his encouragement. But he never answers.

What in the world happened to me? Why am I, right now, *here*? I can't take it in—including this reality I'm a part of. No matter how you look at it, I shouldn't be here. I made up my mind, said good-bye to my shadow, and should have been left behind, by myself, in that walled-in town. So why am I back here, in *this* world? Have I been here the entire time? Did I never leave? Was this all just a long dream?

That said, I do have a shadow now. A shadow attached to my body. Wherever I go, the shadow will accompany me. If I come to a halt, so will my shadow. And I feel relieved, and thankful for that fact—that my shadow and I are literally one flesh. Only people who've lost their shadows can understand this feeling. Most likely.

And on nights when I can't sleep, I go over everything I saw in that walled-in town, all that happened to me, reliving it in vivid detail.

The faint light of the canola oil lamp in the library, how you looked as you carefully crushed the herbs in a little mortar, the click of the hooves of those poor unicorns on the flagstone street, the river willows on the sandbank quietly rustling in the wind— I picture all of it. The Gatekeeper's horn ringing out morning and night, the sad call of the unseen night birds, the path along the river you and I took every night, the old pavement, the sweet apple dish that melted in my mouth. Ancient dreams I held in my hands so they would warm up. The pure white snow falling on the meadow beside the deep pool. That inscrutable high brick wall that surrounded the town without a gap anywhere. No blade could make a mark on it. And more than everything, a lovely girl, dressed in plain, immaculate clothes. This was the scene that had been promised me. And was the promise kept? Or not kept?

Some power might have separated me into two at some point. I can't help thinking that at times. Maybe there's another me, in that town behind a high wall, even now, spending his days quietly. Going every evening to the library, drinking the green herbal tea she makes, sitting behind that thick desk, intently reading old dreams.

I can't help but think that makes the most sense, that it is the proper conjecture. At a certain point I was given a choice between two alternatives. And the me who's here now chose to be *here*. And somewhere is another me who chose to be *there*. Somewhere— most likely in the town surrounded by a high wall.

In the *real world* on this side I was on the verge of what's called middle age. Just a man with nothing special about him, nor a "specialist" anymore with the skills I possessed in that town. My eyes weren't wounded, and I wasn't qualified to read old dreams. I was nothing more than a cog in one of the systems that made up a gigantic society. A tiny, replaceable cog. I couldn't help feeling some regret for that.

After I came back here—and I believe I *did come back*—for a time I acted like nothing had happened, riding the train every morning to work at the company, giving a simple greeting to my colleagues as usual, attending meetings, voicing the appropriate opinions (none of which made a difference), afterward sitting at my desk in front of a computer doing my work. I sent out directives to branches around the country and received all sorts of requests from them. Occasionally I'd go out from the office for meetings with bookstore managers and publishing supervisors. A certain amount of experience was needed to do the work, though it wasn't especially difficult. I was just a tiny, fixed cog.

And then one morning I handed my boss a letter of resignation. I couldn't go on doing this job. I had to remove my body and mind from the track I'd been on—even if I hadn't found a new track to try.

My boss was surprised by my sudden request. Up until that moment, I'd given no indication that I was unhappy. He thought I'd been recruited by a rival company. I tried to explain as best I could. Not an easy thing to do, but somehow I did end up convincing him. His next gambit was speculating that I must be having some psychological issues—a breakdown or midlife crisis.

"If the work's wearing you out you should take some time off," my boss said, calmly trying to convince me. "You have a lot of accrued paid vacation time, so why don't you go to Bali or somewhere for a couple of weeks, let your hair down, recharge, then come back? And then you can think it over again."

I had a pretty good relationship with my immediate boss, and I think he kind of liked me. So I felt bad telling him this. But nothing could convince me to stay. This was as clear to me as the first rays of morning sunlight.

I simply felt that *this reality* wasn't suited to me. It was the same as saying the air in this place wasn't right for my lungs. Stay here any longer, and I'd choke. So I wanted to get off this train as quickly as I could, at the next station—that's all I wanted. It was necessary, what I *had* to do.

But if I said that to my boss (and to my colleagues, too, I imagine), they wouldn't understand. The visceral sense that *this reality isn't a reality for me*, and the deep sense of estrangement that it produced, wasn't something I could share with anyone else.

After I quit my job, I still had no particular plan about what to do next. For the time being as much as I could, I thought about nothing, and did nothing, just hanging out, alone, in my apartment. There was nothing else I could do. It felt like a heavy iron ball that had lost all inertia and lay there, discarded on the ground, unmoving. Though that actually wasn't such a bad feeling.

During that time I slept really well, at least twelve hours a day. When I wasn't asleep, I lay in bed, staring at the ceiling, listening to all the sounds filtering in through the window, gazing at the shadows moving along the wall. Trying to read something into them. But of course there wasn't any kind of message there for me.

I didn't feel like reading books (which was pretty unusual for me), and I didn't feel like listening to music, either. I barely had any appetite. I also didn't want to drink. I talked to no one. I went out to shop for food every once in a while, but the landscape there was something I couldn't take in. An old man walking a dog, people on ladders trimming trees, children on their way to school—I'd see them, but they didn't seem like events taking place in the real world. Instead, to me they seemed like scenery neatly put together to fit the situation, a clever flat scene made to look three-dimensional.

The only scenes that felt real to me were the path along the river, the river willows growing on sandbanks, a clock tower with no hands, unicorns in winter trudging along through the falling snow, the eerie gleam of the hatchets the Gatekeeper had neatly honed.

But I had no way to return to that world.

Financially I had no pressing problems. I had some savings (as I said, I'd lived a simple bachelor life for years), and five months' worth of unemployment insurance. For the past ten years I'd lived in a rented apartment in Tokyo that was convenient for commuting, but I could always move to a cheaper place. Actually, I could move anywhere in Japan. But I couldn't think of a single place I'd want to go.

I was nothing but an iron ball that had come to a stop on the ground. A heavy, self-contained iron ball, my thoughts tightly locked away inside. Not much to look at, but plenty heavy. Unless someone passed by and tried hard to push me, I wasn't going anywhere. Or budging an inch.

Many times I asked my shadow, *Where should I go now?* Predictably, he never replied.

MY STAGNANT LIFE went on for about two months after I quit and started living free and easy. Day after day of an endless lull. And then one night I had a long dream. I hadn't had any dreams for a while. (Come to think of it, during those two months, I had slept long and deep, but had never really dreamed. It was like I'd lost the strength for it.)

The dream was vivid down to the smallest detail—and it was a dream about a library. I was working there, but it wasn't *that* library in the walled-in town, just an ordinary library you'd find anywhere. The shelves there weren't lined with dusty, egg-shaped old dreams, but with books, made of paper, with covers.

It wasn't a very large library. More like a local public library. At a glance, like most similar facilities, it seemed to be getting by on a shoestring budget. All the equipment in the library, and the books on the stacks, reflected this, as did the well-used chairs and tables. Computers for searching out information were nowhere to be seen.

To liven things up a little, a large ceramic vase was set on a central table, but all the cut flowers in it were a few days past their prime. Still, oblivious to the belt tightening, the sunlight shone in brightly through the vertical windows with their old-fashioned brass fittings, past gaps in the sun-faded white curtains.

Tables and chairs for readers were set up next to the windows, where a few patrons were seated, reading books or taking notes. They seemed comfortable enough there. The ceiling was high, vaulted, with thick black beams up above.

I was working in that library. I don't know what my duties there were, exactly, but I didn't seem all that busy. There was nothing I was pressed to finish quickly, no now-or-never matters I had to resolve immediately, and I worked at a leisurely pace.

A few female employees handled the patrons directly (I couldn't see these women's faces) while I was behind a desk in my own office, handling paperwork. Checking lists of books to order, arranging bills and receipts, reviewing documents that needed my signature.

I didn't feel particularly fulfilled working there, at this workplace in my dream. But I wasn't dissatisfied or bored either. I'd dealt with books for years and was used to the work. I'd mastered the necessary skills. I handled the work at hand, took care of any issues, the time generally passing by smoothly.

At least there, I was no longer a heavy iron ball rooted in one spot. It might have been minimal, but I was headed somewhere. Where I was headed, though, I didn't know. But I didn't get a bad feeling from it.

Then I realized something. There was a hat on a corner of my desk. A dark, navy-blue beret, the kind artists invariably wore in old movies. It seemed to have been worn for a long time, the cloth soft and cozy looking—like an old cat napping in the sun. *Still Life with Beret*—and that beret seemed to somehow be *mine*. Which was odd, since I rarely wear hats and (as far as I can recall) have never even tried on a beret. What would I look like with it on? I glanced around the room for a mirror but couldn't find one. Did I have to wear that beret? And why?

And right then, with a start, I woke up.

When I woke up from that long dream, it was before dawn. It took quite some time for me to realize it had been a dream—time to tear my body away from that dream world and return to reality. Subtle adjustments needed to be made to gravity.

After that I relived the dream over and over in my mind, checking each detail. I didn't want to forget anything, so while the memories were still fresh, I wrote as much as I could recall in a notebook. Fine lines with a ballpoint pen over many pages. The dream seemed to hold some critical suggestions for me, seemed to be attempting to get *something* across. Like when individuals who are close send out very heartful messages to each other, and then explain them very kindly, in great detail.

It finally grew light outside the window, the birds began to chirp, and I came to a conclusion.

I needed a new place to work.

I had to get moving. I couldn't stay here, stuck like this forever. And my new workplace had to be a library—*nothing other than a library would do.* A library was the only place I should go to. So simple, yet why hadn't I realized it until now?

Finally I was gaining some momentum to start moving. The ability to gradually move ahead. Urged on by my vivid dream.

WORK IN A LIBRARY.

But how to find that kind of job? For years I had been in charge of book distribution, but libraries were handled by a specialty division, and I had almost nothing to do with them. And after I graduated from college, I don't think I've ever used any place you could call a library.

Just a rough estimate on my part, but if you put together all the facilities that fell into the category of library, big and small, public and private, there must be several thousand of them operating, in Japan. (Hmm . . . am I overestimating? I don't know.) Among all those libraries, which would be the right fit, the kind of library I was looking for? And would that library have a position for me?

I hauled out my computer for the first time in ages and searched online for libraries. I stopped by libraries in my neighborhood, perusing specialized materials regarding libraries. But I couldn't find the kind of information I was looking for. Everything I found out was either too vague and broad, or focused on practical details. One or the other.

After wasting a week in this pointless exercise, I gave up trying to get information from outside sources and went back to the information my own memories provided. That lengthy dream I had—what kind of library did I see there? What kind of place did my imagination suggest?

I reread the notes I'd taken right after waking up, mentally reconstructing the library from my dream. I retraced my memories to see if that place provided any hints. The voices of the people talking, the posters on the walls . . . but I couldn't make these out. The people were silent (it was a library, after all), and the fine print on the posters was too far away to read. For some reason, though, I knew this place was far from Tokyo. I could sense that from the way the air felt.

I focused on the room where I'd been working in the dream, studying it carefully again, so as not to overlook anything.

It was a rectangular room that went back quite a ways, with a wooden floor and a large old area rug that was getting threadbare in spots (though it might have been quite wonderful back when it was new). On the wall in back were three vertical windows, with the same antique brass fittings as the windows in the hallway. Fluorescent lights on the ceiling. On top of the office desk along the wall, which faced forward, was an old desk lamp, a document tray, a daily calendar, an old-fashioned black phone, a ceramic pen holder, a glass ashtray that seemed to never have been used (now a receptacle for paper clips), and, on one corner, that navy-blue beret. Near the front door were four chairs and a low table. And a coatrack. All of them quite plain. A classic clock topped a wooden cabinet. No computer in sight. That was it. Nothing to give a hint of location.

Sunlight slanted in through the windows, but the faded curtains were drawn, and I couldn't see what lay outside. There was a calendar on the wall, with a photo of a mountain and a lake. The mountain was reflected in the surface of the lake. But I couldn't make out what month it was. I couldn't tell where that mountain and lake were located. A lovely scene, but basically the typical kind of mountain and lake you might find in any tourist spot. From the scenery on the calendar, though, I guessed that this place was somewhere inland.

Of course it wasn't a given that the photo on the calendar depicted scenery near the library, but the quality of the light shining in through the window, and the air I breathed, told me this library wasn't located near the sea but somewhere in a mountain valley. And I felt—it was nothing more than a personal impression—that a beret would suit a mountainous region more than near the sea.

That was the extent of the information I could glean from retracing my dream. I could recall all the details of that scene very clearly but had no idea what the name of the library was, or where to find it.

I needed someone's help—the expertise of a specialist.

I called the company I'd worked at until recently and asked to speak to a man I knew from the library division. Oki was his name. He'd been three years behind me in college. We weren't particularly close, but we'd gone out drinking a few times after work. He was the quiet type, not so friendly, but someone I felt I could trust. He could really hold his liquor, and his face never showed it, no matter how much he put away.

"Hello, how are you?" Oki asked. "To tell the truth, I was pretty surprised that you quit so suddenly."

I apologized for not dropping by to say good-bye when I retired. There were personal reasons, I explained. Oki didn't ask any more and didn't say anything. He waited for me to tell him why I'd called.

"I wanted to ask you a little about libraries."

"If I can help, I'd be happy to."

"The thing is, I'm thinking of working at a library."

Oki was silent, then said, "What type of library did you happen to have in mind?"

"If possible, a smaller library in a regional town, a library that isn't so big. I don't care if it's far away from Tokyo. I'm single, so I can move anywhere."

"A small, regional library . . . well, that covers a lot of territory, doesn't it."

"My personal preference would be for something inland rather than near the sea."

Oki laughed. "What an odd wish. But I get it. Let me check things out and get back to you. It might take a while. But even if you count only regional libraries, there are tons of them. Even if you only include ones that are inland."

"I have plenty of time."

"Do you have any other preferences?"

I wanted to tell him I'd prefer a place with a woodstove, but of course I didn't. There were probably no libraries nowadays that had woodstoves.

"Not particularly. As long as I can work there."

"By the way, do you have the qualifications to be a librarian?"

"No, I don't. Do I have to?"

"Not necessarily," Oki said. "It'll depend on the size of the library and the type of work. Maybe I shouldn't say this, but positions like that won't pay well. It'll be a pittance, like you're a volunteer. You don't mind that?"

"I don't. I'm doing okay financially."

"Alright. I'll look into it and get back to you."

I told him my home phone number, thanked him, and hung up.

I felt surprisingly relieved to leave it all in Oki's hands. No guarantee what results we'd get, but the simple fact that things were moving ahead felt like a fresh breath of wind. At long last I got out of bed and started to get going physically, at least gradually. I cleaned my apartment, washed the sheets, went shopping, and cooked meals. I organized my clothes and books so I could move out quickly, and donated things I didn't need to a local organization. I didn't own all that much to begin with, but all these little tasks kept me busy, kept my thoughts from swirling around in my head too much, at least during the day.

Yet when night fell and I was in bed with my eyes closed, my heart returned to that town surrounded by a high wall. I couldn't stop it (not that I tried very hard). There a light autumn rain fell without stop, and she wore an oversized yellow raincoat that made a rustling sound every time she walked beside me. In that town my shadow could talk. Like he was my alter ego. It came back to me so vividly—the flavor of the thick herbal tea, the sweet taste of the apple dish she made.

The call came in from Oki a week later, after eight o'clock one night. I was seated, reading a book, but sprang to my feet at the phone suddenly ringing. It was so still around me, and it had been ages since the phone rang.

Hello, I said, my tone dry, my heart pounding.

"Hello. Oki here."

"Ah."

"Is that you? Your voice sounds different."

"My throat's been feeling a bit weird," I said, coughing lightly, and clearing my throat.

"It's about jobs at libraries," Oki began. "It wasn't so easy. To be a staff member at a public library, an official, public position, in most cases you need the necessary qualifications, or experience working in libraries. Becoming a civil servant midcareer isn't easy. But you've worked for years in a job related to books and you have plenty of specialized knowledge, so I'm sure you'd have no trouble handling the work. There were several libraries looking for people with that kind of background. It would be hard to be hired as an official library staff member, but they'd welcome a person in a more versatile position."

"So there are possibilities if it's not full-time employment."

"You could say that. Honestly the pay won't be much, and don't expect any benefits. But if they think you're doing a good job, they might hire you full-time."

I gave it some thought. "I don't mind if it isn't full-time, or if the pay's low. As long as I can work in a library. So if you find any position that I'd fit could you let me know?"

"If you're fine with that, I'll look for some. I already have a few potential candidates. In a couple days I'll show you a list of their locations and specifics. It might be better to meet and talk directly rather than over the phone."

We decided to meet in three days and set a time and place.

Oki gave me a list of four regional libraries that were looking to hire. They were in Oita, Shimane, Fukushima, and Miyagi Prefectures, and three of them were run by larger cities, while one was a smaller town library. The conditions were all about the same, but for some reason I was intrigued by the town library in Fukushima. I'd never heard of the town before, but according to Oki, Z** wasn't far from the city of Aizu. At the Aizuwakamatsu station you changed to a local rail line, and it took about an hour from there. The population was around fifteen thousand. Like many regional towns, its population had steadily decreased over the past two decades as young people moved to cities to seek better educational and work opportunities. Also, of the candidates on the list Z** was the farthest from the sea, and the smallest library. The town was in a small basin surrounded by mountains, with a river ringing the town.

"This library in Fukushima looks interesting," I said after looking through the list.

"So would you like to go there to be interviewed?" Oki asked. "If you'd like, I could arrange for an interview. You should do it soon. They're advertising for a head librarian, so could you send me your résumé before they decide on anyone else?"

I have it ready, I said. I passed a copy, in an envelope, to Oki, and he stowed it away in his leather briefcase.

"To tell the truth," he said, "I also thought that Fukushima library might suit you best."

"How so?"

"Officially it's a town-run library, but the town isn't actually involved in its operation. So you can avoid all the complications you'd have with being a local government employee."

"It's a town library but the town doesn't run it?"

"That's right."

"So who does operate it?"

"Agriculture's the only industry in the town, and there aren't any tourist attractions. A small onsen hot springs is nearby, but that's all. And the local government is, like many others, chronically underfunded. Maintaining a town library is hard for them, with the building aging and fire code problems, and at one time they thought of closing it for good. But the owner of a sake brewery insisted that a library is a necessary cultural facility and that losing it would hurt the town, so ten years ago he created a fund and invested enough to keep the library up and running. The library moved to a new place, and when it did, the town used that as the opportunity to officially delegate the operation to that entity. I couldn't find out any more details beyond that. If you'd like, you can ask people directly when you get there."

I'll do that, I said.

"You'd describe it now as a library that's been privatized," Oki said. "I think it might be easier for you to work in a place like that. I haven't actually been there, but I get the sense it's a sort of laid-back area."

■

Two days later Oki contacted me again to say that I could visit the library on any day that was convenient for me, other than a Monday, at three p.m.

"A day convenient for me?" I asked.

"You can choose the day. They said they can see you any day."

I found that odd but had no reason to complain.

"And they'll interview me there?"

"I would think so," Oki said. "They seemed surprised that someone like you, in the prime of your life, with such a solid work background, would come all the way from Tokyo to apply, but I did my best to explain it to them. Said you're getting tired of the rat race in Tokyo, and so on."

"Thank you for all your kindness. I really appreciate it," I said.

After a moment he said, "Maybe I shouldn't say this, but I always felt there was something unusual about you. Unpredictable, perhaps, or hard to fathom . . . and the same goes for all this. Why leave your job so suddenly, and take some sketchy job in a remote library? Frankly, I don't get it. But you must have your reasons. Someday I'd love to hear the whole story, if you feel like sharing." He cleared his throat. "At any rate, I hope your life in this new place will be rewarding."

"Thanks," I said. Then I ventured to ask, "By the way, have you ever worried about your shadow?"

"My shadow? You're talking about the dark shadow I cast?" On the other end of the phone Oki thought this over for a while. "No, can't say I ever have."

"I can't help worrying about mine. Especially these days. I feel a sort of sense of responsibility, as a person, toward my shadow. Like whether I've been treating him right, or fairly."

"Has . . . this been one of the reasons for you changing jobs?"

"It could be."

Oki fell silent again, and then said, "I understand . . . Well, honestly, I'm not sure I totally get it, but I'll think a bit more about my shadow. About what's right, and fair."

TRAVELING FROM TOKYO to Z** took longer than I'd expected. I left Tokyo at nine a.m. on Wednesday and arrived at the local station there close to two p.m. The interview was set for three.

I rode the Tohoku Shinkansen to Koriyama, where I took an older line to Aizuwakamatasu, and then I changed to a local line. The train soon entered the mountains, where it wove its way through, gently curving as it followed the land, through one tunnel after another. Some long, some short. I was amazed, wondering how far the mountains went on. It was early summer and the surrounding mountains were enveloped in a vivid green. A breeze blew in from somewhere, and the air I breathed was fragrant. In the sky a number of black kites circled, their sharp eyes carefully scanning the ground.

I'd requested a place inland, so of course there would be mountains, but now that I thought about it, I realized I'd never once lived in a mountainous region. I'd been born and raised by the sea, and ever since moving to Tokyo had lived on the flat Kanto Plain. So it felt strange to think that (maybe) I'd settle down in a place like this, surrounded by mountains. At the same time, it felt like a fascinating new development.

It was noonish so there weren't many passengers on the train. At each station we stopped at, a few people got off and a few boarded. At some small stations no one got on or off, and at some there weren't even any station employees. I wasn't hungry, so I skipped lunch, instead gazing at the endless mountains rolling by, and occasionally nodding off. When I woke up, I felt anxious. *What in the world am I doing here? And what am planning to do?* As I reconsidered these questions, I felt the decision axis inside me waver slightly.

Was I really heading to the right place for me? Or was I making a wrong choice as I headed in the wrong direction? My muscles stiffened as these thoughts came to me. I had to clear my head of any thoughts and trust my instincts—a sense of direction that defied logic.

But you must have your reasons, Oki had said to me. I had to believe there were, and go with it. Believe that there was an important reason behind all this.

Oki had also said there was something *unpredictable* about me, something *hard to fathom.* That surprised me, since I'd never imagined people see me that way. At my company I'd never acted unusually, always trying to seem like your average person. I wasn't very outgoing but socialized with colleagues like everyone else. Admittedly reaching my mid-forties still a bachelor was unusual (I was alone in this at work), but aside from that I don't think anything else set me apart from my colleagues. But a part of me inside probably didn't open up to others. It was like there was a line on the ground I didn't want others to step past. And people sensed that in a subtle way when we'd been together for a long time.

There was something *hard to fathom* about me—I could see that. Because I myself didn't have a good grasp of who I was. I thought about this as I gazed at the mountain scenery passing by. Maybe the person most puzzled about me was . . . me.

I closed my eyes and took some deep breaths, trying to calm myself. A little while later I opened my eyes once and checked out the scenery outside. The train crossed over a beautiful winding river, entered a tunnel, then emerged. Entered another tunnel, then emerged. This deep in the mountains the winters must be freezing, with tons of snow. Snow brought back thoughts of those poor beasts. The unicorns, one after another breathing their last in the falling white snow. Laying their gaunt bodies down, quietly shutting their eyes, awaiting death.

In front of the Z** station was a small plaza, and a taxi stand and bus stop. There wasn't a single taxi at the taxi stand, and no sign of one about to show up. And no one was waiting for a bus. I checked the location of the library on a map I'd brought with me. It looked to be a ten-minute walk from the station. So I figured I'd stroll through town to kill time until I had to be there. But it took only fifteen minutes to see the whole town. There was really nothing to see. There was a small shopping area in front of the station, but half the stores had their shutters closed, while most of the ones that were open looked asleep.

I thought I'd drop by a coffee shop, have some coffee, and read a book I had brought with me, but couldn't find any place I felt like going into. It was nice not to see any fast-food chains, but there didn't seem to be any appealing (or even reasonable) alternative choice. Local people probably drove their nondescript little minivans or super-compact cars outside the town to a nondescript shopping mall to shop and eat. A typical local town you can find anywhere in Japan. *Local color* might already be a defunct term.

I bought hot coffee in a small convenience store and decided to pass the time at a tiny park near the station. Two young mothers had brought their children there to play. Kids not yet in elementary school. One boy and one girl. While the children played on the equipment the mothers stood next to each other, engrossed in conversation. I sat down on a hard bench and half watched this little scene. Suddenly I remembered back in high school, meeting my girlfriend in a park near her home. My head was soon filled with memories of those times.

That summer I was seventeen. And inside me time had actually come to a halt. The hands of the clock moved forward, marking the passage of time, but real time for me—the clock buried in the walls of my heart—had come to a complete stop. And it felt like the nearly thirty years that had passed had just been spent filling in the gap. There was a need to fill in the empty parts of me with anything, and I did so with whatever happened to catch my eye around me. There's a need to keep on breathing, yet people do it unconsciously even while fast asleep. It was the same thing.

I suddenly wanted to see the river. That's right, I thought, the first thing I should have done when I got here was go see the river, since I had plenty of time on my hands.

I reached into my pocket and took out the map I'd printed out from the internet and saw that the river gently curved as it flowed outside the town. What kind of river was it? What kind of water flowed in it? Were there fish? And what kind of bridges spanned it? But I didn't have enough time. I figured that after the interview, if I still felt like it, I could take my time viewing the river.

I finished the tasteless coffee and tossed the paper cup into the garbage can in the park. The two young children were still enjoying playing on the playground equipment. The two young mothers were still there beside them, still wrapped up in their conversation. A single crow alighted at the drinking fountain and cast a sidelong glance at me. It seemed to be carefully observing me, this outsider, watching my movements. I waited until the crow flew off before leaving the park and heading to the library.

The library was a two-story wooden building and looked like an older building that had recently been renovated. The roof tiles—new and shiny—gave it away. The building was at the top of a low hill, with a neatly kept garden and some large pine trees proudly casting their deep shadows on the ground. It looked less like a public facility than like some rich person's old villa.

Not as bad as I'd thought it would be. I was impressed. On one of the two old stone pillars at the entrance hung a large, old carved wooden sign that read z** TOWN LIBRARY. If that hadn't been there, I might have walked right past the place without realizing it was the library. Since it was a small, underfunded town library, I'd been expecting an average, shabby-looking building.

No one else was around. I passed through the huge open steel gate, gravel crunching under my shoes, and walked up the curving gentle slope to the entrance. On a branch of one of the large pine trees was a pitch-black crow, this one too eyeing me warily. Was this the same crow as back in the park? I had no way of knowing.

I opened the door, walked through the foyer, which reminded me of an older home, and went inside to find a spacious, open area. It had a high, vaulted ceiling, thick square pillars, and curved beams that together supported this sizable house, a role they must have silently shared for the past hundred years. Early-summer sunlight pleasantly shone in the high horizontal windows above the beams.

The room just past the foyer was a sort of lounge, with sofas and a wall rack neatly lined with newspapers and magazines. A large arrangement of white flowers on branches sat in a large ceramic vase on the table in the middle of the room. Three patrons were seated on chairs, quietly perusing magazines. Men in their sixties and seventies, no doubt retirees with time on their hands. This was the perfect place for people like them to spend an afternoon.

Behind this was a counter, where a slim woman with glasses was seated. Her face was on the bony side, with a smallish, thin nose. Her hair was tied up in back, and she wore a white blouse with a simple design. She would have been perfectly at home knitting in front of a fireplace. But here she was seated at the counter, noting something in a thick ledger with a ballpoint pen. On the wall behind her was a small painting by Léonard Foujita of a cat stretching, in a sturdy-looking frame. It had to be a reproduction. If it wasn't it would be quite a valuable painting, and I found it hard to believe that such a valuable work would be casually displayed here like this. Still, the frame was too expensive-looking for a reproduction.

I checked my watch. It was just before three p.m., so I went over to the counter, told her my name and that I had an interview at three. She asked me to repeat my name, which I did. Her eyes reminded me of a cat's. Ever-changing, and inscrutable.

She was silent for a time, studying me closely, as if checking something. Like she was temporarily at a loss for words. After a pause, she said, her voice sounding somehow resigned, "Do you have an appointment?"

"I was told that, other than on a Monday, I should come for an interview any day after three."

"Excuse me, but whom did you make the appointment with?"

"I'm afraid I don't know the name. There was a go-between. But I was told to speak with the person in charge of the library."

She adjusted the bridge of her glasses, was silent again, and finally said, in a flat tone, "I haven't heard anything about an interview, but that's alright. Go up those stairs and you'll find the head librarian's room just to the right. Please go there."

I thanked her and headed to the stairs. The confused silence of the woman at the counter must mean something, and of course it bothered me, but now wasn't the time to worry about that. I needed to focus on the interview.

At the top of the stairs, a simple rope was strung across, with a sign reading AUTHORIZED PERSONNEL ONLY. Only part of the first floor, including the lounge, had a vaulted ceiling that had replaced the second floor—the rest of the building was two stories. The only place the ordinary patrons could use, apparently, was the first floor.

I climbed the slightly creaky wooden stairs, and just as the woman at the counter had told me, on the immediate right was a door with a metal plate that read HEAD LIBRARIAN OFFICE. I checked my watch again, saw it was just past three p.m., took a deep breath, and knocked—like a traveler checking the thickness of the ice on a lake before venturing across.

"Yes, please come in," a man's voice said from inside. As if he'd been waiting some time for the knock to come.

I opened the door, made a small bow at the entrance. I could feel the blood pulse in my temples. I felt more tense than I'd imagined. I hadn't been interviewed since back in college when I made the rounds of companies looking for a job. It felt like I'd gone back to that time, to that age.

The room wasn't very large, and directly opposite the door was a long vertical window, the sunlight filtering in. In front of the window was a largish old desk, behind which the man was seated. Because of the light, though, his face was in shadow, and I couldn't make it out well.

"Excuse me," I said, standing at the door, my voice dry. And I said my name.

"Please, ah, come on in. Come on in. I've been looking forward to this," the man said. His voice was a calm baritone, and he sounded as if he were speaking to some strange animal deep in the woods. No hint of a local accent.

"Please, ah, sit there in that chair."

The chair was on this side of the desk, so we faced each other directly. Still, though, backlighted as he was, his face was in shadow. He was seated, so I couldn't tell how tall he was, but he didn't seem to be that large a man. He had a roundish face and seemed to be on the chubby side.

"Thank you for coming all this way out here," the man said. And he lightly cleared his throat. "It must have taken a long time."

Nearly five hours, I replied.

"Is that right," the man said. "The Shinkansen has cut down the time, but I don't go out much so I don't really know. I haven't been to Tokyo in ages."

The man's voice had a strange quality to it, like the feeling you get touching a well-used soft cloth. I'd heard a voice very much like it a long time ago but couldn't recall when or where it had been.

As my eyes adjusted to the sunlight, I could make out that the man was probably in his mid-seventies. His gray hair had receded quite a bit. His upper eyelids were thick, and at first glance he looked sleepy, but his eyes below that were bright, unexpectedly lively.

He opened a desk drawer, took out a business card, and passed it to me across the desk. Printed on the white paper in black ink it said "Tatsuya Koyasu, Head Librarian, Z** Town Library, ** County, Fukushima Prefecture." And then the library's address and phone number. A very plain business card.

"My name is Koyasu," Mr. Koyasu said.

"It's an unusual name," I said. I felt I needed to make some comment about it. "Is it a common name around here?"

Mr. Koyasu smiled as he shook his head. "No, not at all. We are the only ones with the name Koyasu. No one else has it."

I took out a business card from my former company and passed it to him.

Mr. Koyasu put on reading glasses, glanced through my card, then placed it in the drawer. He removed his glasses and said, "Ah, I looked through the résumé you sent. You have no experience working in a library, and no qualifications, so at first we were thinking of turning you down. Since we were advertising for someone with experience in managing a library."

Of course, my expression said as I nodded. As I wondered how many people this word *we* included.

"Still, for several reasons we decided to keep you in the running." Mr. Koyasu picked up a thick fountain pen and twirled it between his fingers. "One reason was your invaluable track record dealing for many years with book distribution. Plus, you're still young. I don't know the circumstances, but you quit your job very early. Most of the others who applied for this job are elderly people who'd already retired. You're the only young person."

I nodded again. At this point I couldn't think of any response I might make.

"Thirdly, I read the letter you included with your résumé, and I could see how very interested you are in working at a library. And not in some large city but in a smaller, regional branch. Is this a correct interpretation?"

I believe so, I replied. Mr. Koyasu cleared his throat again and nodded.

"Frankly, I don't understand how working in a country library like this, deep in the mountains, holds such special meaning for you. Library work can be pretty dull. And there's hardly anything in this town in the way of entertainment facilities. And no cultural stimulation. You're sure you'd be fine being here?"

I don't need any cultural stimulation, I said. What I need is quiet surroundings.

"Well, quiet it is. In the autumn you can even hear the calls of deer in the mountains," Mr. Koyasu said, smiling. "I was wondering, could you tell me about your duties in that book distribution company?"

When I was young, I went to bookstores all over Japan to learn more about book sales at the ground level. When I got to a certain age I stayed back in the company headquarters, taking care of book distribution and acting as a kind of controller, issuing directives to different departments. No matter how well things went you always count on there being complaints, but I think I did a decent job of handling the work.

As I was running through this explanation, I suddenly noticed something—a hat set down at a corner of the largish desk. A navy-blue beret. Clearly used over a long period, it looked nicely broken in, soft and worn in a nice way. And this was *exactly the same* beret—or at least it looked exactly the same—as the one in my dream. And it was placed in the same spot. I gulped.

Something's connected here.

Time came to a halt at this point. The hands of the clock froze as they intently marked a critical memory from the distant past. It took some time before it restarted.

"Is something the matter?" Mr. Koyasu asked, looking worried.

"No, nothing's wrong. I'm fine," I said. I lightly cleared my throat a couple of times, pretending something was stuck in my throat. And then, as if nothing had happened, I went on explaining about my work at my former company.

"I see. So you've studied about books and sharpened your skills over the years. Acquired the requisite social skills and learned the ins and outs of an organization, how it operates." Mr. Koyasu said this once I'd finished talking.

I glanced at the beret and then back to him.

Mr. Koyasu explained how the library operated, and what duties the head librarian had to perform. It wasn't a long explanation, since the scope of the work wasn't that extensive. He also mentioned the salary. It wasn't much, but I'd been steeling myself for even less. As long as I lived alone, frugally, the pay should be enough to live here.

"Ah, would you have any questions?"

I had a few, of course. "Let's say I did take over from you—when I make decisions, whose directions should I follow?"

"You mean, who's your boss?"

I nodded. "Exactly."

Mr. Koyasu picked up the thick fountain pen again, checking its heft, then went on, choosing his words carefully.

"On paper this library is the town library, but in practice the operation is done through a fund set up by interested parties in town. The fund has a board of directors and a board chair, and in theory that person has decision powers, but the position is entirely honorary, and the chair hardly ever speaks."

Mr. Koyasu stopped there. I waited for him to go on, but he didn't seem about to.

I was silent, and in the silence Mr. Koyasu blinked a few times and laid the fountain pen back on the desk.

"It's a long story, so I'll explain more about this at a later date. For the time being, though, if there's any problem that arises, just consult me. I'll make sure it's taken care of. How does that sound?"

"I still don't understand what's going on, but are you saying you'll be resigning as head librarian?"

"Yes, that's correct. Actually, I've already stepped down, so the position is vacant."

"And even after you retire as head librarian, you'll still act in an advisory role?"

Mr. Koyasu inclined his head sharply just a fraction, like a waterfowl listening intently.

"No, being an adviser is not an official position. It's just that, in my humble opinion, while duties are transferred it is, to an extent, necessary. I think that during the handover period it would be good for me to help you, entirely on a *personal basis*. As long as that's not inconvenient for you, of course."

I shook my head. "No, of course not. In fact, I welcome it. It's just that it sounds like the decision's already been made that I will be your successor."

"Well, yes, I guess so," Mr. Koyasu said, looking surprised— as if nonplussed that I hadn't understood this already. "That was our intention from the very start, you see. Actually, we privately spoke to a former colleague, who said, ah, that you have a solid reputation. That you were a capable worker, and that you're honest and trustworthy, like a tree in a forest."

Like a tree in a forest? I doubted what I was hearing. I couldn't think of any of my former colleagues who would have used an expression like that. *Like a tree in a forest?*

Mr. Koyasu went on. "Which is exactly why we invited you to come all the way out here. We thought that before we made the official decision, we should meet you and talk with you once. But we'd already made up our mind. That we would definitely offer you the position."

"Thank you very much," I said, my voice off-kilter, as if I'd misplaced its center of gravity. I took a slow, deep breath. A breath of relief, no doubt.

After this we discussed some practical matters having to do with my taking on the position of head librarian. I had to vacate my Tokyo apartment and find a place to live here. If you'll leave it up to us, Mr. Koyasu said, we can find a suitable place. There are several vacant houses in town, and the rent will be next to nothing compared to Tokyo. And we'll manage to come up with the household goods and things you'll need.

After a half hour, when we'd pretty much finalized things, Mr. Koyasu stood up from his chair, picked up the navy-blue beret on his desk, and put it on. I have something I need to do, he said, so I have to return from where I came.

Return from where I came was a strange expression. But I didn't worry about it—his way of talking was a little odd to begin with.

"What a nice hat," I ventured.

A pleased smile came to his lips. He took the beret off, examined it, carefully adjusted it, then put it back on. It looked like an even more intimate part of him now.

"Yes, I've been using this beret a lot since about ten years ago. It can't be helped, but as I've gotten older my hair's thinned out and I find it hard to do without a hat. Especially in the winter. My niece was traveling in France, and I had her buy me one from a top retailer in Paris. Ever since I was young, I've loved French films and have always loved the look of berets. In an out-of-the-way place like this I'm the only one who ever wears one, and at first I was a bit embarrassed to, but you get used to it. I know I did, and so did other people."

And I noticed one other unusual fact about Mr. Koyasu—in terms of eccentricity, it was even more eccentric than the beret. He wasn't wearing trousers, but a skirt.

Later on, he explained, very kindly and in detail, why he wore a skirt.

"One reason is that when I wear a skirt I, ah, feel like I've become a few lines from a beautiful poem."

NOT LONG AFTER THIS, I vacated the apartment in Nakano ward I'd lived in for over ten years, said farewell to Tokyo, and moved into a new place in Z★★. I had a moving company take away any bulky furniture or appliances, not that I owned many nice ones. I sold most of the books that overflowed from my shelves to a used bookstore. I figured that working in a library, I should have plenty to read. I donated my old suits and jackets to a used-clothing store. I was about to live a new life, and I wanted to get rid of everything redolent of the past. Thanks to which, everything I had fit into a small moving van, and I felt, for the first time in ages, free.

This sense of freedom reminded me of something I'd experienced before, and I tried to remember. It was a little like the feeling I had when I first lived in that walled-in town. When I first entered that town, I had nothing with me. Literally just the clothes on my back (and I had even jettisoned my shadow), but the town provided me with everything, from a place to live to clothes to wear. Everything was plain and simple, but I had everything I needed.

Compared to then, now I dragged along a small truckload of belongings with me from the past, but I did share with that time a sense of lightness, of liberation.

A real estate agent with an office near the station took me to see a house for rent. He was a small, friendly, middle-aged man named Komatsu. The library had asked him to take care of all my housing arrangements.

The place we looked at was a cozy one-story home not far from the river. It was surrounded by a dark brown fence and had a small garden. There was one old persimmon tree growing in the garden. And a well, though it was no longer in use and partly filled in. Next to the well grew Japanese kerria bushes, and in the back of that clump of bushes was a small stone lantern covered in a thin layer of moss. The garden had been weeded, the azalea bushes neatly trimmed. No one had lived in the house for half a year, and a couple of days before they'd had a gardener come to whip the yard into shape.

"Maybe this wasn't necessary, but around here, gardens are quite significant," Mr. Komatsu said.

"Of course," I said, making the expected reply.

"One other thing is that the persimmon tree bears wonderful fruit, but it's way too tart to eat, sad to say. But at least then the neighborhood children won't sneak into your garden to steal the fruit."

"You're saying that everybody knows that? That the persimmon tree here might look nice but the fruit's too tart?"

Mr. Komatsu nodded several times. "That's right. People around here know everything going on around here. Up to and including a single fruit on a permission tree."

The house had been built fifty years before, yet didn't seem old. I liked its coziness, the way it didn't stand out. An elderly woman had lived there before me.

"She was a neat and orderly person, so the inside of the house is well maintained," Mr. Komatsu said. He didn't say what had happened to that old woman, where she'd gone, and I didn't venture to ask. The place didn't have many rooms but was just the right size for a person living alone. The rent was about one-fifth of what I'd been paying in Tokyo, and it was only a fifteen-minute walk to the library.

"If you don't like this place," Mr. Komatsu said, "don't hesitate to tell me, since I can find another. There are plenty of other unoccupied houses in this area."

"I appreciate that. But from what I can tell I don't see any problems with this house."

And there weren't any. As I'd been told already (Mr. Koyasu said I could literally come empty-handed), the place was furnished already with everything from a refrigerator to dishes, cooking utensils, a simple bed and bedding—all the day-to-day things I'd need. None of them seemed new, but not too old either, and quite serviceable. At the library's direction, Mr. Komatsu had arranged for everything. I thanked him for this. It must have been quite a chore to prepare everything.

"Not at all, not at all," he demurred, waving a hand. "Happy to do it, since we don't get many outsiders moving here."

In this way, my humble new life in Z** began. After eight every morning I left home, walked along the river road, heading upstream, then down the road into the main part of town. Unlike when I worked in a company, I didn't have to wear a suit or a tie, or uncomfortable leather shoes. That in itself made it worth changing jobs. Only now that I'd given up that life did I understand how many restrictions I'd put up with all those years.

The river made a pleasant sound, and if I closed my eyes I had the illusion that it was flowing within me. The water, streaming down from the mountains, was clear, and I could see tiny fish swimming here and there. A slim white heron had stopped on a rock and was patiently gazing at the water's surface.

The river in this town looked very different from the river flowing through the *town surrounded by a wall*. Here there was no large sandbank, and no river willows. Nor an old stone bridge spanning the river. No unicorns, of course, chewing on the leaves of Scotch broom. On both sides of the river were bland concrete retaining walls. The water, though, was equally clear and pristine, the sound of cool summer water. I felt happy to be living near such a charming river.

As the town was in a basin surrounded by high mountains, it was hot in the summer and cold in the winter. I moved to the town at the end of August, and though autumn would soon descend on this mountainous region, and the screech of the cicadas of summer was mostly absent, the summer heat lingered, the sunlight bluntly stinging the back of my neck.

With the people at the library helping me, I gradually got used to the job of head librarian. Though I was in charge, there was another librarian directly below me, Mrs. Soeda (the woman behind the counter the first time I visited, the one wearing metal-frame glasses with her hair tied back), and a few part-time women, which meant I had to handle a lot of the sundry tasks of the library.

Mr. Koyasu made the occasional visit to my office. He'd sit across from me and review in detail my duties as head librarian: selecting books, administration, keeping the daily ledger (official accounts were kept by an accountant who came once a month), personnel management, dealing with patrons. There were a few things I needed to learn, but since it was a small facility, none of them were that complicated. I remembered each point he taught me and took care of them without any fuss. Mr. Koyasu was very kind (it seemed that this was his natural personality), and he loved this library dearly. He would usually arrive in my office without warning and leave before I realized it. He reminded me of some cautious woodland creature.

And bit by bit, I got to know the female staff members. At first, they seemed on their guard with me, and who could blame them—I was, after all, a complete outsider who'd swooped in from Tokyo—but as we spent time together, and talked about everyday things, they gradually opened up. Most of them were local women in their thirties or forties, married with families. I think they found the fact that I was in my mid-forties and still unmarried a bit different, and a little exciting.

"Well, Mr. Koyasu was a longtime bachelor, but you know how he is," Mrs. Soeda told me.

"Mr. Koyasu was a bachelor?" I asked.

Mrs. Soeda nodded silently. She wore an expression that looked as though she'd put something in her mouth that she shouldn't have, and I could tell it was best not to ask any more (at least for now).

It seemed that there were several important facts about Mr. Koyasu she wasn't talking about—or at least not telling me. Not yet.

EVERY THREE OR FOUR DAYS, Mr. Koyasu would arrive at the head librarian's office at random, probably just when he felt like it. He would quietly (making hardly a sound) open the door, come in, have a friendly talk with me for about a half hour, then leave, just as quietly. It felt like being grazed by a pleasant breeze. When I thought about it later, I realized I never once met him anywhere outside the library. And we were always alone, just the two of us. No one else was ever present with us.

Mr. Koyasu invariably wore his navy-blue beret with a wrap-around skirt. He had several types of skirts, some made from plain fabric, others checked. Most of them were in flashy colors. Or at least not very subdued ones. And he always wore form-fitting black tights beneath his skirt.

After seeing him dressed like that many times, I got used to it and no longer found it odd. I did wonder how people looked at him, how they reacted, when he walked around in town (naturally he would walk). Most likely they were like me, used to his outfit, and no longer thought anything of it. Plus in this town, Mr. Koyasu was a prominent local figure. No one was going to point or make fun of him.

One time, though, as we were talking about something else, I decided to ask him about it. When did you start wearing skirts? And that's when he said that line. Cheerful, smiling, as if it were all quite natural.

"One reason is that when I wear a skirt I, ah, feel like I've become a few lines from a beautiful poem."

I'm not sure why, but I didn't find his explanation surprising, or odd, and just accepted it. Wearing a skirt every day must have fit his feelings best. And whatever those feelings were, whatever the reason he did it, the sense that he'd become a few lines of a beautiful poem was itself a wonderful thing. Not that it motivated me to try wearing skirts myself. This was a question of personal taste and nothing else.

I liked Mr. Koyasu, and I suspect that he had favorable feelings (or something like them) toward me. But my relationship with him was limited. He'd show up at the head librarian's office out of the blue, and give me suitable advice when I wasn't sure how to proceed with my duties. Without his help it would have taken me much longer, and much more effort, to grasp the essentials of the job. The work itself wasn't complicated, but there were some intricate local rules that had to be taken into account.

We'd talk enthusiastically about the library's operations, drinking tea in between. Mr. Koyasu apparently didn't like coffee. Inside a cabinet in the office was a white porcelain teapot reserved for his use alone, and a special blend of tea leaves. He would boil water in an electric kettle and, ever so carefully, add the tea leaves to the teapot. I joined him in drinking the tea, which had a wonderful color and fragrance and an enrapturing flavor. I prefer coffee myself, but enjoying tea with him was one of the small pleasures of life for me. He looked quite pleased when I complimented its flavor.

Despite these times together, we never saw each other outside the library. I assumed he didn't much like being with people during his private time. And truthfully, I was thankful for that.

Once my work was done at the library I'd return home, whip up a simple dinner, then sit in my reading chair and immerse myself in reading. I didn't have either a TV or a radio at home, just a transistor radio for emergencies. I owned a laptop but had never been fond of using it. My only pastime was lounging in my chair and reading.

While I read, I liked to have one or two glasses of scotch on the rocks. As I drank, I'd grow sleepy and usually go to bed about ten p.m. I was a good sleeper, so once I fell asleep, I never woke up until morning.

In the morning and evening, when I didn't have anything in particular to do, I liked to walk around the outskirts of town. The path along the river, with its lovely sound of rushing water, was one of my favorite routes.

There was a paved walking trail along the river, though hardly anyone used it, and I only occasionally passed a jogger or someone out walking their dog. The path continued several miles downstream, then it branched off from the river into a broad field and turned into a dirt path. I continued on, undeterred, and after a short time, maybe ten minutes, even that narrow footpath petered out and disappeared. I found myself standing, alone, in the middle of a meadow. The green weeds were tall, and the silence rang in my ears. A flock of red dragonflies flitted about me without a sound.

I looked up at the clear pure-blue sky. Hard, white autumn-like clouds were set there like fragmentary episodes in a tale. When I breathed in, I smelled the robust fragrance of grasses. This was really a grass kingdom, and I was a boorish intruder unable to fathom the grassy significance of it all.

Standing there alone, I always felt sad, a deep sadness I'd felt before, long, long ago. I remembered that sadness very well. A sadness that can't be explained, that doesn't melt away over time, that quietly leaves invisible wounds, in a place you cannot see. And how can you deal with something you can't see?

I looked up, listening carefully to see if I could catch the sound of the flowing river. But I heard nothing, not even the wind. Clouds were pinned in place in the sky. I quietly closed my eyes, waiting for tears to well up and trickle down my face. But that unseen sadness wouldn't even allow me to cry.

I gave up trying, and silently went back down the path I'd taken.

I met Mr. Koyasu often in the library, yet for a long time knew next to nothing about him as a person.

He was a bachelor, that much I'd heard, but had he never had a family? "Well, that's the kind of person he was," Mrs. Soeda commented. What did *the kind of* mean? And why the past tense?

The more I thought about it, the more I needed to know about him. Yet at the same time, and I can't explain it well, it occurred to me that maybe it was better to know nothing.

The women who worked at the library were generally pretty chatty. Because it was a library, of course, they stayed as quiet as they could when they were out on the floor. When they needed to convey something they did so as quietly, and in as few words, as they could. But once they were in private in the back rooms of the library, perhaps in response to their public reticence, the words gushed out. It was mainly women whispering to each other, so I tried to stay clear.

For all their chattiness, they hardly ever mentioned Mr. Koyasu when I was around. On other topics (the library, the town), they had no problem providing me with plenty of detailed information, but mention Mr. Koyasu and they hesitated and turned evasive. Whether it was their individual opinion, or a general consensus, they treated the subject like dirty laundry.

All of which meant I was unable to gather any information about Mr. Koyasu as a person. His background remained a mystery. Why they didn't gossip more about this unorthodox, small old man in a skirt was beyond me. It felt like some sort of taboo topic, like the proscription against peeking inside one of those tiny shrines in a forest surrounding a larger shrine. A simple enough type of taboo, yet one that has permeated deep into one's consciousness.

I didn't want to put the women on the spot, so I intentionally avoided the topic of Mr. Koyasu with them. And besides, Mr. Koyasu's background, at least at present, made no difference to my duties in the town's library. Mr. Koyasu very kindly, and efficiently, passed down the essentials of the job, as a result of which I was able to smoothly take over the duties he'd performed. Maybe you're better off not knowing things you don't have to know. Maybe.

The librarian, Mrs. Soeda, was married to a man who taught in a public elementary school in town, and they didn't have any children. She was born in Nagano Prefecture but had left her hometown for Z** after she married. About ten years had passed since then. Even so, she was generally treated as an outsider. Not many people came and went here in this isolated mountain region. Locals didn't exactly exclude others, yet the townspeople weren't all that openly receptive to anyone from the outside. At any rate, Mrs. Soeda was an extremely capable woman, and handled nearly all the sundry administrative tasks that came up at the library. Her judgment in everything was quick, decisive, and accurate.

"If Mrs. Soeda weren't here," Mr. Koyasu said, "the library wouldn't last a week." And as I spent more time there, I saw how right he was.

She was, in a word, the mainstay of the library. Without her, the system would have slowed down and ground to a halt. She stayed in close contact with the town office, managed staff assignments, kept a sharp eye on what was happening there—handling everything from broken hot water pots to burned-out light bulbs, making sure the library ran smoothly so there were no complaints from patrons. She supervised the part-time staff and quickly resolved any issues that arose. When any special event took place at the library, she'd make a checklist of things that needed doing and take care of each and every one. She also had to keep an eye on the maintenance of the trees in the garden. She was basically in charge of everything that was needed to operate the library.

Wouldn't it be best if she were the head librarian? I thought, and even said this to Mr. Koyasu. Wouldn't the library run well with a woman this capable in charge?

Mr. Koyasu looked at me, his face a bit troubled. And then said, "I told her that myself. That her taking over after me was the best thing. But she turned me down flat. She said she preferred being a supervisor. I tried everything I could to convince her, but she wouldn't go for it."

"Is she a very humble person, then?"

"I suppose so," Mr. Koyasu said cheerfully.

Mrs. Soeda seemed to be in her mid-thirties, with clear features and an intelligent air about her. She was about five foot three inches tall, and her figure, like her face, was slim. Her posture was excellent, her back always erect, her gait graceful. In college she had played basketball, she said. She always wore a skirt that came down to just below her knees, and low-heeled shoes that were easy to walk in. She wore almost no makeup, yet her skin was lovely. Her earlobes were round and smooth, like small pebbles on a shore. The nape of her neck was thin but didn't look fragile.

She liked black coffee, and there was always a large mug on her desk behind the counter. The mug had a drawing of a colorful wild bird, its wings spread. She didn't seem like the type of person who opened up to people she was meeting for the first time. Her eyes always had a cautious glint, a hint of defiance on her tight lips. For all that, the first time I met her I had the feeling we'd get to be close before long. Perhaps as fellow outsiders in this town.

Without saying much about it, Mrs. Soeda accepted me as her boss, as if it were all quite natural. Nothing could have made me happier. Nothing is more draining than uncomfortable relationships at the workplace.

Mrs. Soeda didn't like to talk about herself. Still, she had a healthy curiosity about others, and as time passed and she grew more used to me, she wanted to know more about my past. Like the other staff members, she was most curious about why I was in my mid-forties and still unmarried. If I'd said the reason was that I couldn't find the right partner, then she might step up and introduce me to someone who was the right partner. Since I was an older single person, this wouldn't be the first time.

"I didn't get married because there's already someone in my heart," I would explain simply. My standard response to that question.

"But for some reason you couldn't be with her? Was there a reason?"

I nodded, vaguely, without a word.

"Because she was married to someone else or something?"

"I don't know," I said. "I haven't seen her for a long time, and I have no way of knowing where she is or what she's doing."

"But you loved her, and even now you can't forget her?"

Another vague nod from me. This was the safest explanation to give to people. And it wasn't entirely a made-up story, either.

"I wonder if that's why you left the city and moved to this rural little town. So you could forget her?"

I smiled and shook my head. "No, nothing so romantic as that. The situation's the same whether I'm in the city or the countryside. I'm just going with the flow."

"But she must have been a wonderful person, right?"

"Was she? Who was it who said loving someone is like having a mental illness that's not covered by health insurance?"

Mrs. Soeda laughed quietly, and lightly pushed up the bridge of her glasses. She took a sip of coffee from her personal mug and went back to the work she'd been doing. That was our last conversation that day.

EVEN THOUGH IT WAS a small-town library, since I'd taken on the job of head librarian I'd been prepared to make the rounds in town, introducing myself and being introduced to local dignitaries and so on. Social niceties weren't exactly my forte, but I could handle them when the job required it. After all, I'd worked for over twenty years in a company.

But contrary to my expectations, these visits never occurred, not even once. I wasn't introduced to anyone in town, and never visited anyone to pay my compliments. Mrs. Soeda did assemble the part-time women staff members (there were but four of them), and introduced me as the new head librarian; we sat down and had tea and cupcakes together. Each of them briefly introduced herself. That was the extent of it. Short and sweet.

Naturally I was thankful things were kept so simple, but I did feel a bit let down, and baffled. I wondered if something important, something critical, had been overlooked.

One time, when Mr. Koyasu and I were in the head librarian's office, drinking tea together, I asked him about it.

"This library is officially named after Z**, so shouldn't I drop by the city office and at least introduce myself?"

When he heard this Mr. Koyasu half opened his small mouth and made a face like he'd accidentally swallowed a bug.

"Ah, by introduce yourself you mean—"

"In other words . . . wouldn't it be good for me to at least establish a connection with them, meet the people in charge in town? Just in case something happens?"

"Establish a connection," he repeated, looking put out.

I waited, silently, for him to go on.

Mr. Koyasu cleared his throat awkwardly and said, "I don't think that's, ah, necessary. This library has no real connection with the town. It's completely independent. It does have the town name attached, but that's just because it would be too much trouble changing it, so we left it as is. So there's no need at all for you to stop by to introduce yourself. Actually, that would complicate things."

"Don't I need to introduce myself at a board meeting?"

Mr. Koyasu shook his head. "No, there's no need to. And there won't be any opportunity to, since they hardly ever meet. As I explained before, the board is just a formality, a token."

"A board that's a formality," I said.

"Ah, that's right," he said, beaming all the more. "There are five board members, not a single one of whom cares about this library. We just use their names because the system requires that we have a board. So therefore, yes, there's no need for you to go introduce yourself."

I didn't get it. A library operated by a pro forma board.

"If something comes up and I need to consult somebody about it, then who should I go to?"

"I'm here. You can ask me about anything at all. And I'll give you an answer."

All well and good, but I didn't know his address or telephone number, or email address. How would I get in touch, then?

"I'll be stopping by here once every three days or so. Things keep me from coming every day, but I should be able to come that often. If anything arises, please ask me then." He sounded as if he'd been reading my thoughts.

"And also, Mrs. Soeda's here. I'm sure she'll help you. She knows just about everything. So there's nothing, ah, for you to worry about."

I asked him about something that had been on my mind for a time.

"But you require adequate funds to continue running this library. Even a small-scale town library needs to pay utilities and salaries, and funds to make monthly purchases of books. If the board of directors doesn't fulfill its function, who shoulders those costs, and oversees them?"

Mr. Koyasu crossed his arms and tilted his head, looking a bit perplexed.

"I think as you go about your work here day to day you'll gradually come to understand all that. Like the dawn arriving and sunshine streaming through the window. At this point don't let it concern you, and just focus on learning the ins and outs of the job. And acclimating yourself, physically and mentally, to this little town. Right now, there's nothing for you to worry about. It's all under control."

He reached out and lightly patted my shoulder, like encouraging an adorable dog.

Like the dawn arriving and sunshine streaming through the window, I repeated to myself. A nice turn of phrase, that.

One of the first tasks I set myself to as the newly appointed head librarian was getting a handle on what kind of books the library patrons read and checked out. By doing that I could see what kind of books the library should purchase, and grasp a kind of guideline for operating the library. Doing that, however, meant going through, by hand, all the visitor logs and all the lending cards. Requesting books to read in the library and checking them out was all analog, without the aid of computers.

"In this library we keep all those records without using any computers," Mrs. Soeda explained to me. "It's all done by hand."

"No computers at all are used here?"

"Correct, none at all," she replied, as if nothing could be more natural.

"But doing it all by hand takes time, and isn't it a lot of trouble to manage all that? If you use barcodes it can all be finished in an instant, you won't need a place to store the documents, and it'll be easy to organize information."

Mrs. Soeda adjusted her glasses with the fingers of her right hand, and then said this: "This is a small library, and not all that many books are read or checked out. We can manage very well using old-fashioned methods. None of it takes all that much time."

"So you're fine continuing this way?"

"I am," Mrs. Soeda said. "This was already decided and that's how we've always done it. Isn't that a more human approach? And the library patrons have never complained. If you don't use machines, you have fewer technical glitches, and your expenses are less, too."

The library didn't have wi-fi so I was only able to access my computer at home. Even so, there wasn't anyone I regularly corresponded with by email, and I wasn't into social networking, so I never felt this setup was inconvenient. And I could read a number of newspapers at the library so there was no need to check information online.

All of which is to say that I grasped the gist of the library's activities by going through, one by one, the pile of handwritten lists of books read and cards for books checked out. Not that this time-consuming process led to any startling, useful information. The books people read and checked out were for the most part bestsellers at the time, most of these being practical guidebooks or light entertainment. Though occasionally people would check out more weighty works—novels by Dostoyevsky, Thomas Pynchon, Thomas Mann, or Ango Sakaguchi, Ogai Mori, Junichiro Tanizaki, or Kenzaburo Oe.

Most people in the town weren't what you'd call devoted readers, yet among them (a minority, I would think) there were some who'd regularly come to the library, had a healthy intellectual curiosity, and were quite serious readers—this was the conclusion I reached after going through all those cards by hand. I had no idea whether the proportion of such devoted readers there was, compared to the national average, something to be celebrated or lamented. I could only accept it as the present reality. Since this town existed, and functioned, as a reality that (at least for now) operated apart from any of my hopes or intentions.

When I had free time, I'd wander around the stacks and peruse the books. I pulled damaged books to be repaired. I got rid of those that had outdated information and the ones I figured nobody would be interested in, or I stored them in the warehouse in back and replaced them with others. I checked lists of newly published books and purchased titles I thought would appeal to our patrons. The budget I was given for monthly purchases of new books was more generous than I'd imagined (even though still not enough), which surprised me a bit.

I'd spent every day of my life up to now dealing with books, and this new routine gave me a new kind of happiness. I had no boss here, no need to wear a tie. No annoying meetings, and no entertaining of business clients.

I met with Mrs. Soeda and the part-time staff to discuss how the library should be run. I made a few modest proposals, but the women didn't seem too keen on new policies or regulation. We should continue as we've been doing, they said, since there haven't been any complaints from the patrons. So why change anything? They all were dead set against introducing the internet to the library. In short, they wanted to keep things just as Mr. Koyasu had had them.

But about my proactive reorganizing of the stacks, and of the library's inventory—modernizing things, in other words—they had no comments or complaints. They left that up to me. They weren't all that interested in those kinds of matters—maybe that's all it was. I got the impression that they didn't care one way or the other about what happened to books on the shelves, or what sorts of books the patrons read. Though they did all work hard and seemed to enjoy working in the library.

I had little opportunity to come in contact with the library patrons directly, and we never spoke. Were the people who frequented this library even aware there was a new head librarian? Who knows. After I was appointed to the post I wasn't introduced to anyone, and no one spoke to me. Other than the handful of women who worked in the library, a newcomer like me seemed of no interest to anyone in town. No one seemed to notice, or care.

This was a small town and everyone should have heard about me taking over from Mr. Koyasu as head librarian. The news had to have made the rounds. A newcomer from the city coming here, in this town where few ever came and went, had to arouse the curiosity of the residents.

But not a single person showed, by their expression, any of this. They came to the library as if nothing had changed, did things there as always, and even if I peeked into the reading room, no one even glanced in my direction. They'd sit in the lounge's chairs, reading newspapers and magazines, or in the reading room turning the pages of books they'd borrowed, and I could walk right past them without anyone showing a flicker of interest. It was as if they'd all agreed not to notice me.

I was truly puzzled. Were people *really* not aware I'd taken over as Mr. Koyasu's successor? Or for some reason—what reason I couldn't imagine—had they all agreed to ignore me, and treat me like someone who didn't even exist?

I couldn't figure it out. It was baffling, though it didn't cause immediate, practical problems for me. With Mr. Koyasu and Mrs. Soeda's help, I steadily mastered the essentials of the job. So I didn't let it bother me, figuring things would eventually settle down. Like Mr. Koyasu had said, things would become clear over time. *Like the dawn arriving and sunshine streaming through the window.*

The library opened at nine a.m. and closed at six p.m. I arrived every day for work at eight thirty and left the library at six thirty. It was Mrs. Soeda's job to unlock the door in the morning and lock it again in the evening. I had a set of keys, too, but hardly any chance to use them. I left that to her, as they'd been doing. When I arrived at work in the morning the library was already open, with Mrs. Soeda at her desk, and when I left in the evening, she was still there.

"Please don't worry about it. It's my job," she explained when I looked apologetic for leaving before she left.

Seeing Mrs. Soeda there inevitably reminded me of the library in the town surrounded by a wall. There, too, it was *her* job to unlock and lock up the door. The girl always carried around a large bunch of keys. The only difference was that there, after the entrance to the library was shut, I walked her back to her house. We'd walk together, silently, along the river at night, heading toward the Workers' District.

But when the library closed for the day in this little town in the mountains, I walked home alone down the path along the river. Alone, lost in random thoughts, there was a similar murmur of flowing water, but no rustling willow leaves, no calls of night birds. "In the fall you can hear the cries of deer," Mr. Koyasu had told me, but I couldn't hear those either. Maybe it had to be deeper into fall. But then again, what kind of calls did deer make, anyway? I had no idea.

Not too long after I started my job as the head librarian, Mrs. Soeda led me in a tour of the whole library. They used to brew sake in this high-ceilinged building. The sake manufacturer moved to a different facility, and for a long time this old building was vacant, but it was valuable as a historic structure and it would have been a waste to tear it down, so a foundation was set up and the old brewery was reborn as a library.

"That must have cost a lot," I remarked.

"It must have," Mrs. Soeda said, tilting her head slightly. "But the land and the building were owned by Mr. Koyasu, and since he donated it all to the foundation it didn't cost anything."

"I see," I said. That explained a lot. Mr. Koyasu personally owned and operated the library.

The part of the building in back, the area not used as a library, had a complicated layout of rooms, so much so that it took multiple trips to grasp the whole structure. There were dark, winding hallways, slightly raised areas, a minuscule inner garden, and small, mysterious rooms. There was a storage room, too, filled with old, oddly shaped tools the purpose of which I couldn't figure out.

Behind the building was a large old well. It was covered with a thick lid with a heavy stone on top to weigh it down. "So no child will open the cover and fall inside," Mrs. Soeda explained. "It's terribly deep." And in a corner of the rear garden stood a small stone *jizo* statue with a gentle face.

"The building was renovated to make it into a library, but the budget only allowed for partial renovation," Mrs. Soeda explained. "So this unused part of the building, the part we can't use, has been left as is. Right now we only use about half of the whole building as the library. Though of course we're thankful to be able to use half."

Her voice was utterly devoid of emotion. Rather than sounding neutral, however, I detected some tension, as if she were afraid of someone overhearing. (I couldn't help glancing around me.) So I couldn't decide if her feelings were negative or positive toward the building.

The part of the two-story building below the stairs consisted of the magazine lounge, the reading room, the stacks, storage rooms, and a workroom. In the workroom, staff created cards for books and repaired damaged books. In the middle of the workroom was a huge worktable carved from a thick slab of wood (probably used for something special back when the place was a sake brewery), the top of which was a jumble of all sorts of tools used to repair books, as well as office supplies.

The reading room for patrons had vaulted ceilings and several skylights, but most of the rest of the rooms were windowless, the air a bit chilly and dampish. Those rooms must have been used to store all kinds of ingredients used for brewing.

The second floor, which non-staff didn't use, consisted of the cozy head librarian's office (where I spent most of my time), a sort of dimly lit drawing room for guests with heavy drapes, and a breakroom for staff. There was a thickly upholstered sofa and easy chair set in the drawing room, but the room was hardly ever used. "If you'd like," Mrs. Soeda said, "you can use the sofa to take a nap." But the room was musty with a smell from a forgotten age. And the color of the curtains and fabric of the sofa set felt sort of ominous, as if they had absorbed the unhappy secret of something that had taken place here in the past. Even if I was dying to fall asleep, it would be the last place where I'd ever want to take a nap.

The staff breakroom was farthest back on the second floor and was known by all as the rest area. It contained lockers, a small kitchen, and a table for simple meals. It wasn't exactly off-limits to men, but in reality, only women used the room. They changed their clothes behind a partition in back, exchanged whispered gossip, ate sweets they'd brought with them, and drank tea or coffee. Occasionally their happy voices would filter down to my room.

This rest area was a kind of sanctuary. Unless it was some pressing matter, I hardly ever stopped by this room at the end of the hall. I had no way of knowing what sort of conversations they had there, of course. I would guess, though, that gossip about me (hopefully nothing too bad) was a small part of it.

So my days at the library passed by uneventfully. Actual day-to-day practical tasks were taken care of by Mrs. Soeda and the team of women she led. The work I had to do as head librarian was nothing too laborious. Handling the purchase and disposal of books, checking the day-to-day income and expenses, and a few simple authorizations. As Mr. Koyasu had told me early on, even though the library was, officially, the Z** Town Library, the town had nothing to do with its operation whatsoever. So it was only rarely that I needed to contact the town hall. And even then, when I phoned the town Education Section to ask a question, the response was, if not cold, quite half-hearted. Whatever I asked, the reply was always along the lines of *Whatever it is, just do what you like.* I got the impression that the town hall wanted to have as little to do with the library as possible. Not that they were antagonistic, but they clearly weren't trying to create a friendly relationship. Why, though, I had no clue.

The upshot for me, however, was that this situation was to my advantage. Even in the tiniest rural town you can't avoid all kinds of bureaucratic complications. Actually, the smaller the local government, the fiercer the territorial skirmishes. So avoiding those conflicts was a welcome change.

As Mr. Koyasu had stated, he visited the head librarian's office every few days. The time he appeared depended on the day. Sometimes he'd come early in the morning, and sometimes toward the evening. We had friendly chats, but as before, he hardly ever spoke about himself. I knew nothing about where he lived, about his everyday life. I figured he didn't like to discuss personal things, so I refrained from asking. What he spoke about in that calm (and unique) tone of voice was confined to business matters related to the library's operation.

The first thing he did when he came into my office was remove his beret, adjust its shape carefully, and then place it on top of the desk, in one corner, always in the exact same spot, facing the same way. As if doing otherwise would lead to dire consequences. He was completely silent as he went about this meticulous process. His lips were tight, the ceremony was performed solemnly, in utter quiet. Once this was accomplished, his face broke out in a smile, and he said hello to me.

While he always had on a skirt, from the waist up he wore what could be called conservative men's wear. A white shirt, buttoned to the neck, a good old-fashioned tweed jacket, and a plain, dark green vest. He didn't wear a tie, but his somewhat old-fashioned outfit was always neat and clean. This combination of garments took some getting used to, but Mr. Koyasu himself seemed not to care one bit.

In this way my days in Z** passed uneventfully. I gradually acclimated, mentally and physically, to this new life. The late-summer heat ended, fall came on, and the autumn leaves in the mountains surrounding the town turned a variety of beautiful colors. On days off I liked to tramp down mountain paths, taking in the brilliant art that nature had etched into the hills. And as I did, signs of winter began to take shape around me. Fall was short-lived here in the mountains.

"It'll begin snowing before long," Mr. Koyasu said one day as he was leaving. He was standing by the window, studying the movements of the clouds. His smallish hands were clasped tightly behind his back.

"You can smell it in the air. Winter comes early around here. It'd be best to buy yourself some snow boots."

AFTER WORK THE EVENING of the first snowfall (near the end of November), I went into town to do just that. The snow was just a light sprinkling, but once it became heavier, the flimsy shoes I'd brought from Tokyo would have me slipping and sliding all over the place.

Whether I wished it or not, the first snowfall brought to mind that town surrounded by a wall. It snowed a lot there in the winter. And many unicorns died in the snow.

Okay, but what kind of shoes had I worn in that town?

The town had provided me with shoes (and all my clothes and everything else), and I'd worn those as I walked every day down the snowy roads. The snow didn't accumulate much, but the road surface did freeze over and become slippery. But I never had a problem walking on it. I must have been given shoes that were made for walking on snowy roads, but I couldn't recall anything about their shape and color. I wore them every day, so why was it that I couldn't remember them?

There were lots of things about the town where my memory was fuzzy. Several things I could vividly remember, too vividly, yet as hard as I tried, some things had faded. And my snow boots were one of those. This spotty memory had me flustered and confused. Did I lose the memories over time, or did they not exist from the first? How much of what I remembered was the truth, and how much was fiction? How much had really happened, and how much was made up?

Not long after this, Mr. Koyasu showed up one day at the library. It was a little after eleven a.m. That day was gray and cloudy, and a light snow was falling. There was a gas stove in the head librarian's office, but it wasn't enough to heat up the whole room, so I had on a wool jacket and a scarf as I checked the account book. The slight chill in the room, though, didn't bother me much. Downstairs the reading room was comfortably heated, and if it wasn't crowded (it usually wasn't) I could warm myself there for a short time.

And if pressed, maybe I like a touch of cold—where you can still stand it. Since that's something I experienced all the time in that town behind a wall. The cold air surrounding me brought back the feelings I had living in that town.

On this day, Mr. Koyasu knocked at the door and came in. The first thing he did, as always, was remove his beret, adjust its shape, then place it on the fixed spot on a corner of the desk. He then smiled broadly at me and said hello. But he didn't remove his scarf and gloves. Just his beret.

"This room's always a bit chilly," he said. "This little stove's not enough to warm it up. You need to put in a bigger one."

"Perhaps I find a little cold bracing, physically and mentally," I said.

"When the full-blown winter starts, it'll get even colder. I doubt you'll be able to say you like a *little cold* then. I don't think a city person like you can imagine how freezing cold it really gets around here."

Mr. Koyasu removed his gloves, folded them, and put them in his jacket pocket, then rubbed his hands together in front of the stove to warm them up. Then he said, "When I was the head librarian, how do you think I got through the winter cold?"

"How did you?" I had no idea.

"This office was a bit too chilly for me," Mr. Koyasu said. "I was born and raised here, but, how shall I put it? The cold does get to me. So, ah, during the winter I retreated to another room. I worked out of there."

"Another room?"

"Yes. Another room that's considerably warmer than here."

"Is it in this library?"

"It is. It's in this library."

Mr. Koyasu removed the well-used checked scarf, meticulously folded it, and placed it beside the beret.

"It was, in a way, my little winter refuge. Would you care to see it?"

"Is that *refuge* warmer than here?"

Mr. Koyasu nodded several times. "Indeed, indeed. Consider-ably warmer than here, and quite comfortable. Ah, do you have a set of keys for the library?"

"I do." I took the key ring with the set of keys from my desk drawer and showed it to him. Mrs. Soeda had given it to me the first day of work.

"Ah, splendid. Bring that and follow me, if you would."

Mr. Koyasu briskly walked downstairs. I hurried to keep up. We walked through the sparsely populated reading room, passed in front of the main counter where Mrs. Soeda was seated, walked through the workroom (where a staff member was pasting regis-tration labels on new books, with a look of utter concentration on her face), and continued down the corridor in back. No one looked up when we passed by. As if they didn't even see us. It felt pretty strange. Like I'd become invisible.

Past the workroom was an area not used by the library, which Mrs. Soeda had shown me on our little tour. The hallway made a series of complex turns until we emerged in a dimly lit spot that I could hardly recall seeing before. Mr. Koyasu, however, knew where he was going and quickly walked down the hallway and stood before a small door.

"This is it," he said. "The keys, please."

I took out the hefty ring of keys. There were twelve keys, in dif-ferent shapes, and other than a few main ones, I had no idea which doors they opened. Mr. Koyasu took the key ring, immediately chose one of the keys, stuck it in the door's lock, and turned it. With an unexpectedly loud click the door unlocked.

"The room's half underground. It's a little dark, so please watch your step."

Inside it was, indeed, dark. The stairs were wooden, and each step produced an unsettling creak. Mr. Koyasu went ahead and took each step cautiously. He walked down six steps, then reached up and, with a practiced hand, turned what seemed to be a knob there. With a snap, yellowish light appeared from a bulb hanging down from the ceiling.

The room was square, about thirteen feet per side. Wood floor, no carpeting. Across from the door, up on the wall, was a horizontal skylight window. That window must have been just above ground level. It hadn't been cleaned for some time, apparently, as the glass was cloudy and grayish, and you could hardly see outside. Light shone in only faintly. There was a metal security grill on the outside, but it didn't look very sturdy.

Inside the room was a single old wooden desk and two mismatched chairs, all of which looked like discards collected from here and there. That was the extent of the furniture in the room. Not a single decoration, the walls a light yellowed stucco, a single light fixture hanging from the ceiling. There was a small milk-colored shade covering the bulb, which was the sole source of illumination in the room.

What this room had been used for, I had no idea. Yet I felt a sort of enigmatic, suggestive feeling in the air. As if, long ago, a person had whispered some vital secret here to someone . . .

And then I spotted it. An old-fashioned black woodstove in a corner of the room.

I gasped. Reflexively I shut my eyes, took a deep breath, and then opened them again, and checked to make sure it really did exist. No mistake. This was no illusion. The stove was exactly the one—or maybe only looked like it—in the library in that town surrounded by a wall. A black cylindrical chimney ran from the stove into the wall. I stood there for a long time, rooted to the spot, speechless, staring at the stove.

"Is something the matter?" Mr. Koyasu asked me, his voice doubtful.

I took another deep breath. And then said, "Is this a woodstove?"

"Yes, as you can see. Your classic wood-burning stove. It's been here forever. But it's surprisingly useful."

I stood there still, eyes riveted on the stove.

"You can actually use it?"

"Of course. Of course, it's available to use," Mr. Koyasu declared, his eyes sparkling. "Actually, I kept it roaring away every winter. There's plenty of firewood stored in a different site on the grounds. So there's no need to worry about that. An apple farmer nearby closed his business and was good enough to provide the wood from the old trees he'd cut down. A lumber dealer kindly sawed these into logs for firewood. When you burn them, it has a very pleasant apple tree fragrance. Ah, truly a wonderful fragrance. What do you say—shall we bring some firewood over and light it up?"

I gave it some thought and then shook my head. "No, it's not worth it. It's not that cold right now."

"I see. But when you do need it, ah, you can use it right away, whenever you like. You can move out of that chilly office on the second floor and move in here. You'll be able to work better here, too. Mrs. Soeda is well aware of all this."

"What was this room originally used for?"

Mr. Koyasu tilted his head slightly and scratched his earlobe. "Well, I'm afraid I don't know the answer. As you're aware, this building used to be a sake brewery. Over half of it was renovated to use as a library, but the remainder, this section, was left as is. It was so long ago, so I'm sorry to say I don't have any information on what this room was used for."

I scanned the little room once more.

"But it's okay for me to use both the room and the stove?"

Mr. Koyasu nodded emphatically.

"Of course you can. This is a part of our library, and you can use it however you wish. Ah, I'm sure you'll like this woodstove. It's quiet and very warm, and I can tell you that the sight of its red flames will warm you to the core."

Mr. Koyasu and I left the square room, returned to the dimly lit corridor, passed by the counter where Mrs. Soeda sat, cut through the mostly deserted reading room, and arrived back at my second-floor office. And just as before, no one looked up as we passed by.

That afternoon my mind was filled with thoughts of that squarish room and the black, old-fashioned woodstove. And all the next day as well.

THE FIRST REAL COLD FRONT hit town at the beginning of December, with snow fluttering down. I decided to move the head librarian's office to that square subterranean room. When I told Mrs. Soeda, she remained silent for a moment. A short, yet strangely weighty silence, like a small iron weight sunk at the bottom of a lake. Then, as if reconsidering, she merely said, "Alright. I understand." She had no opinions or questions.

So I asked, "Will my changing rooms cause any problems?"

She quickly shook her head. "No, there won't be any problems."

"And I can use the woodstove, I assume?"

"It's fine for you to use it," she replied, her tone oddly flat, expressionless. "But let me get the chimney cleaned out first. Please wait two days before lighting a fire there. Birds build nests inside sometimes, and if you lit it, it could cause problems."

"Of course," I said. "The chimney runs up aboveground?"

"Yes, to the roof. So we need to have a contractor look at it, one who specializes in that sort of thing."

"Are there other rooms in this building that use a woodstove?"

Mrs. Soeda shook her head. "No, it's the only one. There were other woodstoves, but when the place was renovated, they took them all out and got rid of them. That stove alone was left, per Mr. Koyasu's request."

I thought it odd. When Mrs. Soeda had given me the tour of the building, I don't recall her showing me that room. If I had seen it, I would have remembered. I wouldn't have missed the woodstove.

So why hadn't she shown it to me? Did she think there was no need? Or had she simply overlooked it? Perhaps it was too much trouble to search through the keys to unlock it so she had deliberately omitted it. It was hard to believe, though. She was very methodical. No matter how much trouble it took, once a routine was set, she followed it to the letter.

Another thing—why was that room locked, anyway? From the

sound when Mr. Koyasu unlocked it, it had to have been a pretty substantial lock. Yet there wasn't a thing in there worth stealing. So why the hefty lock?

But I put aside these doubts and didn't mention them to Mrs. Soeda. I figured that at this point it was better not to.

I waited two days, until the chimney had been properly cleaned, and then began using that subterranean room as my own. Mrs. Soeda notified the staff, and no one questioned it, since up till now Mr. Koyasu had made the same move every year.

It was easy to move my things—just a file cabinet and a standing lamp. There was no phone jack in the room, so I didn't take a phone. Not having one there wouldn't affect anything, I decided.

My first order of business after I established this as my office (I suppose you could call it that) was to bring over some firewood. The firewood was stacked up in a shed in the garden. I stacked some logs in a bamboo basket I found there and lugged it back to the room. Then I placed a couple of logs in the stove, balled up some newspaper, and lit a match. I twisted the knob on the air intake, adjusting the airflow. The firewood was nicely dried out, and I soon had myself a cozy little fire crackling away.

The stove hadn't been used for a long time, so it took a while for it to heat up. I camped out in front of it, entranced as I watched the orange flames leaping quietly and the firewood gradually changing shape. The square subterranean room was utterly silent, not a sound to be heard. Occasionally something would pop in the stove, but other than that, complete silence. The four, speechless bare walls surrounded me.

Eventually the whole stove warmed up, and I put the filled kettle on top. It was soon chuckling away, exhaling white steam, and I set to making tea. You could use the same tea leaves, but to me, tea made with boiling water from a kettle on a stove was always more fragrant.

As I sipped my tea, I closed my eyes and pictured that walled-in town. In the evening when I went to work, the stove was always roaring, the large black kettle on top puffing out steam. And the girl, dressed in simple, sometimes faded and frayed clothes, was preparing herbal tea for me. The herbal tea she brewed was certainly bitter but distinct from what we (in this world over here) would normally label as bitter. A uniquely bitter taste I can't describe. A bitterness, I imagine, only to be tasted—or known—behind those walls. I fondly recalled that indescribable flavor, and longed to taste it again, if only once.

Here, the silently burning stove, the darkish, twilight-like room, and the occasional rattling of the old kettle brought that town closer to me than ever before. Eyes still shut, I immersed myself in the illusion of that lost town.

But I couldn't sit there, steeped in that illusion, idly spending the whole day in front of the burning stove.

I finished my tea, took a deep breath, pulled myself together, and set about the day's work. I needed to choose the new books the library would purchase that month, within our allocated budget. I was the only one who could choose, but I couldn't just buy books that appealed to me personally. I needed to choose some popular bestsellers, books that people were talking about, titles that patrons had requested we acquire and that would increase interest in this region, books that a public library should have in their collection, and on top of that books I hoped that people in this town would read . . . so I made my selections carefully with those categories in mind and developed a list. Then I'd show it to Mrs. Soeda and take her suggestions under advisement (her opinions were always valuable) and finalize the list. It was then up to her to make the actual orders.

That was my main job that day. With my pencil in hand in that square subterranean room, glancing at the fire in the stove from time to time, I created the purchase list. The room had warmed up enough, and I removed my jacket and rolled up my sleeves to my elbows as I worked.

No one stopped by my room. This was my world alone. I'd get up sometimes to toss another log on the fire, adjust the air intake so the fire wouldn't flame up too much, and go to the sink to add water to the kettle. And I tried my best not to think about *that town*, and *that library*. It was dangerous to think about them. When I did, I was quickly pulled deep into an illusion and when I came to was resting my chin in my hands, eyes closed (the pencil I'd been holding disappearing in the meantime), wandering aimlessly down a labyrinth of thoughts. Wondering why I was here, why I wasn't over *there* . . .

This is my workplace, I told myself. Here I have a responsible position as head librarian. I couldn't throw over that responsibility to immerse myself in a one-man illusory world. Yet despite my efforts I found myself, before I realized it, back in that walled-in town. A world where unicorns roamed down the street, their hooves clicking on the stone pavement; where old, dust-covered dreams were lined up on the shelves; where the thin branches of the river willows swayed in the wind and a clock tower without hands overlooked a plaza. Of course, it was my heart only that had transitioned there. Or my consciousness. My actual physical body always remained in this world—probably.

Just before noon I left that warm room, went to Mrs. Soeda's counter, and discussed with her a couple of administrative issues.

She never asked a thing about the new office—whether I found it comfortable, whether the stove was warm enough. She remained, as always, expressionless, briskly exchanging work-related information, making decisions on a few matters that needed tending to. The library was a quiet zone, so as a rule we never chatted about non-work-related matters. Yet that day I got the sense that Mrs. Soeda was deliberately avoiding the topic. I caught a hint of an unusual tension in her voice. But I had no clue why, or what it might portend.

Mr. Koyasu made his first visit to my new office at two in the afternoon three days after I'd moved in.

As always, he had on a skirt. A long, wine-red wool wraparound skirt that came down below his knees. Below that he wore black tights, and he had on a light gray scarf. And of course his navy-blue beret. His jacket was a thick tweed, and he seemed quite at home in this outfit. He didn't wear a coat. He must have hung it up at the entrance.

He had his usual broad smile, and after saying hello made a beeline to the stove, and without taking off the beret, warmed his hands there for a while. Like this was the most important ceremony there was. Finally, he turned to face me.

"Well then," he said. "How are you finding the room?"

"It's quite warm, quiet, and peaceful."

He nodded several times, as if saying *I knew you would*.

"A stove's fire is such a wonderful thing," he said. "Truly it warms you, body and soul, to the core."

"Yes, definitely. My body and soul do feel warm," I said.

"The smell of the applewood is also quite pleasant. It's—how would you put it—*aromatic*."

I agreed with him. When you lit the wood, a faint fragrance of apples would fill the room. But along with the pleasant smell, there was an element of danger. Because that fragrance, before I knew it, seemed to draw me deeper into a dream world. There was a sense of being pulled into a world without a framework.

There was an apple grove outside the wall of that town. The Gatekeeper would pick apples and give them to the townspeople, since no one besides him was permitted to venture outside the wall. And the girl in the library used the apples to make a sweet dish for me. I could still taste it. The right amount of sweetness, crisply sour, the wholesomeness of it slowly flowing through me.

Mr. Koyasu said, "I tried different types of firewood, but wood from old apple trees is the best. It lights well, and the smoke is quite fragrant. I'd say we're lucky to get this much of it."

"You're right," I agreed.

After he'd warmed himself in front of the stove, Mr. Koyasu came in front of my desk and sat down in a chair. His feet hardly made a sound as he walked. I noticed he had on white tennis shoes. Deep winter was on the horizon, yet here he was still wearing thin-soled tennis shoes, an odd choice. Most people had already changed to their lined, thick winter shoes. I knew that it was pointless, though, to try to apply the normal rules of society to anything Mr. Koyasu did.

We began to talk about the library. His explanations regarding library operations were always clear, concrete, and on point. He might be an old man with some offbeat tendencies, yet when it came to the work of the library, he was invariably sensible and practical. When the conversation turned to pragmatic issues, even the look in his eyes changed. Deep down there was a twinkling, as if a pair of jewels had been buried within. His deep affection for the library was more than evident.

He removed his jacket and hung it on the back of the chair, unwound his scarf, took off his beret, and, as always, carefully laid it down on the desktop (a different desk from before). And like a cat relaxing, he plunked his hands down on top of the desk. Being here, just the two of us, in this little square subterranean room, felt entirely natural.

But at a certain point I suddenly noticed something that took me aback. The wristwatch he had on had no hands.

At first I doubted my eyes. Maybe the light was momentarily playing tricks, hiding the hands for a second. But it wasn't. I casually rubbed my eyes and took another look. And sure enough— the antique wristwatch he wore on his left wrist, the kind you had to wind by hand, I imagined, had no hands on its face. I couldn't see any hands at all—not the short one that showed the hour, the long one indicating the minute, or the thin one showing the seconds. Nothing. Just a dial with numbers around it.

I was dying to ask him about it. *Why doesn't your watch have any hands on it?* If I did, he might readily explain the reason or circumstances. Perhaps I should have asked, but something told me it was better not to. I changed the topic and cast a few furtive glances at his left wrist.

Just to be sure, I glanced at my own wristwatch too, worried that maybe something had happened to time in general. But the dial on my own watch on my left wrist had all the usual hands, the hands indicating that it was 2:36 and 45 seconds in the afternoon. That changed to 46 seconds, then 47. So time still existed in this world, and without a doubt marched on. In a clocklike manner, at least.

It's the same as *that clock tower*, I thought. The same as the clock tower in that walled-in town, in the riverside plaza. *There is a dial, but no hands.*

I had a sense of a *twist* warping, ever so slightly, space and time. The feeling of two things mixing together, as if part of a boundary had collapsed, become vague, with something else mixed in, here and there, with reality. Was this confusion internal, produced by something inside me? Or had Mr. Koyasu's presence played a part? I couldn't tell. I did my best to calm myself, to not let my confusion show on my face, but it wasn't easy. I couldn't think of what I should say, and our conversation petered out.

From the other side of the desk Mr. Koyasu studied me, his face not showing any particular expression. Like a white sheet in a notebook with nothing written on it. Both of us remained silent for a time.

Suddenly, though, it seemed like Mr. Koyasu had noticed something. Or had remembered something. His eyes brightened, his bushy eyebrows fluttering once. And his mouth opened a fraction. As if rehearsing what he was going to say, his small lips formed a few soundless words. A faint but certain desire to say something. He was trying to tell me something—something that had to be important. And I sat on the other side of the desk, awaiting those words.

But right then some firewood in the stove crumbled with a loud clatter, and as if in response the black kettle on top let out a burst of steam. Mr. Koyasu instinctively turned toward the sound (with an uncharacteristic swiftness), checked out the flames with a sharp look, making sure nothing was wrong, then turned his gaze back to me.

But the words he had been about to speak—what they were I didn't know—were lost. His eyes revived their softer gleam. He had nothing he needed to say. As if the red flames burning away in the stove had destroyed the words that should have been there.

After a while Mr. Koyasu slowly rose from his seat. He took

a deep breath, rested his hands on his hips, and stretched, as if loosening his stiff joints one by one. He picked up the navy-blue beret from the desktop, carefully adjusted it, and put it on. And wrapped the scarf around his neck.

"I really must be going," he said, as if to himself. "I can't hang around here forever and interrupt you. The stove feels so cozy I overstayed my welcome. I must be careful of that."

"Don't worry, please stay as long as you'd like. There's so much more you can teach me."

But Mr. Koyasu smiled and, without a word, shook his head. He silently walked up the stairs, bowed, and disappeared.

This old man, always decked out in a skirt, wearing a wristwatch without hands—what did this enigmatic person signify? I wondered. It felt like there was a kind of message involved. A message meant for me . . . But as I pondered all this I grew terribly drowsy, and fell asleep seated in the chair. The hard little chair wasn't suited for napping, but I went ahead and slept anyway. A short yet deep sleep, of such intensity there was no room for even fragments of dreams to intrude. In my sleep I heard the kettle exhale steam again. Or maybe only thought I did.

A while later I left the room, went to the reading room, and spoke to Mrs. Soeda behind the counter. Has Mr. Koyasu already gone home? I asked.

"Mr. Koyasu?" she said, frowning slightly.

"I was talking with him downstairs until about thirty minutes ago. He came just before two."

"Hm, I didn't see him," she replied, her tone oddly lackluster. She picked up a ballpoint pen and went back to the task she'd been working on. Strange, I thought. Mrs. Soeda hardly ever left her post behind the counter and was so observant she wouldn't miss anyone passing by. That's who she was.

Her curtness made it abundantly clear the topic was over. At least it felt that way to me. So our conversation about Mr. Koyasu ended right there. I went back to my perfectly square subterranean office and, feeling vaguely disconcerted, went back to work in front of the stove.

So what was it Mr. Koyasu was about to tell me? And why did that log, as if anticipating that moment, choose that instant to split apart? Like it was deliberately trying to interrupt and warn the speaker. I ran through all kinds of scenarios in my mind, but every thought and inference I came up with ran smack into a thick wall, blocking the way forward.

WINTER DEEPENED day by day. As the end of the year approached, Mr. Koyasu's prediction came true, with ever more frequent snow in this little mountain town. Thick snow-filled clouds blew in on a north wind, one after another. Sometimes quickly, sometimes so slowly that their movement was imperceptible.

In the morning the ground was covered with needle ice, which made a pleasant crunch under my new snow boots. The sound was like when you stepped on a piece of candy that had fallen on the floor. Wanting to hear that sound, I sauntered along the river early in the mornings. My breath was a hard white lump in the air (so hard it looked like you could write on it), the clear morning air forming countless transparent needles that pierced the skin.

Such bone-chilling cold was both a new experience for me and a pleasant stimulus. It was a fresh sensation, as if I'd set foot in a world that originated elsewhere. My life had changed location, though it was too soon to tell in what direction these changed surroundings would lead me.

Along the river just after dawn a pure field of snow spread out before me, untrampled by anyone's footprints. The amount of snowfall wasn't all that much yet, but even so the broad, verdant branches of the evergreen trees admirably held up the new snow that had fallen at night. An occasional blast of wind came down from the mountains among the trees beyond the river, producing a sharp, painful sound that presaged the coming of an even more severe season. This manifestation of nature filled my heart with a frustrating sense of nostalgia and a touch of sadness.

Most of the snow that fell was hard and dry. If you caught the flakes in your palm they would hold their shape for a long time. It was as if, as they passed over high mountains on their journey down from the north, the moisture had been stolen from all the snow clouds. The falling snow was hard and dry and lay on the ground for a long while without melting. It reminded me of white powder sprinkled over a Christmas cake. (When was the last time I'd eaten a Christmas cake? I wondered.)

A thick coat and warm underwear, a wool hat and cashmere scarf and thick gloves became necessities. But once I got to the library that old-fashioned woodstove awaited me. It took a while for the room to warm up, but once the fire was blazing away it felt nice and warm. As it gradually warmed up, I'd take off one layer of clothing and then another. First my gloves, then off came my scarf, and then my coat, and lastly I'd be left wearing a thin sweater. Sometimes, by afternoon, I'd be in shirtsleeves.

In that town surrounded by a wall, the girl always lit the stove before I showed up. In the evening when I opened the door to the library the room was already nicely warm. On top of the stove a welcoming column of steam rose from the large kettle. But here no one took care of that. It was up to me. The subterranean room in the back of the library was, in the early morning, frigid.

I crouched in front of the stove, lit a match, lit balled-up newspapers, and with that some thin firewood, and then on to thicker pieces, gradually getting the fire going. Sometimes it didn't go well, and I had to start over. It was a solemn operation, like some kind of ceremony. Something people had, from ancient times, continued to perform (though of course there were no matches or newspapers back in the past).

Once the fire was roaring nicely, while I waited for the stove itself to warm up, I placed a black kettle filled with water on top. When the water had boiled, I brewed tea in the ceramic tea set Mr. Koyasu had given me. Then, seated at my desk, I savored the hot tea and let my thoughts wander to the walled-in town, and the girl in the library. I couldn't help it. In this way a half hour on winter mornings passed with me lost in thought, my mind shifting back and forth between two worlds.

But then I'd pull myself together, take a few deep breaths, and—like latching a hook through a loop—secure my consciousness to the world on this side. And begin the work I needed to do in this library. No more reading of old dreams for me. The tasks I needed to perform here were more prosaic, more clerical. Reading over documents and paperwork, filling out forms, carefully reviewing daily income and expenditures, and creating a list of tasks that needed to be done to keep the library going.

All the while the stove continued to burn away, the sweet aroma of old applewood filling the small room.

The phone call from Mr. Koyasu came at home after ten p.m. Since I had arrived in the town my phone had never rung this late, and it was quite rare for Mr. Koyasu to call me. (I can't recall exactly, but that time might have been the first.)

I was in my reading armchair (the one Mr. Koyasu had procured for me from somewhere), and, in the light from the standing floor lamp, was reading Flaubert's *Sentimental Education*. The old print was tiring out my eyes and I was starting to think of going to bed—the same ritual as always.

"Hello," Mr. Koyasu said. "Koyasu here. I'm sorry to call so late. Did I wake you?"

"I'm still up," I said. Though I was about to go to bed.

"I realize this is selfish of me, but would you consider coming to the library now?"

"Right now?" I asked, checking the alarm clock next to my bed. The hands showed ten minutes past ten. I remembered Mr. Koyasu's wristwatch without hands. Did he know what time it was?

"I understand how late it is. It's past ten p.m.," Mr. Koyasu said, as if reading my mind. "But it's something kind of important."

"And it's not something you can discuss over the phone?"

"Yes, that's right. It's not simple enough to discuss over the phone. You can't count on a phone."

"Alright," I said. I scanned the clock by my bed once again, just to make sure. The second hand indeed marked the passing time. In the deep silence I could detect the faint click of each passing second.

"Yes," I said, "I can get to the library. But where are you now, Mr. Koyasu?"

"I'm waiting in the subterranean room. The stove is already plenty warm. I'd like to wait here until you come, if that would be alright?"

"That would be fine. I'll meet you there. But I'll have to change my clothes, and it might take me thirty minutes or so."

"Not a problem. I don't mind waiting. I have plenty of time, and I'm used to staying up late. I won't get sleepy. No need to rush. I'll just take it easy here until you arrive."

I hung up, puzzled. How could Mr. Koyasu have gotten into the library? Did he have his own key to the front door? He'd retired as head librarian and had been very hands-on when it came to library operations, so maybe it wasn't so odd that he still had keys.

I pictured him alone, in the room deep in the bowels of the darkened library, in front of the stove, waiting for me to arrive. A weird scene, you would think, but to me it didn't seem so. I was starting to have a hard time judging what was weird and what was not.

I put on a duffle coat over my sweater, and a scarf and wool cap. And tugged on wool-lined snow boots and, lastly, gloves. The night was cold, but it wasn't snowing. There was no wind, either. I didn't see any stars, so the sky must have been covered with a thick layer of clouds. It looked like it might snow at any time. The only sounds were the murmur of the river and the crunch of my feet. It was like the overhead clouds had absorbed all other sound. The freezing air stung my cheeks, and I tugged my wool cap down below my ears.

From the outside, the library was pitch dark. Other than the old lamp at the gate, all other lights were out, like a wartime black-out. I'd never seen the library like this before, and it looked like a completely different building from the one I was used to seeing during the day.

The entrance was locked. I took off my gloves, pulled out the heavy key chain from the pocket of my coat, and, fumblingly, unlocked the sliding door. Two types of keys were needed to unlock it. I realized that this was the first time I'd ever used them.

I went inside, shut the sliding door, and relocked it, just to be on the safe side. Inside, the emergency light cast a faint, greenish glow over the interior of the library. With that light helping me, I carefully shuffled my way across the lounge, past the check-out counter (where Mrs. Soeda reigned), and through the reading room. I proceeded down the winding hallway toward the subterranean room. There was no emergency light in the hallway, and it was very dark. With each step the floorboards gave a small, snappish shriek. I kicked myself for not bringing a pocket flashlight.

Dim light filtered out from the subterranean room. A faint glow from the tiny frosted-glass window in the door illuminated the hallway, just a bit. I knocked lightly on the door and heard an answering cough. Then Mr. Koyasu's voice saying, "Please come in."

Mr. Koyasu was seated in front of the stove, which glowed red with embers. The single old bulb hanging from the ceiling cast a strange yellowish light over the room. On the corner of the desk was the navy-blue beret.

The scene there was exactly as I'd pictured it when I hung up the phone. A small old man, ensconced in a room deep in the library, waiting for me (with grayish whiskers and wearing a checked skirt).

The scene also reminded me of a page from a picture book I'd read as a child. In it was a premonition—that something was about to change. Turn a corner and find something awaiting me there. A feeling I often had as a boy. And that *something* there would tell me a critical fact, which would force a suitable transformation in me.

I removed my wool cap and placed it and my gloves on the desk. I unwound my cashmere scarf and took off my coat. The room was already warm enough.

"Well, would you care for tea?"

"Yes, that would be nice," I said after a slight pause. If I drank strong tea now I might not be able to go to sleep. But I felt a powerful urge to drink something, and always found the aroma of the tea he brewed hard to resist.

Mr. Koyasu stood up and lifted the steaming kettle from the top of the stove. Dexterously, he swirled it in the air to allow the boiling water to settle. The kettle, nearly full, must have been heavy, but he moved it easily. He carefully measured out the right amount of tea with a spoon, placing it neatly in the warmed white ceramic teapot. Then he deliberately added hot water. He put the lid on the teapot, shut his eyes, and stood, at attention, like a well-trained palace guard. The usual procedure. No, less procedure than a ritual.

Mr. Koyasu seemed to have an internal clock that told him the exact right amount of time to steep the tea. Convenient devices like the hands of a clock weren't necessary for him.

Finally, when he felt that the perfect amount of time had passed, he relaxed his stance, like a spell had been broken, and began to move about. He poured the tea into two cups he'd warmed. He lifted up one cup, checking the fragrance arising from the steaming tea, conveying that olfactory information to his brain, and then gave a satisfied nod, small but decisive. The series of actions had been successful.

"Ah, just right. Please go ahead."

We never used any sugar or milk or lemon. The tea was perfect on its own. The temperature, too, was just right. Rich, aromatic, warm, refined. Something about it soothed the nerves. Add anything else and that perfection would be lost. Like a soft morning mist vanishing in the sunlight.

I always found it strange that he could use the same hot water, the same ceramic teapot, and the same tea leaves, yet brew tea that tasted so different from when I made it. I had tried to imitate him many times, following the exact same procedure, every step, yet my experiment always ended in failure.

Neither of us spoke for a while as we enjoyed the tea.

"Ah, I must really apologize for pulling you out here this late at night," Mr. Koyasu said a few moments later, indeed sounding quite apologetic.

"Do you often come here at this hour?" I asked.

He didn't respond for a minute, took a sip of tea, and closed his eyes, contemplating something.

"I like this stove more than anything," he finally said, as if revealing some great secret. "The flames, and the faint scent of the applewood, warm me to the core, both my body and my spirit.

That warmth is precious to me. What warms this fleeting soul of mine. I'm just hoping that—my stopping by here like this—isn't a bother to you."

I shook my head. "No, no bother at all. I don't mind whatsoever. But I'm just wondering, does Mrs. Soeda know about this? That you visit the library after hours? I mean, she's the one who actually runs the library, so if she isn't aware of it . . ."

"No, Mrs. Soeda doesn't know," Mr. Koyasu said quietly, though not uncomfortably. "She doesn't know that I come here late at night. And she probably won't know it, and if I might venture to say, ah, there's no need for her to know."

I had no idea what to say to this and remained silent. *No need for her to know?* What did he mean by that?

"Explaining all the reasons would take a long time," Mr. Koyasu said. "I really should have told you the facts, bit by bit, much earlier than this. But I never found the right moment, and now time has passed and the seasons have turned. I'm to blame, I suppose."

Mr. Koyasu drained his tea and put the empty cup on the desk. The faint clatter echoed through the small room.

"My story may sound very strange to you. Most people, I suspect, would find it hard to believe. But I am sure that you of all people will accept what I have to say. Since you possess the qualifications to believe it."

Mr. Koyasu took a breath, rubbing his hands together on his lap as if checking the warmth the stove had provided him.

"The word *qualifications* might sound a little inappropriate. It's—how to put it—a clichéd expression. But I can't think of any more apt way to put it. I was sure of this from the moment I laid eyes on you. That this person is someone who would take in, and understand, what I was trying to say, and what I had to say. A person who had those qualifications."

A log in the woodstove fell over with a cracking noise. A small, sudden sound like an animal shifting positions.

I stayed quiet, unable to follow what he was saying, gazing at Mr. Koyasu's profile, lit up red in the flames of the stove.

"Let me tell you exactly what's on my mind," Mr. Koyasu said. "I'm a person without a shadow."

"Without a shadow?" I repeated.

He went on, his voice expressionless. "Yes, that is correct. I'm a person who has lost his shadow. I do not have a shadow. I was sure at some point you would notice."

I looked over at the white wall of the room and, sure enough, he cast no shadow. There was only my own black shadow. Illuminated by the yellow light of the bulb dangling from the ceiling, my shadow stretched out, slightly diagonally, to above the wall. When I moved, he did too. But Mr. Koyasu's shadow, which should have been lined up with mine, was nowhere to be seen.

"That's right, as you can see, I have no shadow," Mr. Koyasu said. As if to emphasize the point he held out a hand in front of the light and showed me how it cast no shadow on the wall. "My shadow left me and went somewhere else."

I chose my words as carefully as I could. "When did this happen? When your shadow left your body?"

"It was when I died. I lost my shadow at that time. Probably forever."

"When you *died*?"

Mr. Koyasu gave a few small, vigorous nods. "Yes. A little over a year ago. Since then, I've been a person without a shadow."

"You're saying that you're already dead?"

"That's right, I no longer live in this world. I'm as dead as a cold iron nail."

"THAT'S RIGHT, I no longer live in this world. I'm as dead as a cold iron nail."

I thought about what he'd said. *As dead as a cold iron nail?* I had to say something but couldn't find the words.

"Are you certain that you're dead?" I finally was able to say, but once I did, it sounded like a very stupid question.

But Mr. Koyasu nodded firmly, his expression serious.

"Yes, there's no question I'm dead. It's my life and death we're talking about, so I have a very clear memory of it, and there should be a public record of it in city hall. Plus there's a small grave in a temple here in town. They read sutras over me, and though I don't rightly recall what it is, they gave me one of those posthumous Buddhist names they give to the departed. There is no question about the fact that I'm dead."

"But I'm sitting across from you, and talking to you. You certainly don't strike me as dead."

"It's true, I do look the same as when I was alive. And I can carry on a coherent conversation, too. But none of that changes the fact that I am dead and no longer of this world. Without hesitation, I'd say that although it's rather dated and convenient, you could call me a ghost."

A deep silence descended on the room. A faint smile played on his lips, and he gazed at the flames in the stove as he rubbed his hands together on his lap.

This guy might be joking, pulling my leg—the possibility crossed my mind. In a normal situation, that was entirely possible. Some people like to tease others with a straight face. But I just couldn't see Mr. Koyasu as the type of person who would enjoy fooling people. And above all there was the simple fact that he really didn't have a shadow. It goes without saying, but you can't make your shadow disappear as a prank.

The word *reality* had lost its original meaning. It was unraveling me. I no longer possessed a set standard with which to determine what was real. Confused, I slowly shook my head, and my long black shadow on the wall did the same, the movement seeming a bit more exaggerated than my actual movement.

Was I scared? Not particularly. I wasn't sure why, but even if this old man in front of me was a ghost, I didn't feel frightened at all sitting there, across from each other, talking like this in the middle of the night. Because it was entirely possible. What was wrong with speaking with a dead person?

I still had my doubts, though. An obvious point being that there are so many things we don't know about ghosts.

"Yes, there are so many things I don't know either," Mr. Koyasu said, as if reading my mind. "I don't get it myself—why I didn't go back to nothingness after I died, but remained conscious, with this transient shape, and stayed in the library."

I wordlessly gazed at his face.

"Consciousness is a strange thing. And it's an even stranger thing having a consciousness after dying. Somewhere I read that 'Consciousness is the brain's self-awareness of its own physical state.' Would you say that's a correct definition? What do you think?"

Consciousness is the brain's self-awareness of its own physical state.
I mulled this over.

"If you put it that way, it might be right. Sounds logical."

"If that's the case, then it means my brain still exists. Right? If there's consciousness, then there's necessarily a brain. But is that possible? For the body to be gone but the brain to exist? Can that really happen?"

It took some effort to follow what he was saying. Since the logic was so far removed from the level of the everyday. I paused a moment, then asked, "Mr. Koyasu, are you saying your body doesn't exist anymore?"

Mr. Koyasu nodded emphatically.

"Correct, my body doesn't exist in this world anymore. For now, I've taken on Koyasu's form, but I can't keep this up for a long time. After a set time has passed, I'll vanish into thin air like smoke, and become nothingness. This is but a fleeting, temporary form. The way I look is nothing to boast about, but at this point there's no other form I can take on."

"But your consciousness continues?"

"Yes, it does, as is. Even without a physical body, I have my consciousness. Which is a huge mystery to me. That there's no body, and without the body, of course there is no brain, yet my consciousness continues to function. I find it strange that after death, there are still things I can't understand. When I was alive, I had the vague notion that after you died you'd have nothing more to do with the mysteries of being alive."

"Apart from the brain and the body, don't you think there's also a soul?" I asked.

Mr. Koyasu pursed his lips and gave it some thought.

"Yes, I guess I have thought about the soul. But the more I think about it, the more mysterious the soul becomes. Even after I died and became a ghost—or perhaps I should say *because* I became a ghost—I understand it even less. Lots of people like to use the word *soul*, yet no one can clearly define or explain what it is. The word is used in so many situations that people have come to believe, however vaguely, that the thing we call a soul definitely exists within our bodies. But what I've learned after dying is that you can't see the soul with your eyes or touch it with your hands. You can't use it to do anything special. In my opinion, what we actually *can* rely on is consciousness, and memories."

I didn't give any opinion. A dead person appears before you and says he doesn't know whether the soul exists or not—what sort of comeback could you possibly have?

"I was wondering how it came about, Mr. Koyasu, that you passed away?" I asked. "And how did you become a—well, you know—a ghost?"

"I remember when I died very well. The direct cause was a heart attack. At any rate, I died very quickly. In the blink of an eye, you might say. I didn't even think *I'm dying.* There was no time. People often say that when you're dying, your life flashes before your eyes, but I did not experience anything like that."

Mr. Koyasu sat there for a while, his arms crossed, head tilted. And then he continued.

"My heart was never terribly healthy, but I'd never had any major problems, and just a week before, I'd had my annual physical at a hospital in Koriyama City. The doctor told me nothing had changed. So I wasn't thinking I'd die of a heart attack. But then one morning it happened, totally out of the blue. From my own experience, I'd say the important things in life usually happen unexpectedly. And dying would, I think, count."

Mr. Koyasu chuckled a bit.

"That morning I was taking a walk in the mountains nearby. I was using a walking stick, with a bell attached to it to scare away bears. It was fall, and bears are known to wander down to populated areas then to eat before they go into hibernation. But if you ring a bell while you walk, you needn't fear them attacking you. At least that's what I've been told. Walking in the mountains was my one little form of exercise. But as I was walking, everything suddenly went white before my eyes and it felt like my consciousness was slowly fading away. This can't be good, I told myself, and leaned back against a nearby pine tree, but even then, I couldn't prop myself up and slid down to the ground. I remember my heart pounding in my chest. It was like a large group of dwarves lined up on a far-off hill, all of them beating away at drums—that kind of sinister sound. The dwarves were far away, their faces hidden in the shade so I couldn't see them. But their arms were amazingly powerful, and the drums sounded like they were pounding right next to my ears. I couldn't believe my heart could pound that loud."

Mr. Koyasu closed his eyes a bit, as if recalling it.

"The next thing that came to my mind—why, I don't know— was a vision of me in a boat that was flooding, furiously bailing it out with a small bucket. I was in a rowboat by myself in the middle of a large lake, but there was a hole somewhere in the hull with cold water rushing in. There I was, dying in the mountains, so I have no idea why I'd had those thoughts. But at any rate I had to bail out the water, otherwise the boat would soon sink to the bottom. That was the last scene I saw in my life. Pretty strange, if you think about it. Ah, is that all there is to one's life? Finally, though, nothingness came. Complete, utter nothingness. And I didn't see any clever thing like my life flashing before my eyes. Just a dilapidated old rowboat barely afloat and a tiny bucket—that's it."

Silence.

"So you died right away?"

"Yes, death came on all too quick," Mr. Koyasu said, nodding. "As far as I remember there was no physical pain. It was all so sudden and—how shall I put it?—much too *simple*, so that I didn't have any awareness that I was dying, or losing my life. Because of that, even though I'm a ghost now, I still have trouble grasping the fact that I am actually dead."

"After you died," I asked, "were there stages you went through to get to where you are now—as a ghost?"

"No, no stages. When I next became aware of things, I found myself like this. I died just over a year ago, and I recall that it was a month and a half after my death that I took on this form, a consciousness without an actual physical body. I died, and after there was a funeral, after my body was cremated and the bones put to rest in a grave I became a ghost and came back to earth. I don't know what happened in between, what stages took place."

It took some time for me to wrap my head around what he was saying. But basically I just had to accept it as fact.

"You didn't come back because you had some lingering attachments to the world or anything?"

"Generally, people think that's what ghosts are, but in my case I don't have any particular lingering attachments or regrets. Looking back on my life, it wasn't anything special, just an ordinary life with its share of peaks and valleys."

"But before you knew it, after your death your consciousness came back here."

"Yes, that's correct. I didn't become this kind of being because I wanted to. I did have a personal attachment to this library, my own feeling of affection for it, and I guess those feelings could play a part. But that doesn't mean I have something I feel was left undone when it comes to the library. In fact, I don't."

"People in town all think you're dead and gone."

"Exactly. Or they don't even think about it, because I actually *am* dead and gone. And only certain special people are able to see this fleeting form I'm in now."

"Mrs. Soeda does seem aware that you appear in the library, doesn't she?"

"Yes, Mrs. Soeda basically understands that I've become a ghost. She and I have known each other a long time and, in a sense, understand each other at a deep level, and she accepts that I've become a ghost as a kind of natural phenomenon. Though at first she was a bit shocked by it, as you might imagine."

"But the other staff can't see you, right?"

"That's right. Mrs. Soeda's the only one, other than you. She can't see me all the time, but she can see me as needed. Everyone else thinks I'm dead and no longer here. Well, that's true enough, since I *am* dead and no longer here . . . So when there are other people around I refrain from talking with Mrs. Soeda or you. If somebody saw that, it'd strike them as very weird."

Mr. Koyasu laughed lightly, as if he found this funny.

"So you mean that even after you died, you were here and able to work still as the head librarian, as you'd been doing."

"Yes, when Mrs. Soeda had some administrative things to consult me about, I'd give her advice and make decisions. You're right, basically the same as when I was alive and was the head librarian."

"But still, if a dead person becomes a ghost and works as the actual head librarian you can't tell anyone, and you need someone living to take responsibility for all the day-to-day tasks. So you advertised for someone from outside—an appropriate person with an actual physical body. Do I have that right?"

Mr. Koyasu nodded emphatically a few times, as if thankful I'd conveyed his intentions in the appropriate words.

"Yes, indeed, that pretty much sums it up. And when you came here for the interview, I took one look at your appearance and I knew: Ah—there's something special about this person. This person will completely get the way I am, a consciousness with a temporary body, and surely he'll accept that. This was, how should I put it, an unexpected, miraculous encounter."

As he warmed his small body in front of the woodstove he looked right at me, like some wise old cat. And for an instant there was a glimmer from deep down in his eyes.

"I very carefully observed your actions, what you said and did. I wasn't sure if I should reveal the truth to you. This is a very delicate matter, a person's life and death. I think you understand this, but it's not that simple to reveal that you're a ghost. An appropriate amount of time needs to pass. So summer came and went, then our short-lived fall here in the mountains, and then the harsh winter was upon us, the season when we light the stove here in this room. And finally, I felt sure. That you were the perfect recipient."

With my mouth closed, I gazed at Mr. Koyasu's placid face. The face of this man who was a consciousness with a temporary body.

MR. KOYASU hunched over in front of the stove, eyes shut, for a long time maintaining his silence as if turning things over in his mind. He remained utterly motionless.

"You're a person who's lost his shadow once," he finally said, breaking the silence. He straightened up, opened his eyes, and looked at me.

"How do you know that? That I'm a person who once lost his shadow?"

Mr. Koyasu shook his head twice. "I am a ghost. A consciousness without life. As a result, I can see things that ordinary people cannot see, and understand things ordinary people cannot understand. I could tell at a glance you once lost your shadow."

"What does it mean, when a person loses their shadow?"

Mr. Koyasu narrowed his eyes, as if focusing on something very bright.

"I see—so you don't understand this, do you?"

"I really don't. I didn't know what it meant at the time, and I still don't. I was just carried along, unresisting, by the flow of things. And in that process you can't determine anything with certainty, and as all this happened, my shadow and I were separated from each other. In a town where no one had a shadow."

Mr. Koyasu said nothing, and just kept on stroking his chin. And then, slowly, he opened his mouth to speak.

"As I said earlier, even though I'm dead, there are still many things I don't understand. Just like back when I was alive. Unfortunately, dying doesn't make you any wiser. So sadly, I don't think I can give a definite answer at this point. There are still things in this world that can't easily be explained."

Mr. Koyasu lifted his left wrist and glanced at his watch without hands. From his expression it seemed that even without hands, it served his purposes as a watch. Or perhaps he was just keeping up habits from when he was alive.

"I will need to excuse myself pretty soon," Mr. Koyasu said. "I can't maintain this temporary form for long. I can remain longer on the earth at night than during the day, and I've reached my limit. It's about time for me to vanish. Let's get together and talk again. Well, that is, if you would like to. If it's too much trouble, then I won't appear before you."

"No," I hurriedly said. To emphasize that word, I shook my head several times. "No, it's no trouble whatsoever. I would like to see you again. There's so much I'd like to talk with you about. What would be the best way for us to see each other?"

"Unfortunately, I can't just appear before you whenever I want to. The opportunities are limited. And I can't stay very long. So I have no idea myself when I'm able to meet with you. It's not a matter of free will, of me thinking, 'Okay, I'll take on a visible form now.' If it's alright with you, ah, I'll call you at home like I did today. And let's meet here, in this room, in front of the stove. It'll probably be at night again. As I said before, it's easier for me to materialize after it's dark. Would that be alright with you? It's a little selfish, I know."

"That would be fine. Anytime is fine with me. Just call me, and I'll come."

Mr. Koyasu thought this over for a while, and suddenly raised his head as if remembering something. "By the way, have you ever read the Bible?"

"The Bible? The Christian Bible?"

"Yes, that's right."

"No, I haven't really. I'm not a Christian."

"Neither am I, but I enjoy reading it, apart from any faith. Since I was young, I've liked to read parts of it, and it's become a habit. It's an intriguing book, and I've learned and felt many things from reading it. In the Psalms there are these words: 'People are like a breath; their days are like a fleeting shadow.'"

Mr. Koyasu stopped, grabbed the knob, opened the door of the stove, and rearranged the logs with fire tongs. And slowly repeated his words, as if telling himself.

"'People are like a breath; their days are like a fleeting shadow.' Do you understand that? Human beings are as insubstantial as an exhaled breath, and what they do in their lives is but a moving shadow. Well, these words really got to me when I was younger, but it was only after I died, and became what I am now, that I truly understood them. It's true, we humans are but a breath, and I, dead now, don't even have a shadow anymore."

I looked at him, without saying a word.

"You're still alive," he said, "so cherish your life. Since you still have a dark shadow with you."

Mr. Koyasu stood up, put on his soft beret, and wrapped his scarf around his neck.

"Well, I'd best be going. It's about time for me to disappear. Let's meet again before long."

As he left the room I called out.

"Mr. Koyasu—in the place I mentioned, the town where no one had shadows—I worked like I do now, in a library. In a small library with a woodstove just like this one."

Mr. Koyasu glanced back at me and nodded once to show he'd heard. But he gave no comment. He was silent, with just the one nod. He walked up the stairs and left the room, closing the door behind him.

I thought I heard footsteps retreating down the corridor, but I might have been imagining it. Maybe I really heard nothing. If I did actually hear footsteps, they must have been very subdued.

After Mr. Koyasu left, I stayed for a while, alone in that subterranean room. Once he was gone, I felt assailed by a strong doubt— maybe the whole idea that he had been here was an illusion? Maybe I'd been alone the whole time, lost in aimless thoughts? But this was no illusion, no fantasy. Proof was in the two empty teacups on top of the desk—one of them mine, one of them Mr. Koyasu's (or his ghost, or his consciousness with a temporary body).

I let out a sigh, rested both hands on the desk, closed my eyes, and listened to the sound of time passing. Though of course I couldn't hear that sound. All I heard was a log crumbling inside the stove.

THERE WERE SEVERAL things I needed to ask Mr. Koyasu, and several things I needed to tell him. What I, as a living person, should know, and things I wanted him, as a dead person, to know. But before that, there was a lot I had to sort out in my mind.

The window of time when Mr. Koyasu could take on human form and materialize in front of me was—according to his explanation—not so long. And he couldn't appear that way whenever he wanted to. We needed to discuss all kinds of things within the confines of that limited amount of time. Lots of topics that defied logic, things that belonged to the conceptual realm. So it was necessary, to some extent, to gather my thoughts and plan out how to approach our talks. Otherwise, there was a strong possibility that I would wander forever, aimlessly, in a dark, enigmatic world, casting around for clues.

The next day, after one p.m., I asked Mrs. Soeda to come to the head librarian's office on the second floor. There's something we need to talk about, I told her.

Mrs. Soeda and I spoke nearly every day at the first-floor counter about matters related to the library's operations, but I realized that we'd had almost no opportunities to speak alone. It wasn't like Mrs. Soeda was intentionally avoiding those opportunities, but she was clearly also not seeking them out. Perhaps (now that I think about it, I mean) that might have been because she wanted to avoid the topic of Mr. Koyasu when we talked.

Mrs. Soeda had on a thin, light green cardigan, a simple white blouse, and a bluish-gray skirt. She wore low heels made from dark brown buckskin. Her outfit was neither expensive nor cheap, neither old nor well worn. All were clean and neatly taken care of, her blouse carefully ironed, crisp, and wrinkle free. She usually wore light makeup that didn't stand out, yet today her eyebrows were drawn on thick and sharp, as if to emphasize a strong will. Everything about her suggested an experienced, capable librarian.

I sat behind my desk, and she sat across from me. I caught a trace of tension in her expression. Her thin lips, shaded with a refined pink lipstick, were set in a taut line, as if she'd decided ahead of time not to say more than was necessary.

Outside the window a fine, soundless rain fell, and the room was chilly and dampish. There was only a small gas stove, so the room never warmed up much. The rain had been falling like this, unchanged, since morning, and from the chill in the air it looked like it could snow at any time. The room was dim, the ceiling light only emphasizing the gloom. It was only one p.m. yet seemed like evening.

"I'd like to talk with you regarding Mr. Koyasu," I said, launching right into it. I felt it best with Mrs. Soeda just to get straight to the point. Her expression was unchanged as she gave a slight nod, her lips remaining tight.

"Mr. Koyasu has already passed away, hasn't he," I said, coming right out with it.

Mrs. Soeda maintained her silence for a time and finally exhaled slightly, as if giving in, and reluctantly spoke.

"Yes. You are correct. Mr. Koyasu did pass away some time ago."

"But though he's dead he still sometimes appears in the library, looking like he did while alive. I'm correct, yes?"

"Yes, that's correct," Mrs. Soeda said. She lifted her hands from her lap and adjusted her glasses. "But not everybody can see him."

"You can see him," I said, "and I can too."

"Yes, that's right. *As far as I know*, up to this point the only ones who've been able to see Mr. Koyasu, and speak with him, are you and me. The rest of the staff can't see anything and can't hear his voice."

Mrs. Soeda seemed relieved to finally be able to unburden herself of this secret she'd held on to for so long. She must have had doubts, too, about her own sanity at times.

"Actually, until last night," I said, "I didn't know he was already dead. Ever since I took up this post in the library, I've been sure he was alive. No one told me otherwise. Last night he revealed the truth to me himself, and as you can imagine, I was shocked."

"Of course you were," Mrs. Soeda said. "I'm very sorry, but I couldn't tell you myself that he is no longer of this world."

I ran through an abbreviated version of the previous night's events for her. How around ten p.m. Mr. Koyasu had called me, summoning me to the library. And how we'd sat in front of the warm stove in the subterranean room in the rear of the library, and as we sipped hot, fragrant tea (which Mr. Koyasu had boiled and made himself) he disclosed to me that he was, in his words, already a dead person.

Mrs. Soeda remained silent. Behind the lenses of her glasses, her eyes remained steady on my face, as if trying to read something behind my words—if indeed there was anything to read.

"I believe Mr. Koyasu is personally fond of you," she said quietly when my story was done. "I think there's something about you, or about something you're carrying around in your heart, that he's concerned about."

Something I'm carrying around in my heart, I repeated to myself.

"As far as you know," I said, "until I started work here you were the only one who could see Mr. Koyasu after he died. That's what you mean?"

"Yes, I am probably the only one here who could see him. When Mr. Koyasu appeared in the library, I was the only one he talked to. Just like when he was alive. It wouldn't do for the other staff members to see me talking with an invisible person, so we only spoke when the two of us could be alone. Though what we mostly talked about was office-related matters about library operations."

She pursed her lips, gathering her feelings, mulling over something. And then said, "I think Mr. Koyasu was still concerned over the operation of the library. The library is still officially a town-managed library, but actually it is his personal property. And almost everything to do with the library was managed by him alone. After he died suddenly last autumn I stood in as a temporary substitute until a new head librarian was decided. Needless to say, this was too much for me to handle alone. I'm just a librarian, and there is much about the overall operations of the library, let alone its daily operations, that I don't know about, and cannot make suitable decisions regarding. I think Mr. Koyasu was unable to bear seeing that, so he started to return here after he passed away, in order to lend me a hand."

"So after he died, you ran the library while receiving advice from Mr. Koyasu's—ghost?"

Mrs. Soeda nodded.

"And after a period without a head librarian, I was hired. Correct?"

Mrs. Soeda nodded once. "Correct. In the summer when Mr. Koyasu interviewed you himself in this room, I was, quite honestly, surprised. No—less surprised than taken aback, a bit bewildered. Since he appeared so clearly to you, and on your very first meeting. Mr. Koyasu had been very careful, not appearing to anyone other than myself. I was puzzled and didn't know what was going on. But when I saw that—though I didn't really under-stand the reason for it—I guessed that there was something in you that Mr. Koyasu felt he could trust . . . something that made him think it was alright to appear to you."

I said nothing and just listened. Mrs. Soeda continued.

"And you and Mr. Koyasu had a long, friendly talk here, which resulted in your appointment as the new head librarian, and the library continued to operate as smoothly as before. I felt a great burden lifted from me, which was a huge relief. It seemed like you and Mr. Koyasu built a good relationship, away from anyone else's eyes, and nothing could have made me happier.

"Yet I couldn't tell you myself that Mr. Koyasu had already died. It seemed a little—impertinent of me. I felt if he wanted to tell you that—that he was not a living person—he would do it himself. Not telling you meant it wasn't yet time. So I stayed silent, watch-ing developments, and have kept this critical fact to myself over these past several months. Should I have told you? The fact that Mr. Koyasu isn't an actual living person, that he is a—what should you say—a soul, an apparition?"

"No," I said, "I think it's like you said, that Mr. Koyasu wanted to reveal that to me himself. He was waiting for the right time. So it wasn't wrong for you to keep it to yourself."

We stayed silent for a time. I looked out the window and checked that it was still raining. It hadn't yet changed to snow. Soundless rain, soaking the ground, the garden stones, the trunks of the trees, and adding to the flow of the river.

"What sort of person was Mr. Koyasu?" I asked Mrs. Soeda. "I heard he was born in this town, but what was his background, what kind of life did he have when he was young, and what led him to create this privately owned library? I know next to nothing about him as a person. I have tried asking him many times, but he always sidesteps the questions, like he doesn't want to talk about himself. After a while I gave up on asking personal questions."

Mrs. Soeda kept her legs neatly together, her hands folded on her lap. Her ten slim fingers were delicately intertwined like a ball of yarn.

"Truthfully, I don't know all that much personal information about Mr. Koyasu either. I've worked in this library nearly ten years or so yet have almost never spoken with him about anything personal. Strangely enough, I've grown more familiar with him after he passed away. When he was alive there was a certain, I don't know—aloofness about him, a sense that his feelings were elsewhere. Not cold or arrogant or anything—I'm not saying that. He was always kind and nice to us, but it seemed like he was not quite interested enough in the reality around him, and kept a certain distance between himself and others.

"But after he passed away, after he became a soul, in other words, he'd look me straight in the eye and talk with me quite sincerely. His personality became livelier, with a kindness he hadn't had up until then. It's a strange—he became livelier in a human sense after he died, but it was like something important he'd kept hidden inside finally appeared once he was dead."

"Like a hard shell that covered his heart when he was alive had been taken away."

"Yes. Indeed it felt that way," Mrs. Soeda said. "Like when the snow melts in spring and things underneath it are gradually revealed. Until I got married, I lived in Matsumoto in Nagano Prefecture, and knew nothing at all about this area. My husband is from this prefecture, Fukushima, but he grew up in Koriyama City and has no connections with this area. He just happened to get a job here as a teacher, so we moved here. So most of what I know about Mr. Koyasu is secondhand knowledge. People around me have told me things, bit by bit. Some of it is just rumors, and with some of it it's hard to decide what really happened. But if you're okay with that, I can tell you what I do know about Mr. Koyasu."

According to Mrs. Soeda, Mr. Koyasu was the oldest son of one of the wealthier families in the area. He had a sister who was much younger, and for generations their family ran a thriving sake brewery. He graduated from a local high school and went to a private college in Tokyo. He majored in economics but wasn't enthusiastic about his studies and had to repeat a few years. He really wanted to major in literature, but his father, grooming him to take over the family business, was dead set against it, which is why, reluctantly, he studied management. At college he ignored his studies and instead, with friends, started a little magazine that completely absorbed him, and wrote some short stories, one of which ended up published in a major literary magazine. Yet he never was able to find success as a full-time novelist, and for several years he gadded about Tokyo posing as one of the literati, and his father, who'd run out of patience with him, gave him an ultimatum—meaning he cut off his monthly allowance—and all he could do was return to this little country town.

He worked under his father as the heir apparent to the family brewery, training as the future owner, but they didn't get along. His father was totally devoted to work, and naturally Mr. Koyasu was less than enthusiastic about the sake business operations. Life in this town was, for him, far from fulfilling. His few pleasures were reading and writing in his free time.

Since he was the only son of a well-to-do family, he had many marriage prospects, but he didn't want to settle down, and instead he remained a bachelor for a long time. In his hometown, he was reserved and polite—there was public opinion to consider, and his father's watchful eyes—but rumor had it that he made the occasional trip to Tokyo to cut loose and relax.

When he was thirty-two, his father, who loved to drink, suffered a stroke and was left bedridden, and Mr. Koyasu effectively took over management of the company. In actuality, the devoted longtime head clerk and other employees took over day-to-day operations, and he could get by sitting in a back room, giving instructions as needed, quickly scanning the business's account books, and as long as he kept up social relationships by showing up at business meetings and dining together with influential people in town, that was sufficient. His days were boring and unstimulating, but his nitpicking father could barely speak anymore, and the business continued to do well—even though he didn't devote himself to it. So life was comfortable.

As always, when he had free time he read books, and wrote fiction, yet after he turned thirty, his desire to create, which had once burned like a red-hot flame within him, gradually diminished. Like a traveler who discovers, without realizing it, that he's crossed a great, meaningful divide. There were fewer and fewer days when he sat at his desk, his pen filling in manuscript pages.

A novel . . . what should I write about? He no longer had confidence. In the past he'd had no time to worry over those kinds of questions, as sentences welled up inside him like water gushing out of a crevice between rocks. While he stagnated here in this country town, critical events were happening in Tokyo, leaving him far behind. Over time his exchanges with his former literary friends in Tokyo faded and he became estranged from them.

Out of duty he listlessly plowed through these anxious, frustrating days—he'd turned thirty-five by then—when, by chance, he happened to meet a beautiful woman ten years younger than himself, and immediately he fell in love with her. His heart was full in a way he'd never experienced before. And that sudden rush of emotions was almost immeasurably deep and powerful, confounding him, shaking him to the core. It felt as if all the values he'd had up until then were nothing but an empty box. *What have*

I been living for until now? he asked himself. He was so anxious he wondered if Earth had begun rotating in the opposite direction.

The woman came from Tokyo—she was the niece of a local acquaintance. She was born within the Yamanote Line, the circular rail line around central Tokyo, and grew up there. She graduated from a mission college, where she studied French literature and became fluent in French, then worked as a secretary in either the Tunisian or Algerian embassy. Intelligent and quick-witted, she was knowledgeable about literature and art. She could talk forever about those subjects, never losing interest. Whenever he talked with her, he felt his long-dormant intellectual curiosity revive. He regained a passion for life and couldn't have been more overjoyed.

He was introduced to her when she visited the town during her summer vacation. They saw each other several times that summer and grew close. Later, he found opportunities to travel to Tokyo to go on dates with her. (By the way, at the time he didn't wear skirts and was dressed neatly in normal clothes.)

After they had been going out for a few months, he mustered the courage to propose, but she didn't accept right away. "I'm sorry, I'd like a little time to think about it," she told him. And for several weeks, she was hesitant.

She loved him very much and considered him a trustworthy person. She enjoyed being with him and had no objection to the idea of marrying him (fortunately for Mr. Koyasu, a short time before this she'd broken up with another man). But she was clearly reluctant to give up a career that made use of her language skills, as well as the easy lifestyle of a single woman in the city, so that she could become the wife of a sake manufacturer and settle down in a small town in the mountains of Fukushima as the daughter-in-law in an old, established family.

Finally, after much discussion, they came to a mutual agreement that after they married, she would continue in her present job and come to the town on weekends and holidays, or Mr. Koyasu would visit her in Tokyo when he could find the time. This wasn't a satisfactory setup as far as Mr. Koyasu was concerned, and he tried his best to persuade her otherwise, but her resolve was firm and the last thing he wanted was to give her up, so in the end he had to accept these conditions. They held a simple, token wedding ceremony in his family home. Only a few close relatives and friends were invited, there was no reception, and most people in town were not even aware that he had gotten married.

Mr. Koyasu wanted to give up managing the brewery, cut his ties with this small old-fashioned town, and live a carefree married life with her in Tokyo (how happy he would have been if he could have), but he couldn't just selfishly leave and abandon his longtime employees, his bedridden father, and the family that depended on him. Whether he liked it or not, he had responsibilities to fulfill. Circumstances had forced these on him, but since he had taken them on, he couldn't very well abdicate them.

Also, as a practical matter, if he waltzed off to Tokyo at his age, with no job, no career, and not enough talent to make a living as a writer (he no longer was confident he had such talent), what was he going to do there?

Which is why Mr. Koyasu had to accept her proposal of a commuter marriage. Can't be helped, he thought. Most of life is made up of compromises, anyway, isn't it? After this, they continued this inconvenient, hectic married life for nearly five years.

On Friday nights, or Saturday mornings, she'd take a series of trains to the town and return to Tokyo on Sunday evening. Or he would go to Tokyo for the weekend. During summer and winter vacation, the two of them could spend more days in a row together. If his thoroughly conservative father had been well, he no doubt would have had a litany of complaints about their style of married life, but (thankfully, one might say) he could hardly talk at all. Mr. Koyasu's mother had always been a docile, quiet person whose operating principle was to never make a scene, and his younger sister, about the same age as his wife, found they got along well and had much to talk about, and they formed a close bond. So no one around him criticized his lifestyle, and their atypical, hurried married life proceeded, steady and smooth, for nearly five years.

And actually Mr. Koyasu enjoyed, in his own way, this married lifestyle that the world saw as quite unusual. Even if they could only see each other one or two days a week, being with her was by far the happiest part of his life, so that the time they could spend together was filled with a joy nothing else could equal. Perhaps given that the time he could spend with her was so limited, he experienced with her a joy that was something deeper, more all-embracing. On the days he couldn't see her, his time was filled with a rich, colorful sense of anticipation as he dreamed about the coming weekend.

When he went to Tokyo, sometimes he took the train and other times he drove. He wasn't much of a driver, but when he thought of seeing his wife, soon he didn't find driving all that bothersome or traveling all that way by himself tiring. His heart pounded as he thought, mile by mile, that he was drawing closer to the city where she lived. As if he were young again. Though he'd never experienced, even in his youth, such deep, unconditional love.

Those atypical yet fulfilling days came to an end soon after he had turned forty. His wife found out she was pregnant. Neither of them had planned on having a child, and had used contraceptives, but one day, out of the blue, it was clear she was pregnant. They met to discuss how to deal with this unexpected situation, and had long, sober phone conversations. An abortion was the one thing she said she'd like to avoid, and they decided to respect this wish. Neither of them had much interest in having a child (just being together, the two of them, was more than fulfilling), but since a tiny new life would be born, they wanted to treasure this development. She ended up quitting her job at the North African embassy and moved to the small town in Fukushima Prefecture where he lived. And awaited the birth of their child.

She was comfortable quitting her job at the embassy since the ambassador, who'd been very kind to her, had been replaced when a new administration had come to power, and she didn't get along that well with the newly appointed ambassador. Her passion for her work had faded considerably since then. Another factor was that the weekly trips back and forth between Tokyo and Fukushima were starting to wear on her. And being pregnant would make traveling back and forth take even more of a toll.

She also felt she wanted to live as a married couple under the same roof. Her relationship with his relatives was friendly, and although it was a small, conservative town, she felt she'd be able to live a peaceful life there. If, by chance, any troubles arose, she was confident that her husband would protect her. She had come to trust Mr. Koyasu that much. Her feelings toward him were less a passionate love than a kind of overall respect for him as a person. What she sought from a life partner was not a burning passion but a stable, calm relationship.

Mr. Koyasu's family and relatives welcomed her move to the town with open arms. He prepared a newly built, cozy house not far from his parents' home, and they began living there. At long last he felt they were a normal married couple, which made him relieved. Their commuter marriage had been exciting, for sure, yet he'd been constantly plagued with the fear that eventually she would leave him. He'd never felt confident in his appeal as a man.

As he watched his wife's belly grow, as he gently stroked it, he imagined the child that they were going to have. What kind of child, he wondered, would be born into this world? And what sort of person would that child grow into? What sort of ego would the child have, and what kind of dreams?

Mr. Koyasu couldn't grasp what his own existence meant, but he no longer cared.

He'd inherited a set of information from his parents, which he'd modified slightly, and then would pass it on to his own child—he was, in effect, nothing more than a checkpoint along the way. Just a single ring in an endless chain. But what was wrong with that? Even if he ended up doing nothing meaningful in his life, nothing worth mentioning, so what? He would be able to hand over to his child a kind of possibility, even if it was nothing more than a possibility. Wouldn't that alone make his life until now feel meaningful?

This was an entirely new viewpoint for him, something he'd never considered before. But thinking that way brought him a great sense of relief. Any confusion and melancholy vanished, and for perhaps the first time in his life, he felt at peace. He shelved all of his ambitions, his hopes and dreams, and replaced them with his settled days as the fourth-generation owner of a sake brewery in a rural town. There was hardly anything stimulating, any new changes, around him, yet none of that left him particularly dissatisfied. And with it, the random, frustrated sense he'd had that he was gradually being left behind by all the developments in the wider world disappeared. His life now had a reliable foundation, a little home where his beloved wife and the little baby growing stronger within her were waiting for him.

If he were to put it in a few words, it was as if he had stepped into the midportion of his life and found it to be a flat plateau where the view was magnificent.

Coming up with a name for their child became an obsession. The passion he'd once had to write a novel had now faded. Coming up with his child's name was now the most important, meaningful creative activity. His wife was happy to leave this up to him. Our division of labor, she said, is me having a healthy baby and you giving the baby a wonderful name. Thinking up a good name for a baby was not in her skill set.

Mr. Koyasu pored through all kinds of materials, racking his brain, and after going back and forth he came to a firm conclusion.

If the baby was a boy, he'd name him Shin, the character for "forest." If the baby was a girl, then the name would be Rin, meaning "woods." Perfect names, he felt, for a child born in a small mountain town full of nature.

子易森 Shin Koyasu
子易林 Rin Koyasu

With brush and ink he wrote, in large characters on white paper, the two names, and taped them to his wall. And day and night, as he saw these names, he imagined what the baby to come would look like.

What wonderful names, his wife said, giving her consent. I like the characters visually, too. Wouldn't it be great to have twins, a boy and a girl? But from the size of my belly I don't think that's about to happen. So which do you want? A boy, or a girl?

Either one is fine by me, Mr. Koyasu said. Either a boy or a girl is fine, as long as they're healthy and their name suits them like a well-fitting garment.

This was Mr. Koyasu's honest answer. Either one is fine—a boy or a girl. As long as that child carried on the possibilities he'd passed along, as possibilities.

"THEY HAD A BABY BOY," Mrs. Soeda said. "And as planned, they named him Shin Koyasu. It was an easy delivery, and the baby was very healthy. This was the first grandchild for the Koyasu family, and during his early childhood, the whole family doted on him. Each day was a happy one for Mr. Koyasu and his wife. Their life was stable, with no problems to speak of, and his wife had grown used to life in the town. I hadn't moved here yet myself, so I only know things indirectly, things I heard about later on from people in town. The people who told me this, though, were all trustworthy, so I believe my information is accurate. In a word, there was no hint of trouble whatsoever in Mr. Koyasu's life, with everything going smoothly."

Mrs. Soeda closed her mouth at this point, her eyes blank, and stared down at her hands on the lap of her skirt. A simple gold ring twinkled on the ring finger of her left hand.

But those happy days did not last long, did they, I mused. Her slightly trembling mouth seemed to want to say that.

"But those happy days did not last long. Sadly," Mrs. Soeda said, as if reading my unspoken thoughts.

The boy had his fifth birthday in the middle of May, a lively celebration (incidentally, Mr. Koyasu was forty-five then, his wife thirty-five). The boy received a little red bicycle as a birthday present. He'd really wanted a large, long-haired dog (the boy was crazy about the dog in the story *Heidi*), but his mother was allergic to dog hair, so they held off on a dog and bought him a bike instead. But it was a cute little bike, and the boy loved it. When he came back from kindergarten every day he'd hop on his bike, with its training wheels, and happily pedal around the garden. He loved to sing and was always singing some song as he rode around. Sometimes nonsense songs he'd made up.

One evening, as his mother was preparing dinner in the kitchen, she could hear him singing outside the window. For her this must have been the happiest time of all—twilight in spring, listening to her five-year-old singing as he merrily pedaled around on his bike.

But as she was preparing a stir-fry, she found that the saltshaker was empty and was momentarily distracted as she searched for the salt she'd purchased. She didn't notice for a while that she no longer could hear her son singing. The moment she suddenly realized this, with a start, she heard the screech of a large truck slamming on its brakes. And the dull thud of something being struck. The succession of sounds seemed to come from right in front of their house. This was followed by an eerie silence, as if all sound had been sucked away. Reflexively she shut off the gas range, slipped on sandals, and rushed outside. And went out the front gate.

A large truck sat diagonally across the road, blocking it, after slamming on its brakes, and in front of its tires was a smashed and twisted little red bicycle. Her child was nowhere to be seen.

"Shin!" she screamed. *"Shin-chan!"*

There was no response. The door of the truck opened, and a middle-aged driver stepped out. His face was deathly pale, his whole body trembling.

The child had been thrown to the side of the road some twenty feet away. The impact with the truck had been fearsome, and his body must have been sent flying like a rubber ball. His tiny unconscious body was frighteningly light, like some limp discarded shell. His mouth was half open, as if he had been about to speak but hadn't gotten the words out, his eyelids shut. A thin line of drool had dribbled down from his mouth. His mother raced to his side, picked him up, and quickly checked his body for injuries. He didn't seem to be bleeding anywhere, and she felt slightly relieved. *At least he isn't bleeding.*

"Shin-chan!" she called out to her child. But there was no response. His eyes stayed shut, not moving at all. His hands dangled limply. She wasn't sure if he was breathing. Or if his heart was beating. She brought her ear close to his mouth, trying to detect any breathing. But she couldn't feel anything.

The truck driver came over and stood beside her, obviously shaken. He clearly didn't know what to do, what to say. He just stood there, trembling all over.

She carried her child into the house, laid him on the bed, and called for an ambulance. She surprised herself how calm she sounded. She gave her correct address, telling them a five-year-old child had been a victim of a traffic accident in front of their house and they needed an ambulance immediately. The ambulance and the police soon arrived, sirens wailing, the ambulance carrying the boy and his mother to the hospital. The two police officers and the truck driver remained behind for an on-site investigation.

As she nestled close to her child in the ambulance she wondered whether she'd turned the gas off at their house. She couldn't recall. She remembered nothing. *That doesn't matter now*, she told herself, shaking her head a few times. Yet she couldn't shake the thought of the gas stove still on. That might have been necessary for her at this moment, to keep thinking about whether she'd shut off the gas as she sat next to her unconscious child. To keep from losing her mind.

Her son was in a coma for three days at the hospital, then his heart and lungs gave out, and he quietly took his last breaths. The cause of death was a blow to the back of his head that had struck the curb when the truck had hit him and sent him flying. It was a completely quiet passing, with no bleeding or visible changes to his body. Death came suddenly, before one could think about it. He must not have felt any pain. Mercifully, one might say. Though that was no consolation to his parents.

According to the statement by the truck driver, when the child on the red bicycle had suddenly dashed out from the gate into the road, he'd slammed on his brakes and turned to the right, but not in time, and the child collided with the end of the bumper. The road was a fairly narrow one in town, so the driver wasn't driving that fast, within the speed limit, but since the boy had suddenly run in front of him, there was nothing he could do. But I am so, so sorry, he said. I have a small child myself, and I can feel the pain his parents must be going through. I don't know how I can ever apologize for this.

The police investigated the skid marks on the asphalt, which backed up the driver's statement that he hadn't been speeding.

Involuntary manslaughter charges were filed against him, though it was hard to fault him for being careless. For some reason the child must have raced out the gate onto the road, his head full, perhaps, of some childlike notion. Or perhaps he wasn't used to the bike yet and lost control. There wasn't much traffic in front of their house, but still it was dangerous, and he'd been strictly warned to stay behind their fence and never venture out onto the road. And the gate must have been shut and latched.

The parents' grief was, of course, unimaginable. The child they poured their love into had abruptly vanished. That newborn, healthy life—that warmth and smile and joyful voice—had been snuffed out in an instant, like a tiny flame in a sudden gust of wind. Their despair and sense of loss was awful, and hopeless. When she learned that her child had died the mother went into shock and collapsed, unconscious, and afterward cried her eyes out for days on end.

Mr. Koyasu's grief was no less profound than his wife's. At the same time, he felt a strong need to protect his wife. She sunk deep into shock, almost completely losing her will to live, and he knew he had to somehow save her. Of course, she'd never again be like she was (he knew that was impossible), but he had to try to pull her up onto something close to level ground. She couldn't mourn her child's death forever. Life, after all, was a long, drawn-out struggle. No matter how much sadness there was, how much loss and despair awaited us, you had to steadily move forward, step by painful step.

Day after day he consoled her, encouraged her. Stayed close to her, speaking as many comforting words as he could think of. He loved her deeply, and wanted her to recover, if only a little. Wanted her to find the will to go on living and once more show him that bright smiling face he so missed.

But as much as he tried, she remained sunk in a deep, dark abyss. It was as if she were shut away in her room, the door bolted from the inside. From morning till night she barely said a word to anyone. Whatever he said, whatever he tried to say, the hard shell around her rejected his words. When he tried to touch her, she cringed, as if some unknown man were groping her. This made him desperately sad. It was like a double punch of sadness—first to lose his precious child, and now to be on the verge of losing his beloved wife.

He grew anxious, afraid not just that she was lost in a profound sadness but that the overwhelming shock had made something inside her snap, mentally. Yet he didn't know how to handle this. He didn't think he could easily find a doctor who could resolve her problems, the sadness that created profound issues arising deep within her psyche. As her life's companion, it was up to him to heal these raw emotional wounds. There was no other way. No matter how much time it took, or how much extraordinary effort.

After a month of almost absolute silence, one day, out of the blue, as if a spell had been broken, she suddenly burst into speech. And once she started speaking, she didn't stop.

"I really should have bought him a dog like he wanted," she said quietly, her voice monotone. "If we had bought the dog then we wouldn't have gotten him that bicycle. I told him we couldn't get a dog because I'm allergic to the fur. So we gave him a bike. That little red bicycle as his birthday present. But don't you think he was too young for a bike? We should have gotten him a bike after he started elementary school. And because of that, because of me, he lost his life. If I hadn't been allergic to dog fur, he wouldn't have been in that accident and wouldn't have died. He would still be with us, alive and happy."

That's not true, he said, doing his best to convince her. You're not to blame at all. That's mixing up cause and result. I was the one who suggested we get him a bike if we couldn't get a dog. It was *my* idea. Everything just happened that way. It's nobody's fault. No one's to blame. It was simply a series of unfortunate events. You can only mark it down to fate. Going over all the little details at this point won't bring him back.

But she heard nothing of what he said. It didn't register at all. She just kept on repeating her claims, like an endless tape loop.

If we had bought him a dog then, like he'd wanted, we wouldn't have gotten the bike, and then he wouldn't have died . . . and on and on.

She also fixated on the fact that she'd run out of salt while cooking. I should have realized I'd run out, I should have known where I'd put the new salt I'd bought. It's all on me for being careless. Because I ran out of salt I was distracted and didn't notice he'd stopped singing. Just because the saltshaker was empty as I was making a stir-fry. Something as stupid as that snatched my child's precious life away forever. And then I couldn't even remember if I'd shut off the gas.

Even if you hadn't run out of salt that wouldn't have prevented the accident, and the gas was most definitely turned off. No matter how many times Mr. Koyasu explained this to her, she wasn't convinced. Whatever he said, she droned on endlessly about the dog and the bike, the salt and the gas. She wasn't addressing anyone but herself. These were but empty echoes ringing out in the dark cave that had arisen within her, and Mr. Koyasu could find no space to intervene.

He felt that everything was headed in an awful direction and nothing he did could change it. He had no idea what he should do, how he should approach her. He was at a complete loss. His wife went on forever repeating the same things, completely ignoring and spurning any words of consolation or encouragement. And she refused to let him lay a finger on her. Her sleep was shallow, her waking self hazy and uncertain.

This requires time, Mr. Koyasu thought, steeling himself. This is a problem that only time will solve. People can't do anything about it. Sadly, though, time was not on his side.

Unprecedented heavy rains fell at the end of June. The river quickly swelled and was about to overflow its banks. The river that flowed outside town turned from a gentle stream into a raging muddy brown torrent, sweeping branches and trees downstream.

One morning during this time (it was a Sunday) when Mr. Koyasu woke up after six, he didn't see his wife beside him in bed. The rain was noisily lashing the eaves. Worried, he searched their house, but she was nowhere to be found. He yelled out her name, but there was no response. He had a bad feeling. His heart thumped in his chest. He had no idea why she would leave the house this early, in this driving rain. Since she wasn't inside the house, he could only think she'd gone out.

He put on a raincoat and rain hat and went outside. Wind from the mountains tore through the trees. He searched in the garden, checked the perimeter of the house, but didn't see her. He reluctantly went back inside to wait for her to return. Even if she'd gone out for some reason, she couldn't walk around in this weather for long, in a storm this terrible.

But she didn't return. He went into their bedroom and pulled back the covers of her bed just to check. And instead of her, he found two long scallions lying there. White, thick, splendid scallions. She must have placed them there. He was, naturally, shocked, and frightened by the sight.

Why scallions?

Something was weird, something was wrong. By putting two scallions in her bed, what was she trying to convey to her husband? (This was, unmistakably, some kind of message for him.) As he stared at this uncanny scene, Mr. Koyasu felt chilled to the core.

He immediately called the police. The officer who answered happened to be an old friend of his. Mr. Koyasu summarized the events. When I woke up this morning, I couldn't find her anywhere. I don't know where she went. I can't think of a single reason why she'd go out in this terrible wind and rain at six o'clock in the morning. He didn't venture to mention the two scallions left in the bed. The officer wouldn't understand, and it would only cause more confusion.

"I know you're worried, Mr. Koyasu," the police officer said, "but your wife must have had some reason for going out. I'm sure she'll be back before long. Let's wait a bit more and see."

Unless there was some obvious crime, the police wouldn't get involved for something like this, Mr. Koyasu realized, so he gave up, thanked the officer, and hung up. There must be plenty of wives who, after a fight with their husbands, blew up and left. In most cases they'd cool off, they'd come back home. The police couldn't very well get drawn into each and every marital rift.

But even after eight she hadn't returned. Mr. Koyasu threw on his raincoat and rain hat again and ventured out into the rain. Lashed by gusts of wind, he wandered aimlessly through the neighborhood, but his wife was nowhere to be seen. No one else was walking this early on a Sunday morning, in this weather. Not a single bird was flying. Every living creature had taken cover, it seemed, waiting for the storm to pass. He gave up and went back home, sat down on the sofa in the living room, and, glancing at his watch every five minutes, waited for his wife to return until noon. But she didn't come back.

I'll never see her again, Mr. Koyasu thought. Or, rather, he *knew* it. Instinct told him so. She'd gone somewhere he couldn't reach. Most likely forever.

"Her body was discovered at two o'clock that same afternoon when a fireman went to check the level of the river," Mrs. Soeda said. "She'd apparently thrown herself into the river. She had been swept over a mile downstream from her house and washed up there, entangled in driftwood at a bridge retainer. Her legs were tied up with nylon rope. She must have tied them together herself before jumping into the river. She'd been bashed around as she was swept downriver, and her body was covered with bruises and cuts. The autopsy showed she'd swallowed sleeping pills, though not a fatal dose. A mild sleeping sedative a doctor had prescribed. She'd gathered all the sleeping pills she could find, bound her legs, and then she must have leaped off the bridge near their house and into the river. The cause of death was drowning, and the police determined later that it was suicide. Everyone around her knew she'd been deeply depressed ever since her child's accident, and there was no doubt whatsoever it was suicide."

"The river she jumped into is the one that flows in front of my house?"

"That's right. As you know, it's usually a beautiful, gentle river that doesn't overflow, but once there's a heavy rain, water from the mountains nearby rushes down, quickly filling it up, and it becomes dangerous and raging. Like an angel transforming in an instant into a devil . . . Occasionally a child will be swept away by the river. Unless you've seen it with your own eyes you can't imagine how dangerous the current can get."

She was right—I couldn't imagine the river that violent. Normally it was so peaceful looking, quiet and pretty.

"Everybody in town's hearts went out to Mr. Koyasu," Mrs. Soeda continued. "He and his wife got along so well and seemed such a happy family—no, they didn't just look it, they actually *were* the epitome of a happy family. A beautiful young wife, a healthy, cute little boy, financially all set. Nothing clouding their lives. But that bright, ideal family fell to pieces in an instant. Mr. Koyasu lost his son, and then only a month and a half later, he lost his wife. Neither was his fault. It was nobody's fault. A pitiless fate snatched them from him and carried them away. Leaving him behind, all alone."

Mrs. Soeda stopped at this point and was silent for a time.

"How many years ago was this?" I asked a while later, to break the silence. "When his boy and his wife died?"

"Thirty years ago. Mr. Koyasu was forty-five then. And he remained single until he passed away. Naturally there were attempts to get him to remarry, but he turned them all down and went on living by himself. He did all the housework and never even hired a cleaning woman. He ran the family sake brewery competently enough, but never showed much enthusiasm. He just kept a calm eye on the whole operation to make sure that nothing upset the status quo. He avoided associating with others as much as he could. Other than going back and forth between his home and the company, which was nearby, he rarely ventured out. On the monthly anniversary of his wife's and son's deaths—the days of the month they passed away—he never failed to visit their graves, but other than that, the townspeople never caught sight of him. No matter how much time passed, he never recovered from his child's and his wife's deaths."

His bedridden father finally passed away, and Mr. Koyasu decided to sell the family business to a large corporation that had been, for some time, intent on purchasing it. The family brewery didn't go in for mass production, but since it had steadily maintained its high-quality sake over four generations, its brand was nationally known and they were able to sell the brand and the entire facility for a high price. Workers who had been there for years were given a generous retirement package, and Mr. Koyasu divided the proceeds from the sale fairly, according to how much stock each family member owned. He was well liked and trusted (and everyone was aware how his personality made running a business an awkward fit), so no one raised an objection to the negotiations. After all these payouts were subtracted from the sale, Mr. Koyasu was left with the remainder of the profits, as well as his parents' home, and the long-unused brewery.

"He was finally released from the family business he never enjoyed, and now, as a free man, he could live a semiretired life," Mrs. Soeda went on. "He wasn't all that old, but he led a quiet life shut away in his home. He had a few cats and spent his days almost entirely reading books. For exercise, he went for walks in the mountains. He'd see someone he knew on the street and would smile and say hello, but never seemed to want to go any further. And then his actions became somewhat eccentric."

Eccentric—the word surprised me, and I couldn't help but frown.

"*Eccentric* perhaps is too strong a term," she added, seeing my reaction and seemingly rethinking her choice of words. "If this were the big city it might be just put down as *a little odd*, but this is a small, conservative town and it struck people as bizarre. First of all, he started wearing that beret that his niece had bought him as a souvenir. Mr. Koyasu had apparently asked her to get one for him. After that, he never left the house without it. That in itself might not qualify as eccentric—how should I put it?—but when Mr. Koyasu had that beret on there was an *unusual feeling* about him. There's no stylish person in this town who'd wear one, so he definitely stood out, but it went beyond that. There was an air around him, I'd venture to call—*alien*. It was as if by wearing that beret he was no longer Mr. Koyasu but a different being altogether . . . I know it's an odd way of putting it, but do you see what I'm getting at?"

I didn't offer a response. I just tilted my head a fraction as if to show I wasn't quite sure. Yet I did have a sense of what she was trying to convey, vague though it might be.

One thing was true—for someone with Mr. Koyasu's appearance, a beret was an unusual look. Sometimes it seemed less like he was wearing the beret than the beret was wearing *him*. But he didn't seem to mind that at all. He seemed to welcome it— as if wishing that he himself had disappeared, leaving the beret behind.

"And then, on top of this, the pièce de résistance, you might say, the skirt made its appearance. It's unclear what led up to this, but one day Mr. Koyasu started wearing a skirt instead of trousers. Or, I should say, he *only ever wore a skirt*, never trousers. Talk about shocking the townspeople. There's no rule, of course, that men can't wear skirts, and it's entirely up to them. The Scots, as you know, wear kilts. Even the Crown Prince of England wears one from time to time. A man wearing a skirt doesn't harm anybody, doesn't cause any trouble. There's no reason to make them stop wearing them. But in this little town for Mr. Koyasu—a prominent figure in town, a man in his sixties, intelligent, with a certain social standing—to walk around town, bold as brass, in a skirt was astounding.

"No one knew why he felt he had to wear a skirt. Rumors flew that he was losing it mentally, that he wasn't all there. But no one asked him straight out, *Why are you wearing a skirt, and not pants, around town?* He was, after all, a wealthy man who contributed economically to the town. He was cultured, a calm and amiable man, well liked. You couldn't very well confront a person like that with such a rude, direct question. So people simply remained puzzled, felt awkward about it. Wondering what was going on with him.

"Of course, everyone could well imagine that the deep hurt of losing his son and wife, one right after the other, was the main cause of his eccentricity. Since up till then he'd always dressed normally and lived a normal life. But the strange thing, one might say, is that after he started wearing this odd get-up, beret and skirt, his personality did an abrupt about-face, and he became much more cheerful than before. Like a window that's closed for a long time is thrown wide open, letting spring sunlight stream into a gloomy, damp room.

"He started leaving his house, strolling around town, greeting and talking to people he came across. This seemed to mark the end of his life as a recluse, reading books all the time. People in town welcomed the sudden transformation. They were relieved and pleased to see this change in him. If he grew more cheerful like this, more social, more able to hold a friendly conversation, then who cared if he dressed a little oddly? It didn't hurt anybody. People figured that the passage of time had eased the deep pain of losing the people he loved. And this was good news for everyone. This is what everyone wanted to think—that time solved most problems. Even though this wasn't the case.

"So people in town came to accept Mr. Koyasu's eccentricities as his personal way of doing things that, though a bit deviating from the norm, were well within the boundaries of what was allowed. They were free expression of one's thoughts and beliefs, and were, so to speak, harmless quirks. Some people just pretended not to notice. They made sure, when they ran across him on the street, not to stare at his get-up, or look aside, either, and when children pointed at him, yelled that he looked like a freak, and followed after him, they scolded them and made them stop.

"All the same, children were drawn to him. He'd be simply walking down the street and, like the tale of the Pied Piper, would enchant little children. And Mr. Koyasu himself seemed to enjoy this. When children followed after him, dazed looks on their faces, all he did was smile. Possibly remembering his own child he'd lost in the accident. Not that he ever spoke to the children or played with them."

"In the end, the Pied Piper took all the children away from the town. Isn't that what happened?"

"That's right," Mrs. Soeda said, a hint of a smile playing about her lips. "The citizens of Hamelin hired this flute player to get rid of the rats in town, but after he drove them out, they didn't pay him what they'd promised, and as revenge he used the sound of a magic flute to gather all the town's children and lead them off to a deep cave. The only child left was a little lame boy who couldn't join the procession. So in the end, the flute-playing man became a kind of ominous magical being. Mr. Koyasu never intended to harm anyone, of course. There was never a hint of that. All he did was honestly, sincerely, follow his own feelings, as he understood them. He had no ulterior motives or point to prove. He didn't care if anyone was disgusted with the way he looked, or if they ridiculed him, or if someone found it enchanting.

"With his change in dress, his body, too, underwent a transformation. He'd always had a slim build. (At least that's what I've heard. When I first met him he wasn't thin anymore.) After he began wearing the navy-blue beret, and grew a goatee, and started wearing a skirt, he put on more weight, and got obese. Nice and round. As if with the change in dress he took on a new personality."

"Maybe he really did want to change his personality," I said. "In order to make a break with his life up till then, and to put those painful memories behind him."

Mrs. Soeda nodded. "You might be right. Very soon after that he actually did begin a brand-new life. When he turned sixty-five he donated the old, unused brewery to the town so it could be used as a library. This was about ten years ago. Around the time I happened to move to town.

"The public library operated by the town was deteriorating, and had been an issue for some time, but they didn't have the financial resources to renovate the building. Mr. Koyasu was pained to see this, and he invested his own funds to drastically repair the old brewery and transform it into a library. He also donated his own extensive book collection. The brewery was an old wooden building, but it was sturdily built, with thick pillars and beams, and there were no structural issues. Repairs cost a considerable amount, and Mr. Koyasu paid for most of it himself. And then most of the salaries for the library staff, myself included, were paid from funds from the foundation that he established. As you know, the salaries aren't very high, and it's like we're half volunteers, but even so, running the library through the year takes a considerable amount of operating funds. We need to purchase new books, and utility bills aren't cheap. The town does provide a certain amount of subsidy, but it isn't that much.

"So in fact this library is Mr. Koyasu's own private library, but he doesn't want it to be viewed that way, so he put out a sign that says z** TOWN LIBRARY. In theory, the library is operated by a board of leading local citizens, but that's a formality. The board meets twice a year and there are never any questions or discussion over the accounts statement, which is basically rubber-stamped. Mr. Koyasu makes all the decisions, and no one ever objects. Since the library would never have come to be without his support and leadership.

"Maintaining the ideal library had long been a secret dream of Mr. Koyasu's. To create a special, comfortable spot, to gather lots of books, and to have many people freely read them—for Mr. Koyasu, that was the ideal world. Or microcosm, you should say. When he was young he'd longed to be a novelist, but after he gave up on that dream, and subsequently lost his wife and child, building this library became the sole remaining hope of this life.

"And Mr. Koyasu had no immediate family to whom he would leave his assets. No wife or child, his mother having passed away after his father, with only his younger sister left, but she'd married into a good family in Tokyo and had received her share of the proceeds from the sale of the company, with no desire to inherit anything beyond that. Nor did he have the desire to live a life of luxury—instead, he lived a surprisingly simple lifestyle. Most of the proceeds he received from the sale of the company went into starting the foundation, and then to remodel the library, where he could be in charge. In a sense, his long-held dream was fulfilled, and he built his own precious little world.

"Over the next decade, Mr. Koyasu passed the days in that microcosm, though we have no way of knowing how peaceful and fulfilling he found this period of his life. He always dealt with us calmly, cheerfully, but who knows what he was actually feeling inside.

"Naturally he loved this library, which no doubt became his purpose in life. Being in this library made him happy—that much is certain. But whether this left him satisfied, personally I'd have to think otherwise. I have to think there was a deep hollow inside his heart. An emptiness that nothing could fill."

Mrs. Soeda fell silent, lost in thought.

I asked her, "Have you been working here since the library was established?"

"Yes, I've been here nearly ten years. When we moved to this town, I heard that the new town library was looking for a librarian and I applied right away. Before I got married, I worked as a librarian in a university library and had the certification, but most of all, I really enjoyed that kind of work. I love books and am a kind of precise, methodical person. Working in a library suits me well. It was right here in this room, the head librarian's office, where Mr. Koyasu interviewed me. And he seemed to like me. And ever since, I've worked under him. From the beginning I've been the only full-time staff member. It's a pleasant place to work, and for a small town like this there are actually a lot of patrons, so it's rewarding work. People who live where the winters are long and severe tend to read a lot. In many ways it's been a rich and fulfilling ten years."

"Yet about a year ago Mr. Koyasu passed away."

Mrs. Soeda quietly nodded. "Yes, it was quite unfortunate, but one day, quite suddenly, Mr. Koyasu passed away."

"IT WAS ALL SO SUDDEN, so out of the blue," Mrs. Soeda said. "Mr. Koyasu always seemed so healthy, and though he was seventy-five, he never complained about any ailments. He did tend to be a bit overweight, but he watched what he ate and got regular medical checkups at the hospital in Koriyama. He also went on regular walks through the nearby hills to strengthen his legs. So at first I just couldn't believe it, that he'd had a heart attack while walking there and died on the spot. Lots of people were shocked when they heard the news, and so was I. I felt devastated, like a thick pillar in a building had been snatched clean away.

"I liked Mr. Koyasu on a personal level, and respected him. I worried about him living all alone. Maybe it wasn't my place, but I felt he should have a family again. What I mean is, he was the kind of person who deserved to have a peaceful, warm family. Surrounded by a close family, living a tender, loving life. On a personal and social level, he more than deserved that. So I found it terribly sad that he was all alone at the end. I think he never recovered from the trauma of losing his wife and child. Even if no one noticed it, he still carried around that heavy burden.

"At the same time, I was quite anxious about how the library would carry on without him. And of course for me personally, I was concerned about possibly losing my job. But even more than that, this charming little library might fall under the purview of someone totally unsuited for it, and head in the wrong direction. Or be led by someone who didn't really care about it and therefore lose its unique vitality, winding up abandoned. It really bothered me to think that. Even if I lost my job here, we'd be able to get along on my husband's salary. But when I thought that this wonderful library might never be the way it is again, I simply couldn't stand it.

"Something happened after Mr. Koyasu's funeral, after his bones were laid to rest in the temple cemetery in town. As I was saying, as I was worrying over the future of the library, one night

I had a dream in which Mr. Koyasu appeared. A long, vivid dream. So real that even after I woke up, I thought it had occurred. Maybe it really wasn't a dream. At the time, though, that's the only way I could think of it.

"In the dream Mr. Koyasu was dressed as usual, in his good old navy-blue beret and checked wraparound skirt. He was seated near me on the bed and gazing steadily at my face. As if he'd been quietly waiting there, patiently, for me to wake up.

"I sensed something, woke up with a start, and when I saw it was Mr. Koyasu right in front of me, I hurriedly started to get up, but he gently raised his hands to motion me to stop.

"'It's alright, you can stay in bed,' he said in a kind voice. So I remained lying down.

"'I came here because I have something I need to talk with you about,' Mr. Koyasu said. 'As you know, I'm dead, but I'm not creepy, believe me. I'm the same Koyasu you know so well. So don't be afraid. Alright?'

"I silently nodded. Even with Mr. Koyasu, who should have been dead, in front of me, I wasn't afraid, really. Since at that moment I had no doubts whatsoever that *this is a dream*."

"I've decided to appear like this before you, though I'm dead, because there are several important matters I need to convey to you," Mr. Koyasu said, sounding apologetic. "Matters related to the library. I know it's quite rude to do so late at night while you're resting, and I sincerely apologize. But it was necessary for me to barge in on your sleep."

Mrs. Soeda shook her head. "No, please don't worry about that. If it's something important, then don't hesitate. I'll be happy to hear what you have to say."

"Thank you. I know that you, like me, are concerned about the library's future. I know very well how you feel. It's only natural to be worried. But, Mrs. Soeda, there's nothing to be worried about. I have, in my own way, taken some steps in this regard. When you get to this age, you're always wondering how much longer you'll be here. In my office there's a small safe in the bottom drawer of my desk. It opens with a three-digit code, which is 491. Tomorrow morning after you get to work, go and open that safe, please. Inside are several important documents, including the title to the land and a will with disposition of assets. I'd like you to get in touch with my lawyer, Mr. Inoue—you know him, of course—and hand over the documents directly to him. He will take all the necessary steps.

"There's also a blue envelope with instructions about managing the library. In the envelope there's also a letter regarding the process of selecting my successor as head librarian. With Mr. Inoue present I'd like you to read it at a meeting of the board. Can you do all this?"

"So you want me to assemble the foundation board and, in Mr. Inoue's presence, open the blue envelope and read it aloud?"

"Yes, that's correct," Mr. Koyasu said, and nodded emphatically. "The board members gather, Mr. Inoue is present, and you read the directive. That's the gist of it."

"I understand. I'll do that. The safe's combination was 491, I believe?"

"Yes, that's it. That's all I wanted to tell you today. I'm truly sorry to have bothered you so late at night. But this is a very important matter to me."

"No, please don't say that. I can't tell you how happy I am to see you again, and talk with you, no matter the circumstances."

"As the need arises, I will appear to you again," Mr. Koyasu said. "Not in your dreams like this, while you're resting, but during the day, in real life. I think I can talk face-to-face as a—how should I put it?—sort of ghost. You'll be the only one who can see me then, the only one who'll be able to hear my voice. Will that make you uncomfortable, Mrs. Soeda, or make you afraid, for me to appear like this? If it does, I'll find a different way."

"No, that's perfectly fine with me. Please, appear whenever you want to. I would never be afraid of you. To receive guidance from you is, for me, and for the library, something I'm truly thankful for."

"Thank you for saying that. I feel relieved. Ah, well, this goes without saying, but please, not a word to anyone about this. That

I appear to you like this, though I'm supposedly dead. Let's keep this as our little secret."

"Of course. I won't tell a soul."

And Mr. Koyasu disappeared from her dreams. But Mrs. Soeda couldn't sleep. She lay wide awake under the covers, repeating to herself what Mr. Koyasu had said as she waited for dawn.

I asked Mrs. Soeda, "I assume you then went to this head librarian's office and checked the drawer?"

"First thing the next morning I came here and opened the safe."

I opened the desk drawer and saw there was a black safe there. The door wasn't locked, and nothing was inside.

"I unlocked the safe with the code he'd told me, and everything was there inside just like he said. So yes, that wasn't a dream. Mr. Koyasu had truly returned to our world. Even after he died, keeping the library running smoothly was an urgent mission for him. He might have been a ghost, but I wasn't frightened a bit. Nothing could make me happier than seeing him, whatever form he took. And that allowed us to keep this wonderful library going the way it has been, so the only feeling I have is one of gratitude."

"And then you called the board together and read to them the directives Mr. Koyasu left behind."

"Yes, I did what he asked me to. At the board meeting Mr. Inoue first explained the distribution of Mr. Koyasu's remaining assets. His will stipulated that his personal cash, stocks, real estate, and life insurance be donated in their entirety to the foundation. The foundation would operate the library. In other words, losing Mr. Koyasu was an immeasurable loss to us all, though it led to a substantial financial contribution toward the operation of the library.

"Next the letter addressed to the board was read, which was mainly concerned with specific directions regarding the library's operations. There was an itemized list of detailed directives. Regarding the head librarian position, it said that when he passed away, we should place ads in newspapers to seek applicants. And that I, Soeda, was to be in sole charge of choosing the person.

"As I read this aloud, I was taken by surprise, wondering why such an important task should be assigned to me, a mere librarian. I expect the board members were just as surprised, but since it was all laid out nice and clear in the letter, they had to go along. Naturally the board would need to approve anyone I selected, but that was a formality."

"So you did as Mr. Koyasu directed, placed ads in newspapers, and I applied, and you did the choosing, and I ended up hired. That's how it happened, right?"

"Yes, that's correct. At least ostensibly. But actually, to be precise about it, that's not true. The one who chose you from all the many applicants from around the country was actually Mr. Koyasu. He chose you, and I reported the result to the board as if I'd been the one who made the selection. Can't have a dead person choose his own successor, so I, still alive, stood in his place. Like a ventriloquist's dummy who just moves his mouth and does what he's told. And the board rubber-stamped this and you were appointed head librarian.

"My only role was to convey Mr. Koyasu's decision to the board. As he'd directed ahead of time, I placed the pile of CVs and accompanying letters of applicants on the desk here in the head librarian's office. Somehow when I wasn't there, he looked through them and selected you. And one day he appeared before me and said this person was to be the head librarian. I had no reason to oppose it. It seemed that while he was still alive Mr. Koyasu had a premonition of his impending death. And he must have deeply considered who his successor would be. Which is why he carefully prepared that directive in advance."

"But why did it have to be me, I wonder? What made him single *me* out?"

Mrs. Soeda shook her head. "I really don't know. He didn't tell me the reason. I was just told by him to choose you."

"Has Mr. Koyasu's ghost appeared to you often?"

She shook her head slightly. "I wouldn't say often. Depending on the time, and when it's needed, he'll appear. He shows up, smiling, and tells me to come up to the head librarian's office on the second floor. I'm the only one who can see him, as I said, the only one who can hear his voice. So I act like nothing's up and quietly walk upstairs to the office, taking care that people don't notice. I shut the door and the two of us talk, just like when he was alive. Mr. Koyasu sits there at the desk, and I sit here, across from him. As always, his beret is on top of the desk. I find it hard then to think of him as someone who's dead. When I'm with him it's hard for me to tell the difference between life and death."

I knew exactly how she felt.

"I sort of figured that you and Mr. Koyasu were seeing each other and having friendly talks together. I sensed it. But I said I couldn't bring myself to tell you that the Mr. Koyasu you were seeing wasn't alive, but a ghost. And I figured there must be a reason why the two of you—one alive, the other dead—could have such a good relationship. Though I had no idea what it might be."

"It wasn't just with you, but for some reason when I was talking to others, too, no one mentioned that Mr. Koyasu had passed away. I should have heard, even one time, something like 'Yes, the late Mr. Koyasu . . . ' Why is that?"

Mrs. Soeda shook her head again. "I really don't know. Maybe some special, invisible powers at work."

I looked around the room. Wondering if Mr. Koyasu was here, somewhere. Wondering if indeed some special, invisible power was at work. But all that was there was the still, chilly afternoon air.

"Maybe other people have sensed it too, a bit," I said. "That Mr. Koyasu is not yet truly dead. For instance, even if they can't see him, they have a feeling, a physical sensation, that he's present in the library."

"That could be true," Mrs. Soeda said, as if it were all quite natural.

MR. KOYASU—or his soul, maybe I should say—didn't appear to me for a while after that. I went about my work as head librarian every day, ensconced in my subterranean room. Occasionally I'd look in on the reading room, speak with Mrs. Soeda or the other women working there, observe the patrons reading magazines and books, say a quick hello if I ran across someone I knew, but most of my time was spent in front of the warm woodstove, working alone on administrative tasks at my little desk.

Other than all the day-to-day tasks, the main job I assigned myself was classifying and cataloging our newly purchased books that had not yet been organized. Because of Mr. Koyasu's firm rejection of computerization (this policy, with the strong support of the staff, continued even after his passing), the work was time-consuming and difficult. Instead of a keyboard I used a ballpoint pen, something I wasn't used to, which left my right hand achy. For all that, it was refreshing working in an office without computers, a strange feeling of slippage, as if I'd suddenly wandered into a different world.

At the same time, I was given the duty to revise, in stages, the library's management system. Since this was, from the start, like Mr. Koyasu's own private library, he decided everything at his discretion, and no one ever questioned this. But now, without him, things couldn't go on so easily. It was necessary to manage the library in a way that, to some extent, reassured everyone else. And coming up with this new system was tasked mainly to me, and it wasn't, no matter how you looked at it, a simple job. For one thing, I was still a newcomer (in many matters I had to rely on Mrs. Soeda's assistance), and secondly, I've never been very adept at those kinds of practical tasks.

As I went about this detailed work, day after day, I reviewed my long conversation that day with Mrs. Soeda, writing down a bullet-point memo so I didn't overlook anything or accidentally forget something. And as I reread the memo I mulled over the main points.

There was a lot I still didn't understand. Countless things, actually.

As Mrs. Soeda mentioned, had Mr. Koyasu been aware that he was about to die? Was it precisely because he had a premonition of this that he'd left behind the will in his desk drawer, and directed that a nationwide search be done for a new head librarian? Had he already made plans so he could (while already dead) choose his successor? Was it all foreseen and planned out ahead of time?

Was it possible he'd even known that I would apply for the job?

So many unknowns. I stared at the memo and sighed. The logical order was clearly all jumbled. The context behind cause and effect wasn't clear. When I met Mr. Koyasu before in this little room he'd told me, "You have *those qualifications*, since you lost your shadow once." I don't recall his exact words, but it was something along those lines. Those words sounded ominous, and shook me.

Qualifications? I asked myself. What sort of qualifications?

In the dim subterranean room I gazed at the dancing flames in the woodstove, waiting for Mr. Koyasu's ghost to make an appearance. I had several things I needed to ask him.

Something had led me here. I'd come here guided by *something*. That much was certain. Yet I couldn't decipher the meaning behind it. What was this *something*, anyway? And what meaning, or purpose, lay behind me being led here? That's what I wanted to ask him. Though I had no idea if I'd get an answer.

No matter how long I waited, though, Mr. Koyasu—his soul—didn't appear to me. No phone rang for me.

When a dead person—now an intangible soul—desired to, or perhaps was driven to, appear before someone in some kind of ghostlike form, was it able to do so whenever it wished, via its own free will, its own power? Or was it impossible, without using some outside force, or aid from some higher being? (What that being was I had no idea, though.)

Naturally, I had no way of knowing. Before meeting Mr. Koyasu, I'd never seen anything like a ghost, even once (at least I think so; maybe I did, but just didn't notice), let alone talk with a dead person. What was the process by which a ghost became a ghost? How did it get the qualifications to be one? (It's my own personal conjecture, but I don't think *all* the dead can become ghosts.) I just couldn't figure this out, no matter how much I thought about it. This wasn't the type of problem that logical thinking would solve.

First of all, what's a soul? If there is such a thing as a soul, then my impression of it was of some vague, formless, invisible thing floating around in the air. But that's just a preconceived notion on my part. A stereotype, akin to picturing God as some old man with white hair, a beard, and a staff, dressed all in white.

Mr. Koyasu's soul possessed a consciousness and operated according to it. There was no doubt about it. I remember him quoting someone who said that *Consciousness is the brain's self-awareness of its own physical state.* And he had fundamental doubts about a soul without a brain (himself, in other words) possessing a consciousness, as he did, and operating based on it. Confusing, you could say. The soul of a dead person couldn't even understand the origins of the soul. So how was a living person like myself supposed to?

All I could do—me, with my fragile physical body and imperfect mental powers, a worthless being shackled to the present world— was simply wait patiently for Mr. Koyasu's ghost to appear. This was out of my hands and dependent on his circumstances, what suited him. In that square, silent subterranean room, tossing logs into the old wood-burning stove.

But Mr. Koyasu didn't show up. A week had passed since Mrs. Soeda and I had spoken. In that time winter had deepened, day by day, in that town surrounded by mountains. A sizable amount of snow had fallen, with over three feet piling up in one night. I'd spent most of my life on the warmer Pacific Ocean side of Japan, and I'd never seen this much snow. In the morning I took an aluminum shovel outside and shoveled away the snow from the gentle slope outside the entrance to the library. Shoveling snow, another first.

Other than Mrs. Soeda, the library consisted of part-time female staff, so apart from an old man we hired on a temp basis, I was the only man working there. It felt good to occasionally do something useful like this. The air was bitingly cold, but there was no wind, and it was a beautiful morning, the sky incredibly clear, not a single cloud to be seen. The clouds that had dumped all the snow had moved on elsewhere. Or, having made it snow as much as they could, simply vanished.

I hadn't done any physical work in ages, and it cleared my mind wonderfully. Sweat dampened my shirt, I took off my coat, and under the morning sunlight threw myself completely into the task, silently shoveling away the snow. The shrill cry of winter birds with yellow beaks rent the air. Snow that had piled up on the branches of the pine trees fell to the ground with a heavy, wet thump, like a person, exhausted, letting go. Under the eaves icicles nearly three feet long glistened sharply in the sun, like lethal weapons.

I quietly wished that snow would pile up even more. Then I wouldn't have to worry about the troublesome things around me or wonder about the nature of the soul, but just let my mind go blank and, snow shovel in hand, spend the whole day engaged in physical labor. That might be exactly the kind of life I was seeking now—though there was a limit, of course, to how much heavy labor my muscles could take.

As I scooped up the snow and placed it in the cart, I couldn't help but remember the unicorns dying of starvation and the cold. When dawn broke on winter days, a number of them could be found prone, on the ground of their paddock, blanketed in white snow. It was as though they had taken on the sins of others and died in their stead. Snow wasn't as deep in that town as it was here, yet it had fatal consequences.

As I stood there alone, surrounded by snow, gazing up at the bright blue sky, I didn't understand. Right now, at this moment, which world did I belong to?

Is this world inside the high brick wall? Or outside it?

On Monday, when the library was closed, I had Mrs. Soeda draw me a map, and I went to visit the cemetery where Mr. Koyasu's grave lay. I carried with me a small bouquet of flowers I'd bought at a florist's near the station.

As I walked down the nearly deserted street, I felt like I was no longer the person I am now. As if, for instance, I was seventeen on a clear holiday morning, on my way to see my girlfriend, bouquet in hand . . . It felt like that. A strange feeling, as if I'd strayed from present reality and wandered into a different time and place.

Or maybe I was just pretending to be myself, but really, I wasn't. The me looking back from a mirror might not really be me. Maybe it was someone else who looked just like me, and exactly copied my every movement. I couldn't help but feel that way.

The grave was outside the town, at the foothills of the mountains. I had to climb up sixty stone steps to reach the entrance to the temple. The remaining snow from a few days before had frozen hard, and the steps were slippery in spots.

The grave was on a gentle slope behind the temple, with the Koyasu family gravesite in a plot in the rear. A generous-sized plot, well cared for, speaking to how established and respected the Koyasu family was in the area. And there I found the resting place for Mr. and Mrs. Koyasu and their son.

As Mrs. Soeda had told me, the grave marker was new and large, and I spotted it easily even from afar. When Mr. Koyasu passed away, they probably had brought the bones of all three into this newly built grave. No doubt this is what Mr. Koyasu had wanted above all—that with his passing, they were together once again. I was happy for him. (Perhaps he'd directed it be done this way before he died.)

The gravestone was simple, devoid of any ornamentation, and was smooth and flat, like the monolith in *2001: A Space Odyssey*. The stone it was carved from was obviously costly, and on it read, in straightforward writing, the three names:

TATSUYA KOYASU
MIRI KOYASU
SHIN KOYASU

There were no furigana alongside the Chinese characters to indicate how they were pronounced (I'd never seen a gravestone with furigana), but I was sure his wife's first name, 観理, was read Miri. I couldn't think of any other way to read it. *Miri Koyasu*— I quietly repeated it aloud a few times. The characters meant "to examine reason"—a deep name, to be sure. It was heartbreaking to think that a woman with that name had taken her own life.

Below each name was carved the year of their birth and of their death. The wife and child's year was the same, as they had left this world at nearly the same time. One struck by a truck in the road, the other drowning herself in a raging river. And it was many years later, the previous year, that Mr. Koyasu himself passed away. I stood in front of the gravestone for a long time contemplating those numbers. They themselves told a story. Sometimes numbers can be more eloquent than words.

There was no mistake about it—Mr. Koyasu was no longer a person in this world. The person I had sat across from and spoken with was, in fact, his ghost. Or his soul, taking on the appearance he had when alive. As I stood at his grave, I realized all over again how undeniable this was.

I offered the meager bouquet I'd brought in front of their grave, then stood there, eyes closed, and silently brought my hands together in prayer. Birds screeched sharply from a nearby grove of trees, winter birds I couldn't identify. And before I realized it, a tear had trickled down my cheek. A big tear with a definite warmth. It slowly trickled down to my chin, then plopped like a raindrop onto the ground. The next tear traced the same path. And even more followed. I hadn't cried this much in a long, long time. I couldn't even remember when. I'd forgotten that tears could be this warm.

Tears, like blood, were wrung from the same warm body.

I shook my head and had a thought—maybe Mr. Koyasu, from somewhere, was watching me here at his grave. It was an odd feeling. Normally we visit graves to mourn over people we were close to, and pray that they are at peace. But Mr. Koyasu still moved back and forth between the world of the dead and the world of the living. Probably in order to communicate something to someone, something he still had to tell. At a grave of someone like that, what should I pray for?

I descended the stone steps one by one, watching my footsteps so as not to slip, and returned to town.

I was walking through the shopping district near the station when I spotted a tiny coffee shop sandwiched in between a dry-goods store and a bedding store. I must have walked by it many times but for some reason never noticed it. Probably because I was, characteristically, lost in thought as I walked. (This happened a lot.) It was a bright shop, with a glass front, and from outside I could see that besides seats at the counter there were seats at three tables. I couldn't see any name for the coffee shop. On the door it just said COFFEE SHOP. A coffee shop without a name. It was morning on a weekday so there were no other customers, just a woman working alone behind the counter.

I pushed open the glass door and went inside. I needed to do something to warm up my chilled body after the visit to the gravesite. I sat in the last seat at the counter and ordered hot coffee and a blueberry muffin from the showcase.

The Dave Brubeck Quartet was playing from small speakers set near the ceiling, an old Cole Porter standard on low volume. Paul Desmond's alto sax solo, like a pure, flowing current. I knew the tune quite well but somehow couldn't come up with the title. Even untitled, it was the perfect music for a quiet morning on my day off. A beautiful, pleasant melody that had survived from the distant past. I sat there for a while, my mind a blank, simply taking it in.

The coffee was rich, nicely bitter, and hot, and the blueberry muffin soft and fresh. The coffee was served in a plain white mug. In ten minutes, the chill that had seeped into me was gone.

"Refills are half price," the woman at the counter told me.

"Thanks," I said. "This muffin is really good."

"Fresh out of the oven. From a bakery just down the street," she said.

I paid the bill, brushed away crumbs from my lap, and started to leave. The woman, who was wearing a gingham-checked apron, smiled at me. A warm smile, perfect for a clear winter morning. Not a by-the-book, ready-made smile.

The woman looked to be in her mid-thirties. Slim, and though not particularly beautiful, she nonetheless had a pleasant face. She wore little makeup. If she had wanted to look younger, it would have been easy enough, but she wasn't trying to. Which I found kind of nice.

"I was just at a grave, the grave of a person who still isn't *really* dead," I wanted to tell her. I wanted to tell someone—anyone— about it. But of course I couldn't.

THAT NIGHT I WENT TO BED as usual around ten but couldn't get to sleep. Which was unusual. Normally I fall asleep as soon as my head hits the pillow. I keep a book at my bedside but rarely open it. And most of the time I wake up naturally with the morning sunlight. I must have been born under a lucky star. I've heard more stories than I care to remember about people's insomnia.

But for some reason that night I couldn't get to sleep. My body craved sleep, but it just wouldn't come. I was probably too worked up.

In order to fill the (seemingly) blank space in my mind, I shut my eyes and thought about Mr. Koyasu's grave. The flat monolith-like gravestone at the Koyasu family plot. That smoothly glossy stone. The years noting when the three family members were born and died carved into it. And I thought about the little bouquet I'd brought, the sharp cry of winter birds flitting about the grove, the uneven stone steps of the temple, frozen in spots. I went through these images in my mind, in order, like a series of slides.

And as I did, suddenly—like a bird shooting up out of the grass at your feet—I remembered the title of that piece. The name of the Cole Porter tune that had been playing at the coffee shop near the station. "Just One of Those Things." And the melody played over and over in my mind, a spell plastered on the wall of my consciousness.

The electric clock next to my bed showed eleven thirty. I gave up on falling asleep, got out of bed, threw on a cardigan, switched on the gas stove, took milk out of the fridge, heated it up in a small pan, and drank it. I nibbled on a few cookies that had fresh ginger in them. I plopped down in my easy chair and opened the book I'd been reading but couldn't focus. Images and sounds randomly spun through my head, like messages that made no sense, sent from another world. Soundless bicycle messengers, faceless, left these messages on my doorstep, one after another, and then left.

I gave up, shut the book, and took a few deep breaths there in the easy chair. I focused my mind, expanding my lungs as much as I could, stretching my ribs. To replace every molecule of air within my body. To let go of the tension, even if a little. But none of it made any difference.

The still night, as always, lay all around me. At this time of night there was no traffic on the road outside. No dogs barking. Literally not a sound—other than the endless music on a tape loop in my head.

I needed to get to sleep, but probably nothing I did was going to make that happen. Whiskey or brandy weren't going to help. I was well aware of this. Tonight something was preventing me from getting to sleep. *Something* . . .

I decided to take off my pajamas and put on the warmest clothes I had. I threw on a duffel coat on top of a thick sweater, wrapped a cashmere scarf around my neck, tugged on a wool ski hat and lined gloves. And then I went outside. I couldn't stand it anymore— sitting there, unable to sleep, glancing at my watch every five minutes. Better to wander around in the cold outside.

Once outside, I realized how windy it was. The gentle warmth of the daytime had vanished, the sky now blanketed with a thick layer of clouds. No moon or stars visible, only the sporadic streetlights coldly illuminating the deserted street. Gusts of wind coming down off the mountains whipped noisily through the bare branches of the trees. A cold, damp wind. Like it might snow at any moment.

With no particular destination in mind, I wandered down the path along the river, my breath white. My heavy snow boots trod on the gravel, making an unnaturally loud crunch. The river was half covered in ice, but even so the sound of the flowing water reached me clearly. It was a piercingly cold night, but I rather welcomed the cold. It reached down into my core, squeezing my whole body and numbing, at least for the moment, the aimless, hazy thoughts buzzing around in my head. The freezing air brought tears to my eyes but drove away the rambling melody ringing in my head. A virtue of the winters in the cold north, I suppose.

I thought of nothing as I walked along, my head a pleasant blank space. Or perhaps nothingness. The cold that presaged snow squeezed my consciousness hard, like an arm of steel, and took over. There was no room whatsoever for any feeling other than the cold to slip inside. And then I suddenly realized that my steps were taking me, on autopilot, in the direction of the library. As if the snow boots I had on had a will of their own, a will that was stronger than my own.

In my coat pocket was a bunch of keys to various rooms in the library. I selected the thickest one, unlocked the gate, and entered the library grounds. I walked up the gentle slope and unlocked the sliding door at the entrance. My watch showed twelve thirty. The library was, of course, completely dark and deserted, the only light the faint greenish glow of the emergency Exit sign on the wall.

Following that meager light, I edged forward, careful not to bump into anything, and located the flashlight we always kept on hand behind the counter. I shone the light at my feet and made my way deeper into the library. There was but one place I was heading for. The square subterranean room, of course, with its woodstove.

As I'd sensed deep down, sure enough Mr. Koyasu was already there, waiting for me.

The woodstove was quietly crackling away, the room cozily warm. Neither too cold nor too hot. The red flames licking at the old apple tree logs were neither too strong nor too weak. Mr. Koyasu, somehow predicting (or maybe knowing) exactly when I'd arrive, had warmed up the room for me. Like a smart host, making an important visitor feel welcome. The scent of apples wafted through the room, and I felt a hint of intimacy in the scene, an alert yet unintrusive intimacy.

"Well, welcome." Mr. Koyasu's round face smiled at me as I pushed open the door. "I've been expecting you."

Mr. Koyasu was dressed as usual. His navy-blue beret rested softly on the top of the desk. He wore the gray tweed jacket he'd worn for years, a checked wrapped skirt, thick black tights, and thin-soled tennis shoes. No coat in sight. I imagined he never left the building and walked around in the cold wind. So he had no need for snow boots or a coat.

"I'm glad to see you looking well," Mr. Koyasu said brightly, rubbing his hands together. "Please, take a seat."

I took off my heavy coat in front of the stove, and my scarf and gloves. I sat down in the wooden chair and asked Mr. Koyasu, "So you knew ahead of time that I'd be coming here?"

Mr. Koyasu tilted his head slightly.

"You probably noticed this, but I don't leave this library. What I mean is, I actually cannot leave—whether I take on the form of a person or not. But I had the feeling that you would be coming here tonight, so I made every effort to take on shape, and did my best to prepare to receive you."

"I don't know why, but I couldn't get to sleep. So I thought I'd take a little walk, put on warm clothes and left the house. And ended up here."

Mr. Koyasu nodded slowly. "That's right, you went to the temple cemetery this morning, and saw our grave, didn't you?"

"I'm not sure what to say about it, but I did sort of pay my respects at your grave. Maybe a little too presumptuous of me."

"No, no. Not at all," Mr. Koyasu said, smilingly shaking his head. "I'm very grateful to you for wanting to do that. And you apparently gave us a very nice bouquet as well."

"It's an impressive grave," I said. As I said it, it struck me how it was weird to be praising a dead person's grave to the person himself. "Did you choose that stone yourself?"

"I did. I chose it while I was still alive and paid for it all. I had them carve just our three names and the dates of our births and deaths. I explained to a stonemason I know well how I just wanted that carved on it and nothing else. And he did it exactly as I asked. That would be odd, too, to check myself on how my own headstone came out after I died."

Mr. Koyasu chuckled happily, and I smiled back.

"So in that grave," I said, "the three of you are together again, aren't you."

Mr. Koyasu shook his head slightly. "I understand why you'd think that way, but actually that's not the case. All that's inside the grave is the bones of the three of us, and there's no connection between the bones and the soul. Bones are bones, the soul is the soul—one material, the other immaterial. A soul that's lost a body vanishes in the end. And because of that, even though I'm dead and in the realm after death, I am all alone, just like when I was alive. My wife and child are nowhere to be found. The three names are simply carved on the gravestone, that's all. And this soul of mine, when the proper time has passed, will also vanish, and return to nothingness. The soul is a transitory state and nothing more, but nothingness is eternal. No—it transcends the expression *the eternal*."

I thought of what I should say in response, but nothing appropriate came to mind. But Mr. Koyasu remained quiet for such a long time I felt I had to say something.

"That must be really difficult."

"Indeed. Loneliness is extremely hard. Whether you're alive or dead, the wasting away, the pain is exactly the same. But even so I still have the strong, vivid memories of having loved someone with all my heart. A feeling that seeped into the palms of my hands and still remains. Whether you have that warmth or not makes all the difference in the way your soul remains after death."

"I think I can understand what you mean."

"You, too, loved someone deeply in the past and have strong memories of having loved. And you pursued that person's soul and traveled somewhere far, far away, and have now returned."

"So you knew all that about me?"

"I did. As I said before, I can immediately recognize people who have lost their shadows, even once. Of course you don't find many like that. Especially among people *still living*."

I silently watched the flames in the stove. Inside me it felt like time had grown stagnant, as if some obstacle were blocking its flow.

"You do know, don't you, how very difficult it is for a living person to go over there and return here?" Mr. Koyasu asked. "Going over there is hard enough, but returning here is next to impossible. Can't be done, usually."

"I have no idea how I made it back here," I admitted. "My shadow bid good-bye to me, leaped into a deep pool alone, and was swallowed into a terrifying subterranean waterway. He'd made up his mind to try to make it back to this side, despite the danger. I thought and thought about what I should do, and in the end, I chose to stay in the world over there—in that walled-in town. But the next time I woke up and looked around me, I was back here, in this world. And my shadow was my shadow once more. Like nothing had happened. Like I'd just had a long, vivid dream. But that was no dream. That I'm sure of. No matter who tries to convince me it was all a dream."

Mr. Koyasu, arms crossed, had shut his eyes, listening carefully to my story. I went on.

"I don't know why that happened. I decided, of my own free will, to remain behind in the world over there. But despite my desires, I returned here. As if I were shot back here by a powerful spring. I've thought this over very deeply, and the only thing I can conclude is that there was another will at work, one stronger than my own. I have no clue, though, what kind of will that is. Or the goal of it."

"Do you think that your very entry into the town was the work of that other will?"

"I think so," I said. "One day I woke from a deep sleep to find myself lying alone in a hole I'd never seen before. A hole right near the gate to that walled-in town. The Gatekeeper there found me and asked if I wanted to go inside the town. And I said I did. Someone, or some sort of will, had no doubt carried me to that hole. Though it was my own will that answered the Gatekeeper's question and decided to enter the town."

Mr. Koyasu thought about this for a while, and then slowly began to speak.

"I don't know either what that meant, or what that will intended. I am nothing more than an individual soul without substance. Death hasn't conferred on me any special insight.

"But it sounds to me like it was something you were hoping for. Your heart—in a place you're unaware of—longed for something, and that's why it happened. I know you might deny that. You said you were adamant about remaining behind in that mysterious town. But your real will wanted something else. Deep down in your heart, perhaps, you were actually hoping to leave that town and come back here, back to this side."

"So this will that transcends mine, more powerful than my own, was not something from outside, but was actually inside me?"

"Yes. This is all ignorant guesswork on my part, of course. But from what you've told me, that's the only conclusion I can draw. I think you must have entered that strange town of your own will, and returned to this side, too, through your own will. The spring that bounced you back is a special power that lies within you. The strong will in your heart was what made that tremendous leap back and forth possible. A realm beyond your own logic and reason."

"You know that, Mr. Koyasu?"

"No, it's all conjecture. You shouldn't count on it. But I have a gut feeling about things—though whether a soul after death even has a gut is questionable. And it's telling me that yes, that's very possible. Not that it could happen to just anybody. But it can happen, sometime, somewhere. As long as your will is strong enough, and your feelings are pure."

"I have a question for you," I said, after giving it some thought.

"Of course, please go ahead."

"You loved your late wife and child. Loved them deeply. Am I right?"

Mr. Koyasu nodded clearly again. "Yes, indeed I did. In my meager little life, I loved no one more than I loved the two of them. That is for sure."

"And you built a real family with them and cultivated that love as best you could. A love that was steady and rewarding."

"It might sound like bragging, but you're absolutely right. Not that everything was perfect in our humble little family. We had our share of problems. But apart from trivial things, it was a love that was rich, and rewarding."

"That's truly wonderful. My case, sadly, wasn't like that. I just happened to meet her back when I was sixteen and fell in love. Typical of a sixteen-year-old boy. And happily she came to love me too. She was a year younger. We had many dates, held hands, kissed. It was amazing, like a dream. But that's all that happened. We never came together physically, never slept or lived together. And honestly I didn't know what kind of person she truly was. She talked about all kinds of things about herself, but these were just things she said. I had no way of telling if they were objectively true.

"I was still sixteen, seventeen at the time and naturally didn't understand the world, or myself. But I was so intensely attracted to her, she was all I could think of. A pure love, yet immature, no matter how you look at it. Certainly not the kind of mature, adult love you had, Mr. Koyasu. It wasn't validated over time. Our love encountered no real obstacles, and we were just teenagers sweetly playing at love, that's all. Like a temporary lightheadedness. And nearly thirty years have already passed since then.

"One day she vanished, without a word of farewell, without even a hint that she was leaving. And I've never seen her since. She never got in touch. And now here I am, edging into middle age. Is it really appropriate for a person like that to chase after the love he lost as a boy and shuttle back and forth between this world and the world on the other side?"

Mr. Koyasu—or his soul—sighed deeply, arms still crossed. "There's one thing I'd like to ask you," he finally said.

"Please ask anything you want."

"Have you ever loved anyone else as much as you loved that girl? Had someone who was that precious to you?"

I gave it some thought, though I really didn't need to. "I've met several women over the years and liked some of them. And had fairly intimate relations with them. But I've never felt the same way I did with that girl, not even once. That unadulterated feeling where your mind goes blank, like you're in the middle of a deep dream though it's daytime, like you can think of nothing else.

"I think I've been waiting for that unadulterated emotion to grab me again. Or for the woman, the person, who gave me that feeling."

"It's the same with me," Mr. Koyasu said quietly. "After I lost my wife, I did become friends with a few women. Not that many, really, but with some. A lot of people wanted to set me up with women, the idea being that one of them could be my second wife. When my wife passed, I was still in my forties, and as the successor of an established family, I had a fairly high social position in this little town, so people felt it was only natural that I remarry. And there were women who tried to get close to me.

"But I never felt for any of them what I'd felt for my wife. They might have been beautiful, with lovely personalities, but none of them moved me like my late wife had. And at a certain point I started wearing this skirt. And in a conservative rural town like this nobody's crazy enough to try to set up a woman with a man who walks around town dressed so weirdly."

Mr. Koyasu chuckled, then turned serious again and went on.

"This is what I'm trying to say. Once you've tasted pure, unadulterated love, it's like a part of your heart's been irradiated, burned out, in a sense. Particularly when that love, for whatever reason, is suddenly severed. For the person involved, that sort of love is both the supreme happiness and a curse. Do you understand what I'm getting at?"

"I think so."

"Age doesn't matter, or whether you go through trials, or sexual experiences. The only thing that matters is whether that is, for you, a hundred percent. The feelings of love you had for the girl when you were sixteen and seventeen were truly pure. One hundred percent genuine. You came across your partner at an early stage in life. You had to meet her, maybe I should say."

Mr. Koyasu stopped speaking for a moment and leaned forward, gazing at the fire in the stove, apparently lost in thought. His eyes reflected the color of the flames.

"But one day she suddenly vanished. Leaving behind no message, no inkling or hint of why. You couldn't fathom why that happened. You didn't have a clue.

"My case is similar. After I lost my son, my wife chose to kill herself, but in doing so she never said good-bye, or left behind anything like a final note. On her bedcover, in that little person-shaped depression, she'd left two scallions. Long and white, wonderful, fresh scallions. She deliberately left these on her bed. As if they were a kind of stand-in for her.

"No one knew what those scallions meant, and I had no idea either. It's stayed with me, a stubborn, unsolvable riddle. The vivid whiteness of them remains burned into my memory. Why scallions—why did it have to be scallions? If I ever meet my wife in the afterlife, I'd like to ask her what that all meant. But even in the world after death I am totally alone and the riddle remains."

Mr. Koyasu shut his eyes for a time. As if checking that indeed the afterimage of those scallions remained. Finally he opened his eyes and continued.

"When my wife left this world without a word, it hurt me terribly. You can't see it, but there's a deep wound gouged out in my heart. A gash so deep it runs to my heart's very core. Despite this, I didn't die myself but lived on for a long time afterward. Because at first I didn't understand that this was a hopeless, fatal wound.

It was only later that I realized this, but by then I'd already chosen to survive. The path that led to living on was already laid out before me."

A faint smile rose to his lips.

"And with that it seems like I became a different person. I no longer had enthusiasm for anything of this world. A part of my heart had burned out. That deep, fatal wound had already left me half dead. The only thing I was even half interested in was this library. It was only because of this little personal library that I could survive until a while ago. So I understand your feelings. The wound in your heart is something I can feel, deep down. Perhaps it's a little audacious of me to say, but I can feel it as if it were *my own pain*."

"And knowing that, you chose me to be the head librarian here?"

Mr. Koyasu nodded emphatically. "The first time I laid eyes on you, I knew. That you were the one to succeed me in this post. This is no ordinary library, you understand. It's more than just a public place where there are a lot of books. This has to be a special place that takes in lost hearts."

"Sometimes I just don't understand myself," I admitted honestly. "Maybe I've lost sight of me. I don't have a sense that I'm living this life as myself, as the *real me*. Sometimes I think I'm merely a shadow. When I feel that way, I get this restless feeling, like I'm simply tracing an outline of myself, cleverly pretending to be me."

"The real self and his shadow are essentially two sides of the same coin," Mr. Koyasu said in a quiet voice. "Depending on the circumstances, they can change roles. That's how people can overcome troubles and survive. And tracing something and pretending to be something are very important sometimes. It's nothing to be concerned about. Because the person here right now is indeed you."

With this Mr. Koyasu suddenly clammed up, his face grimacing like he'd swallowed something he shouldn't have. He shook his shoulders several times and took a long deep breath.

"Are you alright?" I asked.

"Ah, I'm fine," he replied after he'd gotten his breathing under control. "Nothing's wrong. Not to worry. I talked a little too much. I'm sorry, but I must be going. The time for that has arrived. What I can say is one more thing—never give up believing. If you can believe strongly, deeply, in something, the road ahead will become clear. And then you can prevent the terrible, inevitable fall to come. Or at least cushion the shock of it."

Prevent a terrible, inevitable fall? Fall from what? What was he talking about?

"Mr. Koyasu, will I be able to see you again soon? There are so many things I still need to ask you."

Mr. Koyasu picked up the beret from the desktop, arranged it with a practiced hand, and placed it on his head.

"Yes, I'll see you again before long. If you don't mind someone like me helping out, I'd like to very much. But I don't know for certain either when we can meet next. There's a subtly shifting flow here that carries me in different directions, and in order to meet with you like this and talk, I need there to be a suitable amount of power stored up. But I'm sure we'll be able to meet before long."

Mr. Koyasu's whole form seemed to be growing fainter, little by little. Like I could see through him. Maybe it was just my imagination, since the lighting in the room was less than adequate.

Mr. Koyasu opened the door and went outside. I heard the door click shut, and then a deep silence ensued. No sound of footsteps.

I WAS RESHELVING books when a teenager came up and spoke to me. It was after eleven in the morning. I had on a beige crew neck sweater, olive-green chinos, and a library ID hanging from a lanyard around my neck. I was removing damaged books from the shelves and replacing them with new ones.

The boy was sixteen or seventeen but small for his age, and was wearing a green parka, faded jeans, and black basketball shoes. All were well worn and looked to be the wrong size. Somebody's hand-me-downs, perhaps. There was a picture of a yellow submarine on the front of the parka. The Beatles' *Yellow Submarine*. The boy had on the kind of round, metal-frame glasses John Lennon used to wear, and they tilted a bit to one side as if too big for him. It felt like someone from the 1960s had mistakenly time-slipped into the present.

I'd seen the boy often in the reading room. Always at the same seat by the window, a solemn look on his face as he was lost in reading. Other than when he turned a page, he never moved. He must really love to read, I'd thought. But I found it odd that he would hang out in the library every day, from morning on. Didn't he go to school?

I asked Mrs. Soeda once about him, whether it was okay that he didn't attend school.

Mrs. Soeda shook her head. "There are reasons behind it, but he doesn't go to school. In a way, the library's his school. His parents are okay with it."

A boy refusing to go to school, I figured. I asked no more. I didn't see any problem with him coming to the library every day and spending his time reading.

But on that day, he didn't have a book in hand but instead was wandering back and forth in front of the shelves, as if lost in thought.

"Excuse me," the boy said, coming to a halt.

"How can I help you?" I replied, books clasped to my chest.

"Would you please tell me your date of birth—day, month, and year?" the boy asked. For a boy his age he sounded too polite, too precise. And toneless. Like he was reading, in a monotone, sentences printed on a page.

With a few books clutched to me, I turned to face him. He looked like he'd been well raised, and had nice features. His ears were bit too big, though. His hair looked to be recently cut, was neatly trimmed, the skin above his ears shaved close. He was short, pale, his neck and arms lanky. No trace of any tan, and I doubted he ever played sports. A strange sort of light was present in his eyes as he gazed at me. A sharp, clearly focused light, as if he were gazing intently at something at the bottom of a deep hole . . . and maybe I was that *something at the bottom of a deep hole.*

"Date of birth?" I repeated.

"Yes, day, month, and year you were born."

I was a little confused, but went ahead and told him. I didn't know what he was after, but I figured there was no harm done in telling him.

"A Wednesday," the boy immediately declared.

Not knowing what he meant, I screwed up my face a fraction. I seemed to have disturbed him a little.

"The day you were born was a Wednesday," the boy said. He said this curtly, as if not wanting to explain the details. And as soon as he got this out, he headed back to the reading room, sat down in his window seat, and went back to the thick book he'd been reading.

It took me a while to figure out what had happened. And then it struck me. The boy was one of the so-called Calendar Boys, who can come up with the day of the week for any date you give them, past or future. He had that special ability. *Savant syndrome* was the accepted term for the condition, like the character in the movie *Rain Man*. In many cases they have mental disabilities yet display an uncanny ability in areas like mathematics and art.

I wanted to check the internet to see if my birth date really was a Wednesday but couldn't since the library had no computers. (I checked my own computer after going home that day, and, sure enough, he was right.)

I called Mrs. Soeda, at the counter, over near the office, and quietly pointed out the boy.

"I wanted to ask about him."

"Did he do something?"

"Is he sort of a savant or something?"

Mrs. Soeda looked at me. "Did he, by chance, ask you your date of birth?"

I explained it all to her.

When I finished she said, blankly, "Yes, he often asks people their date of birth. And tells them right away what day of the week it was. But that's all. He doesn't bother anyone and doesn't cause any trouble. And he never asks anyone a second time."

"Does he ask everyone he comes across?"

"No, not everyone. He seems selective. It depends on the person whether he asks them or not. How he decides, though, I have no idea."

"I see," I said. Unusual, but as she said, it didn't cause any problems. It was just dates of birth and days of the week.

"So what day of the week were you born?"

"Wednesday," I said.

"*Wednesday's child is full of woe*," Mrs. Soeda said. "Do you know the rhyme?"

I shook my head.

"It's a line from the Mother Goose nursery rhyme. 'Monday's child is fair of face, Tuesday's child is full of grace, Wednesday's child is full of woe . . . '"

"I don't think I've heard it," I said.

"It's just for kids. I was born on Monday but don't have a particularly pretty face," Mrs. Soeda said, her face typically serious.

"Wednesday's child is full of woe," I repeated.

"Just a line from a nursery rhyme. Wordplay, that's all."

"Why doesn't he go to school? Was he bullied or something?"

"No, that's not it. He couldn't get into high school."

Mrs. Soeda put down the ballpoint pen she was holding, readjusted her glasses, and then went on.

"Two years ago he managed to graduate from the public junior high in this town, but didn't go on to the nearby high school.

Because his grades were all over the place. In subjects he was good at he'd get a nearly perfect score, but in ones he wasn't good at his grades were close to zero. He'd memorize books he read, with a photographic memory, absorbing so much information, so many details, that it was hard for him to connect it all in some practical way. Most of the information was too specialized to be of any use on the high school entrance exam. On top of which, he totally refused to participate in PE. There was no way he could attend a regular high school."

"I see," I said. "He really does enjoy reading, doesn't he."

"He certainly does, and he comes here about every day, reading books at a furious pace. At this pace he'll have finished most of the books we have by the end of the year."

"What kind of books does he read?"

"You name it. He's not choosy and will read basically anything. He absorbs all the information there like it's a vitamin drink. As long as it's information, he takes it all in."

"That's wonderful, but some information can be dangerous. If you can't make the right choices."

"You're right. So I make it a point to examine every book before he takes it out. I'll take it away if I feel it's information that could cause trouble. For instance, books with depictions of sex or violence that go too far . . ."

"Doesn't that cause problems, forcibly taking away books from him?"

"It's quite alright. He does what I say," Mrs. Soeda said. "Actually, when he was in elementary school, my husband was his homeroom teacher for two years. So I've known him since he was little. My husband really cares about him. Though the boy wasn't always easy for him."

"What kind of family is he from?"

"His parents run a private kindergarten in town, as well as a few juku prep schools. It's a well-respected family. They have three sons, and this boy is the youngest. The other two are real prodigies, graduating from the local high school with top grades and going on to universities in Tokyo. One became a civil defense lawyer after graduating. The other is still in university. In med school, as I recall. But the youngest brother couldn't go on to high school and instead comes to the library, reading one book after another. As I said before, this is his school."

"And he memorizes the books he reads?"

"To give you an example, he read Toson Shimazaki's novel *Before the Dawn*. And once he did, he could recite it all from beginning to end. It's quite a lengthy novel, but he memorized it all. He can quote every word, every line, verbatim. Though I think he probably doesn't understand what this novel is trying to convey to readers, or its significance in Japanese literary history."

I had heard about people with this kind of ability, but it was the first time I'd ever met one.

Mrs. Soeda said, "Some people find his special ability kind of creepy. Especially in a small conservative town, anyone who doesn't fit in or is out of the ordinary is excluded, and most people avoid getting to know the boy. Like avoiding someone with a contagious disease. At least, no one goes out of their way to know him. It's sad, really. He's a very quiet boy, and other than going around asking people their date of birth he never bothers anyone."

"So instead of going to school he comes to this library every day and reads whatever he can lay his hands on. But what's the point of taking in such a huge amount of information?"

"I can't help you there. Maybe no one knows. All I can say is it may be an insatiable intellectual curiosity that drives him on. I can't say whether cramming in all that knowledge will, in the end, be good for him or not. It's unclear whether there's a limit to storage capacity for knowledge. There's so much I don't know about it. But at least I can say that the thirst for knowledge itself is important and meaningful, and libraries exist, after all, to satisfy that."

I nodded. She was right. Libraries existed to satisfy people's thirst for knowledge. No matter what they want to do with it.

"But there must be a school somewhere that would take in a boy like him," I said.

"Yes, there are several specialized schools like that, but none in this vicinity, unfortunately. If he wanted to attend one of those schools, he'd need to move away from this town and live in a dorm. His mother, though, adores him, dotes on him, and would never let him leave her side."

"Which is why this library became a substitute school."

"Right. His mother knew Mr. Koyasu from long ago and asked him to help. The boy's an unparalleled reader, and as long as he can read books, he's quiet and well behaved, she said. Could you please mentor him here in the library? And after discussing it in detail with the mother, Mr. Koyasu fundamentally agreed to take on the role."

"And after Mr. Koyasu passed away you took over that dying wish and took care of the boy?"

"I wouldn't say I take care of him, but I do try to keep an eye on him. I keep a record of every book he reads. I'm very fond of the boy. I know he's a bit odd, and can be stubborn at times, but he doesn't require that much of me. He comes every day, sits in the same chair, and is totally absorbed in reading. His ability to concentrate is astounding. His eyes never leave the pages. As long as you don't bother him, he's quiet and well behaved. He's never once caused any trouble here at the library."

"Doesn't he have any friends the same age?"

Mrs. Soeda shook her head. "As far as I know, there's no one he's close to. For one thing, none of the kids his same age have anything in common they could talk about. Plus in junior high he caused some trouble involving a girl in his class."

"What kind of trouble?"

"He was interested in a girl in his class and followed her around everywhere. She wasn't so pretty and didn't stand out or anything, but something about her really attracted him. And though he followed her, he never did anything strange. Never spoke to her. He just silently followed her around. And not right next to her but at a distance. The girl found it all pretty creepy, of course, her parents complained to the principal, and there was a bit of a to-do about it. Everyone in town knows about it. So no parents are happy about him getting near their children."

After this I was more aware of this boy in his window seat, lost in a book—always keeping my distance so he wouldn't notice.

As far as I could tell, he invariably wore the same green parka with the *Yellow Submarine* picture on it (he must have really liked it). Until then I'd never particularly paid attention to him, but after hearing Mrs. Soeda's explanation, I sensed something out of the ordinary in his figure sitting there, intently reading. Once he opened a book and began reading, he'd sit there, completely still, for hours at a time (I doubt he'd even notice if a horsefly, for instance, had landed on his cheek). His eyes as he followed the words were flat, expressionless, a thin film of sweat forming sometimes on his forehead.

But these were all things I was aware of and observed only after Mrs. Soeda told me about his background. If she hadn't told me and I just saw him sitting there I probably wouldn't have thought anything was different. I'd have merely noted a smallish young boy fixedly reading a book—that's all. I was like that myself as a boy, so lost reading that I'd almost forget to eat or sleep.

And after asking me my date of birth, the boy didn't come to speak to me again. Once he'd asked a person's date of birth (and instantly figured the day of the week), the boy's curiosity about that person seemed satisfied.

It was on a Monday, the day the library was closed, that I saw Yellow Submarine Boy somewhere other than in the library reading room.

THAT MONDAY MORNING I followed my usual routine and paid a visit to Mr. Koyasu's grave, a small bouquet in hand. The sky was clouded over, a feeling of dampness in the wind, as if rain or snow were about to fall at any time. But I didn't take an umbrella with me. Even without one my baseball cap and the hood of my duffel coat would get me through a bit of rain or snow.

I put my hands together and prayed at the grave for the repose of this family of three. For the five-year-old boy who had an unfortunate traffic accident, for his mother, so grief-stricken she threw herself into the raging waters of a river, and for the head librarian, hiking through the woods when he was struck down by a sudden heart attack. I felt strangely close to them, even then, though I never met any of them while they were still alive.

I sat down on the stone wall, faced the smooth black headstone, and spoke out loud to Mr. Koyasu, who perhaps lay out there, somewhere beyond the grave. The winter birds sent out the occasional familiar raucous squawks from the nearby grove. A cry so sorrowful it sounded like they'd just witnessed the earth ripped apart. Other than that, it was still all around. As if the thick clouds had absorbed each and every sound.

I reported to Mr. Koyasu on the doings at the library during the week. Like always, nothing extraordinary, though there were a couple of things worth telling him about. For instance, one sixty-seven-year-old man was reading magazines in the lounge when he started to feel ill. We helped him to rest on the sofa, but he didn't improve, so we called an ambulance. (At the hospital they determined that it was a mild case of food poisoning.) The striped female cat who lives in the garden behind the library gave birth to five kittens. Such cute little kittens. Mother and kittens are all doing well, and after they've grown a bit more, we'll probably put out a poster at the entrance advertising for people to take them. That's about all that's happened. It is, after all, a peaceful little library in a peaceful little town. Nothing much ever happens. (If you don't count the ghost of the former head librarian coming and going.)

Next, I talked about the town surrounded by a high brick wall. How lovely the river was that ran through it, how the unicorns wandered the streets, how sharp the Gatekeeper honed his bladed tools, how strong the herbal tea was that the girl in the library brewed for me . . . I told each and every one of these in careful detail. Maybe I'd already talked about it before. But I went ahead anyway and continued to relate what popped into my head, with my audience the gravestone before me.

The gravestone was silent from beginning to end. Stones don't reply, their expression unchanging. Maybe I was an audience of one. Even so, I continued, haltingly, to tell my tale. There was so much I needed to say about that town. More than I could ever talk about, no matter how long I went on.

The thick clouds were caught by the wind and slowly started shifting south. Watching them, I really got the sense of Earth spinning. Earth slowly, steadily, was rotating, time ineluctably moving forward. As if to prove this progress, the birds flitted from branch to branch, letting out an occasional shrill cry. The faint sadness of the winter morning became a transparent cloak wrapping itself lightly around me.

Just then I noticed a sudden movement out of the corner of my eye. Not a dog or a cat, but a person. A small figure of a person—not a large one. So that the person wouldn't realize I noticed them, I stayed still, just moving my eyes to observe what was going on in that direction.

The person was hiding behind a gravestone, though the gravestone wasn't big enough to completely hide his body. A piece of clothing sticking out from behind the gravestone was that green parka with *Yellow Submarine* on it. I was positive.

No doubt the boy had gone that morning to visit Mr. Koyasu's grave and happened to spot me seated in front of it. And to avoid contact with anyone—human contact being the hardest thing for him—he had hurriedly concealed himself behind a gravestone. I had no idea how long he'd been hidden there.

How much of what I'd said aloud at the grave, this intensely personal monologue, had he overheard? I hadn't spoken very loudly (at least I didn't think I had). And the boy wasn't hidden very close to where I was sitting. Yet it was so awfully quiet and still all around—literally as silent as the grave. But with those oversized ears he possessed, he might very well have caught it all.

But even if he had overheard every word, would that be a problem? Ordinary people overhearing me talk about a "town surrounded by a wall" wouldn't take it as real, but as some kind of fanciful, made-up story. A fantastical kind of fiction. And probably classify me as some starry-eyed dreamer. That's all. But how would all this sound to this boy with photographic memory? How would he absorb it, emotionally?

I eased down from the stone wall, adjusted my baseball cap, looked at the sky to check the weather, and left the cemetery, pretending I hadn't noticed the boy's presence. I intentionally did not look over to where the boy was hidden, but I knew he was still there, behind someone's gravestone, watching me. I couldn't help liking the boy. At least he still had some very strong feelings for Mr. Koyasu. If not, he wouldn't come all the way out here to the temple cemetery on such a cold winter morning.

I walked down the sixty-plus uneven stone steps and, as always, stopped by the nameless coffee shop near the station, had a hot cup of black coffee and a blueberry muffin.

The woman in the gingham apron behind the counter saw me and smiled, a natural, intimate smile that seemed to say *I remember you.* This morning was quite busy behind the counter. She seemed to be running this little shop all by herself. I'd never seen anyone else working there. As before, relaxed jazz at just the right volume filtered out from the speakers on the wall. The song was "Star Eyes." A neat piano trio performance, though who the pianist was I didn't know.

After warming my chilled body at the coffee shop, I didn't go right home but took a detour to the library, and went around to the rear garden to see the cat family. To avoid the weather they'd set up house underneath an old porch. Someone had made a little bed for the cats with a cardboard box and an old blanket. The mother cat wasn't cautious around people (the women in the library gave them food every day), and even when I got near, she merely glanced at me but didn't tense up. The tiny kittens, their eyes still not fully open, relied on their sense of smell to gather, like larvae, around their mother's nipples. The mother cat, eyes narrowed, watched her babies lovingly. I watched this from a way off, never tiring of the scene.

And I remembered something. In that town surrounded by a wall, just as she'd told me beforehand, I never once saw a dog or a cat. There were unicorns, yes. And night birds. But I never saw any other animals. (The night birds I only heard and didn't see.) No, it wasn't just animals—I never saw a single worm there either. Why would that be?

Because they weren't necessary. That was all I could say. Nothing unneeded existed in that town. The only things allowed there were things that were necessary, things that *had* to be there. And I was probably needed in that town. At least for a time.

Back home I heated up some leftover turnip soup. And thought again about Yellow Submarine Boy. What was the purpose of him coming, on an early Monday morning, to visit Mr. Koyasu's grave? Was it just paying his respects to Mr. Koyasu? My gut told me otherwise. And did he know that Mr. Koyasu's soul was still lingering between life and death, and sometimes would appear before us, looking as he had when he was alive?

I wouldn't have found it strange if the boy had known. I knew that Mr. Koyasu's ghost wandered the earth, and so did Mrs. Soeda. It wouldn't be surprising if the boy, whom Mr. Koyasu had taken under his wing, was aware of it, too. Mr. Koyasu had left several things unfinished, and after his death, his soul continued to finish up this remaining business. His mentoring of Yellow Submarine Boy, too, was probably one item on this list of things left undone.

After this the boy came to the library without missing a day, inhaling one book after the next (without even eating lunch). I had Mrs. Soeda show me the list she'd kept of the books from our library that he'd read, beginning two years ago. A surprising number of books, and a surprising variety—everything from Immanuel Kant to Norinaga Motoori, Franz Kafka, Muslim sacred texts, books on genes, Steve Jobs's autobiography, Conan Doyle's *A Study in Scarlet*, the history of nuclear submarines, Nobuko Yoshiya's novels, last years' national agriculture almanac, Stephen Hawkings's *A Brief History of Time*, to Charles de Gaulle's memoirs.

I was astounded to think he could store away all this information and knowledge in his brain. It left me feeling dizzy. And the list I saw was just of books he'd read at our library. Even Mrs. Soeda had no idea how much he'd read outside our library holdings. What did all this enormous amount of knowledge mean to him? What use was all this to him?

But when I thought about it, I realized I was very similar back when I was sixteen or seventeen. On a different scale, of course, but why was I so absorbed in reading back then, reading books that would make you sometimes wonder why I chose them, cramming all kinds of information into my head? I hadn't yet gained the skill and ability to choose what knowledge was helpful and what was useless.

This boy might be doing much the same thing, on a far more magnificent scale. His young, healthy thirst for knowledge was unflagging. He insatiably crammed in knowledge, but it never was enough, since the world overflowed with an outrageous amount of information. Even with his special abilities, of course, there had to be a limit to one individual's capacity. It was like scooping up ocean water with a bucket—though there might be differences in the size of the bucket.

"Does he ever give up on reading a book?" I asked Mrs. Soeda.

"No, as far as I have seen once he starts reading a book he reads to the very end. He never abandons a book halfway. He doesn't judge or pick and choose a book like most people do, based on whether it's interesting or not, or holds their interest. For him a book is a vessel for information that you have to collect down to the last detail, every final piece. Most people who, say, read an Agatha Christie novel and enjoy it might read a few more of her works. But that doesn't apply to him. He doesn't select books according to groupings."

"But how long can such a process like that go on? Is it a phase special to his age group, that settles down in the end? There's got to be a limit to how much information he can cram in."

Mrs. Soeda weakly shook her head. "I have no idea. I mean, what he's doing far exceeds the realm of normal people."

"When he was alive, did Mr. Koyasu say anything about the boy's reading?"

"No, Mr. Koyasu doesn't express any particular opinion," Mrs. Soeda said. Present tense. She pursed her lips. "He just folds his arms and watches him, a big smile on his face. Like always."

EVER SINCE that Monday morning at the cemetery outside town, when I spotted him hiding behind a gravestone, the boy seemed more interested in me. At least, it felt like that. Not that anything in particular happened. He didn't stare at me, but occasionally I sensed him shooting a quick glance my way. Usually I'd feel it from behind. That glance had a strange weight and sharpness to it, as if it penetrated the cloth of my jacket to reach the very skin of my back. But I didn't feel any hostility and malice in it. It was probably more curiosity.

Perhaps he was surprised that I'd pay my respects to Mr. Koyasu's grave, though I'd never met him while he was still alive. And was surprised by my lengthy monologues at his grave. That's no doubt what aroused the boy's interest.

How much had he caught of what I'd spoken of to Mr. Koyasu at the grave? I had no idea. But whether he'd heard it all, or none of it, didn't make any difference. I didn't think he'd tell what he'd heard to anybody, since he wasn't the type to do so, and rarely spoke to anyone. So much so that I had, at first, doubts whether he could even talk.

According to Mrs. Soeda, he only spoke to a limited number of people, and only at limited times. Always in a small murmur, hard to catch, and in as few words as possible. And on days when he didn't want to talk to anyone (which was nearly half the time), he got his message across in writing. So he always carried a small notebook and ballpoint pen around in his pocket. Which goes to explain why, until the day he asked me my date of birth, I'd never even heard his voice. (For some reason when he asked people their date of birth he spoke very distinctly.)

So even if he'd overheard everything I spoke aloud at Mr. Koyasu's grave, and remembered every single detail, I couldn't see him telling anyone else.

One day I looked in on the reading room but didn't see the boy there. There was no open book at his usual seat next to the window, and no coat or backpack. This was unprecedented. He was always there, even skipping lunch, reading intently till three p.m. without raising his eyes from the pages.

"I don't see the boy today. Is something the matter?" I asked Mrs. Soeda at the counter.

Mrs. Soeda smiled faintly. "He went around back to see the cats. He loves cats. But they don't let him keep one at his house. His father seems averse to cats. So he likes to see them here."

I went out to the entrance and made my way around the building to the rear garden. I walked softly so as not to announce my presence. And there I saw the boy, crouched down in front of the porch, gazing at the little cat family. He had on his usual green parka, and on top of that a navy-blue down jacket. He crouched there, not moving a muscle, intently observing the cats, as if watching the very creation of the world and determined not to miss a single detail.

I stood behind the thick trunk of a pine tree and watched him for some ten or fifteen minutes, and all this time he remained crouched there, not moving an inch. Just like when he was in the reading room, lost in a book.

"Does he always look at the cats like that?" I asked Mrs. Soeda after I got back to the counter.

"Yes, I'd say he spends about an hour a day watching them. He's very enthusiastic. When he's into something he doesn't care if it's raining or snowing, or the wind is bitingly cold."

"He just looks at them?"

"That's right. All he does is look. He never touches them, never talks to them. He just watches what they're doing, from about six feet away. With a super-serious look in his eyes. The mother cat is used to him and doesn't go on alert even if he's close by. I doubt she'd mind if he reached out and touched them, though he never does and just squats there at a distance, closely studying them."

After the boy had left, I went into the back garden and crouched down like he'd done, as quietly as possible, and tried observing the cats. The kittens' eyes were starting to open now, their fur a bit more lustrous than before. With gentle, narrowed eyes, the mother was licking their fur. I wanted to get closer and touch their fur but refrained. I wanted to re-create inside me the feelings the boy must have inside to want to watch the cat family so intently, for so long, but of course those feelings were beyond me.

A week later, the women staff took photos of the cats and put up a poster saying LOOKING FOR HOMES FOR THESE KITTENS on the library bulletin board near the entrance. The kittens were certainly cute, and the photos came out well, and people quickly came forward to adopt them. All of the kittens were soon taken away to new homes. The mother cat didn't put up any resistance as her kittens were taken from her, one after another, but when the last one was gone, she fell into a kind of panic, restlessly pacing the garden in search of her offspring. We could hear her calling to them, and though they knew there was nothing to be done, the library's staff all felt sorry for her. A few days later, though, the mother cat seemed to have given up and returned to her usual pre-kitten behavioral patterns. Next year she'd most likely be back under the porch again, giving birth to a new batch of five or six kittens.

I had no clue what Yellow Submarine Boy felt about the kittens all being gone. And neither did Mrs. Soeda. He never said a word about their disappearance, just no longer making a habit of going around back to see the little family. Almost as if they'd never existed in the first place.

When the boy did not wear his *Yellow Submarine* parka he wore a brown parka with a picture of another character from the movie *Yellow Submarine*. A strange creature with a blue face, pink ears, and brown fur over his body. I'd seen the movie but couldn't remember that character's name. He was the Nowhere Man who lived in Nowhere Land. John Lennon sang the song about him. But the name just wouldn't come to me.

When I got home I went online and did a search for "Characters in *Yellow Submarine*" and found out that the blue-faced weird character was named Jeremy Hillary Boob, PhD. He was a master of many things—a pianist, a botanist, a classicist, a dentist, a physicist, a writer of satire . . . A man who could do it all, yet was a nobody.

The boy must really like the movie *Yellow Submarine*, I figured, which is why he always wore that parka. I assumed that his mother would regularly take the *Yellow Submarine* parka from her son in order to throw it in the wash. Half forcing him to hand it over. When that happened, it made sense that he'd wear his backup outfit, the Jeremy Hillary Boob parka. At least that's what I figured.

As I researched more on Jeremy Hillary Boob, I found myself wanting to see the movie *Yellow Submarine* again. It had been more than twenty years since I'd last seen it, and I'd forgotten most of it. So I went to the town's only rental video shop near the station, but couldn't find it there. The Beatles films they did have on the shelves included *A Hard Day's Night* and *HELP!* but that was it. I asked the clerk but was told they didn't carry *Yellow Submarine*. I'd wanted to find out what it was about *Yellow Submarine* that so fascinated that boy.

He wore nearly the same outfit every day. Either the *Yellow Submarine* parka or else the Jeremy Hilary Boob parka. One or the other. And faded blue jeans and ankle-top black basketball shoes. I don't recall ever seeing him in anything else.

According to Mrs. Soeda, though, his family was quite well off, his mother doted on her youngest son, and it would have been easy for her to buy him clean, new clothes. Which could only mean that these outfits were ones he preferred. Or he absolutely refused to wear new clothes he wasn't used to. Who knows.

So he appeared at the library dressed almost the same every day, lugging the same green backpack, showing up right after the library opened. He'd sit in the same seat and plow through his books there without ever speaking to anyone. He never ate lunch, only the occasional sip from the mineral water he brought. Come three p.m., and he'd shut his book, stand up, shoulder his backpack, and again wordlessly exit the library. The same scenario, repeated daily.

Whether he was satisfied with this unvarying everyday routine, or derived any happiness from it, no one knew. You couldn't read any emotion on his face. But I imagine that precisely following a set pattern every day must have meant something vital to him. Perhaps it was less the actions themselves or the direction they took him in than the repetition itself that was the point.

The following Monday morning I again visited Mr. Koyasu's grave. At exactly the same time as the previous week. Again I faced the gravestone, put my hands together to pray for the family, and then started speaking to the gravestone. I talked about a few minor incidents that had happened at the library during the week, and some thoughts that had occurred to me in the course of work, and then went on to talk about the life I'd led in the walled-in town. On this day, the clouds that covered the sky like a lid for so long had lifted, and sunlight shone brightly on the earth for the first time in forever. Patches of snow left over from a snowfall a few days before dotted the cemetery like little white, isolated islands.

As I continued my halting, intermittent monologue, I made sure to pay attention to my surroundings, but couldn't spot Yellow Submarine Boy anywhere, or get the sense that I was being watched. No particular sounds, either, only that of the usual winter birds crying out. They busily fluttered around in the woods that surrounded the cemetery, searching for berries or bugs. And the occasional crack of a woodpecker pounding a tree.

I felt lonely, not seeing the boy there, as if something were missing. I might have been expecting him to be there, hidden behind a gravestone, carefully following my story. Perhaps I wanted not just Mr. Koyasu to hear my story—I wanted the boy to hear it, too.

But why?

I couldn't explain why. I just had that feeling. Pure curiosity, perhaps. Perhaps I wanted to know what the boy would feel, what reactions he'd show, hearing the story of the town surrounded by a wall.

Occasionally, as if a sudden thought arose, a gust of freezing wind rushed through the gravestones. The leafless branches of the trees in the woods raised a wretched howl for a time. I wrapped my cashmere scarf tighter around my neck and gazed up at the sky. The winter sun was doing its best to provide the earth with brightness and warmth, but it wasn't enough. The world—the people, the cats, the souls with no place to go—sought after yet more light, yet more warmth.

So Yellow Submarine Boy didn't appear on that Monday at Mr. Koyasu's grave. Perhaps he didn't want to interfere with my visit (or me paying my respects). Or maybe he didn't want anyone else seeing him coming to that grave. Maybe he chose another time, deciding to visit in the afternoon. Or had found a more clever spot to hide.

I spent my usual half hour there in the cemetery and then left. I stopped by that nameless coffee shop near the station, enjoyed some hot black coffee to warm myself up, and had the usual blueberry muffin. I paged through the morning newspaper and half listened to Erroll Garner's rendition of "April in Paris" playing through the speakers on the wall. My little Monday routine. Repeating the same thing, tracing my steps from the week before. It wasn't just Yellow Submarine Boy who lived a repetitive life, for wasn't my own life equally so? Just like with the boy, wasn't repetition itself becoming something of a goal in my life?

The same held true with clothes. When I worked at the company, I paid close attention to what I wore. I'd iron my own shirts (a week's worth of shirts every Sunday) and wear a new one every day. I chose my ties' color and design to match those. But once I quit and moved to this town, I couldn't even recall what kind of clothes I was wearing at the moment. I'd suddenly realize I'd been wearing the same sweater for a whole week, or the same trousers. And I hadn't even noticed it. So I was in no position to comment about the boy always wearing his *Yellow Submarine* parka.

Not to imply that this lack of interest in clothes meant I was getting slovenly. (At least I don't think so.) I kept things around me orderly and clean. I shaved every morning, changed my underwear, and shampooed every day. I brushed my teeth three times a day. I was, as always, a clean bachelor who put a premium on habit. Yet here I was suddenly realizing that I'd been wearing the same sweater and trousers day after day. Even if it was unconsciously, I was starting to discover a kind of pleasure in that.

Nearly four weeks had passed since I'd last seen Mr. Koyasu, the longest time between sightings.

"It's a temporary phenomenon for my soul to take on this kind of form. Before long, it will all disappear." He'd told me something like this once. After that temporary period passed, then maybe he vanished somewhere. Absorbed into *mu*, nothingness, never to return to the earth again.

A sorrowful thought. Like suddenly losing a dear friend to an accident. But from the first time I met him, he was already someone not of this world. A *dead person*, in short. If his soul were to (once again) vanish forever, didn't this just mean that a person who was already dead goes on to a deeper state of death?

All of that gave me what you might call a metaphysical, strangely muted sadness, a little different from losing someone alive. There was no pain in this loss, just pure sorrow. The thought of a *deeper* state of death made me feel, even more closely, the certain presence of nothingness. So close that if I reached out, I could almost touch it.

The day after the library's day off I went to Mrs. Soeda and asked, in a hushed voice, if she'd seen Mr. Koyasu recently. She looked up and gazed fixedly at me. She looked around her and then said, "No, now that you mention it, I haven't for quite a while. Longer than ever before . . . And you?"

I shook my head slightly a few times, and returned to my office.

We didn't speak anymore about him, but I could tell, from her tone and expression, that like me, Mrs. Soeda missed his visits. Mrs. Soeda and I had become accomplices, sharing the secret between us of the *nonexistent existence* of Mr. Koyasu.

One afternoon around this time, as I was working in the square subterranean room, Mrs. Soeda came to see me. There was a faint knock at the door, I said, "Come in," and she entered. She held a large business-sized envelope in her hand, which she placed on my desk.

"M** gave this to me a short while ago. He asked me to hand it to you."

M** was the name of Yellow Submarine Boy.

"To me?"

Mrs. Soeda nodded. "It seems like it's very important. I've never seen such a serious look in his eyes before."

"What could it be?"

Mrs. Soeda shook her head as if she had no idea. The frames of her glasses caught the light and glittered.

I picked up the envelope. It was very light, almost weightless. At most maybe one or two sheets of A4 paper inside. There was nothing written on the envelope itself, no address, no name of sender. The near weightlessness of the thing left me nervous.

A letter? No, it's not that. A letter would be folded and in a smaller envelope.

"He's been coming here a long time, but this is a first," Mrs. Soeda said, narrowing her eyes to underscore the point. "The first time he's sent anything to anyone."

"Is he still in the library?"

"No, he left after he asked me to give this to you."

"He just said to hand it to me?"

"That's all. Not another word."

"How did he put it, exactly? *Please give this to the new head librarian?*"

"No, he knows your name."

I thanked her, and she went back to her station, her chartreuse flared skirt fluttering as she walked. The image of her healthy-looking calves lingered.

I left the envelope on top of the desk for a time. I didn't feel like opening it just yet. I needed to prepare myself, is what it felt like. I can't explain, though, why I had to mentally prepare, or what sort of preparation that might be. It just felt like I should leave it, unopened, for a while. Like waiting for something hot to cool down. Intuition told me that.

Leaving the envelope unopened, I sat down in front of the stove and watched the flames. It was like they were alive. They gave tiny little shudders, like an accomplished dancer would make. A large sway of the body, the occasional deep, fleeting sigh that sank down only to quickly arise again. It tried to eloquently convey something and then, suddenly, perked up its ears and listened carefully. It raised its eyes sharply, pointedly opening them wide, then shut them tight. I observed the flames, expecting them to tell me something vital, but they taught me nothing. Not even a hint. Time alone passed without a sound. But I didn't care. That's what I needed—the right amount of time passing.

I went back to my desk and picked up the large envelope. I snipped it open with scissors, careful not to damage what was inside. As I expected, inside there was but one sheet of A4 paper. It was a relief to find it wasn't empty. If it had been empty, with only nothingness inside, I might have been completely bewildered.

I gently eased that one sheet of typing paper out of the envelope. On it was some sort of detailed drawing, in black ink. No writing. I laid that drawing out on the desk and gazed at it. And gulped. A shock ran through me—like I'd been slammed in the back with a hard object. And that shock knocked every bit of logic, every bit of the rational clean out of my body. A physical sensation, as if the entire room were swaying. I lost my balance and grabbed tightly onto the desk. For a moment, words failed me, and I couldn't think straight.

On the paper was a nearly accurate map of that town surrounded by a high wall.

I SAT THERE for a long time in front of that map, totally speechless.

This was, without a doubt, a map of that town surrounded by the high brick wall.

The perimeter of the town, kidney shaped, with an indentation at the bottom, the beautiful river gently winding its way through the middle of town. The exit for that flow, that eerie *pool*. The gate, the sole entrance and exit to the town. The Gatekeeper's cabin inside. The three old stone bridges spanning the river (no one knows how old they were), the dried-up canal, the clock tower with no hands on the clock, and the library with not a single book in it.

It was a simple map, a sketch, really (and reminded me of the woodblock prints in medieval European books). When I studied it carefully I saw it had mistaken some of the details. (The sandbanks in the river, for instance, were depicted as much smaller than they actually were, and fewer in number.) Yet it was, overall, surprisingly accurate. How could that boy draw such an accurate map of the town without ever being there? When I'd tried myself several times to draw my own map and could never pull it off.

What I imagine is that he'd hidden himself at the cemetery (even on times when I hadn't noticed him there), had heard what I told Mr. Koyasu, and then drew the map based on the information he'd gathered about the walled-in town. Or he had learned to read lips. This was the best explanation I could come up with.

But was that even possible? When I spoke at the grave it was a disjointed monologue, everything out of order, as I called to mind bits and pieces from my memory. It was all so random—I'd jump from one topic to the next, one scene to the next. Had he taken all this fragmentary, contextless information and brought it all together like a jigsaw puzzle to create this map?

If so, his photographic memory extended beyond the visual to encompass a special auditory ability as well. My memory of savant syndrome was that it included people who were able, upon listening, no matter how complex the composition, to reproduce every note accurately, and perform it and transcribe it. Mozart supposedly had this gift.

Certainly I had spoken of the walled-in town at Mr. Koyasu's grave, but later I couldn't recall much of what I'd actually said, how I'd described it. I spoke of the town as if retelling a vivid dream I'd had—or rather as if actually experiencing the dream all over again. Just as I recalled it, nearly half consciously.

For instance, had I really mentioned the clock tower with no hands? I must have, since the boy's map included it. That clock tower was just a scrawled sketch, yet it looked just like the actual tower. And had no hands on the clock. Though there was no guarantee that my memory itself hadn't changed later on. Isn't it possible that my memory was subtly reworked to line up with the map the boy drew?

The more I thought about it, the less I understood. What was cause, and what was effect? How much was real, and how much had he simply made up?

I returned the map to the envelope, put it on top of the desk, and linked my fingers behind my head, absentmindedly staring into space. Faint afternoon light shone in through the cloudy horizontal window that just cleared ground level, the air in the room filled with a faint aroma of applewood. The black kettle on top of the blazing stove huffed out a burst of white steam, like a big sleeping cat exhaling from deep in its slumber.

I had the vague sense that something around me was gradually changing. It was as if, unaware, I was slowly being led somewhere by some sort of power. But was this a recent development, or something that had been going on from quite some time ago? I had no clue.

About all I did know was that right now I seemed to be hovering on the boundary between the *world over there* and the *world over here*. Just like this subterranean room, though it was neither entirely aboveground nor belowground. The light shining in there was muted and dim. That's where I was situated, in that twilit world. A line that was neither one nor the other. And I was trying to judge which side I was really on, and on which side the real person, the real me, could be found.

I picked up the envelope again from the desk, took out the map, and studied it. After a while I noticed how that map was making my heart tremble. And I don't mean metaphorically. It was literally making my heart, quietly yet definitely, physically shiver. Like a gelatinous substance in the midst of an unceasing earthquake.

As I stared at the map, my mind unconsciously returned to the town. I closed my eyes and could hear the murmur of the river, the sad cry of the night birds in the dark. The Gatekeeper's horn ringing out morning and evening, the streets filled with the dry *clip-clop* of the unicorns' hooves against the flagstone paving. The yellow raincoat of the girl walking beside me, rustling with each step. As if rubbing against the edge of the world.

With a small creaking sound, the reality around me was cracking ever so slightly. Assuming that this was, in fact, reality.

THE NEXT DAY, Yellow Submarine Boy never showed up. Which was more than unusual.

"He doesn't seem to have come today," I said to Mrs. Soeda, who was seated at the counter. I gave the reading room a once-over.

"I don't think he has," she said. "There are days like that. He might not be feeling well."

"Does that happen sometimes?"

"Periodically. It's not like a chronic condition, but sometimes he doesn't feel well, feels weak and can't get out of bed. His mother thinks it's some kind of nervous condition. If he stays in bed for three or four days, just resting, he recovers, she said, and there's no need to have a doctor look at him."

"In bed for three or four days, just resting."

"That's right. Like recharging a drained battery," Mrs. Soeda said.

Something like recharging indeed might be involved here, I thought. His abilities (which surpassed most human intellect) might get overactive and exceed his physical capacity. Like when a fuse automatically blows in a circuit board when it detects excess demand for electricity. Then he needs to take it easy, cool down from being overheated from overwork, and let his body recover naturally. Considering the timing, perhaps creating the map of that town—work that required extra energy—had caused his system to shut down.

Mrs. Soeda went on. "As you know, the boy has extraordinary feelings and abilities, but he's still at the age where he's growing and might not yet have the physical capability, or emotional defenses, to fully support the use of those abilities. I get terribly worried about him sometimes."

"He needs someone to take care of him, to guide him."

"Exactly. He needs someone to teach him how to control those unique abilities himself."

"Which can't be easy."

"Yes, it's very difficult. First they would have to understand each other. But the way I see it, his mother dotes on him too much, and his father is too involved with work to take care of his son. Up till now, Mr. Koyasu kept a close eye on him and took care of him in the library. Perhaps seeing him as a substitute for the son he lost. But sadly Mr. Koyasu passed away and no one is around who should watch over him."

"He hardly ever talks with anyone, yet he does seem to talk with you often."

"True, he does, because I've known him since he was little. Still, our conversations are pretty minimalist, limited to practical matters. I wouldn't say our mutual understanding is such that I can care for him mentally, or help him with any emotional issues."

"Do his family members talk with him?"

"He speaks a little to his mother, but only when it's absolutely necessary. And he never talks to his father. The only time he speaks to people he doesn't know is when he asks them their date of birth. It's only then that he's not timid and will speak to anyone. Looks them right in the eye and speaks clearly. But other than that he never talks to anyone. And if they talk to him, he doesn't respond."

I asked, "I understand that Mr. Koyasu personally took on the boy's care, but did the boy and Mr. Koyasu—when Mr. Koyasu was alive, I mean—go beyond the superficial when they talked?"

Mrs. Soeda narrowed her eyes and tilted her head slightly. "That I don't know. They always went to the head librarian's office, or that subterranean room, shut the door, and spent a long time together there, just the two of them. So I have no idea what they talked about, or whether they had more confidential talks."

"But he was pretty attached to Mr. Koyasu."

"I don't know if *attached* is the right word. But spending hours together, just the two of them in a room, implies a certain level of trust. That was quite unusual for the boy."

There was one thing I had to know. Yet I wasn't confident that this was the time or place (in midmorning sunlight shining on the bright library counter) to broach the question straight on. But I decided to plunge ahead, and ask it as simply as I could.

"Mrs. Soeda, do you think the two of them met even after Mr. Koyasu passed away?"

Mrs. Soeda looked right at me for a few seconds, her expression serious. Her thin nose quivered a fraction. Then she said, each word carefully punctuated, "What you're asking is whether after Mr. Koyasu's death did M** continue to meet him—with his ghost, his soul that took on form—and communicate with him. Do I have that right?"

I nodded.

"Well, I guess that is possible," Mrs. Soeda said after giving it some thought. "Very possible, in fact."

For four days after that, Yellow Submarine Boy didn't show up at the library. Without him, the reading room seemed unsettled. Or maybe it was me who was unsettled. I spent most of those four days holed up in the square subterranean room, lost in random, dreamy thoughts as I gazed at the map the boy had drawn.

The map summoned up amazingly vivid memories of scene after scene I'd seen myself in the world *over there*. Like a visual hallucination machine, the map activated my memory, unearthing details in a precise, three-dimensional way. The tangible feel of the air I breathed, the faint fragrance in the air—it all came back. As if it were all there, right before my eyes.

The map was simply drawn, yet it seemed to contain some sort of power. For four days, alone in my room, with the map before me, I wandered in that *world that isn't here*, caught up so deeply in that visual hallucination machine (type of thing) I gradually couldn't tell which world I belonged to. Like some eighteenth-century aesthetic poet addicted to opium in search of a pure illusion. Though what I held in my hand was merely a rough map, drawn in ballpoint pen on a thin sheet of A4 paper.

So why had Yellow Submarine Boy drawn this map, and had it delivered to me? What was the point? Maybe, though, there was no goal. Maybe it was an act performed purely for the sake of the act (just as he asked people their birth dates and then told them what day of the week they were born on).

If Mr. Koyasu and the boy were somehow communicating, and

working together, was Mr. Koyasu involved in the creation of the map? Was it partly his intention that the map be delivered to me? If so, then why? What did he intend by it?

Lots of questions, but no clear-cut answers. The meaning of it all totally eluded me. Many mysterious doors before me, but no key that fit. What I could somehow understand (or faintly perceive) was that there was an extraordinary, special power at work. This was not just a map of the place I had stayed in for a time in the past, but also served as a rough sketch of the shape of the world to come. As I gazed at it, it felt like something had been entrusted to me, personally.

I used the library copy machine to make a copy of the map and penciled in several corrections I noticed. The library, for instance, was shown as too close to the town square, the river was depicted as too gently meandering just before the pool, the area where the unicorns lived was a little bigger . . . those sorts of things. Seven corrections in all. These were all minor differences, nothing to do with the overall structure of the town. No need, really, to make these corrections (and how accurate was my memory, anyway?), but I surmised that the boy would value accuracy of detail. Also at play was the general principle that every act of expression required critique, and my need to make contact with the boy in some form or another. If the ball's served to me, I need to hit it back. That's the rule.

I put the copy of the map with my corrections in an envelope, sealed it, and handed it to Mrs. Soeda. I didn't go so far as to add a letter. Inside the envelope was a single sheet with the map—the same as when the boy had sent it to me.

"If the boy shows up, I'd like you to give this to him."

Mrs. Soeda took the envelope and looked at it for a moment, inspecting it. Nothing was written on either the front or the back. "Any additional message from you?"

"There's nothing you need to add," I said. "Just tell him it's from me and hand it to him, that'll be fine."

"Alright. I'll do that. I think he's probably recovered by now and should be coming here before long. If previous times are any indication."

Two days later, Mrs. Soeda showed up at my room.

"M** came this morning, so I gave him the envelope you left with me," she said. "He took it without a word and put it in his backpack."

"He didn't open it?"

"No, he put it in without opening it. And after that I didn't see him take it out of his backpack. He sat at his usual seat, intently reading as always."

"Thank you," I said. "By the way, what is he reading now?"

"A collection of letters by Dmitri Shostakovich," Mrs. Soeda replied without missing a beat.

"Sounds interesting."

Mrs. Soeda didn't give an opinion. Instead, she frowned a fraction. She was a woman whose expressions and gestures spoke louder than words.

THE NEXT DAY was a Monday, the library was closed, and I left the house as usual and headed toward Mr. Koyasu's grave. It was a cold morning, with bursts of snow fluttering in the air, the remaining snow on the ground frozen solid. A large truck passed by, its snow chains clattering loudly as they scraped against the road. The north wind blowing down stung my ears, and it was not at all the best weather for a visit to a grave.

Yet the weekly visit to his grave had become more than just a habitual ceremony, but something that I looked forward to. In my life, here in this town, I needed it, very much.

It's a strange way of putting it, but for me, Mr. Koyasu seemed much more alive, someone I felt the breath of life in, more than any of the actual living people around me. This held true not just for this town, but for everywhere I'd ever lived.

I loved his unique personality, and felt empathy toward his unswerving way of life. Fate had not been kind to him, yet he never lapsed into self-pity but did his utmost to make his life—for himself, and for those around him—something meaningful.

His life was quite isolated, yet he cherished his emotional exchange with others. He loved reading above all else, and when the town library was struggling financially he took over, invested his own money, and operated it, making sure that the library's holdings were substantial. As a result, this mostly one-man little town library had an amazing catalog of books, both in quantity and quality. I couldn't help but respect this well-ordered lifestyle of his, and visiting the cemetery every Monday felt less like visiting a grave than going to see a friend who was alive.

But that particular morning in February was so bitingly cold, too cold for me to linger there giving a monologue. I gave up after twenty minutes and headed back, being careful not to lose my footing on the steps of the temple, slippery from the remaining snow. And as always I stopped by the little no-name coffee shop near the station to warm up, enjoying a cup of hot black coffee and a muffin. They had two kinds of muffins, plain and blueberry, but I always had the blueberry.

On this snowy Monday morning, I was the only customer there. The same woman—her hair pulled tightly back, probably in her mid-thirties—went about her tasks behind the counter. Jazz played softly in the background, Paul Desmond on alto sax. When I first dropped by this shop, I recall, the Dave Brubeck Quartet was playing then, too, with another Paul Desmond sax solo.

" 'You Go to My Head,' " I said to myself.

As she warmed up the muffin in the oven, the woman looked up.

"Paul Desmond," I said.

"You mean the music?"

"Yeah," I said. "With Jim Hall on guitar."

"I don't know much about jazz," the woman said, a bit apologetically. She pointed to the speakers on the wall. "I just play a jazz channel."

I nodded. Understandable. She was too young to be fond of Paul Desmond's sound. She brought the warm muffin over, I tore off a piece and ate it, and sipped the hot coffee. Lovely music. Listening to Paul Desmond, watching the snow.

It suddenly occurred to me—in the town I never heard anything like music. But I never felt lonely without it, or felt I wanted to hear any. I didn't even really notice that there was no music. Why, I wonder?

With a start, I realized that Yellow Submarine Boy was standing there, next to my stool at the counter. I'd just finished the blueberry muffin and was wiping my mouth with a napkin. He had on his usual navy-blue down jacket, zipped up to the neck, and a scarf wrapped above his chin, so I couldn't tell if he had on his parka with the *Yellow Submarine* picture. But I bet he did.

I couldn't figure it out for a moment. Why was he here? How did he know I was here at this coffee shop? Had he followed me? Or had he known that every Monday, after I visited the grave, I stopped by here, and he'd come here to see me?

He was standing beside me, but not looking at me. With his back straight, he was gazing at the woman behind the counter.

His eyes were wide open, his chin tucked in tight. *Can I help you?* her expression said, a faint professional smile rising to her lips as she looked at the boy. He was too young to be a customer here, still almost a child.

"Can you tell me your date of birth?" he asked her, politely, and as precisely as if he were reading words written down.

"My date of birth?"

"Date of birth," he said. "The year, the month, the day."

Not surprisingly, the question puzzled her, but finally, having concluded that there was no harm in revealing this, she told him.

"Wednesday," the boy immediately declared.

"Wednesday?" the woman said. She looked unsure of what he was going on about.

"It means that you were born on a Wednesday," I piped in from beside him.

"I didn't know that," she said. She still looked puzzled. "But how can you know that so quickly?"

"Good question," I said. Explaining it all from the beginning would take too long. "At any rate the boy seems to know."

"Would you care for a refill?" the woman asked. I nodded.

"Wednesday's child is full of woe," I said, as if to myself.

The boy took a large envelope out of the pocket of his down jacket and handed it to me. He nodded once as if confirming the handover. I took it and likewise nodded once. Like Indians in a Western sharing a peace pipe.

"How about having a muffin?" I asked the boy. "The blueberry muffins here are delicious, freshly baked."

But he didn't reply, as if he hadn't heard what I'd said, and simply looked up at my face. As if engraving on his memory some information my face was sharing. His round, metal-frame glasses caught the light from the ceiling and glittered. A moment later the boy spun around and headed toward the door without a word. He opened it and left the shop. Into the fluttering, fine flakes of snow.

"An acquaintance of yours?" the woman asked as she watched him leave.

"Um," I replied.

"What an odd boy. He barely said a word."

"You know, actually I was born on a Wednesday, too," I said. I wanted to change the subject.

"Wednesday's child is full of woe . . . ," the woman said, her expression solemn. "You said that a moment ago. Is it true?"

"It's just a line from an old nursery rhyme. Nothing to worry about," I said. Like Mrs. Soeda told me once.

As if suddenly remembering, the woman tugged her cell phone, in a red plastic case, out of the pocket of her soft jeans and with her slim fingers raced over the screen. Finally, she looked up.

"Huh—it's right," she said, sounding impressed. "I was born on Wednesday. It's a fact."

I nodded silently. That's right, of course it's a Wednesday. Yellow Submarine Boy is always spot on. No need to check it. Nowadays, though, anyone can check what day of the week they were born on in less than ten seconds. The boy could come up with the answer in one second. This wasn't a shootout in a Western, but how much practical difference was there between ten seconds and one? I felt a little sad for the boy. The world was, day by day, becoming a more convenient, and unromantic, place.

I sipped my second cup of coffee and opened up the envelope he'd given me. As expected, it was a single-page map. Nothing else was inside. The same A4 paper as before, the same map in black ballpoint pen. A map of the kidney-shaped, walled-in town. All seven corrections I'd made a few days before, though, had now been incorporated into the map. The information shown there was more detailed and accurate now. A kind of revised edition of the town map. I returned the map to the envelope. At least the boy had responded to the message I'd sent. I'd hit the ball into his side of the court, and now he'd returned it over the net. A new development. A meaningful, probably favorable development.

I bought two blueberry muffins to take back, and she put them in a paper bag for me. As I was paying the bill at the register, the woman behind the counter said, "It sort of bothers me, but it can't be true, right, that children born on Wednesday all suffer a lot?"

"No, not to worry. That's not true," I said. I had no definite proof, but probably it wasn't.

The next morning, a Tuesday, the boy showed up at the library. This day he didn't wear his usual green parka with the picture of *Yellow Submarine,* but the brown parka with the picture of Jeremy Hillary Boob on it. His mother had probably taken the submarine parka to wash it, and until it dried he had to wear this substitute. Even with different clothes on, though, his actions fit his usual pattern. He took up his usual position in the reading room in a chair next to the window and read on, utterly focused on his book. He reminded me of a butterfly drinking the last drop of nectar from a flower. A win-win for both the flower and the butterfly. The butterfly gets nutrition, the flower gets help pollinating. A mutually beneficial relationship, which harms no one. One of the wonderful things about the act of reading.

On that day I wasn't in my subterranean room but working in the upstairs head librarian's office. The small gas stove didn't warm up the room enough, but the sun had, for the first time in a while, peeked through the clouds, so I decided, for a change of pace, to work in that bright room with its long, vertical window. I kept the map the boy gave me in the envelope on top of the desk, forcing myself not to open it. I had some tasks that required my immediate attention, and I knew that if I opened up the map and started looking at it, I would never get any work done.

The map that the boy drew had a power about it that was intriguing—bewitching, even. It wasn't just some map in black ink on a A4 sheet. Instead it summoned something from the viewer's heart, something normally hidden deep within, something with an intense power inside. And I couldn't resist that power. So on that day I focused on not taking out the map from the envelope. Today I had to cling to this world—what should probably be called the *real* world. Despite myself, though, my gaze was drawn, like an intermittent wind blowing fallen leaves closer, to the large business envelope on my desk.

Occasionally I'd open the window, stick my head out, look at the scenery outside, and cool myself down. Like a sea turtle or whale regularly surfaces to breathe. But I found it odd that I needed to feel the outside air to cool down on this cold winter day, when the room wasn't warm at all. But for me, on that day, it was a necessary, indispensable act. To confirm that I was living in the world on this side.

Below the window, the cat was making its way through the garden. The mother cat that had raised five kittens underneath the veranda. There were no kittens to be seen now, and the cat was slowly sauntering across the garden, her white breath billowing. She walked cautiously, her tail rigidly upright, heading somewhere. Her steps seemed painful, as if the ground were too freezing for her paws. I followed her slim, graceful figure until she slipped from view. I closed the window, sat down at my desk, and went back to work.

Just before noon, Mrs. Soeda hesitantly knocked on my door.

"Do you have a moment?" she asked.

Of course, I replied.

"M** said he'd like to come see you," she said.

"That would be fine," I quickly replied. "Please bring him over."

Her eyes narrowed in a faint smile, and she nodded.

"If you don't mind, could you bring over two cups of tea? And heat this up?" I said, handing her the bag with two blueberry muffins.

"Ah, muffins," she said, peeking inside the bag. Her eyes gleamed behind her glasses.

"That's right, blueberry muffins. I bought them yesterday, but if you heat them up in the microwave they should still be fine."

Mrs. Soeda headed toward the door with the paper bag. "I'll bring him here first, then bring over the tea and muffins."

"Thanks."

Five minutes later there was another knock and the boy, accompanied by Mrs. Soeda and wearing his Jeremy Hillary Boob parka, eased his way inside. Mrs. Soeda lightly rested an encouraging hand on his shoulder and then left. When he heard the door shut behind him the boy's expression stiffened even more, as if there were a sudden increase in air pressure. If Mrs. Soeda had been by his side he would probably have been more relaxed. He wasn't used to being alone with just me. Yet there was a mysterious reason that he needed to speak with me. Probably.

"Hey," I said to him.

The boy showed no reaction.

"Why don't you come over here and take a seat," I said. I pointed to the chair in front of the desk.

After some thought he approached the desk with measured steps, like a cautious cat, but just glanced at the chair and didn't sit. He stood there next to the desk, his back straight, his chin tucked in.

Maybe he didn't like the chair. Or maybe it was his way of showing he wasn't quite sure enough about me to want to settle in. Either way, if standing suited him better, fine by me.

The boy stood there, silent, staring at the oversized envelope on the desk. The one with his handwritten map of the town inside. The fact that it was on my desktop seemed to draw his attention. His face was expressionless, as if he wore a thin mask, yet it seemed that behind it some sorts of thoughts were racing.

I decided to let him be. I didn't want to interrupt what seemed to be his deep thought process. And Mrs. Soeda would soon be bringing over the tea and muffins. If the boy and I were going to have a conversation, whatever it turned out to be, it could wait until then. Usually it was the job of someone else on staff, not Mrs. Soeda, to bring over sweets for the boss, but I predicted that she'd bring over the tea and muffins herself. Anything to do with the boy seemed important to her.

And sure enough it was Mrs. Soeda who brought it all over, entering the room with a round tray in hand. On the tray were two teacups, a small sugar bowl and slices of lemon, and the two blueberry muffins. The cups and saucers and sugar bowl were all a matching design, older, lovely items. Wedgewood, by the look of it. The spoons and forks were silver and glistened humbly and elegantly. My guess is that these were all personal items Mr. Koyasu had brought from his home. Not at all the kind of things you'd expect to find in a small town library. Tableware only brought out for special guests, I would imagine.

With a soft clatter, Mrs. Soeda arranged the cups and plates and sugar bowl on my desk. Thanks to which my normally drab office suddenly had the refined, quiet feeling of an afternoon salon. The sound of a Mozart piano quartet would have suited nicely.

When the muffins I had bought at the coffee shop near the station were taken out of the paper bag, placed on the plates with their lovely pattern, with the silver forks next to them, they looked like sweets of some noble lineage. White linen napkins folded into triangles and a single red rose would have completed the look, but that was asking too much.

"Thank you so much. It's lovely," I said to Mrs. Soeda.

Mrs. Soeda didn't reply or show any expression, but merely gave a slight nod and exited the room. It was just the boy and myself, alone again.

The boy hadn't spoken a word. When Mrs. Soeda had come in, and then left, he hadn't looked at her at all. He paid no attention whatsoever to the tea and muffins on the desk, or to the elegant tableware and silverware. He kept his gaze riveted on the envelope, his sharp gaze never wavering a fraction. Behind that expressionless face his mind seemed ceaselessly at work.

I picked up a cup and took a sip of tea. The perfect temperature and strength. The tea Mr. Koyasu had made for me was so delicious, but Mrs. Soeda seemed equally adept at brewing tea. She was, I would bet, the type who earnestly pursued things—as long as they were worth pursuing. Intelligent, attentive, a woman diligent at everything.

I suddenly wondered what kind of person her husband was. I hadn't met him, and she'd never said much about him. So I had no mental image. The little I did know was that he was from Fukushima Prefecture (though not from this region), had worked for about ten years as a teacher in an elementary school in town, and used to be Yellow Submarine Boy's homeroom teacher. When would I have a chance to meet him and talk with him, I wondered.

■

The boy's tense look finally relaxed a bit. His thought process seemed to have passed its peak and slowed down a little. I could feel it getting looser. There was still tension, but not as much as before.

The boy's gaze finally left the envelope and took in the tea and muffins neatly arranged on the desktop.

"Blueberry muffins," I said. "They're really good."

The same lines I'd used the day before at the coffee shop. Yesterday he'd totally ignored my invitation, but now he showed some interest. He stared at them for a long time. A sharp, critical eye, like Paul Cézanne assessing the shape of apples piled in a bowl.

His mouth moved slightly, as if starting to form words but then brushing them away. So no words emerged. This might have been the first time in his life he'd ever laid eyes on blueberry muffins, and maybe he was assembling information about them in his mind. But how much information about muffins could possibly be included? I had no clue. There were too many things about this boy I couldn't understand. I cut the muffin in half with a fork, and cut that in half again, and put that quarter of the muffin in my mouth.

"It's delicious," I said. "Best to eat it while it's still warm."

The boy watched intently as I ate the quarter of the muffin. With the same look he had as he watched the mother cat nursing her kittens. He reached out, grabbed the other muffin from the plate, and took a bite. He didn't use a fork, or a plate to catch the crumbs, crumbs spilling down onto the floor, but he didn't seem to care. And neither did I. A quick vacuuming later would take care of it.

The boy downed the muffin in three quick bites. His mouth wide open, noisily chewing away. Blueberry stains appeared around his mouth, but he didn't seem to care. And neither did I. It wasn't like paint or anything. Just blueberry juice. Just wipe it away with a tissue later.

Maybe he was challenging me with his rough behavior, testing me. A thought hit me. Mrs. Soeda had told me he'd been raised in an affluent family, so he should have learned some table manners. Maybe he was intentionally acting rude to see how I'd react. Hitting a new ball back into my side of the court. Or maybe he simply didn't understand table manners—or didn't recognize the need for them. Maybe that's all it was.

Either way, I let it slide. With this boy, the only thing to do was accept what came. Just showing interest in a blueberry muffin and actually picking it up and eating it was an important step forward for our relationship.

I speared another quarter piece and put it in my mouth and quietly ate it. I dabbed at my mouth with a handkerchief and took a sip of tea. Still standing, the boy picked up the cup of tea and, adding no sugar or lemon, slurped it. Again ignoring table manners, even though the tableware looked like Wedgewood. Again, I pretended not to notice.

"They really are delicious muffins," I said to the boy in a carefree voice.

The boy said nothing, and just neatly licked away the blueberries stuck to his lips. Much like a cat licking its whiskers after eating.

"I bought these yesterday at that coffee shop. I was thinking of having them for lunch today," I said. "I had Mrs. Soeda heat them up in the microwave. The blueberries are grown by a farmer in the area, and a neighborhood bakery uses those to bake muffins every morning. So they're fresh."

Again no response from the boy. He stared at his now empty plate. Like a lonely passenger up on deck, gazing at the horizon after the sun has set.

I left half my muffin and held out my plate to him.

"I have half left, so would you like a little more?"

The boy gazed at the proffered plate for some twenty seconds, and finally reached out and took it. After a moment's thought he used a fork this time, cut the piece in half, placed it on his plate, and quietly ate it. Other than the fact that he was standing, his table manners were fine. Once he finished, he took out some tissue from his pants pocket and wiped his mouth.

Had he learned something watching me? Or given up on challenging me? I couldn't decide which. He returned his empty plate to the desktop, and quietly, and politely, drank his tea. The ball was back in my court. Most likely.

The blueberry muffins eaten, the tea all drunk, I put the plates and cups and sugar bowl back on the tray and tidied up the desk. The only thing remaining on the desktop was the envelope with the map inside. Right around the spot where Mr. Koyasu used to place his navy-blue beret. I glanced around the room, my faint hope that maybe he was there, but no one was. The only ones here were Yellow Submarine Boy (though dressed today in his brown parka) and myself.

"I looked at the map that you drew," I said. I took it out and placed it next to the envelope. "It's very accurately done. Almost like the real thing. I was impressed, or . . . maybe I should say surprised. I say *almost* because I myself don't know the exact shape of the town. So it's not your fault."

The boy stared straight at me through his glasses. Other than the occasional blink his expression remained static. No expression at all in his eyes, just momentary shifts in the intensity of light.

"I lived for a time in that town," I said. "The town drawn in this map. I worked in a library there, too. But there wasn't a single book in that library. Not a single one. More like a former library, I guess you should say. Instead of books, my job was to read the old dreams stacked up there on the shelves, one by one. The old dreams were shaped like large eggs, and covered in white dust. They were about this big."

I indicated the size with my hands. The boy gazed steadily at this but didn't comment. Just absorbing the information.

"I don't know how long I lived there. Seasons came and went, but I feel like the flow of time there was different from the changes in seasons. At any rate, time there basically had no meaning.

"While I was living there, I went to that library every day and read those old dreams. I don't recall how many of them I read. But the number wasn't important, since the number of old dreams was nearly infinite. I worked after the sun set. I'd start reading in the evening and usually finish very late at night. I don't know the exact time. There were no clocks in that town."

The boy instinctively glanced at his own wristwatch. He checked that time was indicated there, then turned his gaze back to me. Time seemed to have a certain meaning to him.

"During the day I was free to do what I wanted, but I couldn't go out much, since the sunlight hurt my eyes. To become a Dream Reader my eyes had to be cut, which was done by the Gatekeeper before I could enter the town. So I couldn't walk around as much as I needed to draw a proper map. Also, the brick wall that surrounded the town changed shape a little day by day, like it was making fun of my efforts to create a map. Which is one of the reasons why I couldn't grasp an overall view of the town.

"The wall was made from bricks precisely laid upon each other and was very high. It seemed to have been made in the distant past, but there was not a sign of wear and tear. It was unbelievably sturdy. No one could climb over the wall to go outside, and no one could climb over it to come inside. That sort of unique wall."

The boy took a small memo pad and three-colored pen from his pocket. A vertical, spiral memo pad. He quickly wrote something down in it and held it out to me. I took it from him. There was one short sentence written there.

To prevent an epidemic.

Neat block printing. He'd written it hurriedly, yet it looked just like it had been printed, not handwritten. There was not a speck of emotion in it.

"'To prevent an epidemic,'" I read aloud. And I pondered this as I looked at him. "So the brick wall was built to prevent an epidemic from coming into the town. Is that what you're saying?"

The boy gave a slight nod. *Yes.*

"Why do you know this?"

There was no answer. His lips remained shut tight and he continued to gaze at me, devoid of expression. Probably telling me that *this is not something we need to discuss at this point.*

But if the wall was, as the boy was saying, constructed to prevent an epidemic, this could have many meanings. I don't know when it was, but from the moment it was built that high wall functioned to forcefully, and strictly, keep the residents shut away inside and block nonresidents from getting in. The only ones who could enter and leave the town were the unicorns, who lived in their own settlement; the Gatekeeper; and a handful of people with special qualifications whom the town needed. I was one of those. The Gatekeeper might have had a natural immunity to the epidemic, which would explain why he was the only one who could freely go in and out of the gate.

That wall was no ordinary brick wall. It towered there imbued with its own will, its own unique life force. And the town was completely enveloped in its hands. At what point, and how, had the wall acquired that power?

"But the epidemic had to have ended at a certain point," I said to the boy. "No epidemic lasts forever. Yet the wall went on as before maintaining a strict isolation. No one could come in, no one could go out. Why is that?"

The boy took the memo pad, turned to a new page, and again smoothly wrote something down in ballpoint pen.

A never-ending epidemic.

"'A never-ending epidemic,'" I read aloud. "What's that all about?"

Again, no response from him. I was left to my own devices. Like solving a riddle, and a very difficult one at that. Considering the level of difficulty, there were too few hints. Still, I had to return the ball served into my court. That was the rule of the game. If you could call it a game, I had to return it.

I went ahead and said, "An epidemic that's not really an epidemic. In other words, epidemic as metaphor . . . Is that it?"

The boy gave the tiniest of nods.

"Is it, possibly, like an epidemic of the soul?"

The boy nodded again. Clearly, emphatically.

I gave this some thought for a while. *An epidemic of the soul.* And then I said, "The town, I mean the people who ruled over the town at the time, surrounded the town with a high, indestructible wall in order to shut out the spreading epidemic raging through the outside world. Like sealing it up tight. And they implemented a secure system that lets no one in, and no one out. The construction of the wall must have included some magical elements as well.

"But finally at some stage something happened—what, I don't know—and the wall began to function with its own unique will and power. A power so overwhelming that people could not control it. I wonder if that's what happened?"

The boy stayed silent, staring at my face. No yes or no. But I went on. This was all a guess on my part, but probably went beyond mere conjecture.

"And the wall, in order to completely eliminate all types of epidemics—including what they thought of as an *epidemic of the soul*—reworked the town and the people in it. Reconfigured the town. And created a firmly closed-off system. Is that what you're trying to say?"

There was a knock at the door. Not a loud sound. A terse, simple sound—a real sound coming from the real world. Two knocks, a pause, then two more.

"Come in," I said, in a voice that didn't sound like my own, but someone else's.

The door opened a crack, and Mrs. Soeda stuck her head inside.

"I've come to collect the dishes," she said reticently.

"Please go ahead. Thank you," I said.

She came inside, her steps stealthy, took the tray with the plates and cups, and quickly checked that they were empty. She seemed relieved to see that they were.

She glanced at the muffin crumbs on the floor but seemed to pretend she hadn't noticed them. She could always come back later to clean up.

Mrs. Soeda looked at me with a slightly questioning look, but I nodded that everything was okay, and she took the tray and left. The door shut with a metallic click. And once again the room was enveloped in silence.

The boy opened to a new page in his memo pad and quickly wrote something down in it. He passed the memo pad to me across the desk, and I read it.

I have to go to that town.

"'I have to go to that town,'" I read aloud. I cleared my throat and passed the pad back to him. When he took it, he finally sat down and gazed directly at me, his eyes unwavering, deep beyond measure.

"So you're hoping to go to that town," I said, checking. "The town surrounded by a high wall. That town where people have no shadows, where the library lacks a single book."

The boy nodded emphatically. As if to say there was no room for debate.

Silence continued for a time. A heavy, dense silence. A silence that contained many meanings. And then the boy broke the silence with his slightly high-pitched voice.

"I have to go to that town."

I brought my fingers together on my desktop, and gazed at them for no particular reason, then looked up and asked, "Even if going *there* means you can never be *here* again?"

He gave another emphatic nod.

I mentally pictured the boy passing through the gate, going inside the town surrounded by a wall, and living there. For him this would be "Pepperland." The colorful Shangri-La that appears in the movie *Yellow Submarine*. Deep down inside him, utterly seriously, this sixteen-year-old boy wanted to move to a different realm, rather than continue living in this real world that didn't (seem to) accept him. I couldn't help but feel, painfully, how deadly serious he was.

A time of silence ensued again, and then he spoke again.

"I'll read old dreams. That's something I can do."

He pointed to himself.

"You are able to read old dreams," I mechanically repeated.

"I'll read old dreams in that library. Forever."

Just like when he wrote something in his block printing, his spoken words were neatly distinct.

I silently nodded.

You know, he might just be able to do it. It would be little different from the way he spends each day here in this library. Deep inside that library are the old dreams, dusty, piled up high, that he should read. Countless dreams, perhaps infinite. And each dream singular, one of a kind.

"I have to go to that town," the boy repeated, his voice more distinct than before.

"I HAVE TO GO to that town," the boy repeated.

"You want to leave this world and go inside that wall?" I asked.

The boy was silent, and gave a short, decisive nod.

That town surrounded by a wall, needless to say, was no Pepperland, no imaginary utopia cooked up for an animated film. Beautiful people there, surrounded by beautiful nature, lived beautiful lives. It overflowed with enjoyable music and colorful flowers. A momentary fantasy world with a whiff of the 1960s drug culture. The town behind a wall, though, wasn't like that.

There beasts starve to death because of the freezing winter. The people there live taciturn, shabby lives. The food they are provided is simple and insufficient, their clothes nearly worn to threads. No books, no music. The canal is dried up, most of the factories closed. The communal housing where they live is dingy and dim, on the verge of collapse. There are no dogs or cats. The only living creatures you could see were the birds that flew back and forth over the wall. Far from a utopia. How much did the boy understand about this?

I was thinking I might tell him more of these details but then thought better of it. He was probably already aware of all of that. And, accepting it all, had made up his mind to go there. An unwavering conclusion he'd arrived at after much careful thought. His firm expression told me the seriousness of his decision. But still I needed, even more at this point, to make sure of his feelings.

"Going into that town means discarding your shadow and having both eyes wounded. These are the two conditions to go through the gate. Before long, your shadow will die. And you won't be able to leave that town. Are you okay with that?"

The boy nodded.

"You might not ever be able to see anyone from the world on this side, ever again."

"I don't mind," the boy said aloud.

I took a deep breath. The boy's heart was not at all connected with the real world. In a real sense he had never put down roots in this world. He was like a balloon temporarily tethered here. Floating a little above the earth, seeing different scenery from the ordinary people around him. So it was neither painful nor scary for him to untie himself and leave this world forever.

Unconsciously I gazed around me. Was I myself connected tightly to something here? Had *I* put down roots? I thought of the blueberry muffins. And the tone of Paul Desmond's alto sax coming through the speakers in the coffee shop near the station. And the thin, lonely female cat, its tail straight up, cutting across the garden. Were these things holding my spirit here in this world, if even a little? Or were they simply trivial details, not worth mentioning?

I looked at the boy. Behind his metal-frame glasses he gazed at me with narrowed eyes. As if reading my feelings.

"But how are you planning to get to that town?"

He pointed at me, then at himself, then off into the distance.

I put his gestures into words. "You're saying I'll take you there. Is that right?"

The boy in his Jeremy Hillary Boob parka silently gave an emphatic nod. *Yes.*

"But can I do that?" I asked. "I can't will myself into that town. Let alone guide you there. It was coincidence, *chance*, that took me there."

The boy gave this some very careful thought (or at least he looked like he did). And then, without a word, he popped to his feet. He took a neatly folded white handkerchief from his pocket and politely wiped his mouth again. Perhaps the gesture was his way of thanking me for the blueberry muffin. Or maybe just a habitual act. I couldn't tell the difference.

He put the handkerchief back in his pocket, walked over to the door, opened it, and without a glance back, or a word of farewell, exited the room. Behind him the door closed with a metallic click, leaving me alone.

"I'm to take *you* there?"

In a low voice, I aimed these words at myself.

I pictured pulling the boy by the hand and standing in front of the town gate. Without a moment's hesitation the boy in his green *Yellow Submarine* parka would, I imagined, leave me (without a backward glance) and step right through the gate.

I would probably never again pass through that gate. I'd already been stripped of the ability to do so. I would see the boy off, watch the gate close behind him, and go back alone to the world on this side.

I stood up and went to the window, pushed it up, then stuck my head out and took a few deep breaths. The crisp winter air pierced my lungs. For a long while I randomly gazed at the deserted winter garden. Hard patches of snow dotted the ground like white stains.

Several less than memorable days passed by. The weather continued sunny, windless, the bright sun melting the thick icicles hanging from the eaves. As I listened to the drip, drip of the melting snow outside the window I sat at my desk doing office work, while the boy was in the reading room, as always, immersed in reading. I asked Mrs. Soeda what books the boy was reading now, and she had the answer at her fingertips. He was deep into such as *The Icelandic Sagas*, *Wittgenstein on Language*, *The Collected Works of Kyoka Izumi*, and *The Home Medical Encyclopedia*. All of them thick books. Regardless of the contents, he seemed fond of longer books. Thinner books might be unsatisfying. Like a person with a healthy appetite who orders a restaurant's thickest steak.

The boy and I had no contact in the week following our tête-à-tête in my office. Once again wearing his *Yellow Submarine* parka (probably back from being washed), shouldering his green backpack, he showed up every day as usual in the library, but even when I passed by him in the reading room I didn't speak to him and he never as much as glanced in my direction. He remained fixated by his reading, seemingly uninterested in anything else. And that probably was true. For my part I sat at my desk in the office, taking care of the day-to-day tasks that came my way as head of the library. Boring office work, you could call it, but as long as it involved books, even if it was as mundane as collating classification numbers, I could find an enjoyable aspect of it. We—the boy and myself—were each taking care of what needed to be done here in the real world.

Yellow Submarine Boy wanted more than anything to go to the town surrounded by a high wall, and become one of its citizens. He'd made up his mind, even if it meant never returning to the world on this side. Nothing here in the world on this side had the power to detain him. That much was clear. Yet he wouldn't be able to get to the town under his own steam. He needed my guidance. The only one who knew the way to get there—who had, indeed, followed that way—was me, and me alone.

Yet I couldn't recall the specifics of that route. In the past I had simply gone there. Or to put it more precisely, last time I was, before I was aware of how it happened, *taken there*. Ask me to follow the same path again, and I wouldn't know how.

And there was one other thing I couldn't decide on—the question of whether it was really the right thing to do to take the boy to the world over there. Was it a morally acceptable thing? If the boy did go inside that town, settled down there as the Dream Reader, his existence would, no doubt, be extinguished from the real world.

I hadn't killed my shadow, and had let him escape outside the wall, which allowed me to return to this world (or, more accurately, be sent back here), and my existence here wasn't erased. All conjecture on my part, yet I'd grown increasingly certain of it.

But if the boy had his shadow stripped away, and that shadow subsequently died, the boy's existence in the world on this side would be permanently, decisively lost. Mrs. Soeda told me he had no friends, but surely his parents and brothers would mourn him if he disappeared. Especially his mother, who doted on him so much . . . So was it right for me to invite this sort of situation? No matter how earnestly the boy might wish for it, no matter whether I thought that it was the more natural direction the boy's life should take, wasn't this an unethical act?

I wanted to ask someone about it all. Mr. Koyasu, for example. He understood the situation, had the requisite wisdom, and might be able to advise me on how to proceed. But Mr. Koyasu—or Mr. Koyasu's ghost—hadn't appeared to me in quite some time. And who knew if he would ever appear again. His soul might have already left this earth. It was a distinct possibility. He'd told me that the soul only remains on the earth for a limited time, and that it was no easy task for it to take on human form.

I considered asking Mrs. Soeda, but decided it was next to impossible to explain to people living an ordinary life how, for a time, I'd lived in a town surrounded by a high wall. That could make things complicated. She might end up more anxious about my mental state than about the boy. No, bringing up that town was out of the question. At this point those who would accept what I'd experienced there, what I'd seen and done, were Mr. Koyasu and Yellow Submarine Boy—those two and no one else.

I went over to Mrs. Soeda and, timing it when she didn't seem busy, casually asked her about the boy. About his home life in particular.

"I recall you saying M**'s mother dotes on him?"

"Yes, that's right. She loves him so much, it's like the way you love a pet cat."

"How about his father?"

Mrs. Soeda tilted her head a fraction. "I don't know much about his father. I've never actually met him. What I hear from others, though, it sounds like he's not that interested in the boy. This is all hearsay, though, and I don't know for sure."

"Not that interested in him?"

"I think I mentioned this before, but his two older brothers were at the top of their class at school here, went to famous universities in Tokyo, and have followed an elite path. And the father is so gratified by their accomplishments—these sons who would do him proud wherever they go. Compared to them, the youngest son didn't even attend the local high school, spends every day reading in the library, and, frankly, says some wacky things. They'd prefer he keep a low profile. The father seems embarrassed by all this."

"You said that his father runs a kindergarten here in town?"

"That's right. A quite impressive facility for a kindergarten. But he's also branched out into other businesses—an exam prep school, and classes aimed at adult learners, those sorts of things. Quite the entrepreneur, certainly outstanding, though not what you'd call the education type. At least from what I hear.

"They limit M**'s reading at home. His father argues that reading all the time is unhealthy and will only buy a limited number of books for him. They strictly limit the time he's allowed to read, which has to be hard on him. For him reading is as natural as breathing."

"What about his mother? How much does she understand about the boy? About his special abilities, what separates him from ordinary children?"

"As far as I can see, she's very emotional. She adores him, but probably doesn't really *get* him. She doesn't seem much interested in developing his special abilities, or finding a place where he can put them to good use."

"That's why she doesn't want to let him leave her?"

"Right. Actually, I've proposed this a number of times. Maybe it's not my place, but I gave her my honest opinion. There are several specialized facilities in Japan that take in and educate children like him, I told her, and in a place like that he could develop his innate abilities even more. I don't think there's any future for M** if he stays in this town. But that logic didn't sway her. She totally believes that the only way he can grow is under her care."

I thought about what Mrs. Soeda had said for a time, and then said, "According to what you said, it sounds like his family home is not a warm place for him to be."

"M** never shows his feelings, so I have no way of knowing how he feels about it. But yes, I can imagine that his home is not exactly a very pleasant place for him. There's the father who doesn't care about him, the always hovering mother. Neither one of whom truly understands him or even makes an attempt to do so."

"What about his relationship with his two older brothers?"

"His brothers who moved to Tokyo are too busy, too wrapped up in their own lives. They're young, so you'd expect that. They rarely come back here, much less have the time to deal with their eccentric, dropout kid brother."

"Which explains why he comes to the library every day. Here he doesn't need to talk to anyone and can immerse himself in reading."

"It is pointless to say this now, but if only Mr. Koyasu were still alive," Mrs. Soeda said, "since he was the only one the boy trusted. It's such a pity he's no longer with us. For M**, and for the library."

I nodded. Mr. Koyasu's death left a deep hole in many places.

What Mrs. Soeda told me allowed me to see a lot more details about the boy's family, which left me a little relieved.

The boy did have a reason for wanting to leave his family so much, and to leave this world. If he were to suddenly disappear from this world, his mother would surely grieve. But for his sake, separating the boy from his mother might be a good thing. Just like the point when kittens are separated from their mother and become independent. When the mother cat loses her kittens, she runs around, frantically searching for them, but then she gives up and forgets them. And the cycle repeats. This is the natural path that animals take. Like the changing of the seasons.

The father and the two brothers would, of course, be devastated if the boy were to suddenly vanish somewhere, or pass away. They might feel guilty for not having paid enough attention to him. But they were too wrapped up in their own affairs to lament him for long. The boy, too, had no one you could call a friend. In this world, the boy lived a solitary existence. If he were to vanish, the gap would be filled in no time. Quietly, without a sound, or even a ripple.

Hypothetically, if I were in his position—though as Mrs. Soeda said, being in his shoes and surmising what he was feeling was no mean feat—I think I wouldn't want to stay in this town, but go to live in another world.

A world, say, like a town surrounded by a high wall.

THE NEXT MONDAY, I went as usual in the morning to visit Mr. Koyasu's grave. Facing the gravestone, I spoke about the boy. How he was hoping to go to the town surrounded by a high wall. How he'd asked me to take him there. But it didn't seem like I could make his wish come true. Because, first of all, I didn't know how to get there.

As you are well aware, I told Mr. Koyasu, the boy is totally isolated here. The boy strongly believes that leaving this world to transition to that other town was the natural, happiest choice for him.

And perhaps it was, since this real world was no place for him. No one truly understood him, including his blood relatives. His unique, innate abilities might be put to better use in the world on the other side.

But the thing was—even assuming I could do that—I wasn't at all sure that helping him make that transition was the right thing to do. Or even if I was qualified to do so. I mean, he was, all things said, just a sixteen-year-old boy. Even if they didn't fully understand him, if their emotional bond was tenuous, it was certain that if he was gone his relatives—parents and brothers—would be left deeply saddened. That's why Mr. Koyasu's take on things would be so critical. If at this moment he could hear what I said, I wanted to get his candid advice. I was, frankly, baffled, unsure of a way forward.

After I finished speaking, I sat down on the stone wall in front of the gravestone, waiting for some sort of response. But, as I had half expected, there was none. Just clouds leisurely making their way across the sky, from the ridge of one mountain to the ridge of another. For some reason that morning I couldn't even hear the sound of birds. Only the silence of the grave.

I spent a silent thirty minutes before the gravestone, like sitting alone at the bottom of a dried-up well, hugging my knees to myself. Nothing happened during this time. Only the gray clouds drifting by overhead, and the long hand of my watch making a half circuit of the face. The only things moving were these.

Occasionally I'd look up and cast a quick glance around me, but I didn't spot Yellow Submarine Boy anywhere. No one else was at the cemetery. I got up from the stone wall, gazed up at the winter sky for a while, then redid my scarf and brushed off the bits of leaves from my duffel coat.

Mr. Koyasu's soul had, I imagined, already left this world. A long time had passed since the last time I had seen him and spoken to him. And now Yellow Submarine Boy, too, was hoping to exit this earth. And after the two of them were actually gone (forever), I would have to remain *here*, living on. In what would no doubt be an insipid world, since I had grown fond of, and felt empathy toward, both of them.

As was my wont, on the way home I stopped by the nameless coffee shop near the station. I seemed well on my way to becoming one of those lonely middle-aged men who follow habits without really thinking about them. I sat at my usual spot at the counter, and ordered my usual black coffee and ate a plain muffin. (Blueberry muffins were sold out.) The woman behind the counter gave me her usual sunny smile.

Jazz guitar music was filtering out, quietly, through the speakers, but I didn't know the name of the tune or of the musician. I half listened to the music, letting the hot coffee warm my chilled body, tearing off small pieces of the plain muffin and eating them. Plain muffins had their own merits too.

"I've been thinking for a while how wonderful your coat is," the woman said to me. I looked over at the gray duffel coat on the seat next to me.

"This coat?" I said, a bit surprised. I folded up the morning paper I'd finished reading. "I've worn it for about twenty years. It's heavy as armor, the design is out of date, yet it's not that warm, really."

"But it's lovely. Everyone these days wears the same kind of down coat, so it's refreshing to see yours."

"Maybe you're right. Though it's not really suited to cold around here. I was thinking of buying a down coat before next winter. It's so much warmer and lighter. This is my first winter here, and I didn't know much about the climate."

"I don't know why, but I've always liked duffel coats. I find them attractive."

"I'm sure the coat, too, would be happy to hear that," I said, laughing.

"Are you the type who takes good care of things over the long haul?"

"Perhaps," I said. No one had ever said that to me before, but now that she mentioned it, it might be so. Or maybe I just found it too much trouble to buy a replacement.

I was the only customer in the shop, and while waiting for water to boil for coffee she seemed happy to have someone to chat with.

"You said this is your first winter here, so I assume you're not originally from this town?"

"I just moved here last summer and started living here then," I said. "So I know next to nothing about the town. I'd lived in Tokyo until then."

Other than the period when I lived in the town behind the brick wall, that is . . .

"Did you move here for work?"

"That's right. There happened to be a job opening."

"It's like my situation," she said. "I found a job and just moved here in the spring of last year. I lived in Sapporo before. And worked at a bank."

"Yet you quit your bank job and moved here."

"Quite a change in environment."

"Did you know someone here?"

"No, I didn't know anyone at all. Like you, I came here all by myself."

"And started working at this shop?"

"Actually, I found this property online. A coffee shop for sale. For various reasons the owner needed to quickly sell it. He let it go for way below market value, so I bought it, with everything included, and moved here as the new owner."

"Quite a bold decision," I said, impressed. "Quitting a job in a bank in a big city, moving here by yourself to this far-off little town you knew nothing about, and starting a business."

"There were reasons behind it. Like that boy who was here said? That Wednesday's child was full of woe."

"He didn't say it. *I* did. That it's a line from a nursery song. The boy just said you were born on Wednesday."

"Is that how it went?"

"That boy basically only states facts."

"Only states facts," she repeated, sounding impressed. "That's sort of amazing, isn't it."

She stepped away, turned off the gas, and began brewing some fresh coffee with the water she'd boiled. I stood up and put on my duffel coat. I paid the bill and was about to leave. But something held me back. I stopped and went back inside the shop and spoke to the woman making coffee behind the counter.

"This might sound pretty forward of me," I said. "But I was wondering if you wouldn't mind me inviting you out sometime, for a meal or something?"

The words flowed out, entirely naturally. No hesitation, no reluctance. Though I did feel my cheeks redden.

She raised her face and looked at me. She narrowed her eyes, as if looking at something she wasn't used to seeing.

"*Sometime?*" she asked.

"Today would be fine."

"A meal or something?"

"Like, dinner, maybe."

She pursed her lips ever so slightly, then said, "I close up shop here at six p.m. It takes about thirty minutes to straighten up everything, so I could go after that if that works for you."

That would be fine, I said. Six thirty was a good time for dinner. "I'll be back to get you at six."

I left the shop and walked home. As I walked along, I reviewed each and every word I'd spoken to her, which felt strange. Until that moment came, I'd had no intention of inviting her to dinner, yet the words had come out of my mouth almost on their own.

It had been a long time since I'd invited a woman out for a meal. What could have made me do that? Was I, maybe, attracted to her? Maybe I was.

If so, though, I didn't know what about her attracted me. I'd liked her in a vague sort of way for a while, but this wasn't the kind of feeling that would move me to seek more—a more intimate connection or something. She was a woman in her mid-thirties who every Monday served me coffee and a muffin, that's all. A slim figure who moved briskly as she worked, with a warm, winning smile.

Something about her must have particularly attracted me that day and led me to invite her out to dinner. Something in the abbreviated conversation we had must have propelled me to do that. Or maybe I was just tired of being alone and wanted someone I could have a pleasant conversation with. But that wasn't all there was to it. Intuition told me that.

Whatever the motivation, it was a fait accompli. Half unconsciously, almost reflexively, I'd invited her out to dinner and she'd accepted. Many things in life are like that, though, if you think about it—moving ahead on their own without regard for the intentions or plans of the person involved. To take it a step further, I'd have to say that at this point I was bereft of any intentions or plans.

On the way home, I stopped by a supermarket, bought a week's worth of food, and back home divided this up and arranged it in the fridge, and prepped meals to come. I then vacuumed the house, scrubbed the bathroom clean, changed the sheets and pillow covers on my bed, and washed the clothes that had piled up. And did some ironing while I was at it. The same procedure I followed every Monday. All the tasks done silently, and efficiently. Like always.

After three I'd finished up my chores, lugged my reading chair over to a sunny spot, and opened up a book I'd been reading. Somehow, though, I couldn't focus. This was, after all, not a usual Monday. I'd invited a woman out to dinner. And—after a few seconds' hesitation—she'd accepted. Was this really significant for me? Or was it simply some side episode, a little detour that had nothing to do with the larger flow of things? *The larger flow of things*—was such a thing even a part of my life?

I spent the time until evening vaguely considering all this. I switched on the radio, where I Musici di Roma was performing one of Vivaldi's concertos for viola d'amore. I sort of half listened to it.

The radio commentator spoke between pieces:

"Antonio Vivaldi was born in Venice in 1678 and composed over six hundred pieces in his lifetime. He was a popular composer in his time, also quite active as a superb violinist, though afterward he was completely ignored, a forgotten figure from the past. In the 1950s, however, his reputation once again grew, with the publication of his composition *The Four Seasons*, which proved popular, and over two hundred years after his death his name became, immediately, widely known throughout the world."

As I listened to the music, I thought about being forgotten for two hundred years. Two hundred years was a long time. Two hundred years in which he was "completely ignored, a forgotten figure from the past." No one knows, of course, what will happen in two hundred years. Or even in two days, for that matter.

All of a sudden I wondered what Yellow Submarine Boy was up to at this moment. How did he spend his time on days when the library was closed? If the library wasn't open, he surely had time on his hands. Since, according to Mrs. Soeda, his father strictly limited his reading at home.

At times like that I couldn't imagine how his brain processes operated. Maybe he took the massive amount of knowledge he'd amassed over the week, used that free time to organize it systematically and reorder it. He'd take the fragments he gathered from *The Home Medical Encyclopedia* and *Wittgenstein on Language*, connect them organically, intertwine them to transform them into one part of a massive "Pillar of Wisdom." What would that pillar—assuming it really was formed—look like, and what scale would it be? Was this formed internally, not exposed to others' eyes? I wondered. As an enormous input monument with no exit.

Maybe the order his father forced on him was the right thing to do (if you view the results, at least). It must have been necessary to put a temporary halt to reading (the input process) so the boy would have time to sort out the massive amount of knowledge he'd absorbed and store it in the proper order in the appropriate spot in his brain—like sorting out the food you buy in a supermarket and stowing it away in the fridge. But this was all pure conjecture on my part. The only one who knew what went on in his head was the boy himself.

Even so, I couldn't help but shut my eyes and try to picture this Pillar of Wisdom (as it might be called) that this solitary boy had created within himself. Was it like some massive pillar in a limestone cave towering in the darkness deep below the ground? Unseen by anyone, rising up boldly in the inky darkness where no one's feet had ever walked? In that sort of darkness, maybe two hundred years means nothing.

Perhaps by entering that town surrounded by a wall he might be able to effectively put that Pillar of Wisdom to good use. And find the right method to output this wisdom.

Yellow Submarine Boy . . . *He himself was capable of becoming a freestanding, autonomous library.* This thought struck me, and I exhaled deeply.

The ultimate personal library.

I WENT OVER to the coffee shop near the station a little after six. The woman was closing up when I got there. She turned off the lights, took off her apron, untied her hair, and put on a navy-blue coat. She removed the sneakers she wore while working and exchanged them for some low leather boots. She looked like a different person.

"Dinner or something," she said as she wound a scarf round her neck.

"If you're hungry, that is."

"I'm very hungry, actually. I didn't have time to eat lunch."

The thing was, I couldn't think of anyplace to eat. I'd hardly ever eaten out after I moved here. The food served in the few places I had eaten in wasn't very impressive. The service, too, left a lot to be desired. It was a small town deep in the mountains, after all. Can't expect the kind of smart restaurant you'd find in guidebooks.

I asked her if she knew of any good place to eat. "I still don't know much about this town," she said.

"Neither do I, but there might not be any."

I thought about it, and an idea popped into my head. "How about coming to my place? If you don't mind. I could whip together a simple meal there pretty quickly."

She hesitated, but then said, "What could you make? For instance."

I did a quick mental review of the food I'd put in the fridge earlier in the day.

"I could do a shrimp and herb salad and spaghetti with calamari and mushrooms, if that sounds alright. And I have a Chablis in the fridge that would go well with that. I bought it here in town, so we're not talking top of the line, though."

"Sounds so good, I'm sold," she said.

She locked up the shop and slung a leather shoulder bag over her shoulder. And we began walking together down the dark streets. The heels of her boots made a hard click against the pavement.

"Do you always prepare such nice meals for yourself?"

"It's too much trouble to eat out, so generally I cook for myself. Nothing fancy. Simple, easy-to-prepare meals."

"Have you lived alone for a long time?"

"I guess you could say that. I've lived on my own since I left home at eighteen."

"So you're a veteran of the single life, then."

"I suppose so," I said. "Not that it's anything to brag about."

"You know, I realized I haven't heard what you do for a living."

"I'm kind of the head librarian of the town library. It's a small library, so the title sounds more impressive than it is. We only have two full-time employees, including me."

"I see—a head librarian. That sounds like interesting work. I haven't been to the library yet. I love to read, and I knew there was a library in town, but work keeps me too busy."

"It's a small place, but we have a nice collection. The building is a renovated private home, a former sake brewery, and is quite attractive. You should stop by if you have time."

"What did you do before you became the head librarian?"

"After college, I've always worked in a book distribution company in Tokyo. Because I loved working with books. But for various reasons I quit that job and then just sort of lazed around for a while, but when I heard that the town's library was looking for a head librarian, I went ahead and applied."

"Did you get tired of life in the city?"

"No, that wasn't it. I wanted to work in a library, and looked for available openings, and this town just happened to be advertising for a position. Anywhere would have been good—the city or the countryside, north or south."

"I got divorced two years ago," she said as she carefully watched her step, as if checking to see if the street was frozen. "Things got complicated for a while, and I became pretty depressed. I didn't feel like doing a thing. The thought struck me that I should go far away from Sapporo—where, didn't really matter. As long as it was somewhere where no one knew me, anyplace in Japan would have been okay."

I gave a vague response. I didn't know what to say. She was silent for a while and then said, "And as I explained, I did an internet search and found that a coffee shop near the station in here was for sale. I actually traveled here to check it out and thought it looked good. I calculated the expenses and projected revenue and figured if I owned the shop and worked there, I could manage enough for me to live on. I used to work in a bank so I'm good at calculating those kinds of things. And I thought that if I came here to this remote mountain town, no one would be able to find me. So I quit my job at the bank and used my severance pay and savings to buy the place, and moved out here. Without telling anyone my forwarding address. I was lucky that the money I had on hand was enough and I didn't need to take out a loan."

"That's good."

"You're the first person I've told since I moved here."

"You didn't tell anyone?"

"No, not a soul."

"You never dug a hole, faced the bottom, and confessed everything?"

"Never did. What about you?"

I gave it some thought. "I might have."

Maybe we felt a bit closer, since our circumstances were similar. Two lonely people, outsiders, blown in by the wind to this tiny rural town deep in the recesses of Tohoku. With no friends here. And it wasn't clear if either of us would end up settling down in this place.

As soon as we got to my home, I switched on the heater, took off my coat, opened a bottle of white wine, poured it, and we made a toast.

In the kitchen I sipped my wine while tossing together the salad and spaghetti. She watched curiously as I buzzed around the kitchen. As I waited for the water to boil for the spaghetti, I minced a clove of garlic and sautéed calamari and mushrooms, then minced some parsley. I shelled the shrimp, sliced a grapefruit into even pieces, tossed soft lettuce and herbs together, and added a dressing of olive oil, lemon, and mustard.

"You really look like you know what you're doing. Very efficient." She seemed impressed.

"Well, I am a veteran of the single life."

"I'm still a beginner, and honestly I'm not that good a cook. Though I do like cleaning up the house. A natural trait, I suppose."

"How long were you married?"

"Not quite ten years."

"You were in Sapporo the whole time?"

"That's right," she said. "I was born and raised there. A very peaceful upbringing, in a very peaceful family. My husband was a classmate back in high school. After college I went to work at the bank and got married at twenty-four. I think our marriage was good at first, but then I realized things weren't going so well."

"I'm going to put the spaghetti in to boil. Could you time it for me?" I asked. "Tell me when eight minutes, thirty seconds have passed. And not a second more."

"Got it," she said. She looked up at the wall clock, all business. "Eight minutes, thirty seconds, and not a second more."

I put the spaghetti into the boiling pot, stirred it with a wooden spatula to separate the strands, divided up the salad, and set the table.

We sat across from each other at the small table, enjoying the chilled Chablis, eating salad and spaghetti, and afterward had some coffee. We skipped dessert.

It had been a long while since I had eaten a meal with someone. (It was hard to remember the last time.) To prepare a meal for someone, set the table with decent tableware, and enjoy a dinner and casual conversation together—it was all pretty nice. As we savored the food and sipped the wine we shared more about ourselves. That said, there wasn't much about me to share, so it was mainly about her life.

She had graduated from a cozy upscale women's college in Sapporo and began work at a local bank. She met her husband again at a high school reunion, fell in love rather quickly, and married at twenty-four. It was a lively wedding and reception, with their friends attending. Everyone wished them well on their new start in life. (This was some ten years ago, which would make her thirty-six now, about the same age as Mrs. Soeda.)

Her husband worked for a large food manufacturer, which mainly specialized in the import and processing of flour. They went to Bali on their honeymoon, but right after getting there he came down with a terrible case of food poisoning (probably brought on by eating crabs), had awful diarrhea and vomiting, and spent almost the whole trip in bed. He couldn't eat much, either. While he was prostrate in bed she swam in the hotel pool and read a book she'd brought from Japan. There was nothing else to do. When they arrived back in Japan she had a lovely tan, while her husband was pale and gaunt. Despite the inauspicious beginnings, their married life after that was peaceful and happy. The miserable honeymoon became a memory they laughed about.

"I don't know where things began to fall apart," she said, shaking her head a fraction. She took a sip of wine. "But at a certain point something critical broke down and things went south in all sorts of small ways. We were at odds, no matter what we did. We argued, and it gradually dawned on us that we didn't have all that much in common, and then sex was . . . You get what I mean, right?"

Another vague response from me. I picked up the bottle and poured her more wine. The wine brought a slight blush to her pale cheeks.

"So he ended up having an affair with a female colleague at work, I found out about it, and that was the immediate cause of our divorce. He never was good at hiding things."

"I see," I said.

"But his relationship with that woman wasn't all that serious, apparently. Just a spur of the moment, impulsive thing. He apologized for what he did, promised to never let it happen again. I guess this happens a lot. But I found I couldn't go back to the way I felt before."

I didn't have any particular response and merely nodded.

"But what I found more trying than getting divorced was that

I was no longer sure of my emotions," she said, eyes fixed on the wineglass in her hand.

"I felt like no matter what man I might meet later on, and maybe even marry, and no matter how much I felt I loved him, the same thing might happen all over again. I had never felt that way before."

"You said you knew him since high school?"

"Yes, we were in the same class. But we didn't go out then. We chatted a few times, that's it. Secretly I thought he was very attractive. He was tall, handsome, did well in school. But I was busy with the volleyball club, and he was the captain of the soccer team, and of course we were both studying for college entrance exams, so we really didn't have time to get to know each other one-on-one."

"Handsome and athletic."

"Right, the type that high school girls drooled over. He was, of course, super popular in our class. Anyway, I finished college, and we ran across each other at a high school reunion for the first time in a long while, where we had some drinks and talked, and hit it off right away. Like . . . The sort of *I liked you from a long time ago* type of thing. It happens a lot."

"Oh, does it?"

"Yeah, it does happen a lot, that kind of thing. I mean . . . have you never been to a class reunion?"

I shook my head. "Can't say I have, no. From elementary school all the way to college."

"You don't want to remember the past?"

"It's not that. Honestly, I never felt like I fit in at school or with my class. And there's no one in my classes I felt like meeting again."

"Wasn't there any attractive girl you liked in your class?"

I shook my head. "I don't think so."

"So you liked solitude from way back then?"

"I don't think anyone likes solitude. Anywhere, I think," I said. "Everyone's looking for something, for someone. The way they do, though, is a little different."

"Yes. You may be right."

After we had coffee, after we'd washed the dishes in the kitchen (I washed, and she used a towel to dry), the clock on the wall showed that it was almost nine. I'd better be going soon, she said. Work starts early again tomorrow. I brought over her coat and scarf and helped her into her coat. She tucked her straight black hair under the collar of the coat.

"Thank you for dinner," she said. "It was delicious."

"I'll walk you home," I said.

"That's okay. I'm a grown-up and can get back safely on my own."

"I feel like walking."

"On a freezing night like this?"

"Cold is relative."

"There were nights colder than this?" she asked.

"And a colder place, too."

She looked in my face for a time, then nodded assent. "Okay, then. I'll take you up on that."

We walked side by side on the road along the river. Occasionally the heels of her boots would step on a frozen patch and make a hard crunchy sound. As I heard that I couldn't help but think of when I used to walk the girl from the library home in the walled-in town. *There* I could hear the murmur of the river, the periodic cries of the night birds, the branches of the river willows fluttering in the wind. The old raincoat *she* wore made a dry rustling sound.

Time seemed all jumbled together inside me. The tips of two different worlds were overlapping, ever so slightly. Much like the mouth of a river at high tide when the seawater and river water flow up and down, back and forth, and mix together.

It was windless, but chillingly cold. The daytime had been fairly warm for the end of February, but once the sun set the temperature plummeted. We wrapped ourselves up tight in our coats and wrapped our scarves up above our chins. Our breath was white, breath so hard and pure you'd swear you could write on it. But I welcomed the cold, since it cooled down some of the confusion swirling around within me.

"I get the feeling I talked about myself and nothing else this evening," she said as she walked along. "Now that I think of it, you said hardly anything about yourself."

"There's not much in my life up till now worth talking about."

"But I'm interested. How you got to be the person you are now. I'd like to know."

"It's not all that interesting. I was born in an ordinary family, did ordinary work, and lived a quiet life by myself. A run-of-the-mill sort of life."

"You don't seem like a run-of-the-mill person, to me at least," she said. "You never thought of getting married?"

"A few times," I replied. "I'm an ordinary person, so yes, I did feel like that sometimes, like everyone else. But each time that possibility arose it never worked out. It got to be too much trouble to go through the same thing over and over."

"You mean falling in love?"

I had no good reply to that. Silence reigned for a time. That silence hung there in the air, shaped like a blank sheet of breath.

"Anyhow, thank you. It's been a long time since I've had dinner and had a nice talk with someone like this. It's the first time since I've moved to this town."

"I'm glad."

"The wine made me talk too much, I'm afraid. But I think you're a very good listener."

"When I drink wine, I always wind up wanting to hear what other people say."

She chuckled. "Though you don't say much about yourself, do you."

We found ourselves standing outside her coffee shop.

"This is where I live," she said.

"Here?"

"Yes, there's a living space upstairs. It's small but has what I need, and I manage. I'm thinking of moving to somewhere better, but I just can't find the time."

"Well, it *is* convenient."

"True enough. My commuting time is zero. It's not the kind of place I'd like to show to anyone, though."

She unlocked the door and went inside the shop. She switched on the light behind the counter.

"Can I invite you out again?" I asked, standing just inside the doorway. The words just slipped out without thinking. Just like some skillful ventriloquist was moving my mouth and talking.

"I mean, if it isn't any trouble for you." That much I managed to add on my own.

"If you make a delicious dinner for me again," she said, her expression serious.

"Of course. I'll be happy to."

"I'm joking," she said, and laughed. "I don't mind if it's not for dinner—please invite me again."

"What day is your shop closed?"

"I take off every Wednesday," she said. "The other days the shop's open from ten in the morning until six in the evening. How about your library?"

"It's closed every Monday. Other days it's open from nine in the morning until six in the evening."

"Seems we can only meet after the sun's gone down."

"Like a pair of owls."

"Like a pair of owls deep in a dark forest," she said.

"You should change your day off to Monday. You're the owner, so you're free to have your day off any day of the week you like."

She inclined her head and thought about this. "You're right. I should consider that."

She walked briskly over to me, stretched up, and gave me a quick kiss on the cheek. Very unaffectedly, as if it were utterly natural. Her full lips, perhaps because they'd been wrapped in her scarf, were surprisingly warm and soft.

"Thank you for walking me home. I haven't done this for so long, and I enjoyed it. Feels like a high school date."

"On a first date in high school you wouldn't drink Chablis or talk about how a divorce came about."

She laughed. "Ah, you got that right. But still—"

"Good night," I said. I tugged a knit cap out of my coat pocket and put it on. She waved to me and locked the door from inside.

A faint feeling of her lips on my cheeks remained. To hold on to that feeling, I wrapped my scarf up to just below my eyes. I looked up at the sky but didn't see any moon or stars.

Clouds must have emerged.

MAYBE IT WAS because I was lost in thought, but when I looked up, I realized my feet were carrying me to the library. It was nine forty by my wristwatch.

I was perplexed for a moment, but I decided to go ahead and stop by the library. Talking with someone so long, which I hadn't done for ages, and the feeling of those soft lips on my cheek made me want to get my thoughts in order, but not back home, where traces of her still lingered. It had been a long time since I'd felt this way.

Feels like a high school date, she'd said. Maybe she was right. She and I were still like *beginners*, in many senses of the word, as far as being in this region was concerned. Our minds and bodies still not used to this new environment. Like not being used to wearing new clothes. Our movements and speech were still a bit awkward around each other. And as I got so worked up over a thank-you peck on the cheek that I took the wrong direction home, I guess maybe I was not much better than some high school student.

I extracted the key chain from my coat pocket, unlocked the iron gate at the library's entrance a crack, then shut it. I walked up the gentle slope and opened the sliding doors at the entrance. Inside the library was dark and quite chilly. The green emergency light on the wall faintly lit up the inside. This was the third time I'd visited the library at night. I wasn't nearly as tense as the first time. I let my eyes adjust to the dark, and guided by the pale emergency light made my way to the counter and picked up the flashlight we always kept there. I shone the flashlight at my feet and walked toward the subterranean room down the hallway.

I quietly opened the door to the subterranean room, which was dark inside. There was a fire burning in the stove, though. Not huge flames shooting up, but several thick logs were indeed giving off an orange glow. And the air had its usual fragrance of old apple tree wood. The room's white stucco walls caught the firelight and were dyed a slight orange.

I looked around. Someone had filled the stove with firewood and lit it. It must have been Mr. Koyasu. And he must have been waiting for me here. But I couldn't see him in the room. Just the silently burning flames. The fire seemed to have been started quite some time ago, since it was burning so evenly and the little room was comfortably warm. I took off my scarf and gloves and sloughed off my duffel coat. I stood in front of the stove warming my chilled body.

"Mr. Koyasu," I ventured. There was no response. My voice didn't resonate and was absorbed by the four walls. Had Mr. Koyasu known ahead of time that I would go in the wrong direction tonight and stop by here? Or had he willed my feet to bring me here? In order to tell me something? I had no clue what powers a soul might possess.

But no matter how I scanned the room, he was nowhere to be found. No doubt about it. I stood there, alone, silently gazing at the orange flames, warming myself, observing time passing.

Those orange flames gave my heart a quiet warmth and sense of peace. Our ancient ancestors must have been like this, deep in a cave, in front of a fire, the flames giving them a sense of calm, at least for the moment knowing they were protected from the piercing cold and the fangs of ferocious animals. On a cold night a flickering reddish fire had the power to summon up a collective memory etched deep into our genetic makeup.

Mr. Koyasu had been here until a little while ago—that much I knew for sure. He'd put the firewood in the stove, lit it, adjusting the air intake valve so the fire was just right. He'd prepared ahead so that around the time I came the room would be a pleasant temperature. Mr. Koyasu was the only one who would do that. And yet he himself was absent. He'd gone off somewhere, leaving the fire in the stove.

Maybe some emergency came up all of a sudden. What kind of emergencies did the dead have? I had no idea, but something had come up and he couldn't stay here and wait for me. That must be it. Or maybe when he was lighting the stove his strength as a soul gave out (like a battery fading) and he could no longer maintain the appearance of a human being anymore? To take on human form, he'd said, in other words to appear as a ghost in this world, took a great deal of energy to pull off.

But all I was able to do right now was gaze at the fire in the stove and wait for something to happen. So I waited. From time to time, as if punctuating the deep silence, or as if testing if my voice could still be heard, I called out, low, into the blank space.

"Mr. Koyasu."

But there was no reply. Or nothing even close to hinting at a reply. The silence enveloping the room was heavy and dense, unflinching, like some thick cloud settling heavily in a spot in the winter sky. I opened the door of the stove and added more firewood.

I stood in front of the stove and thought about the coffee shop owner. (And what was her name? Why couldn't I recall hearing her name? And why hadn't I told her my name? Were names, for the time being, not an important issue?) Her slim body, her straight black hair, her face with but a hint of makeup, her full lips that sometimes curled up sarcastically. Was there something special about her that had attracted me? It wasn't that she was extremely young or beautiful (though, admittedly, she was ten years younger than me).

At any rate, she had settled down comfortably in a corner of my mind (in a spot where I could definitely see her) and she wasn't about to move. What—or who—was she reminding me of? But I just couldn't make a connection between her and something, or someone, else. She was her own person, quietly settled into a spot inside me.

An honest question for myself—did I have sexual desire for her?

I'd have to say I did. As a man with a healthy (I would guess it's healthy) sexual appetite, I did desire her sexually. No doubt about that. But this desire wasn't so strong I couldn't control it, and wasn't so sure of itself that it made me forget all the possible problems that expressing this desire could bring about. It was just a possibility, subtly changing its form, quietly knocking on the door to my heart. My ears could hear it knocking. A sound I'd heard before.

Let me come back to the main point.

Was I in love with her?

Most likely the answer was no. I wasn't in love with the woman from the coffee shop. I liked her, but that was different from love. I think the emotional and physical function needed in order to love—the kind of overarching impulse to give your whole self to another—had burned out in me long ago. I remember Mr. Koyasu telling me this once.

"You came across your very best partner at an early stage in life. You had to meet her, maybe I should say."

And that was probably the truth. Some bitter experiences I'd been through in life had taught me this very clearly. Driven them home to me, you could say. I'd learned this the hard way . . . paying more than a little to learn that lesson. I never wanted to go through that again if I could help it. The experience of unwillingly hurting someone else and being hurt myself as well.

That said, I still couldn't help imagining sleeping with her. I got the feeling that if I really asked for it, she might respond. And I pictured it—she would take off her clothes, the two of us would hold each other in bed. I imagined her naked body, the feeling of holding that body close. The same as when I was seventeen, in the train on the way to see *her* and imagined taking her clothes off. And I got the same guilty feelings I had back then. I couldn't separate the sexual desire I had back then from the desire I felt right now. The two of them intertwined, entangled into one inside me. And this left me more than a little confused.

I thought about the swell of your breasts, about what lay underneath your skirt. Imagining what was there. I'd fumble with the buttons on your white blouse one by one, fumble, too, to undo the hook of your white bra I picture you wearing. My fingers slowly reach out under your skirt. I touch your soft inner thighs and then . . .

I shut my eyes and tried to erase this reconstructed image from my mind. Or shove it aside to somewhere unseen. But the image wouldn't vanish so easily.

No. That's not it. That's not something now. Not something

that's from this place here. It's something that's already lost, already disappeared somewhere. I was just arbitrarily overlapping two separate images, from different times and different places. Not exactly the right thing to do.

My watch showed that it was just before midnight. I stood there, in the little square subterranean room in the bowels of the deserted library, before the woodstove, lost in thought as I warmed myself. A burned-up log fell with a clatter that rang out through the room. I glanced at the stove and then gazed about the room again.

"Sorry to have kept you waiting," Mr. Koyasu said.

"SORRY TO HAVE kept you waiting," Mr. Koyasu said.

Startled, I hurriedly looked around me. Mr. Koyasu was seated on an old wooden chair in a dark corner. Navy-blue beret, checked skirt, tweed jacket. And thin white tennis shoes. The usual outfit. He wasn't wearing a coat.

"Sorry about taking so long. I was planning to come here much sooner, but something prevented me from doing so."

I nodded silently, unable to find the right words. I turned to face him, my back to the stove. His face was paler than usual and seemed sad, somehow.

"I haven't been to the library in quite some time," Mr. Koyasu said. "And wasn't able to be seen by you. It's getting harder for me to take on human form. Perhaps the time is approaching for me to leave this earth."

Now that he mentioned it, he looked a bit smaller than usual, less substantial. If I looked at him long enough it was like I could almost see through him. Like the first stage in a movie fade-out.

"It's been a while," I said. "It makes me feel lonely not seeing you."

A faint smile rose to his lips. The changes in expression were muted.

"I'm very happy to hear that, but after all, I'm already dead. I'm only able to meet for a brief time. I've been granted a special grace period, that's all."

Been granted, I repeated to myself. But by whom? Asking him would draw things out, though. Before that I had something vital I needed to ask.

"A couple of things happened while you weren't here," I said.

"I believe I have a grasp of the gist of it all, but it might be best to hear it directly from you. So I don't misunderstand."

I told him about the boy in the *Yellow Submarine* parka and us exchanging a few words. About the boy wanting to leave this world and move over to the town surrounded by a wall. Arms crossed, Mr. Koyasu listened silently to what I said. No *I see* or *Is that right?* Only the occasional hint of a nod. His eyes remained closed the whole time, and I almost thought he was asleep. But of course he wasn't. He was minimizing his movements to conserve energy.

I finished what I needed to say, and Mr. Koyasu, arms still crossed, contemplated this. Or at least it seemed like it. He didn't stir an inch. He looked like he wasn't even breathing. But if you think about it, he was already dead. Nothing strange about not breathing.

Maybe people die twice. There's a fleeting, trivial death here on the earth, then the death of the actual soul. Though of course not everybody has that kind of death. Mr. Koyasu must be a special case.

"I'm happy the boy was able to talk with you," Mr. Koyasu said, finally speaking. "He doesn't talk to just anybody. Or rather, he hardly speaks to anybody at all."

"I call it a conversation, but it was mainly silent gestures and written messages on his part. He spoke very little."

"That's fine. Our conversations were mostly like that too. That's the usual way he speaks. That sort of disjointed communication is natural for him. At least in *this world*."

From inside the stove came a whooshing sound, like a cat growling, and I turned to look at it. But there was no change in the firewood. Maybe wind had whirled through the air intake pipe. I turned back to Mr. Koyasu. He sat there as before, his eyes barely open.

"He wants very much to go live in the walled-in town," I said. "The town I lived in in the past. To do so, though, you have to erase yourself in the world on this side. Since people who've lost their shadow wind up losing their existence in this world."

Mr. Koyasu nodded. "Yes, I'm aware of that. After all kinds of things happened, you could return to this world and recover your shadow. But what the boy is hoping for is to go over completely to that other world."

"It seems like it."

"As you are probably aware, this world is not suited for that boy. There's no place for him here."

"I sort of get it, too, how he's not suited for this world. But does that mean I should help him get over to that other world? Don't you think later on he might regret going there, that he might think it's better he never went there? I mean, he's only sixteen, and it's questionable whether he can decide for himself the ultimate path he's going to take in life."

Mr. Koyasu gave one slow nod. As if to tell me he got what I said, loud and clear.

"That town," I said, "once you enter is nearly impossible to leave. You have the high wall around you, and a powerful Gate-keeper who severely controls any movement in and out. And you can't say that the lives of the people there are very fulfilling. Winters are long and cold, and lots of beasts die from starvation or the cold. It's no paradise."

"Yet you chose to live there. And in that town surrounded by a high wall you were able to live the kind of life you'd been seeking. Even when your shadow asked you to leave, you chose to remain behind by yourself. Correct? Apart from how it all turned out."

I took a slow breath, and then let it out. Like a person who'd floated up from the bottom of the sea.

"Yes, that's correct. But I still struggle with whether I made the right decision or not. Whether I should have stayed in that town, or come back here. In the end, I was bounced back here despite my decision . . . So I can't predict whether that boy, if he gets to that town, will blend into the life there or not."

Mr. Koyasu's eyes, wide open now, were gazing at a corner of the ceiling. As if something special were lurking there. I followed his gaze but didn't spy anything out of the ordinary. Just the corner of the ceiling.

"So you are struggling over what to decide," Mr. Koyasu said.

"I really am struggling over it. Whether it's right to help his desires come true. Whether it's right to help that boy, to help a human being vanish from this world."

"If I may," Mr. Koyasu said, holding one finger up to emphasize the point, "there's no need for you to struggle over a decision. Because there's no need for you to make a decision."

"But he's asking me to guide him to that town. He doesn't know the way to get there."

"You can't do that. You've gone to that town, but that doesn't mean you know the way to get there."

"Exactly."

"So there's no need for you to struggle over a decision," Mr. Koyasu repeated quietly. "That's what I'm saying. Can you choose the dreams you have at night?"

"I don't think so."

"If that's true, then can you choose for another person the dreams that they'll have?"

"I don't think so."

"It's the same thing."

"So what you're saying," I said, "is that the walled-in town was nothing more than something I saw in a dream?"

"No, that's not it. What I'm getting at is in the realm of metaphor. The town behind a wall most definitely does exist. What I want to say is that there isn't a set route to get there. The path to get there differs from person to person. So if you decided to go ahead, you wouldn't be able to take him by the hand and lead him there. He has to discover, through his own power, his own personal route."

"So all my struggling over the decision and everything isn't going to find a way to help him transition to that town. Is that what you mean?"

"Exactly," Mr. Koyasu said. "He'll find his own way to get there. He will no doubt need your assistance in doing so, but what form that assistance takes is also something he has to find on his own. There's no need for you to decide a thing."

I thought over what Mr. Koyasu said yet couldn't grasp it completely. The logical sequence was beyond me.

Mr. Koyasu continued.

"Listen, you've already been a big help to him. You're the one who erected that town surrounded by a high wall in his mind.

Now the town is vividly alive within him. Much more real to him than this world."

"So you mean the memory of that town inside me has been shifted over to his consciousness as is? Like it was three-dimensionally transcribed."

"Yes, we know about his innate ability to absorb everything. As best I could, I might have been of some help to him, too."

"But it can't be an exact transcription. First of all because my knowledge of the town was incomplete. And second because it's hard to say my memory is accurate."

Mr. Koyasu nodded. "True, the town erected in his mind may differ in lots of small ways from the one you actually lived in. The basic structure is the same, yet the details have been changed so it's a *town made for him*. Since it's a town that exists *for that purpose*."

Maybe so. From when I lived there, the wall of the town was changing by the moment. Like the inner wall of an internal organ.

Mr. Koyasu paused for a moment, then spoke. "Be that as it may, well, there's no need for you to worry over which world the boy chooses. He'll choose himself the life he'll lead, based on his own judgment. He might not look it, but he's a tough kid. I have no doubt he'll survive in the world that's best for him. And you need to live the life you chose, in the world you chose to be in."

He crossed his arms again in front of his chest and looked me right in my face.

"You've done a lot of good for him already. You've provided him the possibility of a new world. And I am certain that's a good thing for him. It's like—how should I put it?—a kind of inheritance, maybe. Like how you succeeded me in this library."

It took a while for me to fully digest what Mr. Koyasu had said. Succeed? What have I passed down to Yellow Submarine Boy?

Mr. Koyasu unclasped his arms and brought them back to his lap.

"Well, I'm afraid I must be going soon. I'm just about out of time. There's a place for me, and I have to go there. So we might not have a chance to meet like this again. Most likely."

Mr. Koyasu's figure started to grow faint, right before my eyes, and finally vanished. Like smoke sucked up into the air, leaving only the old wooden chair behind. I gazed at that chair for the longest time, hoping against hope that he would appear again and apprise me of something he'd left unsaid. As much as I waited, though, he didn't show up. The old wooden chair sat there, forlorn in the silence.

The realization came to me that he had, without a doubt, vanished forever. Left this world for good. I could think of nothing more painful, or more sad. Sadder, even, than if anyone among the living had passed away.

The stove made another of its catlike howls, while the wind swirled around outside. I made sure the fire in the stove was out, then left the library and went home.

THE NEXT MORNING, when I slid open the front doors of the library and stepped inside I knew it was a different place from the library I had known before. The sensation of the air on my skin had changed, the color of the light shining in from the window was unfamiliar, and sounds resonated differently. All because Mr. Koyasu had disappeared from existence—forever, and totally. Though probably I was the only one who knew it.

No—Yellow Submarine Boy might know it too. He knew a lot of things intuitively, and had been close to Mr. Koyasu, so he might have sensed, naturally, that Mr. Koyasu's soul had exited the world. Or perhaps, as he had done with me, Mr. Koyasu had told him directly that he would no longer be here.

If I asked the boy about it, though, I doubted he would respond. He only spoke about what he wanted to speak about, and only when he wanted to, plus his speech was fragmentary, and symbolic. The only time you could have a conversation of sorts with him was when he wanted it to happen.

Mrs. Soeda still seemed unaware of what had taken place. At least, she didn't act any differently when she saw me that morning. She greeted me as always, a calm, faint smile on her lips. As with every morning, she briskly went about her work, directing the part-time staff when needed, and dealing with library patrons.

It was Tuesday morning. The sun, which we hadn't seen for a while, brightly lit up the earth. Icicles hanging from the eaves sparkled, and patches of frozen snow began to melt at a leisurely pace.

In the late morning, I went to the reading room and looked around. There were six patrons seated at desks, either reading or taking notes. Three were elderly people, and three looked like students. The old folks had plenty of time on their hands and used it to read, while the young people, in a perpetual race against the clock, sat there, notebooks and reference books before them, pens in hand. But I didn't see Yellow Submarine Boy among them. His usual spot was occupied by a fat, white-haired man.

I went over to the counter to speak with Mrs. Soeda. I had a few work-related items I needed to run by her, but then, as if it had suddenly occurred to me, I asked about the boy.

"I don't notice M** here today."

"Yes, he didn't seem to come today," Mrs. Soeda said casually. Occasionally the boy didn't show up at the library.

I was about to ask her about Mr. Koyasu but thought better of it. Instinct told me to avoid the topic. Best to leave a departed soul alone. And best not to even mention his name. I don't know why, but I just had that feeling. I figured it was also best to forgo my visits to his grave for a time.

Yellow Submarine Boy didn't show up at the library the next day. Or the day after that.

On Thursday morning, when I saw that, once again, he wasn't in his usual seat, I went over to Mrs. Soeda to ask about it. The boy hasn't been here for three days running, I said. What was up with him?

"I think he might be in bed, resting for a while," she said. "He reads so intensely his brain gets overloaded."

"But it hasn't been that many days since the last time his batteries ran out."

Mrs. Soeda lightly pushed up the bridge of her glasses. "You're right about that. The interval in between does seem shorter than usual."

"There's probably nothing to worry about, but I do feel a bit concerned if I don't see him for a few days."

Mrs. Soeda pursed her lips for four or five seconds, then said, "Now that you bring it up, I've been a little worried myself. Why don't I call his mother later and find out how he is." Then she went back to work.

After lunch Mrs. Soeda showed up at my subterranean room.

"I phoned his house during lunch break," she said. "I spoke with his mother, but it was all quite baffling."

"Baffling?"

"Yes, I couldn't really understand what she was saying. She seemed distraught. Something had definitely happened, but I got nowhere over the phone in finding out what had taken place. It might be best to visit them and ask directly."

"I agree," I said. "Why don't you go there. I'll spot you behind the counter."

"Alright. I'll go see what's happened. Thank you for taking over."

She went to the staff room, put on her coat, and scurried out of the library. I stood in for her at the counter on the first floor for about an hour. There was little to do, though, it being a weekday afternoon. People in the warm reading room went on reading quietly or taking notes.

Mrs. Soeda returned just before two p.m. She went to the staff room and removed her coat, then came over to me, her cheeks a bit flushed. Her voice was tense.

"The bottom line is, the boy seems to have disappeared last night."

"Disappeared?"

"From Monday morning he had his usual fever and was resting in bed. This morning when his mother went to his room to check up on him, she found his bed empty and the boy nowhere to be seen. His mother flew into a panic, but piecing together what she told me, that's pretty much it."

"So he left their house in the middle of the night?"

Mrs. Soeda shook her head. "His mother insisted that wasn't the case. M** had gone to sleep, dressed in pajamas, and no other clothes of his had been taken away. No coat, or sweater, or trousers— nothing. In other words he disappeared, at night, wearing only pajamas. It was freezing last night and you can't go out like that, but even if he had, he would have frozen to death by now, she said. And all entrances and windows were locked from the inside. She said before she goes to bed, she always makes sure they're locked. So he couldn't have opened a door or window and gone outside that way. Yet there it is—the boy vanished. Like smoke."

I tried to put all this in some kind of order in my mind. "If that's true, then isn't the boy hiding somewhere inside the house?"

Again Mrs. Soeda shook her head. "They turned the place upside down, checking under the floorboards and all the way to the attic. But there was no sign of him."

"Very weird indeed," I said. "Did they ask the police to search for him?"

"Yes, they reported it to the police right away. But because it had only been a few hours since they realized he was gone, and there was no sign of a kidnapping, the police told them to wait for a while and if there still was no sign of him to get back in touch. That's the extent of their response. Like they expected he would eventually pop up from somewhere . . ."

All I could do was fold my arms and give it some thought.

"His family's been scouring the area outside all morning, canvassing the neighbors to see if anyone saw him. But no clues so far. The boy suddenly vanished from a house where everything was locked up tight. And dressed only in pj's."

"Was that *Yellow Submarine* parka also left behind?"

"Yes. His mother insists that other than pajamas no other clothes are missing."

If the boy had indeed run away from home, he would have surely worn his favorite *Yellow Submarine* parka. Of that I was certain. Something about that well-worn parka had a calming influence on him. Leaving that behind meant he hadn't walked out of the house. Which could only mean that in the middle of the night, wearing only pajamas—clothes that made no sense— he had moved on to somewhere else. Or was *transported* there. Somewhere—like the town surrounded by a high wall.

I shut my eyes and tried to think. But emotions swelling up from inside scattered those thoughts in every direction. I just couldn't pull it all together in any coherent way.

"And also," Mrs. Soeda said, "the boy's father said he'd like to come talk with you, if you're available."

"With me?" That was a surprise.

"Yes. He said he'd like to meet you and speak with you directly."

"That's no problem, of course. But what exactly should I do?"

"He said he'll come to the library today at three, so would that be convenient for you?"

I glanced at my watch.

"That'll work. Have him come to the second-floor office."

But when I met the boy's father, what should I say? I certainly couldn't say anything about the town surrounded by a high wall. Mentioning anything about the boy leaving this world to transfer over to another world was, needless to say, out of the question.

If only Mr. Koyasu could be here, I thought, wishing it with all my heart. Now more than ever I needed his deep wisdom and words of advice. But it was more than likely that he no longer existed here, in this realm, anymore. He'd vanished, gone somewhere else forever. I looked up at the clock on the wall and let out a deep sigh.

The boy's father arrived at the library shortly after three. Mrs. Soeda led him to the office on the second floor. We briefly introduced ourselves, I handed him a business card, and he did likewise.

He was tall and nearly bald. I'd put him at mid-fifties, and he had long ears, thick eyebrows, and wore sturdy black-frame glasses. To me his facial features seemed wonderfully symmetrical. That was my first impression of his face—that the left-right symmetry was perfect. He stood straight with excellent posture and seemed strong willed. I could picture him as an orchestra conductor. He was running a preschool and juku, an after-school prep school, now, but I imagined he'd taken command, conducting numerous situations throughout his life, always with the utmost self-confidence. He and Yellow Submarine Boy shared no features at all, as far as I could see.

He twisted his body as he shrugged off his overcoat. Beneath it, he wore a checked wool jacket and a black turtleneck sweater. I beckoned him to take a seat at our little guests-only sofa set, and he nodded and sat down. I sat in a chair across the table from him.

Mrs. Soeda came in and placed tea on the table before us, bowed, and left the room. Once the door was shut we sat there, facing each other, silent for a time. As if making sure no one else was in the room other than the two of us. Then the boy's father spoke.

"I was very close to Mr. Koyasu, the head librarian who preceded you here, since long ago. My son's been frequenting the library now for a while, and Mr. Koyasu was kind enough to keep an eye on him."

"It's quite sad that he passed away," I said.

The father looked at me a little strangely. "So you knew him?"

"No, unfortunately we never met. He had already passed when I took over this position. I've just heard a lot about him from people and got the impression from what they say that he was an outstanding person."

"Yes, he was a wonderful person. He used his own personal fortune to establish this library and did everything he could for it. No one in this town has ever spoken ill of him. Except—" he began to say, and found it hard to continue. He set to work trying to come up with the appropriate words. "Except . . . how should I put it . . . there was something a bit *different* about his speech and behavior. Eccentric, you might say. Especially after he lost his son and wife. Nothing, though, that ever caused any particular issues."

I nodded vaguely.

"But I came here today about my son M**," he said.

I nodded vaguely again.

"I'm sure Mrs. Soeda has told you the gist of it, but my son disappeared last night. The last time he was seen was ten p.m., and this morning, before seven, when my wife went to his room to check on him, his bed was empty. It showed signs of having been slept in and was soaked in sweat. My son had had a high fever the whole night, apparently. But he wasn't there. My wife frantically looked for him, calling out his name. And I joined in the search. But we didn't find him."

He removed his black-frame glasses, gazed at them for a while, as if checking the thick lenses, and then put them back on.

"There was no sign of him having left the house. The doors and windows were locked tightly from the inside, and all his clothes were still there. My wife keeps a close eye on all his clothes and is positive nothing's missing. And needless to say, it's impossible that he went out on that cold a night wearing only pajamas."

The boy's father was silent for a time, as if mulling over his own words.

I asked him, "In other words, during the night, M** vanished from your house. But you don't know how? Is that correct?"

The father nodded. "Yes, my son vanished like smoke from us. I can't explain it any other way."

"Has he ever vanished suddenly like this before?"

He shook his head. "As I'm sure you've noticed, M** was born with some peculiar tendencies. He's not an ordinary child, and sometimes his behavior is quite odd. But he's never caused a problem like this before, going out without telling us. He values his daily habits above all, and once a habit is established, he insists on it, like a train on a fixed track. He never deviates from his habits. If they get messed up, he gets confused, even angry at times. So he's never gone missing like this, even once."

I tilted my head. "It's a very strange thing, isn't it. I can't figure it out."

"It's incomprehensible. How could he go out like that—without any real clothes on, no shoes, with no sign that he unlocked anything? And on a freezing night in the middle of winter? I've contacted the police, of course, but they don't seem to want to deal with it. All they say is to wait a little more and see what happens. I came here today to ask you if you had any idea at all what's going on. I'm basically grasping at straws here."

"Ask *me*?"

"Yes, I heard that you'd talked with my son."

I chose my words carefully.

"Yes, I did speak with M** once or twice. But it was quite disjointed, gestures and writing and such. Not what you would call a real conversation."

"Still, he was the one who came to you, who initiated the conversation?"

"That's right. He spoke to me first."

He sighed and rubbed his large hands in front of him as if warming them before an imaginary bonfire.

"I'm quite embarrassed to say this," he said, "but for years I've never had a decent conversation with him. When I speak to him, I get no response, and he's never talked to me. He does say a few things to his mother, but only practical, everyday matters.

"The only one he really talked with was Mr. Koyasu. I don't know why, but Mr. Koyasu was the only one he opened up to. And Mr. Koyasu was kind to him, like he was his own child. As parents we were grateful for this. However fragile it was, that was his connection with the outside world."

I nodded, and the boy's father went on.

"I don't know what the two of them talked about. I never ventured to find out. I thought it best to keep it between them. But Mr. Koyasu suddenly passed away last fall, and M** lost his only confidant and was all alone again. He didn't go on to high school, and just spent every day at this library, silently reading books.

"As I said before, M** lacks many of the skills needed to live an ordinary life, but has other special abilities instead. One of these is the ability to race through books at an unbelievable speed, absorbing a huge amount of information. But I just don't get the point of that. And another thing I don't get is whether this kind of extreme behavior is beneficial to him, or harmful.

"I imagine Mr. Koyasu must have grasped this, to some degree at least. And then guided my son the best way he could. But now that Mr. Koyasu is gone, sadly I have no one to ask about what's going on.

"And in the midst of all this . . . now he's disappeared. Just up and vanished in the middle of the night."

I didn't say anything, waiting for his words. After a pause, he went on.

"And then you took over as head librarian here after Mr. Koyasu passed. My wife heard from Mrs. Soeda that our son had quite an interest in you. What I'd like to know is what you and M** talked about. What you talked about might have some bearing on his disappearance. Or at least might provide some hint about it."

I was stumped as to how to respond. I couldn't very well tell an outright lie to his father, who was so (apparently) worried about his son's safety. But neither could I reveal the whole truth. It was all too complicated, too removed from common sense. I had to watch my step about what I should tell him, and what I shouldn't. I braced myself, trying to find words that would at least be close to the truth.

"What I talked about with M** was a kind of fable. I talked about a *certain town*. A fictitious town, as it were. The minute details are all real, yet it's a town based on a variety of hypotheses and suppositions. More accurately, I didn't speak to M** directly about this. I told a *certain person* about it, and M** overheard, so to speak. At any rate he seemed quite enthralled by this town."

This was the truth, as far as I could take it. At least it wasn't a lie.

M**'s father thought long and hard about this. Like someone trying to swallow something stuck in the back of his throat that just wouldn't go down.

"According to his mother," he said, "he spent a few days at his desk, totally focused on drawing a picture of some sort, a kind of map, maybe. He was so into it he forgot to eat, or sleep. Was this connected to that town?"

I nodded vaguely. "Yes, I'd say so. I think he was drawing a map of that town. A map he created based on what I talked about."

"And have you seen this map?"

I hesitated a moment, then nodded. I couldn't lie. "Yes, he showed me the map."

"Was the map accurate?"

"Yes, it was surprisingly precise. And I'd given only the bare outlines of that fictitious town."

"M** has that sort of ability," his father said. "The ability to, in an instant, put together all kinds of unconnected, loose fragments into an accurate overall picture. Like with one of those thousand-piece jigsaw puzzles, he can easily assemble it before you know it. Since he was little, I've seen him display that talent any number of times. As he grew up he became more cautious trying not to expose his special abilities to others."

Yet, I thought, for some reason he couldn't suppress showing his ability to tell what day of the week a person had been born.

His father continued. "I apologize for asking this, but honestly do you think there's some connection between the fictitious town you talked about and M**'s sudden disappearance?"

"At least as far as common sense is concerned I would say no, there's no connection." I chose my words carefully. "What I talked about with M** was only about an imaginary, fictitious town, so what he drew was a detailed map of something that doesn't exist. What we talked about was all based on fiction."

At least as far as common sense is concerned.

That was all I could say, but thankfully his father was the type who lived in a world constrained, and defined by, common sense. So it would never occur to him that his son had actually set foot in that fictional world. Something I should be grateful for.

"Still, M** was extremely interested in that town, wasn't he. Totally absorbed by it, would you say?" His father looked bewildered.

"Yes, it seemed that way to me."

"So in your conversations you spoke of that *fictitious* town to him. Did any other subject come up?"

I shook my head. "No, nothing else. That's all he was interested in."

His father was silent, lost in thought. After many twists and turns, though, those thoughts seemed to arrive nowhere. The tea on the table before us was now cold. Neither of us had taken a sip. His father, apparently resigned, relaxed his shoulders and took a deep breath.

"People seem to think I'm an indifferent, cold father to him," he confessed. "I'm not trying to make excuses, but I wasn't indifferent, really. I just didn't know how to approach him. I tried to get close to him, and did my best as I saw it, but he never reacted to any of my overtures. It was like talking to a stone statue."

He reached out, picked up a teacup, took a sip of the now cold brew, frowned a bit, and returned the cup to its saucer.

"I've never experienced something like this. I have three sons, and the older two are the type of boys you can easily imagine—

they did well in school, never caused any problems or trouble for me. They grew up normally, then went to the city in search of a new world. But M** is, innately, a different story. I can understand that he was born with some special, probably valuable qualities, but as a parent I had no idea how to deal with him, how to raise him.

"I'm known as an educator, of sorts, yet I'm embarrassed to say that as far as the boy is concerned, I felt powerless. What hurt the most was his utter lack of interest in me. We lived under the same roof, parent and child, but it was as if he didn't even know I existed. Being related by blood means nothing to him. Honestly, I envied Mr. Koyasu. I agonized over what he might have that I didn't to connect with my son."

As I listened to him, I sympathized with him. In a sense we were similar. Yellow Submarine Boy wasn't so much interested in me, either, as a person, but in the place I used to live. I might have been nothing more than a passage to that place he simply traversed. When he was with me maybe all he was seeing was that town?

"I'm sorry to take your time when you must be busy," his father said, glancing at his watch. "I'm going to go back to the police now and ask them to investigate again. We're also going to make the rounds again of a few places that might be connected. If you notice anything, please get in touch with me. My cell phone number is printed on the business card I gave you."

He stood up, twisted himself again as he put on his coat, and thanked me.

"I'm sorry I couldn't be of much help," I said.

His father weakly shook his head.

I saw him to the library entrance, then went back to the reception office. I gazed out the window, lost in thought. I spotted the skinny female cat slowly making her way diagonally across the garden. I remembered Yellow Submarine Boy studying the cat and her kittens so intently.

Mrs. Soeda came back to the room, tray in hand, and gathered the teacups.

"How was your talk with him?" she asked.

"He seems quite worried about his son. I'm afraid I wasn't very helpful."

"He probably just needed someone to talk to. It's painful worrying all alone."

"I really hope they can find him."

"But it's so strange, him disappearing at night like that. It was freezing cold then. I'm very worried."

I nodded silently. I could tell she had the same fear as me. The fear that we would never see the boy again . . . I could sense it in her tone.

AND, INDEED, the boy never came back.

After his parents had pleaded with them repeatedly, the town police finally pulled out all the stops to investigate, but could find nothing. Yellow Submarine Boy was nowhere to be found in the town. And, of course, he never showed up at the library. They checked security footage from the railroad station, but there was no sign of him having boarded a train or bus. (Local train and bus lines were basically the only means of public transportation out of town.) In his father's words he truly vanished *like smoke*. As far as the mother knew, the boy had taken no other clothes or luggage, and all he had were a few coins for lunch money. It was totally baffling. Two days passed in this way, then three.

Perhaps the only one who had any idea at all of where he had gone was me. The boy had found a way to get to the walled-in town (though I had no idea how) and had gone there. Like I had done so long ago, he went through a secret passageway inside him, traveling to another world.

This was just personal conjecture on my part, of course. I had no proof and couldn't explain it logically. But I was sure that the boy had already made the transition over to that town. No doubt about it. There was no other explanation for such a complete and total disappearance. He had wanted with all his heart to go to that town, longed for it, and his uncanny, inborn powers of concentration had likely made it possible. Put another way, he possessed the *qualifications* to reach that town. The same qualifications I myself used to have.

I pictured Yellow Submarine Boy entering that town.

He'd meet up with the powerful Gatekeeper at the gate, have his shadow ripped away, and his eyes injured. Just as it had been for me. The town needed a Dream Reader, and I imagined him smoothly taking over as my successor. And probably—no, undoubtedly—he would be a far more able and effective Dream Reader than I ever was. He had the ability to immediately grasp every detail, combined with tremendous powers of concentration that never flagged or lost interest. And through the massive amount of information he'd already infused into his mind, he himself had become a kind of living library—a massive reservoir of knowledge.

I tried picturing the scene of the boy in his *Yellow Submarine* parka, in an inner room in that library, reading old dreams. Would that girl sit beside him? Would she have lit the stove, warmed the room for him, and prepared strong green herbal tea to heal his weakened eyes? A faint sadness came over me as the thought arose. Like colorless water, utterly devoid of warmth, my heart was quietly immersed in that sadness.

On Monday, I got a late-morning phone call at my house. It was my day off, so I was still in bed. I'd been awake for a few hours but just didn't feel like getting up. A long thin line of sunlight slanted in through a gap in the curtains, as if criticizing my laziness.

I never got phone calls. There was really no one here in town who called me. The sound of the phone ringing in the morning on my day off was jarring, unreal. So I didn't get up to answer it. I just lay there, listening to this bell ring on and on. It rang twelve times, then seemed to give up.

A minute later, though, and it was ringing all over again. It sounded a bit louder, more piercing, than before—though I must have been imagining that. It rang ten times and now it was my turn to give up. I got out of bed and answered it.

"Hello," a woman's voice said.

At first I didn't know who it was. The voice of a woman who was neither young nor old. Neither high pitched nor low. I was sure I'd heard it before but couldn't connect the voice with any person. But then the tangled memories somehow linked up, and I knew who it was. The owner of the coffee shop.

"Good morning," I said, wringing out the words from deep in my throat.

"Are you okay? Your voice sounds different from usual."

I gently cleared my throat. "I'm okay. I just couldn't get the words out."

"That's because you've lived alone so long. If you don't talk to anyone for a while it's hard sometimes to get the words out. Like they're stuck in your throat."

"Does that happen to you?"

"Sometimes. I'm just a beginner at living alone."

A short silence followed. And then she spoke.

"This morning two nice-looking young men came to the shop. To have coffee."

"Sounds like the first line in a Hemingway short story," I said. She chuckled.

"It's not that hard-boiled," she said. "To be more precise about it, those two didn't come to my shop to drink coffee. They wanted to talk with me. They ordered coffee while they were at it."

"They wanted to talk with you," I said. "Was this part of a pickup line?"

"No, I doubt it. Unfortunately, maybe I should say. At any rate, the two of them were a bit young for me."

"How old were they? Those two?"

"One was mid-twenties. The other around twenty or so, I'd say."

"So not too young for you."

"Thank you. That's kind of you to say that," she said, her voice nearly devoid of expression.

"So what did the two of them and you talk about? Apart from any possible attraction."

"They are actually the Wednesday Boy's older brothers."

"The Wednesday Boy?"

"You know—that odd boy who barged in here once and asked me to tell him the date I was born."

I shifted the phone to my other hand. And got my breathing under control.

"That boy's older brothers came to your shop . . . But why?"

"They're searching for their missing brother. They've been standing around outside the station, showing everyone a photo of their brother, asking people if anyone's seen him."

"And they came into your shop, ordered coffee, and asked you the same thing."

"They asked me, 'Have you seen this boy?' And I told them, 'Yes, I have.' And I explained, briefly, what happened then. How he asked me my birth date, and when I told him, he said it was a Wednesday. I checked later, and sure enough, it was. But that all happened before he was spirited away, so I don't think it helped much with the search."

"Spirited away?"

"Yes, those were the words they used. Our younger brother disappeared from our home, they said, but it wasn't like he ran away or anything. He vanished in the middle of the night, like he'd been spirited away. That's what they said."

"*Spirited away*—now that's a pretty old term."

"It is, but in a little town in the mountains like this it sounds right," she said. "I assume you're aware of that, that the boy has disappeared?"

"Yes, I'm aware of it."

"When I told them this, they seemed puzzled. Their brother is very shy and wouldn't go into a place he wasn't familiar with. They asked, 'Why did he come into this shop on that day?' So I explained. I said it was probably because you, the new head librarian of the town library, were sitting at the counter, drinking freshly brewed coffee. He must have spotted you from outside, through the window, and came in. Since he seemed to have something he needed from you."

I didn't know how to respond, so kept silent.

"Maybe I shouldn't have said all that?"

"No, not at all. He came into the shop because I was there, and he saw me."

Or maybe he'd been following me that morning.

"And while he was at it, he told me which day of the week I was born on."

"Telling people the day of the week they were born is like his way of saying hello to people he's meeting for the first time. His way of showing closeness to the other person."

"A pretty unique way of saying hello, I would say."

"For sure."

"Those two pleasant young men wanted to know the reason why their unique kid brother was so interested in you, the newcomer."

"They must find that unexpected, since the boy isn't interested in very many people. *Why him?* they must be wondering."

"I suppose so. From the way they talked, it sounded like the boy didn't have much interest in his brothers either. They lived under the same roof but might never have had a good heart-to-heart talk. That's just a personal impression, though."

"You're very observant."

"It's not being observant, but if you work in this business you start to pick up on things. All kinds of people come here and talk about all types of topics. I just listen and nod my head. I generally forget what they talked about, but my impression of them remains."

"I see."

"Which is why I think those two polite, handsome young men might be visiting the library sometime soon to meet you. To pick up a clue about where their missing brother might be."

"I'm okay with that, of course. To talk with the two of them. But it might not help their search."

"Because he was spirited away?"

"I don't know," I said. "From what you said, though, it sounds like those brothers are really doing all they can to find their brother."

"As soon as they heard that their younger brother was missing, they rushed back home from Tokyo to help their parents, who were at a total loss, and helped out in the search. The oldest brother took time off work, as did the younger brother, who took a leave of absence from university, and though they haven't found any clues yet they're doing everything they can to search for him, the two of them working together. It's like they're—how should I put it?—compensating for something."

Like they're compensating for something. Makes sense. I got the same feeling when I was talking with the boy's father.

"Today's Monday, so the library's closed, right?"

"That's right. That's why I'm home at this hour."

"Oh, right. One more important thing I forgot to say," she said as if suddenly recalling.

"What could that be?"

"I just now got in some blueberry muffins, hot from the oven."

I could envision black coffee, steam rising, and soft, warm blueberry muffins. The image roused me, and a healthy appetite returned. Like a stray cat that has wandered back home.

"I'll be there in thirty minutes," I said. "Could you hold two blueberry muffins for me? I'll eat one there, and take the other to go."

"Okay, I'll hold two blueberry muffins for you. One to go."

WHEN I PUSHED OPEN the door to the coffee shop, two customers were already there. Two mid-thirties women, probably settling in for a nice chat after dropping off their kids at elementary school or preschool. They were seated at a small table by the window, whispering to each other, serious looks on their faces.

I sat at the counter, ordered my usual black coffee, and ate a blueberry muffin. The muffin was still slightly warm, moist and soft. In this way the coffee became my blood, the muffin part of my flesh. A precious source of nutrition.

I loved to watch her, nimbly at work behind the counter. As always her hair was pulled tight behind her and she had on a red gingham apron.

"So are those brothers still handing out the boy's photo in front of the station?"

"I would guess so," she said as she washed dishes.

"But they haven't found any clues yet."

"They haven't found anyone who's seen the boy. From what I heard, the way he disappeared was very odd. They can't explain how he got out of the house in the middle of the night by himself."

"It's a mystery."

"He seemed to me to be a pretty mysterious child from the start."

I nodded. "He had some strange abilities. Not your ordinary child, for sure. He saw the world differently from us."

She stopped washing, looked up, and gazed at me.

"Are you free to talk this evening after I close up? If you have the time, I mean."

"Of course I have the time," I said. After the sun set, my only plan was to listen to a classical music program on FM radio while reading.

"Okay, I'll close up shop at six as always, so could you come a little after that?"

"Sure," I said. "I'll be here a little after six."

"Thanks."

The shop got crowded around lunchtime, so I decided to make my exit. She put a blueberry muffin in a paper bag to take with me.

Back home the first thing I did was wash a week's worth of laundry that had piled up. As the washing machine did its thing I vacuumed and gave the bathroom a good scrub. I cleaned the windows and made my bed. When the laundry was done, I hung it out on the frame outside to dry. Then I listened to the FM radio broadcast of an Alexander Borodin string quartet while ironing some shirts and sheets. Ironing sheets took time.

The radio announcer said that at the time Borodin was better known, and more respected, as a chemist than as a musician. At least to me, though, nothing about the string quartet seemed like the work of a chemist. Smooth melodies, gentle harmonies—who knows, maybe there was an element of chemistry to it after all.

Finished ironing, I grabbed my tote bag and went out shopping. I bought food I needed at the supermarket, then, back home, prepped some meals. Washed and sorted out the vegetables, wrapped up the meat and fish in plastic wrap, and put the ones that needed to be frozen in the freezer. I made some soup with chicken bones and parboiled pumpkin and carrots. Doing these household tasks one by one I felt, bit by bit, my usual self again.

Based on my less than stellar knowledge of classical music, Alexander Borodin was one of the so-called Russian Five. Who were the others? Mussorgsky, then Rimsky-Korsakov . . . but I couldn't recall the others. As I arranged things in the fridge, I did my best to recall, but it was a no-go. Not remembering them didn't cause any problems or anything, though.

I left home at five thirty. During the day the gentle sunshine had brought a promise of spring to come, but come sundown a cold wind suddenly blew up, as if winter had won back its lost territory. I buried my hands in my coat pockets and headed toward the station. For no special reason the mental picture came to me of

Borodin doing some complex chemical experiment while lovely melodies played in his head.

After six there were no customers left in the coffee shop, and she was straightening up. She had loosened the hair she'd had tied up, taken off her gingham apron, and was dressed in a white blouse and slim jeans. Her lean figure looked wonderful. Well proportioned overall, and her movements were supple.

"Can I help with anything?" I asked.

"Thanks, but I'm good. I'm used to doing it by myself, and it doesn't take long. Just take a seat and relax."

I did as she said, sat on a stool at the counter, and watched her briskly wrap up for the day. It seemed that there was a set order she did things in. She dried the washed dishes and placed them on a shelf, switched off all the various devices, totaled up the register, and lastly lowered the blind at the window.

After closing, a hush fell over the shop. A silence deeper than necessary. The shop looked like a totally different place from when it was open during the day. All her tasks done, she meticulously washed her hands, wiped each finger with a towel, and came over and sat down on the stool beside me.

"Do you mind if I smoke a cigarette?" she asked.

"Not at all. I didn't know you smoked."

"Only one cigarette a day," she said. "After I close up shop, I sit here at the counter and smoke just one. It's like a little ceremony."

"The other day you didn't smoke."

"I hesitated to. I thought you might not like it."

She took a pack of long-sized menthol cigarettes out of the cash register, extracted one, and stuck it between her lips, struck a match from a matchbook, and lit it. She narrowed her eyes, enjoyed inhaling and then exhaling the smoke. The cigarette seemed mild, and as long as she didn't smoke too many, I figured it wasn't that harmful.

"Would you come to my place for dinner, like last time?" I asked.

She gave a small shake of the head. "I think I'll pass today. I'm not hungry. I might have a bite later, but I'm fine now. If you don't mind, could we just sit and talk for a while?"

"Sounds good," I said.

"Do you drink whiskey?"

"When I'm in the mood."

"I have a really nice single malt. Will you have some with me?"

"Of course," I said.

She went behind the counter and pulled down a bottle of Bowmore twelve-year-old whiskey. The bottle was half empty.

"That's a great whiskey," I said.

"It's a gift from someone."

"Is this also one of your little ceremonies?"

"Sort of," she said. "My own secret ceremony. Each day one menthol cigarette and one glass of single malt. Or sometimes wine."

"Single people need those kind of modest rituals in their lives. To get through each day."

"Do you have those too?"

"Several," I said.

"For instance?"

"Ironing. Making soup stock. Doing ab training."

She seemed to want to give an opinion on this but held off.

"With whiskey," she said, "I don't use ice, just a little water. What about you? If you want some ice, I can put some in."

"I'll have the same as you."

She poured a double into each glass, added a splash of mineral water, and gently stirred them with a swizzle stick. She set both glasses on the counter and came back to sit beside me. We clinked glasses together and each took a sip.

"A very aromatic flavor," I said.

"People say that Islay whiskies have the fragrance of peat and sea breeze."

"Could be. Though I couldn't tell you what peat smells like."

She laughed. "Me neither."

"Do you always drink it this way? With just a bit of water?" I asked.

"Sometimes I drink it straight, or on the rocks. But most of the time like this. It's expensive whiskey, and this doesn't ruin the aroma."

"And you always drink just one glass?"

"Yes, just the one. Depending on the day I might have another just before bed, but never any more than that. Otherwise, it could get out of hand. Living alone, I'm scared of that. I'm still just a beginner."

Silence continued for a time. The silence of the closed-up shop lay heavy on my shoulders. To break the silence I asked, "Um, do you know the Russian Five?"

She shook her head a fraction, and quietly, slowly, crushed out the menthol cigarette in the ashtray, as if rubbing it out. "No, can't say that I do. It is something to do with politics? An anarchist group maybe?"

"No, no connection with politics. It was a group of five Russian composers active in the nineteenth century."

She looked at me curiously. "So . . . what about them? The group of five Russian composers."

"Nothing. I'm just asking. I can remember the names of three of them, but the other two escape me. I used to know them all. It's been bothering me most of the day."

"The Russian Five," she said, and laughed happily. "You're a strange one."

"I think you told me you had something you wanted to talk with me about?"

"Ah, that's right," she said. She brought the glass of whiskey to her lips and took a small sip. "But as time's gone by, I don't know if I should tell you."

I likewise took a sip of whiskey. I savored the sensation as it slowly made its way down my throat, and waited, silently, for her to go on.

"Because if I tell you this you might be disappointed and not want to see me anymore."

"I don't know what you're going to tell me, but if there's a good opportunity to say it, I think it's best to go right ahead. My own rather limited experience tells me that if you let the right opportunity slip by things usually get kind of messy."

"But is now the right opportunity?"

"You've finished work for the day, have had a slim menthol cigarette and a couple of sips of an excellent single malt, so I'd say, yes, this might be the right opportunity."

A faint smile rose at the corners of her mouth, like the moon rising over the ridge of a mountain. She brushed the hair back from her forehead. Her long, slim fingers were shapely.

"If you put it that way, I guess I'll do my best. You might be disappointed when you hear it. Or maybe not disappointed at all, and I'll have embarrassed myself and afterward find myself left all alone."

Afterward find myself left all alone?

No comment from me on this. Since I knew she was about to launch into whatever she had to say.

"I've never told anybody this before."

The thermostat of the AC unit on the ceiling clicked on loudly. I kept silent.

"Can I ask you a direct question?"

"Of course."

"I'm not sure how to put this, but are you—interested in me as a woman?"

I nodded. "I guess I am. Now that you ask me, I'd say I definitely am."

"And that includes a sexual component."

"To some extent."

She frowned ever so slightly. "To some extent, meaning how much, actually? If you don't mind telling me, I'd like to know."

"Well, specifically . . . Let me see. Earlier today I changed the sheets on my bed, and as I was smoothing out the wrinkles, I thought about you lying on the bed. It was just a supposition, a possibility and nothing more, but it was a wonderful possibility."

She swirled the glass of whiskey in her hand. Then she said, "I think that makes me very happy you said that."

"I think that makes me pretty happy to hear that makes you happy. Though I'm sensing a *however* here."

"However . . . ," she said. She took her time choosing the words.

"However, unfortunately I can't respond to that hope of yours, or the possibility there. Though I wish I could."

"You have somebody else?"

She shook her head decisively. "No, no one like that. That's not it."

I silently waited for her to continue. She slowly swirled her glass again and sighed lightly. "The problem is the act of sex itself." She sounded resigned. "I can't do it. I've never wanted to do it, and never have been able."

"Even when you were married?"

She nodded. "I never had sex until I got married. I went out with a few men, but never took it that far. I tried several times, but it never worked. It was too painful. I was optimistic, though, that after I got married and settled down things would work out, and I'd gradually get used to it. Sadly, nothing changed, even after I got married. I did what my husband wanted, regular marital relations. I tried all kinds of things, but all I felt was pain. And finally, I refused to do those things. Needless to say, that was one of the reasons we got divorced."

"Do you know why this happens to you?"

"No. Not really. I never had any shocking experience as a child that became a psychological burden or anything. Never had any experience like that at all. I don't think I have lesbian tendencies either, or have any bias toward sexual experiences. I was raised in a normal home, and was your normal girl. My parents got along well, I had good friends, and got decent grades in school. My life was completely ordinary, typical. Though not being able to have sex—that alone was atypical."

I nodded. She lifted her glass of whiskey and took a small sip.

"Have you seen a specialist about this?"

"Yeah, when I was in Sapporo my husband asked me to see someone, so I went twice to see doctors at a department of psychosomatic medicine. First as a couple, and then by myself. It didn't help. I mean it didn't change anything. Frankly it was painful to talk to someone else about such private things, even if the other person is a specialist."

I suddenly remembered that sixteen-year-old girl. I remembered exactly what she told me that May morning. I was seventeen then. I can still clearly hear her voice, her breathing.

"I want to be yours," the girl said. "In every way there is. Yours from top to bottom. I want to be one with you. I mean it."

"Are you disappointed?" she asked me.

I quickly sorted out my muddled thoughts and somehow came back to reality.

"Are you asking if I'm disappointed that you aren't interested in male-female sex?"

"That's right."

"Hm, I guess I am, a little," I said honestly. "But I'm glad you told me about it beforehand."

"So, will you still see me, even *without that*?"

"Of course," I said. "I enjoy seeing you and having nice talks like this. There's nobody else like this for me in town."

"Same for me," she said. "But I think I can't do anything for you. In that area, I mean."

"I'll do my best to try to forget about that area, then, for now."

"You know," she said, as if confiding in me, "I deeply regret it, too. More than you might think."

"But don't rush things, okay? My heart and my body are apart from each other. In slightly different places. So I'd like you to wait a while. Until I'm ready. Does that make sense? A lot of things take time."

I shut my eyes and thought about time. In the past—for instance, back when I was seventeen—there was literally an inexhaustible amount of time. Like a huge reservoir, filled to the very brim. So there was no need to consider time. But now was different. Time, I knew, was limited. And as I aged, considering time had even greater implications. Time, no matter what, ticked away, ceaselessly.

"What are you thinking about?" she asked me from the seat next to me.

"About the Russian Five," I said, almost reflexively, without hesitation. "Why can't I remember all their names? I used to be able to list all five right away. They taught us that in music class at school."

"You are a strange one," she said. "Why do you care about that right now?"

"It bothers me that I can't remember what I should remember. Doesn't that happen to you?"

"I'm more concerned about things I can't forget but want to."

"To each his own," I said.

"Is Tchaikovsky in that group of the Russian Five?"

"No, he isn't. They formed the group in opposition to the Western-style music that Tchaikovsky composed."

We maintained silence for a time. Then she broke it.

"It's like something's stuck inside me. Because of that, nothing works out."

"Maybe so. But later on, you won't be left alone."

She thought over what I said. And then spoke.

"So you'll continue to see me?"

"Of course."

"*Of course* seems to be your pet phrase, doesn't it?"

"Maybe so."

She rested her hand on top of mine on the counter, her five smooth fingers intertwining with mine. Different sorts of time overlapped there, mixed into one. From deep within my chest an emotion much like sadness, yet somehow different, reached out its tentacles, like a thriving plant. I'd missed that sensation. A part of my heart remained still not fully known to me. A realm that even time cannot reach.

Balakirev, someone whispered in my ear. Like a kind friend seated next to me at an exam secretly telling me the answers. That's right—Balakirev. That makes four. Four of the five-member group. One left.

"Balakirev," I said aloud, as if clearly inscribing the word in the air. I glanced at her, but she seemed not to have heard. Her face was covered with both hands, and she was silently weeping. Tears dripped down between her fingers.

I quietly laid a hand on her shoulder and let it rest there a long while. Until the tears stopped.

THE BUSINESS CARD the young man handed me had the name of his employer on it, a law office. The name of the firm was of three lawyers. "Hirao, Takubo, and Yanagihara, Attorneys at Law." His name wasn't one of them.

"I'm a lawyer," the young man explained, smiling, eyes trained right on mine, "but still just an underling. Kind of an intern, an errand boy, an apprentice, you could say." He sounded used to giving this explanation, something he said often, so it didn't come across as particularly humble.

I motioned the young man, and the younger man with him, to take a seat in the reception room. They settled ever so gently into the chairs, as if unsure the chairs would hold up.

"This is my younger brother," the man said, introducing him. "He's in medical school in Tokyo. He'll be busy training soon."

"I'm very glad to meet you," the younger brother said, making a deep, polite bow. Very well mannered.

The older brother was, if anything, on the small side, while his younger brother was, if anything, more sturdily built. Their faces were very similar, though. I could tell at a glance they were brothers (they'd inherited the unusual shape of their ears from their father). Both had calm, collected, well-proportioned features and were clearly raised well. The way they were dressed, too, was urbane and refined. The older brother had on a slim-cut navy-blue suit, a white shirt, a tie with green and navy-blue stripes, and a black wool coat. The younger brother wore a perfectly sized gray turtleneck sweater, beige chinos, and a navy-blue peacoat. Both of them had their hair cut to the perfect length, and although it had product in it, it was arranged quite naturally.

The coffee shop owner had called them "nice-looking young men," and this was an apt description. Both were clearly neat, intelligent, but not at all stuck-up, and made a good impression. The two of them together looked like they could appear in a magazine ad for men's cologne.

"Thank you for always taking care of M**," the older brother began.

"Yes, he came here almost every day, totally engrossed in reading," I said. "When he suddenly disappeared everyone who works here was quite worried. I hope he can be located as soon as possible."

"Our family is doing everything we can to search for him," the older brother said. "We printed up a leaflet with his photo on it and have been handing it out all over. But so far, not a clue. Not a single person has come forward saying they saw him. It's very odd. The town is in such a small basin, surrounded by mountains, and he had barely any cash on him, so he couldn't have gone far. If he really had run away from home, surely someone would have spotted him."

"It really is quite uncanny," I agreed.

"Dad says it's like he was spirited away," the older brother said.

"Spirited away," I said.

"Yes, apparently in this region in the past something like being spirited away took place. Usually it was young children suddenly vanishing for no apparent reason, and never coming back. There are some legends about it. Dad said maybe that could have happened, because there's no other good explanation for it."

"Assuming it's a case of being spirited away," I said, "is there some way to get the children back?"

"Dad asked a Shinto priest he knows at a shrine to offer up prayers every day. Prayers to God to bring him back safely. To me it's just some fable, just some legend, but Dad obviously needs to cling to something. There's nothing else to rely on. It's like he's entreating God."

"As I'm sure you're aware," the younger brother, the med school student, said, "M** is not what you'd call an *ordinary* child. He lacks some of the skills needed to function in society, and perhaps to make up for that he was born with some other special abilities. Abilities unimaginable for ordinary people. In that sense you might say he's in something close to a divine realm. It might mean he's beloved by God or, conversely, violating what God forbids."

I said, "You mean that compared to ordinary people he's closer to the spiritual realm?"

"I do think it's possible to think that way," the younger brother said. "So perhaps the idea of being spirited away that my dad mentioned isn't so far off the mark. Putting aside, of course, the question of whether such a thing actually happens."

The older brother shot his brother a glance but kept his opinion to himself. It was clear they weren't on the same page.

"That's a fascinating hypothesis," the older brother said, "but we need to think more practically here."

What you'd expect a practicing lawyer to say. The notion of *spirited away*, impossible to prove logically, wouldn't fly in a court of law.

He went on. "We don't care what they are, but we need *concrete* clues. A hint to help us solve this inexplicable case of our brother disappearing. The more time passes, the more difficult the search will get, which is why we came to you. I realize how busy you are, and that it's an imposition, barging in like this."

"I'll make as much time as you need. If I can be of help, I'm happy to do whatever I can," I said.

The older brother nodded a few times and touched the knot of his tie, as if to check that it was still in the right spot. "According to what I've heard," he said, "M** felt close to you."

I tilted my head a bit. "I don't know if *close* is the right word. Our talks were never that personal or anything. As I told your father, M** mostly conveyed his ideas to me through writing or gestures."

"Yes, but you need to understand how big a deal that is," the younger brother interjected. "We've lived together all these years, yet he hardly ever did that with us. We'd talk to him, but he basically didn't respond. The same goes for our father. He'd speak to our mother, the bare minimum to get by, but we could never hope for anything more."

The older brother nodded. "He's right. He never spoke to us first. He was closed away in his own world, like an oyster at the bottom of the sea. Yet he initiated conversations with you."

"True enough," I said. "He did come and speak to me."

"And when he spotted you in that coffee shop near the station he went inside. That's totally unimaginable for a person like him."

"It does seem that way."

The brothers said nothing for a time. I stayed silent, too, waiting for them to go on.

The older brother spoke up. "Forgive me if this sounds rude, but what about you attracted him? What was it? Our brother was certainly close to Mr. Koyasu and spoke to him often. But Mr. Koyasu had known him since he was a child, kept an eye on him, and was very fond of him. So I can understand him being close. They must have had a mutual understanding on some level. But after Mr. Koyasu passed away, you moved here from Tokyo and only recently took over as the new head librarian. What about you could have attracted our brother?"

"As I told your father the other day, I told someone about a fictitious town and your brother happened to overhear that."

"Yes, our father told us that. M** was really taken by the story of that town and even drew a map of it."

"He did."

The younger brother asked, "And that's a fictitious town created out of your own imagination?"

"Exactly," I said. "It's a world that doesn't really exist that I came up with back when I was young."

"Do you have the map?"

"No, I don't have it here. M** took it away." Which was a lie. The map was in a drawer back in my house. But I didn't feel like showing it to them.

The brothers exchanged a look.

"If it's okay with you, could you tell us about that fictitious town, too?" the older brother asked.

The younger brother in med school added, "We'd like to know what M** was attracted to before his disappearance."

I gave them the short version of the town surrounded by a high wall. They were doing all they could to locate their brother, and I couldn't very well refuse.

I told them what you could see in the town, how it was laid out, always speaking of it as a fictional construct. (I didn't tell them everything, of course. I touched on the girl who took care of the library only in passing and omitted the part about having my shadow ripped away, my eyes stabbed, and the ominous pool. I didn't want to convey a sinister impression.) The brothers listened intently, asking a few questions along the way, succinct, on-target questions. Both of them seemed to have keen intuition and quick minds. I couldn't keep things as simple as when I spoke with their father, and when I finished, the silence lay thick and heavy. The younger brother was the first to speak.

"I think M** wanted to go to that town on his own. Listening to you, I get that impression. Once he zeroes in on something, his powers of concentration are unbelievable. And he seemed very drawn to that town of yours."

Silence again descended on us. A heavy, stagnant silence with no outlet. I turned to the younger brother, choosing my words carefully.

"But this is, above all, a made-up town I thought up on my own. It doesn't really exist. So M** can want to go there as much as he wants, but he won't be able to."

The younger brother, the med school student, said, "Okay, but the fact is that he disappeared. On a freezing night, dressed only in pajamas, with barely any money on him. The way he vanished is so unreal that all kinds of unreal theories are running through my head. Just as possibilities, of course."

"What do the police say?" I asked, trying to change the subject.

The older brother, the lawyer, said, "The police think that in the middle of the night he changed his clothes, took some cash, left the house, and found some way—hitchhiking, for instance—and left town. Typical case of a teenage boy runaway. Our mother is adamant that no other clothes are missing and he couldn't have taken any cash, but the police don't seem to put much stock in her words. Since she's in shock, and a little hysterical, I think you'd say."

"The police officer said he might get in touch when he runs out of money, or might just show up back home as if nothing had happened." This from the younger brother.

"Well, that's what most people would think," the older brother said, sighing.

"But I don't agree," the younger brother said. "Mom is very detailed oriented. She does get flustered easily, but when it comes to practical matters, like the number of clothes or any missing cash, she's extraordinarily accurate. She wouldn't make mistakes with those, even if she's a bit shaken and confused by what happened."

"And about the house being locked up tight from the inside," the lawyer brother said, "the police insist someplace must not have been. Logic would dictate that. And everybody in town knows that M** is a bit of an eccentric, not your *ordinary* child. People think he'd do something unpredictable. My father is well known in town and the police have responded attentively, but that's the extent of what they've done."

"Nothing could be better than if he just showed up at home again," I said.

"Our parents said the same thing," the older brother said. "But we can't just sit around hoping he'll return. He doesn't have any social skills whatsoever. When I think about where he might be, what he might be doing, it tears me up."

"To go back to the town surrounded by a wall," the younger brother interjected. "What aspect of your town do you think he was most drawn to?"

I was stuck for a reply. How should I respond to that?

"I'm afraid I don't know, since he never told me. He was just caught up in drawing a map. But my personal impression is that he was drawn to a town where the social skills you mentioned weren't necessary. All he needs to do in that town is go to the library and read some special books. Basically the same process he's been doing in this town, in this library. Nothing else is required. And in that town reading those books is extremely significant."

"What do you mean by *special books*?" the older brother, the lawyer, asked. An obvious question to ask. "Why is reading those so important for the town?"

I sighed. For some reason the image of that skinny female cat slowly cutting across the library garden came to mind. And the picture of Yellow Submarine Boy gazing, never tiring of it, at the cat and her five kittens. It all felt, though, like something from the far-off past.

"What that involves, what meaning reading them could have, I can't really explain. All I can say is they're mysterious books."

"But that situation is all something you created with your imagination, isn't it?" the younger brother asked.

"Yes, that's true," I said. "I believe so. But there are still lots of things there I can't explain logically. Since they rose up on their own from inside me, back when I was a teenager."

More precisely, the town was created by me, as a seventeen-year-old, and by her when she was sixteen. A joint creation, not something I made on my own. Not that I could bring that up here.

The brothers sat there for a time, each contemplating what I'd said.

Finally the younger brother spoke. "Do you mind if I give a personal theory?"

"Of course, please go ahead. Whatever you'd like to say."

"I think the wall surrounding the town is the consciousness that creates you as a person. Which is why the wall can freely change shape apart from any personal intentions. A person's consciousness is the same as a glacier, with only a fraction of it showing above the water. Most of it is hidden, unseen, sunk in a dark place."

"You're studying medicine, I understand. What area are you specializing in?"

"I plan to be a surgeon. If possible, I'd like to specialize in neurosurgery. But I'm also interested in psychiatry and am taking several courses in that area. It overlaps with neurosurgery."

"I see," I said. "Did M** have an influence on your going in that direction?"

"I suppose so. There is some connection, though it's not the only reason."

"It goes without saying," the older brother said, "but neither of us is thinking that our brother actually stepped into that fictitious town. That's science fiction, not something that actually happens.

So we're not blaming you, or asking you to take responsibility. Yet to be honest, I can't help feeling that that fictitious town you told him about was somehow an impetus for his disappearance."

"Impetus in what way?"

"For instance, M** might have felt that he discovered a passageway to take him to that town. He had a high fever then, remember. And then he got out of his sickbed and left home, in search of that passageway. I don't know how he went about exiting a house that was locked up from the inside, but somehow he made it outside. Dressed just in pajamas. Naturally, he didn't find that passageway anywhere. Plus it was a bone-chilling night . . ."

The younger brother took over. "He might have gone into the nearby mountains and lost consciousness due to the extreme cold. That's the most plausible theory we can come up with."

"And did you search in the mountains?" I asked.

"Yes, we walked around as much as we could, looking for him, but of course we can't search everywhere, without exception. The town, after all, is surrounded by mountains," the younger brother said.

The older brother said, "It would be ideal to gather a lot of people and form a search party, but that's hard at this stage."

The older brother, the lawyer, said, "We plan to stay a few more days in town, searching for him. We'll do our best. But it's hard for us to stay beyond that. We feel bad about it, but we both have to get back to Tokyo, and back to work and school."

I nodded. They'd sacrificed a lot already to leave Tokyo for a week and come here. Everyone has their own life that keeps them busy. The younger brother took out a pocket notebook, wrote something down with a ballpoint pen, ripped out the page, and handed it to me.

"This is my cell phone number. If you remember anything about this town surrounded by a wall, no matter how small, could you please get in touch?"

"Of course. I'll do that."

He seemed to hesitate, then spoke, his voice serious, confessional. "Metaphorically, symbolically, or suggestively, I don't know, but

I can't help but think M** found a passageway to that town and went into it. Deep below the surface, you might say, a dark realm of the unconscious."

I neither agreed nor disagreed, just silently looked at him.

"If we go there, we might find our brother. But realistically we can't," the younger brother said.

If, hypothetically, Yellow Submarine Boy did discover that passageway, he probably wouldn't want to come back to this world. But I couldn't say that to his brothers.

The brothers politely thanked me and quietly exited the room. After those well-mannered, obviously intelligent young men had gone I went over to the window and gazed out for a long time at the deserted garden. Birds were on the leafless branches, chirping for a while, but then flew off in search of who knows what.

"Metaphorically, symbolically, or suggestively, I don't know," the younger brother had said.

No, this wasn't metaphorical, symbolic, or even suggestive, but could be an unshakable reality. I pictured the *real* Yellow Submarine Boy walking down the streets of that *real* town. And I felt a palpable sense of longing. For the boy, and for that town.

THAT NIGHT I had a very long dream. Or something close to a dream.

I was walking down a path in the woods. On a heavy, overcast winter afternoon, a light dusting of white hard snow swirling in the air. I had no idea where I was. I was just aimlessly walking on and on. Searching for something, apparently, but what, I didn't know. But that didn't bother me. Whatever I was looking for, I was sure I'd know it when I found it.

In the densely deep forest, all I could see was the thick trunks of trees. The dull sound as I trampled over fallen leaves, and the occasional squawk of birds high overhead, but no other sounds. No wind was blowing.

Eventually I emerged from the trees onto a flat, open glade and found a small, old, abandoned building. Perhaps used as a little mountain lodge in the past. No one had taken care of it for a long time, and now the roof leaned over at an angle, the pillars termite-eaten and half decayed. I climbed three suspect-looking steps. The door creaked as I carefully opened it. The inside was dim and musty, with no sign of anyone inside.

One look told me, instinctively, that this was the place I'd been aiming for. I'd made my way through the thick forest in order to arrive here. Pushing aside thickets, crossing over a frozen stream as birds' sharp warnings rang in my ears.

I quietly stepped inside the cabin and looked around. The windows were dusty and I could barely see outside, but not one was cracked (a minor miracle considering how dilapidated the building was) and a faint light shone through the windowpanes. It was a simple, one-room cabin. I had no idea who had used it, and for what purpose. I stood in the middle of the room, carefully scanning the inside as my eyes adjusted to the dimness.

The cabin was literally empty. There was no furniture or other implements. Or any decorations or ornaments. At some point people had vacated the cabin and the building was abandoned.

The wooden floorboards bowed as I stepped on them, groaning loudly, as if sending out a vital warning to the creatures in the forest.

I had a vague memory of having seen this cabin. I'd been here before . . . but when and where I couldn't recall. An overpowering sense of déjà vu hazily numbed my entire body, as if some unseen foreign object had infiltrated the blood coursing through me.

On the wall in the back was a small wooden door. A storage area or closet by the look of it. I decided to open it. Not knowing what was inside, I didn't want to open it but couldn't resist. I'd come all this way in search of something, and I couldn't go back without opening the closed door. I tiptoed as carefully as I could to the door, trying not to make a sound, and stood in front of it, taking a few deep breaths. I steeled myself, grabbed the rusty doorknob, and slowly pulled it toward me.

The door made a dry, grinding sort of creak as it opened. As I had thought, it was a kind of storage space, a place to store tools. Narrow and deep, dark in back where the light didn't reach. Unopened, I imagined, for ages, it had a rotten, stagnant smell. The sole object inside was a doll. Since it was dark, it took a while for me to realize that it was a wooden doll, a quite large one, over three feet tall. The doll's legs were bent, like a person slumped to the floor, exhausted, its back resting against the wall. Once my eyes had adjusted to the dark, I saw that the doll was wearing a kind of parka. A green parka with a *Yellow Submarine* drawing on it.

I leaned forward to study the doll's face. The paint had faded a lot, but it was definitely M**'s face, a caricatured face like the clownish face of a ventriloquist's puppet. Its expression was neither here nor there, as if it had started to smile but thought better of it.

And then it struck me. *This* was what I had been searching for. No doubt about it. I'd come here in search of that doll. Clambering up steep slopes, making my way through a thick forest, avoiding the eyes of darkish beasts. I stood there, breathing quietly, staring straight at that wooden doll.

This was M**'s cast-off skin. I was sure of it. Deep in this mountain forest, M** had sloughed off his body, which then changed into an old, faded wooden doll. And his soul, liberated from the confining prison of the physical body, had transitioned to the town surrounded by a high wall. That was a fact I had wanted to verify.

But what should I do with this leftover wooden doll, the boy's cast-off shell? Should I take it back to town to show his brothers? Or just leave it right here, as it was? Or dig a hole somewhere and bury it? I couldn't decide. Leaving it alone might be the best choice. The boy might be able to use it in some way later on.

Just then I noticed something. The doll's mouth was moving ever so slightly. It was dark, and at first I thought it was an illusion. Maybe I was seeing things that weren't really happening. But it was no illusion. I looked more closely and saw that the doll's mouth was moving, albeit just a fraction. As if trying to say something. The mouth seemed made to only move up and down, just like a ventriloquist's puppet.

I thought I needed to hear what it was saying, so I focused and listened as alertly as I could, but all I could catch was a windy rustling, like a broken old bellows. But soon that sound of wind seemed to form words.

More . . . , it seemed to be saying.

I held my breath, totally focused, waiting for the next words to emerge.

More . . . the word, or a vague sound close to a word—repeated in a faint, hoarse voice.

Maybe I was mishearing. Perhaps it was a different word. But to my ears that's what it sounded like. *More.*

"More *what?*" I said aloud to the wooden doll, the corpse of Yellow Submarine Boy. What did he want me to do *more* of?

More . . . the same word, intoned in the same way.

Maybe he wanted me to get closer. Maybe an important, confidential message was waiting there, from a faraway world. Undaunted, I brought my ear closer to that mysterious mouth.

More . . . , the mouth repeated. More loudly than before.

I brought my ear even closer.

And right then the doll leaned its head forward with surprising speed and bit my ear. So forcefully, so deeply, I was sure that my earlobe had been ripped off. It hurt like hell.

I screamed, and that scream woke me up. It was dark all around. After a time I knew it was a dream, or something akin to a dream. I was lying in my own bed, in my own house. I'd been having a long, graphic dream (or dreamlike experience). This hadn't really happened. Yet my right earlobe still ached from the bite. This was no illusion. It throbbed something terrible.

I got up, went to the bathroom, switched on the light, and checked my right ear in the mirror. But no matter how closely I examined it, I found no trace of a bite. It was the usual smooth earlobe. The only thing that remained was the pain of having been bitten. But the pain was real enough. That wooden doll—or someone who'd taken on the form of that doll—had snapped down hard on my ear. In a flash, hard and deep. Had this taken place in my dream? Or in some deep, submerged part of my unconscious . . .

The clock showed three thirty a.m. I took off my pajamas and underwear, heavy with sweat, tossed them into the hamper, and gulped down several glasses of cold water. I toweled myself dry, took out a fresh pair of underwear and pajamas from the dresser, and put them on. That calmed me down, though my heart was still pounding like a hammer banging a board. The shock of the memory had my muscles tense and tight. I could recall the images of what I'd seen down to the smallest detail, and the pain that still buzzed through my earlobes was actual, honest-to-God pain. And that acute sensation didn't back down as time passed.

The boy bit my ear to pass on some kind of message. That's why he wanted me to come closer—that's the only way I could see it. But what could he possibly be trying to tell me by biting my ear? Was there something disturbing in that message? Or by biting my ear was he (in his own unique way) expressing a kind of closeness? I couldn't say.

Even so, despite the pain, deep down I felt, somehow, relieved. Deep in that out-of-the-way forest, inside that dilapidated old cabin, I had finally discovered *it*. The body that Yellow Submarine

Boy had left behind. Or, he had shed his skin. A valuable clue to explain the puzzling question of the boy's disappearance (or spiriting away).

Not that it looked like I could report all this to his brothers. The news would only trouble and confuse them. And above all, this had only happened in a dream (probably). Yet they had the right to hear about this, as a piece of information. Several times I took out the piece of paper the younger brother, the med school student, had written his cell phone number on. I was unsure what to do. In the end, I didn't call him.

During lunch break that day I walked down toward the station and went inside the coffee shop. The place was more crowded than usual. I sat at my usual seat at the counter and ordered black coffee and a muffin. The woman had her hair neatly tied behind her, as always, and was working briskly behind the counter.

The pain in my earlobe had mostly faded, yet I still felt traces of the dream. An ache still pulsed in time with my heart, faint yet beyond question.

A Gerry Mulligan solo was playing from the small speakers in the shop. A performance I'd heard a lot in the past. Sipping black coffee, I searched my memory and came up with the title. "Walkin' Shoes," I was sure. A performance by a piano-less quartet, with Chet Baker on horn.

After a while, when the other customers all seemed set, she had a free moment and came over. She had on slim jeans and a plain white apron.

"You look pretty busy," I said.

"Yeah, for a change," she said, smiling. "I'm happy you came. Are you on lunch break?"

"Right, so I don't have a lot of time," I said. "There's something I'd like to ask you to do for me."

"What is it?"

I pointed to my right earlobe. "Would you take a look at this earlobe? See if you can see any mark? I can't really see it well myself."

She rested both elbows on the counter and leaned forward. She closely examined my earlobe from different angles, like a house-wife checking out broccoli at a supermarket. She straightened up and said, "I don't see a mark or anything. What kind of *mark*?"

"Like something bit me."

She frowned, as if on her guard. "Someone bit you?"

"No," I said, shaking my head. "Nobody bit me, but when I got up this morning my earlobe hurt like it had been. Like some big bug had stung me, or bit me, in the night."

"Not a bug in a skirt by any chance?"

"No, not that kind."

"Good to know," she said, and smiled.

"If you don't mind, could you touch my earlobe?"

"Sure, I'd be happy to," she said. She reached over the counter and took my right earlobe between her fingers, gently rubbing it.

"It's a big, soft earlobe," she said, as if impressed. "I'm envious. Mine are so small and hard. Seedy-looking."

"Thanks," I said. "You touching them makes me feel a lot better."

Which was true. After she gently stroked it, the pain in my ear—the faint vestiges of the dream—vanished without a trace. Like morning dew dispelled in the fresh sunlight.

"Would you be okay having dinner with me again?"

"I'd love to," she said. "Just say the word, whenever you'd like to invite me."

I walked back to the library, and as I went about my daily tasks at my desk in my office, my mind was filled with thoughts of that dream. I tried not to think about it but couldn't help it. Memories were plastered on the walls of my consciousness, not about to come off anytime soon.

Why did Yellow Submarine Boy have to bite my earlobe so hard?

I focused on that. That question had rattled me since morning, fraying my nerves. *Why did Yellow Submarine Boy have to bite my earlobe so hard?* It had to be some kind of message. And to convey that message to me, he'd led me into the forest.

Or maybe the boy wanted to leave a clear trace on my mind, and imprint on my body, a vestige of the fact that he indeed had existed in this world. Indelibly imprinting it on me with a physical pain not easily forgotten. That's how painful it was.

But why? Wasn't the fact that he existed in this world already clearly etched in my mind? I wasn't about to forget him, even if he vanished from here forever.

This world, I thought.

I looked up and gazed around at my surroundings. I was in the second-floor head librarian's office. The ceiling, walls, floor I was used to seeing. Several vertical windows set into the wall, afternoon sunlight brightly shining in.

This world.

But as I gazed at them, I knew that their overall scale was a bit different from usual. The ceiling was too wide, the floor too narrow, which made the walls buckle under the pressure. A closer look showed that the whole room was wriggling, wet and slimy like the inner walls of an internal organ. The window frame expanded and contracted, the glass undulating unsteadily.

My first thought was that we were having a massive earthquake. But it was no earthquake. The shaking was coming from inside me. The shaking inside me was merely projected in the external world. I rested my elbows on the desk, covered my face with my hands, and closed my eyes. I slowly counted to myself, patiently waiting for the illusion to pass.

A while later—two or three minutes, something like that—when I removed my hands from my face and opened my eyes, the feeling had gone. The room was back to normal, its usual stationary self. No shaking, no moving, everything to scale.

Still, it seemed like the shape of the room had changed a fraction, the measurements of all its components transformed, ever so slightly. Like the furniture had been moved somewhere else and then lined up again in its same position. It had been very carefully moved back to where it had been, but subtle details were changed. Nothing major. Most people wouldn't have noticed the difference. But I did.

But maybe I was just imagining it. I might be overly sensitive. Maybe my dream from the previous night had put my nerves on edge. The borderline between inside the dream and outside it was no longer clear.

I gently tried touching my right earlobe. It was soft and warm, with no more pain. The pain that remained was all in my mind. And that pain, that vivid residual memory, might not disappear. It felt like that. It was like a hot seal, an actual painful mark that made it possible to cross over the border from one world to another. And one that would most likely remain a part of me for the rest of my life.

LATE THAT AFTERNOON I called the coffee shop and invited her to dinner.

"Is your ear better now?" she asked.

"No problem now, thanks to you."

"I hope no more bugs bite you," she said.

"If you don't mind, could I see you later today?"

"Sure. I have nothing going on. Why don't you come to the shop after I close up, whenever works."

I hung up, checked what I had in the fridge, and ran through a menu of what I could make. Nothing fancy, by the looks of the ingredients I had, but I could throw together an impromptu dinner. I could make some clam sauce, and I had a chilled bottle of Chablis in the fridge.

As, one by one, I mentally listed the details and steps of a menu, my mind began to calm down. Being occupied with practical issues like this helped me to forget any other problems. Like when I remembered the title of that Gerry Mulligan tune.

Just before evening, when I saw Mrs. Soeda, she told me that both of Yellow Submarine Boy's brothers planned to return to Tokyo tomorrow.

"They're quite discouraged to not have found any clues about M**'s whereabouts. But they have work and studies and can't stay here forever."

"I feel sorry for them, but I guess it can't be helped," I said. "Are there any leads in the police search?"

Mrs. Soeda shook her head. "I'm not saying the police here are incompetent, but neither can you say they've been much help. This is a small town, without many people coming and going, and the only crimes they deal with are domestic disturbances and traffic accidents. They're understaffed, too, and don't really know what to do."

"A thought occurred to me," I said. "Say the boy really did run away somewhere far away, no matter where he went, I think he'd wear that *Yellow Submarine* parka. It's like a second skin for him. I can't see him leaving it behind."

"I feel the same. If he did go far away, he'd wear that parka. It makes him feel safe."

"But the parka was left behind."

"Yes, that's what his mother said, that the parka was left behind. That sort of bothered me, so I asked her a number of times to make sure, and she insisted that he didn't wear it."

After I finished my work at the library and arrived at the coffee shop, it was just after six thirty. The long winter was finally drawing to a close, the sun clearly setting later than before, the cold a degree less biting. Clumps of snow along the road had shrunk in the noontime sunlight, and the runoff from this had made the water level rise in the river.

A Closed sign hung on the glass door of the coffee shop, and the blinds were lowered. I pushed open the door and went inside. She was alone on a stool at the counter, reading a book. Not a paperback but a thick hardcover book. She shut the book, turned, and smiled at me. The bookmark showed that she'd nearly finished.

"What are you reading?" I asked as I shrugged off my duffel coat and hung it on the coatrack.

"*Love in the Time of Cholera*," she said.

"You like García Márquez?"

"I think so. I've read most of his books, but I especially like this one. This is the second time I've read it. What about you?"

"I read it a long time ago. When it first came out," I said.

"I like this particular passage," she said, opening the book at her bookmark and reading it aloud.

> Fermina Daza and Florentino Ariza remained on the bridge until it was time for lunch. It was served a short while after they passed the town of Calamar on the opposite shore, which just a few years before had celebrated a perpetual fiesta and now was a ruined port with deserted streets. The only creature they saw from the boat was a

woman dressed in white, signaling to them with a handkerchief. Fermina Daza could not understand why she was not picked up when she seemed so distressed, but the Captain explained that she was the ghost of a drowned woman whose deceptive signals were intended to lure ships off course into the dangerous whirlpools along the other bank. They passed so close that Fermina Daza saw her in sharp detail in the sunlight, and she had no doubt that she did not exist, but her face seemed familiar.

"In his stories the real and the unreal, the living and the dead, are all mixed together in one," she said. "Like that's an entirely ordinary, everyday thing."

"People often call that *magical realism*," I said.

"True. But I think that although that way of telling stories might fit the critical criteria of magical realism, for García Márquez himself it's just ordinary realism. In the world he inhabits the real and the unreal coexist and he just describes those scenes the way he sees them."

I sat down on the stool beside her and said, "So you're saying that in the world he inhabits, the real and the unreal are equivalent and that García Márquez is simply recording that."

"Yes, I think that might be the case. And that's what I like about his novels."

While working, she always had her hair tied back, but now had let her hair down, and it fell straight down to her shoulders. When she brushed back her hair, I caught a glimpse of small silver piercings in her ears. She never wore them while working. Her earlobes were, as she said, small and hard-looking.

Talking about García Márquez's novels made me think of Mr. Koyasu. If she had met him, I think she might have simply accepted the fact that he was already dead. Unconnected with magical realism or postmodernism or anything.

"You like to read, don't you," I asked.

"I've read a lot since I was young. Work keeps me busy now so I can't read much, but I get a bit of reading in when I can. After

I came here, I had no one I could talk to about the books I read, which made me sad."

"I could be someone you talk to, I think."

She smiled. "Well, you *are* a head librarian, after all."

"How about your daily routine—the one cigarette and the glass of single malt?" I asked.

"I've already smoked the cigarette. Haven't got to the whiskey yet, though. I was waiting until you got here."

"Shall we go to my place and have dinner? I can whip up something simple."

She tilted her head a fraction, eyes narrowed as she considered this. "If you don't mind, could we order in pizza instead, and have beer? I'm in the mood for that, somehow."

"Sure. Pizza sounds good."

"Margherita's okay?"

"Whatever you feel like having."

She punched in a number on her speed dial and ordered the pizza, like she'd done it before. She added three types of mushrooms as a topping.

"It'll be here in a half hour," she said, glancing at the clock on the wall.

During the thirty minutes we waited for the pizza, we sat beside each other at the counter and talked about books we'd read recently. All the while sipping on single malt.

"Would you like to see my room?" she asked after we'd finished the pizza.

"The apartment upstairs?"

"Yeah, it's small, with a low ceiling and cheap furniture, a totally nothing room, but it works for me. If you don't mind going."

"I'd love to," I said.

She cleared away the pizza box and plates and switched off the lights in the shop. She led the way up a narrow staircase beyond the kitchen. The room upstairs wasn't as terrible as she'd suggested. It was cramped, with low ceilings, but felt like a clean, neat attic room. There was a sofa bed (a sofa at this point), compact electric cooking equipment, a table and chair by the window as a work-space, with a laptop computer on the desk. A chest of drawers and a closet, books in a small bookcase. No TV or radio as far as I could see. The bathroom was the size of a large phone booth, but you could manage to take a shower there (moving around would take some doing, however).

"Most of the furniture was already here. Things the previous tenant had. The only thing I bought new was bedding, so I could basically start living here without bringing anything with me, which I was grateful for. Laundry and cooking I can do down-stairs, and when I want to have a nice soak, there's a public hot springs nearby. The quality of life could be improved, of course, but I can't really complain."

"And you're close to work, that's for sure."

"It is convenient, I'll give it that. I can buy things online, most of the things I need for the shop are delivered, and anything else I need I can pick up at the neighborhood stores, so there's little need to go out. But living like this for so long makes me remember *The Diary of a Young Girl* by Anne Frank. The room she hid out in in Amsterdam. With low ceilings and tiny windows . . ."

"But you're not being pursued by anyone, and don't need to stay out of sight. You just need to go ahead and live the life you've chosen."

"But living in such a tiny place, going back and forth from the first to the second floor, I get that feeling sometimes. An obsession with being chased, maybe, the feeling that someone, or some-thing, is doggedly after me and I'm kind of in imminent danger and have to hide."

She took two chilled cans of beer from the fridge and poured them out for us. We sat next to each other on the sofa, drinking beer. Not the most comfortable sofa, but I'd seen lots worse.

"It'd be nice if I had music here, but I don't," she said.

"No worries. I like the quiet," I said.

Holding her and kissing her just happened naturally. She didn't resist—in fact, she leaned closer to me. But she didn't want to take it a step further, and I knew that. I just held her, and we kissed, that's all. It'd been ages since I'd kissed anyone. Her lips were soft and warm, and slightly moist. It'd been a long time since I'd felt that—how warm a body can be and how that warmth can be felt by another.

We stayed that way for a long while, arms around each other. Each lost in our own thoughts, I imagine. I stroked her back with my palm, and she stroked mine with hers.

But as we did, I couldn't help noticing something. Her entire slim body seemed to be tightly bound up with *something*. The twin peaks on her chest in particular were carefully guarded by some kind of rounded, artificial material. This dome-like material wasn't metal, but a little too hard to be called clothes. Resilient, but plenty strong enough to repel anyone. I went ahead and asked, "Why does your body feel like this? It's like you're wearing a bodysuit of armor."

She laughed and said, "It's a special undergarment that fits tightly against my body."

"I don't exactly get it, but isn't it sort of uncomfortable?"

"It can be uncomfortable, but my body's mostly used to it, so maybe I don't really feel it anymore."

"So you always wear this bodysuit underneath? This special undergarment?"

"Yes, this all-in-one underwear. I do take it off when I want to relax and when I go to bed, but when I'm with anyone else, I always wear it."

"But you're quite slim, with such a nice figure. You don't need to force yourself to wear something that tight."

"Maybe not. We're not in Scarlett O'Hara's time. But wearing it makes me feel at ease. Like I'm completely protected. Safeguarded."

"Safeguarded from . . . me, for instance?"

She laughed. "Let me put it this way—I'm not that worried about you. I don't think you'd force anything on another person. What I'm protecting myself from is something more generic."

"More generic?"

"More hypothetical."

"*Hypothetical Things* vs. *Special Underwear.*"

She laughed and shrugged in my arms.

"So what you're saying, to put it plainly, is that taking it off isn't easy?" I asked.

"No one's actually tried it, but I imagine it would be complicated."

"Wearing your special armor, you're completely protected from all things hypothetical."

"There you go."

Silence continued for a while, and my mind flicked backward, on its own, to when I was seventeen. Like a castaway carried along by a strong tide. Inside my mind, the scene around me switched tracks.

I started thinking about your body. About the swell of your breasts, about what lay underneath your skirt. Imagining what was there.

But as I was imagining all this I suddenly realized a part of my body was totally stiff. Like some indecent marble ornament. Inside my tight jeans my erect penis was terribly uncomfortable. If it didn't simmer down, I doubted I could stand up.

But when it gets that hard, it doesn't go right back down, as much as I try. Like a big jumpy dog that never listens, ignoring the leash you're tugging on with all your might.

"What are you thinking about?" she whispered in my ear.

My consciousness was pulled back to the present. The second floor of the coffee shop, her cozy little dwelling. Us hugging on the sofa. Her body tightly constricted by her underwear, diligently defending her against *all things hypothetical*.

"I'm sorry I'm so useless," she said. "I really like you and want to help you if I can. I mean it. But I just can't bring myself to do so."

I pondered this in the ensuing silence. And I tried verifying the thought that came to me.

"You don't mind if I wait?" I asked.

"By waiting . . . you mean waiting until I feel more proactive about that part of life?"

"It doesn't have to be proactive."

"You mean feeling more receptive to it?"

I nodded. She gave that proposal some serious thought. Then she looked up and said, "I'm very happy you'd say that, but it might take a long time. Whether proactive or receptive, I might never feel that way again. There are a few issues I have to work through first."

"I'm used to waiting."

She thought about this again.

"I wonder if I'm worth waiting for."

"That remains to be seen," I said. "But there's a certain value in wanting to wait, even if it takes time."

She said nothing and pressed her lips against mine. Her lips were warm and soft and, unlike the rest of her body, were open to me.

As I walked home, I thought about the feel of the warm, soft parts of her, and the hard, protected parts. The moon was beautiful that night, and I was still a bit tipsy from the whiskey and beer.

"I'm used to waiting," I'd told her. But was I, really? My breath hung there in the air like a white, hard question mark.

Was I used to waiting, or was it that I just wasn't given an alternative?

And *what is it* I have been waiting for all this time? Did I really grasp what it was I was waiting for? Was I simply patiently waiting for it to become clear what I was waiting for? Like a series of nested wooden boxes, a smaller box inside a larger one, an endless succession of exquisitely crafted boxes one after the other. The boxes grew progressively smaller—as did what lay at the center of it all. In my forty-some years, was this the true state of affairs of my life until now? What was the starting point, and where did the destination lie—if indeed there was one? The more I thought about it, the less sure I was. *At a loss* was more the right expression. The crisply clear, cold moonlight illuminated the surface of the river, gurgling along with all the water from the melted snow in it. There were all kinds of water in the world. And they all flowed from high to low. A self-evident, unhesitant fact of life.

Maybe I'd been waiting for her.

The thought suddenly struck me. Waiting for this thirtysomething woman who ran a nameless coffee shop all on her own, wrapped up tightly in her special protective bodysuit, defending herself from all the hypothetical things (presumably) lying in wait around her, this woman who was unable to respond to any sexual acts.

I liked her very much, and I knew she liked me. Of that there was no doubt. In this small town surrounded by mountains we were (probably) both seeking each other. Yet something kept us apart—something impenetrable, something like, for instance, a high brick wall.

Had I been waiting until now for her to appear? Was this the new wooden box I'd been given?

My feelings for her were not the same as the ones I had at seventeen for that girl. That was clear. Those overwhelmingly powerful feelings, a laser-like focus on one object, etching it into me, would never return (and even if they did, I doubt I could handle the intensity). The feelings I had for the coffee shop woman were more diffuse, more sensible, wrapped in soft clothing, restrained by a certain wisdom and experience. Something to be grasped over a longer time frame.

And another important fact was this—I was not seeking all of her. Her entire being wouldn't fit, perhaps, in the small box I possessed now. I was no longer a seventeen-year-old boy. Back then, I had all the time in the world. But not now. The time I have now, and the ways I can use it, have become so limited. What I sought now was the gentle warmth that lay inside, beneath her defensive wall. And the rhythmic beat of the heart that lay pulsing beneath.

At this point was I asking for too little? Or too much?

A nostalgia for Mr. Koyasu came over me. If he were here now, there was so much I would tell him, so much advice I could seek. And I'm sure he'd give me valuable suggestions. The sort of mysterious, ambiguous advice befitting a bodyless soul. And like a gaunt dog chewing on a bone, I would savor that advice for a long time.

I realized I had only known Mr. Koyasu as a dead person. Yet he was so full of life, and I had only vivid, vibrant memories of his presence, his personality. I wondered how he was doing. Did he still exist somewhere—where, I couldn't even imagine—or had he returned to nothingness?

> Fermina Daza could not understand why she was not picked up when she seemed so distressed, but the Captain explained that she was the ghost of a drowned woman whose deceptive signals were intended to lure ships off course into the dangerous whirlpools along the other bank.

García Márquez, a Colombian novelist who had no need of the distinction between the living and the dead.

What is real, and what is not? In this world is there really something like a wall separating reality from the unreal?

I think there might be. No, not *might*—there *is* one. But it's an entirely uncertain wall. Depending on circumstances and the person, its texture, its shape transforms. Like some living being.

THAT NIGHT IT SEEMED I passed over that uncertain wall. Or maybe I should say passed *through it*. Like swimming through a thick, jelly-like substance.

I suddenly realized I was on the other side of the wall. Or maybe on *this side*.

This was no dream. The scene there was entirely logical, continuous, coherent. I could see, and recognize, each and every detail. I stood there in that world, checking over and over, every way I could think of, that this was no dream (which people don't do in dreams). And this was no dream. If I had to label it, I'd say it was a concept existing on the periphery of reality.

The season was summer. Intense sunlight, the air filled with the clamor of cicadas calling out. The peak of summer, probably August. I was walking in a river. I'd rolled my pants up to my knees, was holding my white sneakers, my bare feet in the water. The water, winding its way down from the mountains, was bitingly cold, and crystal clear. I could feel the flow of the river on my ankles. It was a shallow river. There were deep spots, but as long as you avoided them, you could walk downstream. In those spots little silvery fish formed schools. The shadow of an occasional dragonfly flitted low over the surface of the water. The air was filled with the strong fragrance of summer grass.

I'd seen this river before. It was the river I'd played in as a child. Catching fish, enjoying the feel of the water. Yet I was no longer a child. It was *me as I was now*, in my mid-forties. I was walking through the river by myself. The strong sunlight made the back of my neck tingle, yet I wasn't sweating at all, and wasn't thirsty. I made my way forward, careful not to slip on the moss-covered rocks. I was in no hurry. The wind blew fluidly over the surface of the river. There was a clump of white clouds far off near the horizon, but nothing disturbed the clear blue sky overhead.

I continued upstream, against the current. I had no particular goal in mind as I forged ahead, no apparent place I was heading toward. I just walked along, barefoot in the water, drinking in the nostalgic scenery. My goal, then, was simply the act of walking.

Yet as I walked along, I suddenly understood something. As I followed the river upstream, very gradually I was undergoing a transformation. Not a change in consciousness or awareness, nothing sensory or abstract. It was a more concrete, visible, tangible change. A material, actual physical transformation.

I'm being physically transformed.

One step after another, with each step this change continued. It was no illusion. No misunderstanding. I could feel the definite rhythm of this change with my whole body.

At first, I didn't know what type of change this was. But when I touched my face I could tell it was a clear transformation in appearance. My skin was smoother, the loose skin under my chin gone, the outline of my face more trim overall. I looked at my arms and legs and saw the skin had regained a healthy tautness. And most of the wrinkles were gone. Several scars, too, had vanished.

No mistake about it. Compared to before—*before* meaning just a few hours prior—my skin had clearly been revitalized, my body had become lighter, as if a weight had been lifted. The chronic tightness and ache in my shoulder blades had vanished, and I could move them smoothly and lightly. Even the air I breathed into my lungs felt fresher, more invigorating. The natural sounds I could hear, too, struck me as more distinct and alive.

I wish I had a mirror, I thought. Then I could see the actual changes taking place in my face. The face in the mirror would, I imagined, be the same as back when I was young. The face I had in my late twenties. My hair fuller, chin tauter, cheeks tighter. Completely healthy, and (viewed from the present perspective) probably a bit foolish-looking (and it probably actually was foolish). But, of course, I didn't have a mirror with me.

What was happening to me? My powers of understanding, of course, couldn't conceive of it. The only hypothesis that did occur to me was that the farther upstream I followed the river, the younger I'd become.

A peculiar hypothesis for sure. But I could think of no other explanation. I gazed at the scenery around me, looked up at the cloudless blue sky and down at the clear water flowing by at my feet. But nothing seemed strange, nothing there was out of the ordinary. It was your typical, midsummer-afternoon scene. Despite its seeming ordinariness, though, this river might hold some special significance. And I might have unwittingly set foot in it.

I decided to walk farther upstream. If doing so made me even younger, I could prove my hypothesis.

But what about after? At a certain point if I turned around and headed back, went downstream, in other words, would I go back to my original age? Or was this a flow that didn't allow you to backtrack? I didn't know. Anyway, at this point the only thing was to keep on going upstream. Curiosity led me on.

I went under several bridges that spanned the river, walking on through shallow spots in the riverbed. I didn't pass anyone else. The only things I saw were a couple of small frogs, and a white egret on top of a rock. The egret stood there on one leg, motionless, vigilantly monitoring the river's surface.

I did see some people crossing the bridges, but only a handful, and none of them stopped to look down at me. Some had parasols, or hats pulled down low to block out the intense summer sun. Their clothes and hats all seemed a bit old and odd, but that could have been my imagination, since I was seeing them from far below, in the strong sunlight.

One time only a small boy leaned out over the handrail on a bridge and shouted out something to me, though I couldn't catch it. He seemed to be trying to tell me something very important, but only scraps of his words carried. Before long a heavyset woman, his mother apparently, appeared from behind him, and yanked the shouting boy away from the railing and took him away. She didn't even glance once in my direction. It was like I didn't even exist in her eyes. Other than that small boy, no one else paid any attention to me as I splashed my way upstream.

Stopping occasionally to check on my transformation, I continued walking through the river. There was no doubt about it now—as I followed the river upstream my body was slowly, yet most assuredly, growing younger. I was going back in my twenties, getting closer to the watershed moment of turning twenty, adulthood. I rubbed my arm and found it silky, even smoother than before. And my vision, impaired through years of reading, was as clear as if fog had lifted, and the extra pounds I'd put on were falling away. Which told me that, though normally careful about my weight, I'd still put on a few pounds over the years. I put my hand to my head and found the hair thicker, and fuller. My legs and body were now full of energy, and I didn't grow tired, no matter how much I walked.

As I continued upstream, the scenery around me was clearly changing. I seemed to have left the plain and gotten close to a valley. The number of bridges decreased, and the greenery around me grew more intense. No one was to be seen. The river sloped upward much more. Here and there were small weirs, retaining walls to contain the flowing sand, which I had to clamber over.

As I made my way upstream, I must have passed through age twenty (not a particularly happy time in my life, now that I thought about it) and entered my teens. My body grew slimmer, the lines of my jaw more angular. My waist became more compact, and I had to cinch my belt up tight. I touched my face, and it didn't seem like my own. More like someone else's face. Maybe I actually was a different person in the past.

But these changes occurring as I went back in time seemed confined to my physical body. My thoughts and memories remained those of the *present-day me*. My feelings and all my memories over time remained intact, as my body continued to return to that of a teenager, or boy.

Up ahead was a sandbank. Quite lovely. Made of white sand, covered in thick summer grass, *and she was there*. She was sixteen. And I had gone back to being seventeen.

You'd stuck your low, red sandals in your yellow plastic shoulder bag and were walking from one sandbank to the next, just ahead of me. Blades of grass were pasted to your wet calves, wonderful green punctuation marks.

∎

She kept on walking ahead of me. She never glanced back once, as if sure of my presence. As if focusing solely on walking through the water. Occasionally she'd hum snatches of some song in a small voice (one I didn't recall) and walked on.

Our youthful bare feet silently splashed through the clear cold water that had flowed down from the mountains. As I walked right behind her, I gazed, eyes narrowed, at her shoulder-length black hair swinging, pendulum-like, from side to side—as if watching some brilliantly shining, exquisite piece of craftsmanship. Mesmerized, I couldn't take my gaze from that lively, lovely, subtle movement.

Then, as if remembering something, she came to an abrupt halt and looked around. She stepped up, barefoot, out of the water and onto the white sandbank. Then, as if carefully folding her light green dress, she sat down on an open spot surrounded by summer grass. Without a word I sat myself down beside her. A green grasshopper fluttered up from the nearby grass, its wings buzzing shrilly as it flew away. We followed its path as it sped away.

Yes, that's how the two of us came to stop at that spot, coming to a halt in the world of a sixteen- and seventeen-year-old. In the midst of verdant summer grass, on a white sandbank, a river flowing all around us. We would go no farther. For me, and for her, there was no need to travel further back in time.

My memories and my reality overlapped here, blending together as one. And I was watching this happen.

You plunked yourself down on the summer grass, wordlessly gazing up at the sky. With a screech a pair of small birds flashed across the sky. In the silence that followed, a hint of bluish twilight began to entwine itself around us. As I sat down beside you, I had an odd feeling, as if thousands of invisible threads were finely tying your body to my heart.

I tried speaking to her, but no words came. As if my tongue had been stung by a bee and had swelled up. In this world on the edge of reality, my body and my heart were not yet joined.

Yet I knew. That I would stay here like this forever. Neither going on further, or going back. The hands of the clock had stopped, or maybe the hands had vanished, time coming to a complete standstill. My tongue was finally able to move normally again, and one by one I found the right words to say.

I shut my eyes. For a short time I remained there, in that interim darkness, then opened my eyes once more. Quietly, carefully, trying not to accidentally wreck anything, I gazed around, making sure that that world had yet to vanish. The sound of cool flowing water reached me, and the intense fragrance of the summer grass. Countless cicadas called out something to the world as loudly as they could. Her red sandals and my white sneakers rested side by side on top of the sand, like small animals taking a rest. From our ankles down, our feet were covered with fine white sand. The color of the sky told us that summer twilight was fast approaching.

I reached out and touched her hand, and held it tight. She squeezed back. We were linked as one. My young heart thumped out dryly, deep inside my chest. My feelings became a sharp-edged wedge driven with a mallet unfailingly into the right gap.

And right then I realized something. Before I knew it, my shadow was gone. The sun sinking in the West cast clear, long shadows of everything else onto the ground, but mine was nowhere to be found. So at what point had I lost my shadow? And where did he go to?

Strangely enough, that didn't make me feel particularly anxious, or fearful or confused. My shadow must have vanished from here of his own accord. Or, for some reason, had temporarily moved somewhere else. But it would be back sometime. Since we were *one*.

The wind silently blew over the surface of the river. Her slim fingers seemed to be secretly telling me something. Something vital, something that words couldn't convey.

At that time neither you nor I had names. The radiant feelings of a seventeen-year-old and a sixteen-year-old on the grass of a riverbank, in the summer twilight, were the only things that

mattered. Stars would soon be twinkling above us, and they had no names either.

She looked right at me, as if peering down at the bottom of a clear, deep spring, with eyes that couldn't be more serious. And then she whispered out a confession, our hands still entwined.

"Did you know that? The two of us are nothing more than someone else's shadows."

And right then I snapped awake. Or was yanked back to an unmistakable plateau of reality. Her voice still ringing clearly in my ears.

Did you know that? The two of us are nothing more than someone else's shadows.

PART THREE

PART THREE

IN THE EVENING, as I followed the usual path to the library, I saw a strange boy.

He was standing all by himself beyond the bridge. A light sheen of evening fog lay over the surface of the river, the kind of fog that often arose in the spring because of a difference in water and air temperature. The fog prevented me from getting a good look at the boy. His clothes, though, were unusual, and caught my eye. He was wearing a kind of green parka, with a yellow illustration on the front. A gust of wind cleared away the fog for a moment, revealing the picture on it. A picture of a round-looking submarine.

That yellow submarine that appeared in the Beatles' animated film of the same name.

All the people moving along the street (and there weren't that many) were dressed in old, dull-colored clothes, and this brightly colored parka stood out. And it was also the first time I'd laid eyes on the boy. If I'd seen him before, I surely would have remembered him.

Likewise, the boy seemed to be intently gazing in my direction. Hard to say for sure, though. He was standing way on the other side of the bridge, and the wind had stopped and fog once again lay over the river. My eyes, too, hadn't fully recovered from the wounds I had received when I entered the town. I felt it, though, on my skin—the feeling of being watched. Perhaps the boy had something he wanted to tell me. Maybe I should cross over the bridge and talk to him? Ask him, *Do you have something you want to say to me?*

But I was on my way to the library, had no clear-cut reason to talk to him, and didn't want to deviate from my set path. So I continued on down the road on this side of the river, heading upstream.

With the approach of spring, the clumps of white snow that lingered on the sandbanks in the river had begun to melt. The snow melt made the river level rise. Instinctively sensing that spring was near, the unicorns gazed around with dreamy eyes, patiently waiting for the green buds to appear on plants. They'd lost quite a few of their number during the harsh winter, mostly elderly beasts or young ones not yet strong enough to survive. Even those who'd somehow survived the winter were gaunt from chronic malnutrition, with none of the lustrous yellow fur they displayed in the fall.

With my hands stuck in the pockets of my coat, I continued down the road along the river, maintaining my usual even pace that never flagged. My mind, though, was far from calm. For some reason the image of the boy in his *Yellow Submarine* parka wouldn't leave me.

A couple of questions nagged at me. In this dull-colored town, why did this boy alone have such colorful, eye-catching clothes? And why did he stare at me so intently? The people here tended to lower their eyes whenever they saw someone else, as if trying to avoid the gaze of something ominous—like that of large, dark raptors circling high overhead—and hurried along. Never did they halt to take a long, hard look at anyone.

Before I came to this town surrounded by a wall, when I was still in the world over there, I'd seen that animated film. *Yellow Submarine.* So I was familiar with that drawing. And the song, too. What the film was about, though, I couldn't recall at all. *We all live in a yellow submarine* . . . It means something, and at the same time, it doesn't.

The boy had somewhere gotten hold of that old parka as a hand-me-down—where, though, I had no clue. I doubted that he knew what the illustration on it meant, since no one in this town surrounded by a high wall could listen to the Beatles' music. No, not just the Beatles, but any kind of music. And they had no idea what a submarine was all about.

I walked down the twilit road, vaguely thinking about all this. I passed in front of the clock tower, and as I did, I habitually glanced up at the clock. As always, the clock had no hands. It wasn't a clock that told time, but a clock that showed the meaninglessness of time. Time hadn't come to a halt, but it had lost any significance.

There were no other clocks in the town. The sun rose in the

morning and set in the evening. Who needs any more detailed division of time than that? The difference between one day and the next—if indeed there was a difference—who cared about that?

And I was one of them, a resident who likewise didn't need to measure time. When twilight came, I changed clothes, left home, walked the same way down the same path to my workplace, the library. The number of steps I took from one day to the next varied little, I would guess. And in the stacks in a back room of the library, I set to reading old dreams. Until my fingers and eyes grew too tired and I could read no more.

Time had no meaning there. Like the seasons came and went, so did time. Going round and round. In the same spot? That, I don't know. In its own way, time was advancing forward bit by bit. But honestly, *going round and round* is the only way to express it. The rest can just be left up to time.

Yet that evening, seeing that boy on the far bank in his *Yellow Submarine* parka, the usual sense of time was thrown into confusion. The sound of my footsteps on the pavement of the road sounded different, somehow. And the way the branches of the river willows on the sandbanks quivered and shook—that, too, seemed changed, ever so slightly.

As always, the girl was waiting for me in the library. She arrived before me and got everything ready. In cold seasons, she lit the stove and, facing the counter, steeped herbal tea, a special blend to help heal my injured eyes. The tea wouldn't completely heal them, yet it lessened the pain. As the Dream Reader, I had to keep my injured eyes functioning.

And as long as I was the Dream Reader, I'd be able to see the girl every day and spend a few hours with her. She was sixteen. For her, time stood still at that age.

"On the way here, I saw a boy standing on the other side of the river," I told her. "He was wearing a parka with a yellow submarine on it. He's about the same age as you. Do you know him?"

"Parka? Submarine?"

I explained as best as I could. I don't know how much she understood, though I think I got across what they mostly looked like.

"I don't think I've ever seen him," she said. "If I had, I'm sure I'd remember him."

"Maybe he's new to the town."

She shook her head. "Nobody new has come here."

"Are you certain about that?"

As she crushed the green leaves with a pestle, she shook her head decisively. "I am. No one has entered after you did. No one at all."

People in town seemed familiar with all the others who lived there. If anyone else showed up here they'd be sure to notice. And the only entrance was tightly guarded by the able and imposing Gatekeeper.

I didn't get it. That was no mistake or illusion—I'd seen that Yellow Submarine Boy with my own eyes. But I decided to put him out of my mind. I had work to do.

I drank down the last drop of the thick herbal tea she had prepared for me, then went to the stacks in the back of the library. And held the old dream she'd picked for me and silently began the task of reading it.

"What happened to your ear?" the girl suddenly asked. "The right earlobe."

I touched my earlobe and felt a sharp pain. I winced a bit.

"It's reddish black. Like something bit you hard."

"I have no memory of it," I said.

And I really didn't. Until she mentioned it, I hadn't felt any pain. But now it ached in time with my heartbeat. Like her pointing it out made my ear suddenly remember.

She moved closer and examined my earlobe from a number of angles, and gently touched that part. And being touched by her like that made me so happy. Even if it was but a tiny fingertip grazing my earlobe.

"You'd best put on some medicine. I'll make a cream you can use, so just wait a moment." She hurried out of the stacks.

I closed my eyes and waited for her to return. My heart beat on, hard and regular, like the sound a woodpecker makes in the woods. I had no idea what had happened to my earlobe. Had something really bitten me? No, if I'd been bitten hard enough to leave a mark, I would have noticed it when I got bitten.

But say I had been—then what had done it? An animal? An insect? But there weren't any animals or insects in this town that I'd ever seen. (The exception being the unicorns, but I couldn't picture them sneaking up on me in the middle of the night and biting me.) I just didn't get it.

The girl finally returned, carrying a small ceramic bowl. A simple bowl, the rim slightly cracked. Inside was a mustard-colored ointment.

"I just whipped this up, so it might not work all that well, but it's better than nothing."

She put her finger in the ointment and gently, softly spread some on my earlobe. It felt cold, chilly.

"Did you make this?" I asked.

"Yes, that's right. I picked some good herbs from the garden out back."

"You really know a lot."

She modestly shook her head. "Most people in town can do this. There are no shops that sell medicine, so you have to make do by yourself."

After a while the pain in my earlobe lessened. The cold feeling remained, and that seemed to ease the pain. When I told her this she smiled happily.

"I'm glad," she said. "When you've finished work, I'll put some more on."

I sat at my desk again and focused on reading the old dreams. The flame in the oil lamp on the desk flickered. But our shadows were not cast on the wall.

No one in this town had shadows. Including me, of course.

I SAW THE BOY again the following day. A small, skinny boy in a *Yellow Submarine* parka. Wearing round metal-frame glasses. His hair came down to his ears, and his limbs were thin and lanky, so thin it made me worry if he was eating enough. He was standing in the same spot as yesterday, beyond the bridge, gazing straight at me. As if appealing to me about something. There was no one else around.

There was no fog on the river that day, so I could make him out much more clearly. And as I'd thought, I'd never seen him before. I'd never seen any other teenage boy in this town, for that matter. Other than the girl working in the library, the only other people I'd seen on the streets were adults, middle-aged or on the verge of being elderly. (At least I think that's true. Most people kept their heads down as they walked, hiding their faces, so I had to guess their ages from their gait and physique.)

For a second, I was struck by the impulse—stronger than the day before—to cross the bridge and talk to him, but thought better of it. Unless it was some very important matter, people in this town would never speak to someone if they didn't know them, especially out on the street. They never looked at each other, either. This was a code of manners they felt they had to follow. And as I lived there this state of mind had naturally seeped into me. A road was for walking down, as quickly and simply as one could.

So for that boy to come to a halt on the other side of the bridge, not go anywhere, and silently stand there staring at me was quite out of the ordinary. It was impossible. And it didn't just happen once, but twice. Had he been standing there all that time, waiting for me to pass by? But why? I couldn't think of a reason. I felt strangely shaken.

Even so, I never stopped but kept on walking along the river on the road to the library.

That night, with my (dream reading) work over for the day, as always I accompanied her back to her home (walking side by side on the flagstone path along the river, rarely speaking, the sound of the rhythm of our footsteps in sync). Yet even after I got back to my own home the figure of Yellow Submarine Boy wouldn't leave me. In the afterimage I had, he gazed steadily in my direction. Even while I slept, he appeared to me in dreams. And there he was again, standing on the other side of the stone bridge, the river between us, gazing at me. Nothing beyond that happened. Just him standing there, looking at me. Motionless.

At night my right earlobe pulsed with a dull pain in time with my heart. That odd boy across the river and the pain in my earlobe had arrived simultaneously. There had to be a connection. Both were quite out of the ordinary, inexplicable, and had appeared at nearly the same time.

I woke up many times that night, which was unusual for me. Since I had come to live in this town I'd never woken up at night. Once I crawled into bed nothing disturbed me and I was able to get a good rest, physically and mentally, until morning. Yet that night, because of the appearance of the boy in my dreams and the ache in my earlobe, I couldn't sleep well. And even when fitful sleep came I couldn't really relax and recharge. I had to fluff up my pillow over and over, straighten out the covers I'd kicked around, and wipe away my sweat with a towel. I tossed and turned, dozing and waking, until morning came.

Was something about to happen?

I wasn't hoping for anything to happen. I needed nothing to happen, for my present situation to go on forever. But once a change began—whatever kind it was—I didn't think it could be stopped. I had that kind of premonition.

The next day, at the same time—at least I think it was the same time; there weren't any clocks in the town so I couldn't be sure—

I passed in front of the bridge. But on this day Yellow Submarine Boy was nowhere to be seen. And his absence confused me all the more.

Why isn't he there today?

My emotions were contradictory. I wasn't hoping he would be there. And yet, his absence perplexed me. Why is that? I decided to stop thinking about him. I blanked out my thoughts and trudged along toward the library. But this time I couldn't make my mind a void, as I usually could. I kept on seeing the boy in the *Yellow Submarine* parka.

In front of the glowing stove, the girl looked at me uneasily. She came over, closely examined my right earlobe, and touched it lightly with her fingertip. "Somehow it seems more swollen than yesterday," she said.

"It ached all night long. I couldn't sleep well."

"You couldn't sleep well?" she said, a frown on her face. In this town that must be something that shouldn't happen.

"I woke up many times during the night."

She shook her head. "I asked people I know about that kind of swelling of the earlobe, but no one had ever seen a case of it. So I don't know the cause or the treatment. But I brought a different kind of ointment, so let's try that."

She opened the lid of a small label-less jar, dipped a finger in the sticky, dark brown ointment, and massaged some into my earlobe. It stung. A much different feel from that earlier ointment.

"We'll see how this does. I hope it helps."

This was the first time I'd seen her look worried. The girl was always calm, never flustered or confused, quietly, matter-of-factly, going about her tasks at the library. Her worried look made my own vague anxiety worse. Maybe my swollen earlobe was not a simple case of an insect bite but a symptom of some more serious disease.

And perhaps that was the reason why that night I couldn't do a good job of reading the old dreams. The old dreams didn't smoothly rest in my palms like usual. They woke from their sleep and appeared to me, but hesitated just before they gave them-selves up to me and disappeared somewhere. Perhaps returning to their shells.

"Things aren't going well today," I said to the girl after many failed attempts.

She nodded. "Maybe because your earlobe is swollen and hurts. So you can't focus. Getting that swelling down is the first priority."

"But no one knows what caused it, nor how to treat it."

She nodded again. The glimpse of sorrow that flitted across her face made her look much older, as if she were no longer a girl but a grown woman. And that perplexed me a little. How she seemed, marginally, different from before.

We closed the library a little earlier than usual since there was little more we could do then. And, as always, I was going to see her back to her house. But she turned me down.

"I'd like to walk back alone today," she said.

My chest tightened up when I heard this, and I had trouble breathing. From a few days after I first visited the library I'd seen her home, without fail, every time after work. We'd walk along the path beside the river to her old communal housing in the Workers' District. This was the most important part of my day. And now that routine was being disrupted, like someone had taken away a step from a ladder.

I asked her, "Is this because I wasn't able to read the old dreams? Or because my earlobe is swollen?"

She didn't answer that.

"I have some things I need to think about," she replied.

Her voice had a self-contained sound to it, cutting off all further questions. So we said good-bye at that point with no more words between us. She walked upstream, I downstream, both toward our homes. The sound of her footsteps slowly faded away, and then I couldn't hear them at all. All I could hear was the flow of the river. It was hard to imagine a lonelier sound than a river flow-ing at night.

I felt a bit gloomy, lost, as I plodded down the street by myself toward home. This unusual parting made me realize how very alone I was. And my right earlobe chose this moment to begin aching something fierce.

Somehow I had to get my old life back. Return to the way things should be. First I'd need to heal the wound in my ear. And then wipe that Yellow Submarine Boy from my mind.

Okay, but how?

Back in my room I changed clothes, snuffed out the lamp, and climbed into bed. I tried to blank out my mind but the ache in my ear continued unabated, and the figure of Yellow Submarine Boy wouldn't leave me. It was as if they had settled down inside me, a pair of inexplicable events I couldn't cut loose.

MY SLEEP THAT NIGHT was again unsettled.

And when I suddenly shot awake, I realized there was someone right beside me. And that someone was silently gazing down at me from above. I felt that piercing stare stinging my skin. I had no idea what time it was, of course. But I knew it was the dead of night. When the night couldn't get any deeper.

I cracked my eyes open a slit as I lay there, trying to figure out who was there. It took a while for my eyes to adjust to the darkness. The only light source was a slight band of moonlight slanting through a gap in the shutters. Trying not to let him know I was awake, I slowly, and quietly, breathed through my nose, letting my eyes get accustomed to the dark.

You would think that lying there defenseless like that in a dark room, with some stranger right beside you, might produce anxiety and fear, yet it didn't. My heart rate managed to stay normal. And the sound of that regular heartbeat kept me calm.

What is *going on*? I wondered. I wake up in the middle of the night to find someone sitting right next to me, staring down at my face. I should be more freaked out, terrified. That's a natural reaction. But I was oddly calm. Why?

That unknown person seemed to read my thoughts.

"You were born on a Wednesday," that person said. A young man's voice, a little high pitched. As if it hadn't been long since his voice changed.

I was born on a Wednesday?

"It was a Wednesday when you were born," the person said.

I tried getting up out of bed but didn't have the strength. I felt as if I were tied down, with no feeling in my arms and legs. I no longer felt the ache in my earlobe. Some change must have occurred in my nerves. Unable to do anything, I lay there, prone, in bed.

Did being born on a Wednesday have some significance for me?

"No. It's just a simple fact. Wednesday is just one day of the week," the young man said. He said it matter-of-factly, unemotionally, as if explaining an immutable mathematical theorem.

I still couldn't make out his face in the dark. Was this the boy in the *Yellow Submarine* parka? I wondered. No other possibility came to me. He'd come here to see me in the deepest part of night—with this "simple fact" of my being born on a Wednesday his little present in place of a normal greeting.

"Don't be afraid of me," the boy said. "I'm not going to hurt you."

I gave a small nod, tilting my chin a couple of degrees. I couldn't open my mouth to attempt any words.

"I'm sure I startled you, showing up in the middle of the night, but there was no other way for me to talk with you, just the two of us."

I blinked several times. Blinking I could handle. And moving my chin a little. Other than that, no parts of my body were following orders.

"I have a request," the boy said. "That's why I came here. Passing through the wall."

Without getting permission from the Gatekeeper?

"Yes, that's correct," the boy said, reading my thoughts. He was able to do that.

"I came into this town without the Gatekeeper knowing, and without getting my eyes injured. So I'm not officially allowed to be here. That's why I came here at this time of night, so no one will notice."

Do you have a shadow? I asked. People with a shadow aren't allowed inside this town.

"No, I don't. I left my shell back in the world over there. I imagine it would be called my shadow. Or maybe, conversely, the me here is a shadow. The real me might be there in that other world. Either way, I hid that discarded shell deep in the forest so no one will find it. So I could enter this town."

And he had a favor to ask of me.

"That's right. I have a favor to ask of you. I have to become the Dream Reader. That's the only thing I ask, that I be allowed to read old dreams. But since I'm not a resident of the town I have no hope of officially taking on that job. So I want to become one with you. If we become one, I can, as you, read old dreams every day."

Become one with me?

"Yes, that's right. It might sound outlandish, but it isn't. In fact, it's only natural. You and I joined together. Since I am, from the start, you, and you are, from the start, me."

That deeply puzzled me. From the start I am him, and he is me?

"Yes, that's it. Please believe me. We were originally one. But things happened and we were separated into two entities like this. But in this town we can become one being. I will become one part of you. I will become the Dream Reader, and can continue reading old dreams."

Him reading old dreams . . . Did this mean I didn't have to read them anymore myself?

The boy said, "No, it doesn't mean that. You will continue to read old dreams in the back of the library like always. Since I am you and you are me. My power will become yours. Like water blending with other water. Becoming one with me won't change your personality or your everyday life. And your freedom won't be restricted."

I tried my best to wrap my head around all this. And in my heart I asked him, *Why do you want to read old dreams that much?*

"Reading old dreams is my calling. I came into this world in order to become the Dream Reader. Yet I just couldn't find a way of becoming one in the world I belonged to. Finally, like this, I was able to run across you. Please believe what I say and become one with me—and help me live in this town. I can be a real help to you as the Dream Reader. If you wish to, you can continue going to that library, and seeing that girl."

If I wish to.

Alright, but how do I actually *merge* with you?

"It's quite simple. Please let me bite your left earlobe. If I do that, we will become one."

So you're the one who bit my right earlobe?

"Yes, that was me. Biting your right earlobe in the world over there allowed me to come to this town. And biting the left in this world will let me merge with you."

I needed time to figure out right from wrong. I had to get my confused thoughts in order, had to get my paralyzed body back to normal. Whether to become one with Yellow Submarine Boy or not was for me a critical decision, one that might drastically change my life. This boy was basically a stranger, so why should I believe him? Wasn't I missing something vital here?

"I'm sorry, but there's not much time to think this over. I'm a trespasser in this town. If the Gatekeeper learns I'm here, things will get sticky. Someone in town might spot me and inform him. He'd waste no time in grabbing me. He has that much power. So I need to merge with you as soon as possible."

I still didn't get it. *Why is this boy me, and me this boy?* What did that mean?

I don't know why, but even though I couldn't fathom the logic of what this boy was saying in his calm tone, I started to feel like I could accept it.

"Yes, please believe what I say. By becoming one with me you'll become more your true self, the self you were meant to be. I won't let you regret it, I promise. And when the time comes when you think you need to leave, then you can. You're free as a bird flying through the sky."

Free as a bird flying through the sky?

I agonized, but couldn't get my thoughts straight. My mind got more and more hazy and finally I couldn't think at all. I seemed to be falling asleep again.

"Don't fall asleep," he said sharply in my ear. "Stay up a little longer and give me permission. Permission to bite your left earlobe. This is the one and only chance. It's absolutely critical for me."

I was terribly sleepy. So desperate for sleep I didn't care what happened. All I wanted was to fall asleep as soon as I could and sink back into that pleasant world of rest and oblivion. With no one bothering me.

Okay, it's alright with me, I muttered in a trance. *You want to bite me that much, be my guest.*

In an instant the boy bit my left earlobe. So hard it might have left teeth marks.

And I fell into a world of deep, deep sleep.

LATE THE NEXT MORNING I woke up as always, the same old me. The paralysis of the night before was gone, and I could move my arms and legs. Daylight shone faintly in through gaps in the shutters, and everything around me was perfectly still. Just like every morning.

As soon as I awoke, I remembered Yellow Submarine Boy from last night, and immediately tried touching my earlobes. The right earlobe, then the left. Neither one, though, was swollen, and I felt no pain. Situation normal—a soft, healthy pair of earlobes.

Last night the boy had bitten me so hard. So hard and deep there had to be toothmarks. I could still remember the pain, yet now there was none, and no marks. Which was pretty odd.

I replayed our entire conversation. I could recall it all accurately, verbatim, like it was all transcribed.

He got my permission and bit my left earlobe, and that action, perhaps, allowed him to merge into one with me. Yet I felt nothing strange about my body or my mind. I shut my eyes hard, searching my consciousness in the darkness as deeply as I could. I took a deep breath and stretched out the joints of my legs till they cracked. I gulped back a few glasses of water and had a good long pee. No matter how I looked, though, nothing was different about me this morning from the night before. Was the boy really able to meld with me? Wasn't it all just a vivid dream?

No, that can't be. That awful pain was real when he sunk his teeth into my left earlobe (despite the pain, I'd fallen straight asleep right after), and I could reproduce, word for word, our entire conversation. That couldn't be a dream. No dream could ever be that clear.

However—there isn't just *one* reality. Reality is something you have to choose by yourself, out of several possible alternatives.

Winter was nearly over, and the day was bright and sunny. I lowered the shutters and spent the afternoon hours until evening in the dimly lit room, mulling over random thoughts about my own existence.

If Yellow Submarine Boy and I had really merged into one, there should be some apparent changes in me as a person—how I was, what I thought. A new personality had taken up residence inside me, after all. But I couldn't detect any such changes, no matter how carefully, how attentively, I scrutinized myself. Nothing felt out of place. This was the usual me here. The me I always thought of as myself.

I didn't think, though, that the boy had just made up some baseless story. What he said as he sat next to me had to be true. He'd tried as hard as he possibly could to convince me, his eyes glowing with sincerity. He'd insisted that by biting my left earlobe he and I would meld into one, and he'd done it. I'd given him authorization to. The way he bit me was so very intent and focused. This *melding* he spoke of must be completed now. Why would I doubt it?

So that's what had happened—deep at night, as I lay asleep, Yellow Submarine Boy and I had merged. Like water blending together with other water. Or, to put it another way, we were *restored* to our original state.

Would it take some time for me to psychically feel the changes brought on by becoming one with him? Or could I only wait, quietly, for these changes to manifest on their own? Or did *melding* mean that I could no longer sense these changes? Did my new self just feel natural?

I am he, and he is me, the boy had declared. The two of us becoming one was, he said, entirely natural, and by doing so I could become more the *essential, real me.*

Had I become more the real me? Is this—the me here now—the essential, original me? But who's to decide? How can you distinguish a subject and object that meld together? The more I thought about it, the less I understood about who I am.

As evening approached, I changed my clothes, left my house, and headed toward the library. I took the dimly lit road along the river to the town square. I stopped, looked up at the clock without hands, checking the nonexistent time. I didn't see anyone on the other side of the bridge. No unicorns either. The only thing moving were the river willows, swaying slightly in the wind. I closed my eyes and asked myself, my question directed at Yellow Submarine Boy.

"Are you there?"

No response, just a deep silence. I asked again.

"If you're there, could you say something? Anything, just a sound."

Again, no answer. I gave up and set off again along the riverside road toward the library.

We must have completely become one. Or were *restored* to being one. Which meant I was talking to myself. So how could I expect a reply? If I did hear anything in response it would be but an echo.

When the girl in the library saw me, she came over and checked out my earlobe. Without a word she observed my right earlobe that had been swollen. She gently held it between two fingers, caressing it. And she checked out the left earlobe, too, just to make sure. Then the right one again. As if all this held some profound significance. She tilted her head a fraction.

"It's odd. The swelling from yesterday is totally gone. The color is back to normal, too. It's like nothing ever happened. And it was so swollen and discolored. Are you having any pain? Does it still ache?"

No pain or aching, I replied.

"So one night's sleep was all it took for the swelling and pain to disappear?"

"That new ointment you applied last night may have helped."

"Perhaps," she said, not sounding convinced.

But I couldn't tell her about Yellow Submarine Boy showing up in my house last night. Or how he'd bitten my left earlobe, making us into one being. The boy wasn't permitted to enter the town. Maybe by becoming one with me his illegal status was no longer an issue. Still, for this town he was an alien who, if discovered, would be eliminated in no uncertain terms by the powerful Gatekeeper. And since I was one with the boy I might be kicked out as well—no, no doubt about it. I would most definitely be excluded from the town. So I couldn't reveal to anyone what had taken place the night before.

Now I had a secret I was keeping from the girl. And a significant one at that. Up till then I'd never had anything I had to hide from her . . . and having one now made me more than a little anxious.

As always, she made some hot, green herbal tea for me. I took my time drinking it, letting it soothe my nerves. I watched her as she quietly moved around the room, her graceful movements as she briskly went about her tasks, and savored the time we could spend together, just the two of us. Nothing there had changed. The calm stillness, the warm comfort . . . Today was a complete repeat of yesterday, and tomorrow would be a repeat of today.

That made me feel relieved. Nothing around seemed changed. The air there was the same air as always, the light the same. The sound of the kettle beginning to boil, the faint creak of the wooden floorboards, the smell of the canola oil lamp. Everything was in its rightful place. With nothing to disrupt the harmony.

After I'd finished the herbal tea, the girl and I, without a word, moved to the stacks in the rear and began the task of reading old dreams. I settled down at the old desk and held the old dream she'd brought to me in both palms as I gently, cautiously, coaxed the dream to emerge. Over time I'd grown used to the work and mastered it, and could get the dreams to be less wary. They silently slipped out of their shells, emitted a faint light, and I could feel their warmth in my palms.

I could sense how relaxed they were, how they let down their guard and gave themselves up to my hands and began relating their tales. The tales that had been locked away—how long a time, I wondered—inside those shells.

Strangely enough, though, on this day I couldn't directly hear the voices as the old dreams told their stories. I could only sense the distinct, faint vibration they made as they began to speak. They were speaking, that much I knew, yet their voices eluded me.

My guess was that the boy was the one reading their dreams. I was the one who woke them up and got them talking. But the one who actually could hear their voices was the boy. In other words, we'd divided up the work of dream reading. No, that wasn't it. He and I had become one and were already a single entity. Labeling it a *division* of labor wasn't correct. I was simply *separately using* several parts of my body in the appropriate way.

Honestly, I never fully understood the stories the old dreams related. Their voices were small, and they spoke fast, in most cases their words were hard to catch, their stories hard to organize. I understood little of what they said, so I let most of their words just flow on past. I came to see my job as Dream Reader as helping them open their hearts and speak freely, but not to accurately read the content. Not understanding what they said didn't cause any particular problems, though, and I never regretted it. So if the boy could understand what they said, I should welcome it. I imagined him precisely hearing all the details of their tales, and all this content steadily storing up inside him. All I did was gently warm up the old dreams I held in my palms and coax them out of their shells.

Once a dream had spoken everything about itself, it was peacefully freed. It would hang there vaguely in the air, then disappear without a sound. Leaving an empty shell in my hands.

"You're moving right along with your work today," the girl said. She was seated across from me, gazing into my eyes, and she sounded impressed.

I just nodded. No words came out of my mouth.

"You must have mastered the skill of dream reading," she said, smiling tenderly. "Nothing could be better. For this town, for you, and for me."

"I'm glad," I said. *I'm glad*, Yellow Submarine Boy inside me whispered as well. At least I felt like I could hear that whisper. Like an echo from deep in a cave.

That night we read five dreams in all. Until now we'd been able to get through only two, or at most three, so this was a major step forward for me, one that made the girl happy. And—need I say it—her bright smile made me happy too.

After we closed up the library, I walked her home as usual. The click of her shoes on the flagstone road along the river seemed lighter and more cheerful than usual. I didn't say much as we walked, merely entranced listening to her footsteps.

"Reading old dreams is no easy task," the girl confided. "It's not something anyone can do. I'm so happy to know you're so well suited to it."

I watched as she was enveloped by the door to her home, then set out down the riverside road, and as I walked I directed a question to Yellow Submarine Boy. Or to myself, rather. *Hey, are you there?* I asked.

But there was no answer. No echo, either.

THAT NIGHT Yellow Submarine Boy appeared in my sleep.

We were in a small square room. Four blank walls, and not a single window. In the middle of the room was a small, old wooden desk, and the boy and I sat there across from each other. On top of the desk on a small dish was a small, thin candle, whose flame flickered as we breathed out.

"What is this place?" I asked him after gazing around me.

"A room inside of you," Yellow Submarine Boy said. "Deep down in your consciousness. Not the most attractive place, for sure, but for now this is the only place where we can meet and talk."

"I can't see you anywhere else?"

"That's right. We are already one being, so we can't be easily separated. This is the only place where we can be two people."

"So if I come here I can see you."

"Yes, if we come to this special place, we can see each other and talk together. Up until this little candle burns out."

I nodded, and said, "That's good. I was thinking I needed to talk with you again."

"Yes. There are a few things we should talk about. Though words are, after all, just words."

I looked at the candle, checking its length, and after a pause said, "So . . . at the library tonight you read the old dreams in my place, didn't you? Five dreams altogether."

The boy gazed straight into my eyes. Then said, "Yes, I read the old dreams instead of you. Like I was usurping your job, and I hope it didn't make you feel bad."

I shook my head several times. "No, it didn't. I actually felt thankful. Up till now I've called forth the old dreams and they pass through me, but I've only been able to catch a shred of what they're talking about. It's like listening to something in a foreign language."

The boy gazed into my eyes without a word.

"But you're able to understand what they're saying, aren't you?" I asked.

"Yes, I understand quite well. The meaning of what they're saying passes through me very distinctly, each and every part. As clearly as following words in a book. But I'm still not good at leading them out of their shells. At this point that's something only you can do."

"Only I can?"

"Yes, your hands lend them a sense of peace, warming them up, gently, naturally guiding them out. Like a butterfly emerging from a chrysalis."

"So you and I sort of supplement what the other's lacking. Is that it?"

The boy nodded emphatically. "By becoming one, we complement what's missing and lacking in the other."

"I warm the old dreams up in my hands and lead them out of their shells, while you read the tales they tell. And from now on we will do that work as a kind of cooperative unit."

"Right, and I came to this town to make that possible. By becoming one we're able to accomplish that."

The little candle on the dish had gotten smaller and would soon burn out.

Yellow Submarine Boy said, "Reading is my life's work. And the old dreams here are special books that only I can read. So *I* have to read them. That's my duty, and the most natural thing for me to do."

"So how long will our—*cooperative unit* last?"

"How long?" the boy repeated in a flat voice. "That's a meaningless question. Because the clock in this town has no hands."

"So time here doesn't progress."

"Exactly. Time here stopped."

I gave this some thought and then said, "So if there's no time, nothing ever accumulates?"

"Right, where's there's no time there's no accumulation. What looks like accumulation is nothing but a transitory illusion cast by the present. Imagine turning pages in a book. The pages change but the page numbers do not. There's no logical connection between the new page and the previous one. The scenery around us may change but we're glued to the same spot."

"An eternal present?"

"Exactly. The only time that exists in this town is the present. There is no accumulation. Everything is overwritten, renewed. That's the world we belong to now."

As I pondered what he'd said, the candle's flame flared up once, then went out. Complete darkness descended on the room, and along with it time also vanished.

WINTER DEPARTED, and spring came. Even if time stopped, the seasons marched on. Even if everything we could see now was nothing more than a temporary illusion projected by the present, no matter how many pages you turned without the page numbers changing, still one day followed the other.

The snow scattered here and there on the ground began to melt, and the runoff of melted snow raised the level of the river. New buds sprang out on the barren trees, and day by day the beasts' fur took on its former luster. Before long the mating season would be upon them, the males viciously hurting each other with their sharp horns. Considerable blood would be shed, staining the ground dark, the blood making lots of colorful flowers blossom.

I was finally liberated from my armor-like heavy coat and now wore a wool jacket as I went to and from work at the library. It was a worn-out coat someone had probably worn for years but, oddly enough, it fit like a bespoke jacket.

I was grateful that spring had come. The long winter was finally drawing to a close. And an extraordinarily long winter it had been. Of course, living in this town it was hard to measure what was long and what was short, but my own sense of it was that it had been an unusually long winter. So long it made me feel like winter was the only season this town had. Which is why I was so thankful that spring had finally arrived.

By then I was quite used to being one with Yellow Submarine Boy. It didn't feel uncomfortable or weird at all. We functioned as a close single unit—in the boy's words, *inseparable*. Nothing unnatural about it. The girl in the library probably didn't even notice the change.

In the evening we walked along the riverside road toward the library. At the desk in the stacks I warmed up the old dreams with my hands and led them out of their shells, and the boy then fervently, greedily read them. For us as one being—conscious of each other's existence—this was our sole division of labor, but this joint work was seamlessly smooth, and never stagnated.

Now *we* were able to read through six, even seven old dreams in a night. The girl was deeply impressed, and pleased, by the startling progress of the work. As a reward—I would guess it was a reward—she baked apple sweets for us several times. And we enjoyed them.

"Have you ever read the book *The Papalagi*?" Yellow Submarine Boy asked me. We were in the little room deep belowground, seated, the candle's flame between us.

"I read it when I was young," I said. "So long ago I can't remember the details. All I recall is that it was an early-twentieth-century story of a Samoan Island chief relating his experiences traveling in Europe to his fellow villagers back home."

"That's right. But we know now it was purely fiction, the German author making up the story as if the village chief were telling it. A forgery, in other words. But back when it was widely read it was taken as a true account. Which is understandable. It was well done, a humorous and wise critique of modern civilization."

"I always thought it was a real account," I said.

"Real or fake, that doesn't really matter. Facts and the truth are two different things. That aside, the book talks a lot about coconut trees. In the island where the village chief lives, coconut trees are very important in the lives of the islanders, with coconut trees always being used to compare things, since they're so familiar.

"There's a description in the book that goes like this. The village chief spoke to the assembled villagers and said, 'Anyone can climb up coconut trees using their legs, but no one's ever climbed up higher than a coconut tree.' He probably said this to make fun of Europeans, who build skyscrapers and go up and up, ever higher. *Anyone can climb up coconut trees using their legs, but no one's ever climbed up higher than a coconut tree.* It's a very specific, easy-to-grasp expression. An allegory anyone could understand. And full of many implications. The audience there listening to the chief's talk—of course there's not actually an audience—would no doubt

433

nod in agreement since no one, no matter how skilled they were at climbing, could climb higher than a coconut tree."

I waited, silently, for the story to continue. Like a Samoan islander waiting for new knowledge to be imparted.

"But to contradict what the chief said, you could think of it this way. You can't say there aren't any people who have climbed a coconut tree higher than a coconut tree. Wouldn't we—you and I—be that kind of people?"

I tried to picture that scene. Me climbing up to the very top of the highest coconut tree (as high as a five-story building or thereabouts) growing in the Samoan Islands. And then trying to climb even higher. But the tree, of course, ends there. Beyond is just the blue sky of a southern island. Or just nothingness. You can see the sky, but you can't see nothingness with your own eyes. Since nothingness is, in the end, nothing but a concept.

"So you're saying we've left the tree and are in empty space? Where there's nothing to hold on to?"

The boy gave a short, hard nod. "Exactly. We're floating in empty space. There's nothing we can grab onto. But we haven't fallen yet. In order to start falling, you need the flow of time. If time is stopped, then we keep on floating there in empty space forever."

"And time doesn't exist here in this town."

The boy shook his head. "Time exists here. It just has no meaning. Which in the end amounts to the same thing."

"So if we remain in this town we can stay there, suspended in empty space?"

"Logically, at least, yes."

"But if for some reason time starts moving again," I said, "then we'll plummet from that height. And it might be a fatal fall."

"Probably," Yellow Submarine Boy said simply.

"Then to maintain that existence we can't leave the town. Is that what it means?"

"We probably couldn't find a way to prevent the fall," the boy said. "But there is a way to keep it from being fatal."

"Like what?"

"Believing."

"Believing in *what*?"

"That someone on the ground will catch you. Believing that from the bottom of your heart. Without holding back, absolutely unconditionally."

I pictured that scene in my mind. Someone with powerful arms waiting under the coconut tree to catch me when I fell. But I couldn't make out any face. Probably some imaginary person who didn't really exist.

I asked him, "Do you have someone like that? Someone who will catch you?"

He shook his head firmly. "No, I have no one like that. At least there's no one among the living. So I will stay forever in this town where time has stopped," the boy said, his lips forming a tight line.

I considered what he'd said. Who would catch my fall from such a terrible height (assuming there was someone)? As my imagination spun around pointlessly, the flame of the candle suddenly vanished. And a pitch-black darkness surrounded me.

A WHILE AFTER Yellow Submarine Boy and I had that talk about coconut trees, I couldn't help but sense a subtle change inside me, an uncomfortable feeling I couldn't put into words. In the back of my throat was a small hard lump of air that I couldn't get rid of. Every time I tried to swallow something, it irritated me a bit. There was a faint ringing in my ears, too. Because of this, everyday things I'd done naturally and smoothly became largely awkward and stilted.

Was this sort of new phenomenon because of the change in the seasons? Or because I'd become one with Yellow Submarine Boy? Or was there some other reason? I couldn't tell.

How can I express that uncomfortable, discomforted feeling? If I had to, I'd say it was as if my heart had gone off on its own in a direction completely counter to my will. Contrary to my will, my heart, like a young rabbit in a spring meadow for the first time, craving a wild playfulness that was inexplicable, unpredictable. And I couldn't control that willful, instinctive movement. But what I couldn't understand was why that unknown rabbit had popped up so abruptly inside me, and what it meant. Or why my will and my heart were moving in such conflicting ways.

Despite this, my day-to-day life was, on the surface, calm and unruffled. In my free time in the afternoons before I headed to the library, I read the huge amount of books Yellow Submarine Boy had accumulated in the world outside. This was a personal library provided just to me. The boy had opened up his entire inner library to me.

In those tall, long bookcases, all kinds of books, from all times and places, were lined up as far as the eye could see. My wounded eyes were not yet completely healed, yet I had no problem in reading the books stacked up in my unconscious. Since I could read those books not with my eyes but with my heart. From agriculture annuals to Homer, Tanizaki to Ian Fleming. In this town without a single book, being able to read these formless, thus invisible, books, freely, without any rebuke from anyone, was a source of endless joy.

The boy opened up his inner library to me, and while I read the books there the boy seemed to be fast asleep. Or had temporarily switched off his mind. At any rate I was the only one there, the time there for me alone. During those afternoon reading sessions I turned from being *us* to being *me, myself.*

Even so, the rabbit in the spring meadow inside me never ceased its frisky movements. Such tireless vitality never seemed to need to rest. On occasion it would disturb my concentration while reading, fiercely messing with my nerves with its powerful hind legs. And it unsettled my nightly sleep.

Something out of the ordinary was taking place inside me. Yet I had no clue what this *out of the ordinary* thing meant, I was utterly at a loss.

On occasion, Yellow Submarine Boy and I would sit across from each other in that little square room in my unconscious, the flame of the small candle between us, and quietly talk about all kinds of subjects. All in the darkest, deepest time of night. Gradually, though, the number of meetings decreased, since as time passed our bond became an expected, natural thing, and there was no need to speak to each other in words anymore. Probably.

On that day, though, Yellow Submarine Boy gazed at me with a serious look I'd never seen before. His lips were a tight line, his round metal-frame glasses reflecting the candle flame and glittering in the light.

I had consulted with the boy about the uncomfortable feelings I'd been having. What in the world was happening to me?

"Well, it seems that time has almost come," the boy said, breaking the deep silence.

I couldn't grasp what he was saying.

"That time?"

The boy opened both hands, palms face up, as if waiting to catch the right words when they fell from the ceiling. "The time for you to leave."

"I'm going to leave here?"

"Yes, you must be feeling it in your heart," said the smallish boy wearing a *Yellow Submarine* parka.

Did that lively rabbit inside me have anything to do with this?

"Yes, that's right. That's the rabbit inside you *telling you with all its might*." The boy had read my mind.

"That I will leave the town?"

"Yes, that's right. Your heart is wanting to leave this town. Or rather, it *needs* to leave. I've been feeling this for a while and have been keeping a close watch on your wavering heart."

I mulled over, in my own way, what the boy had said.

"But I myself don't yet understand what that wavering means. Is that what you're saying?"

The boy tilted his head a fraction. "That's right. Since your heart and your mind are in different places."

I looked at his face, silent.

"So I'll be leaving this town?" I repeated.

The boy nodded. "Yes, you will. In the past you let your shadow go outside the wall. Correct? And next time you will leave me behind and depart from this town. You'll be away from me, become one again with your shadow that's outside the wall."

I needed time to clear my head. "But is that even possible?" I asked. "Being together again with my shadow?"

"Yes, it is. If, *from your heart*, you truly want that."

"But I have no way of knowing where my shadow is now, and what he's doing. More importantly, after he left me, has he even survived in the outside world?"

With the candle flame between us, the boy quietly said, "He's fine. No need to worry. Your shadow is alive and well in the outside world. And he's doing a good job in your stead."

I was speechless, just gazing steadily at the boy's face. Finally, I managed to say, "You've met my shadow in the world outside?"

"Many times," the boy said, nodding slightly.

This surprised me and confused me. He'd met my shadow in the outside world?

"Yes, your shadow is doing quite well over there."

"And *I* am hoping to become one with him again."

"That's right. *Your heart* is seeking, and needing, a new direction. Though your mind has yet to fully grasp that. People's hearts are not that easy to grasp."

Much like a young rabbit in a spring meadow.

"That's right," the boy said, reading my mind. "Like a young rabbit in a spring meadow, it eludes the slow-moving hands of one's consciousness."

"So my shadow who escaped from here to the outside world is doing well standing in for me. That's what you said, right?"

"Exactly. He's doing a fine job in place of you, without any mistakes."

"Then we have already switched roles. Meaning he's actively functioning as the real me, while I'm a secondary entity, like I'm *his* shadow. I can't help thinking that. Is that really possible? For the real person and his shadow to switch like that?"

The boy considered this, then said, "Well, I can't really say. Since it's basically your issue. For me, though, I think either way's fine. Whether I'm the real me, or a shadow. Either way, the me here now, the one I see as myself—that's me. There's nothing beyond that. Maybe you should consider it the same way too."

"So you're saying it's no big deal which is the real person and which the shadow?"

"That's right. Sometimes the shadow and the real person trade places, and trade roles. But whether you're the real you or your shadow, either way you're you. That's for sure. Instead of wondering which is real and which is the shadow, it might be best to think how each is the vital other self to the other."

I stared at the back of my hand for a long time, as if making sure of something. As if checking that it was real flesh. "I'm not confident I can make it if I return to the outside world," I confessed. "I've lived in this town for so long and grown used to the life here."

"There's nothing to worry about. Just honestly follow the dictates of your heart. As long as you don't lose sight of that, all will be well. And your precious self will, no doubt, fully support your return."

Was that really true? Were things that easy? I still wasn't certain.

"Let's say I get out of this town," I said. "Then what? You'll stay behind?"

"That's right. I'll remain behind in the town. Even if you're gone, I think I can fulfill the role of Dream Reader. I'm resigned to the fact that someday you'll leave, so I've been preparing for it all this time. The old dreams in the shells trust me now, to some extent. Slowly I've learned empathy. It isn't easy for me, but I have made a small amount of progress. I've learned a lot of things from you."

"And you'll be my successor."

"Yes, I will take over from you as Dream Reader. Please don't worry about me. As I said before, reading old dreams is the calling given to me. I can't live in any other world but this one. That's an unshakable fact."

The boy sounded quite confident.

"But if one day, all of a sudden, you become the Dream Reader instead of me, will the town easily accept that? I mean, you haven't received the qualifications to be in this town."

"No worries. I need this town, and the town needs me. The town isn't workable without a Dream Reader. There's no way they would drive me away. The town, and the wall, will change ever so slightly to fit in with me."

"You're sure of this?"

The boy nodded decisively.

"Okay, say I do want to leave here. Practically speaking, how do I make that happen? It's no easy task to leave this town, with those tightly sealed high walls surrounding us."

"As long as your heart wishes it, it will happen," the boy intoned in a quiet voice. "Wish this in your heart before this little candle burns out, then blow out the candle. Blow it out with one breath, with all your might. Do that, and in the next instant you'll be transported to the world outside. It's simple. Your heart is like a bird flying through the sky. The wall can't prevent your heart from flapping its wings. There's no need to do what you did before, travel all the way to the pool and throw yourself in. And believe from the bottom of your heart that your other self will catch you in the world outside as you fall."

I silently shook my head. And took a few deep breaths. What should I say? No words came. I still hadn't fully grasped the situation I was in.

A deep gulf separated my mind and my heart. At times my heart was a young rabbit gamboling about a spring meadow, at times a bird freely flitting off in the sky. But I still couldn't control it. It's true—the heart is something hard to comprehend, what's hard to comprehend is the heart.

"I think I need some time to think," I finally managed to say.

"Of course. Please think about it," the boy said, all the while gazing deeply into my eyes. "Give it a lot of thought. As you know, there's plenty of time here to think. Paradoxically, the fact that time doesn't exist means there's a limitless amount of it."

The candle flame wavered just then, went out, and deep darkness descended.

EVERY TIME I SAW the girl to the door of her house I always said, "See you tomorrow." A meaningless thing to say, if you think about it, since in that town tomorrow in the precise sense didn't exist. Even knowing that, though, every night I couldn't help but say that to her.

See you tomorrow.

Whenever she heard this, she smiled faintly. But didn't say anything. Sometimes her lips would open a fraction, but no words ever emerged. She'd spin around, and, the hem of her skirt fluttering, she'd be absorbed by the entrance to her pitiful communal residence and vanish.

And I'd revisit the silence between us (silence being the one thing we held intimately in common as we walked, side by side, down the riverside path). As I secretly tasted this sustenance deep in my throat, I walked home. And thus ended the day for me in the town.

"See you tomorrow," I often said aloud to myself as I walked the path along the river. Knowing all the while that tomorrow didn't exist.

But on that final night, I couldn't say those words. Since tomorrow did not exist there. Not in any way, shape, or form.

What I said instead was "Farewell." An odd expression arose on her face, as if this was the first time in her life she'd heard the word, and she gazed steadily at me. This sort of good-bye wasn't what she was used to, and it seemed to puzzle her.

And I, too, gazed directly at her.

And I noticed something. How her overall features had changed slightly. I couldn't say for sure how, though I did notice changes in several details. The outline and depth of her features, like small waves, had begun to transform into something ever so different from before. Like a vibration makes a traced picture subtly off from the original. Very subtle changes, ones most people wouldn't notice.

Perhaps my "Farewell" to her that evening—different from my usual parting words—had brought on these changes in her looks. No—that wasn't it. What was transforming there, and undergoing subtle changes, wasn't the girl's looks but *me*. My own heart, as a human being, might be what was transforming.

"Farewell," I said to her again.

"Farewell," she said. Slowly, carefully, cautiously, as if putting in her mouth some food she'd never laid eyes on before. Always a tiny smile rose to her lips then, but this smile, too, was not the same. At least it felt that way to me.

How would she feel tomorrow when she realized I was no longer in this town? No, I thought—after I was no longer here the girl herself might very well have vanished. Maybe she was a being prepared by the town for my sake alone. So if I disappeared from here, so might she. This was entirely possible. And then someone else would help Yellow Submarine Boy in his dream reading. That thought hurt me, something awful. It felt like my body had turned half transparent. Precious things were steadily going far away from me. I was losing them forever.

Even so, my determination was firm. I knew I had to leave and move on to the next stage. This was a predetermined flow. I understood that now. I didn't belong here anymore. The space that contained me was no more. In many senses of the term.

She finally stopped gazing at my face. And as always she spun around, the hem of her skirt fluttering, and disappeared into the entrance to the communal residence. Quickly, precisely, like a night bird slipping into the darkness. With not a single wasted motion.

Left alone, I stared for a long time at the traces of her she'd left behind. That graceful image faded, disappeared completely, filled in by a blank space left by nothingness.

On my way back home along the river, night birds called out

their lonely night song, the spindly branches of the river willows on the sandbanks trembling in time to this. The sound of the water was louder than usual. Spring had arrived.

Late that night, Yellow Submarine Boy and I met in that small dark room deep in my unconscious. We sat there, the small desk between us, a thin candle burning as always. For a time we silently gazed at the candle. The flame flickered slightly in time to our silent breathing.

"So, have you given it enough thought?"

I nodded.

"You aren't feeling any doubts?"

"I don't think so," I said. I don't think so.

The boy said, "Then at this time I'll say good-bye to you."

"So I won't be seeing you again?"

"Probably not. We probably will never meet again. But I don't know. Who can say for sure?"

I took another close look at the boy in his *Yellow Submarine* parka. He took off his glasses, lightly pressed down on his eyelids, then put the glasses on again. Every time he put his glasses back on, it seemed to me that he became a slightly different person. In other words, he might be growing, moment by moment.

"I'm very sorry, but I'm unable to feel sadness," he confessed. "I was born like this. But if I weren't like this, and were a normal person, I'm sure I would feel sad at saying farewell to you. This is merely my imagination, of course, and I have no way of knowing what sadness is."

"Thank you," I said. "I'm just happy you'd say that."

Yellow Submarine Boy kept silent for a while. And then spoke.

"I guess we won't be seeing each other again."

"Perhaps not," I said.

"Believe in the existence of your other self," Yellow Submarine Boy said.

"That's my lifeline."

"That's right. He'll catch you. Believe in that. Believing in your other self is believing in *you*, yourself."

"Time for me to go," I said. "Before the candle burns out."

The boy nodded.

I breathed in deeply and paused. In those few seconds all kinds of scenes flashed before me. All the scenes I treasured. Among them a scene of a downpour on a broad sea. But I didn't hesitate. I had no hesitation. Perhaps.

I closed my eyes, focused all the power within me, and, in a single breath, blew out the candle.

Darkness descended. A darkness deeper than anything, a darkness ever so soft.

Afterword

I generally dislike adding an afterword to my novels (in most cases, they sound like I'm trying to justify myself), but with this novel I feel I need a word of explanation.

The core of the novel *The City and Its Uncertain Walls* lies in a novella (or long short story) I published in 1980 in the literary magazine *Bungakukai* entitled *The City, and Its Uncertain Walls*. It came to a little over 150 pages of handwritten manuscript pages in length. I published it in the magazine but wasn't satisfied with it (all kinds of circumstances before and after led up to it, and I felt as a novel it was a bit raw), so I never allowed it to be reprinted in book form. Nearly all my fiction has appeared in book form, but this work alone was never published as a book, either in Japan or in other countries.

Still, from the first I felt that this work contained something vital for me. At the time, though, unfortunately I lacked the skills as a writer to adequately convey what that *something* was. I'd just debuted as a novelist then and didn't have a good idea of what I was capable, and incapable, of writing. I regretted publishing the story, but figured what was done was done. Someday, when the time was right, I thought, I'd take my time to rework it, but till then would keep it on the back burner.

When I wrote this shorter novel, I was running a jazz bar in Tokyo. I was handling two jobs at once, life was hectic, and it was hard to focus on writing. I enjoyed running the bar (I loved music, and the place did well), but after I finished writing two novels the desire to earn my living solely by writing took hold of me, so I closed up shop and became a full-time writer.

So I settled down to write full-time and finished my first large-scale novel, *A Wild Sheep Chase*. This was in 1982. I planned to next move on to a complete revision of *The City, and Its Uncertain Walls*, but I realized it would be a stretch to make this story into a full-length novel so instead decided to add a completely different type of story to it and make it a kind of *double feature*.

I wrote the work as two alternating, parallel stories. At the end the two would combine into one—at least that was the rough idea. I had no set plan from the start and just wrote what I felt like writing, so even I, the author, had no clue how the two storylines were supposed to merge.

A pretty haphazard approach, if you think about it, but even so I was always optimistic (or maybe fearless), sure that it would sort itself out. I was confident, I guess, that things would work out well in the end. And sure enough, as I got near the end the two storylines did rather neatly link up, like two crews digging a tunnel, one from each end, breaking through and meeting up in the exact middle.

Writing *Hard-Boiled Wonderland and the End of the World* was a thrilling experience for me. And a lot of fun, as well. I published it as a book in 1985. I was thirty-six then. A period when all sorts of things forged ahead on their own.

As the years passed by, though, and as I gained more experience as a writer and grew older, I couldn't help but think that I hadn't seen this unfinished, or perhaps immature, work, *The City, and Its Uncertain Walls*, through to its conclusion. *Hard-Boiled Wonderland and the End of the World* was one response to the original story, but I thought a different form of response might be worth doing, too. Not overwriting the earlier work but instead creating a story that coexisted with it, so that the two complemented each other.

Yet a vision of what form that *other response* would take still eluded me.

At the beginning of 2020, at long last I felt I might be able to rework *The City, and Its Uncertain Walls*. It was exactly forty years since I'd published it. In the interim I'd gone from age thirty-one to seventy-one. In many ways there's a major difference between a novice writer holding down two jobs and an experienced professional writer (though I find it embarrassing to say so). But when it comes to the natural affection one has for the act of *writing novels* there shouldn't be much of a difference.

One other thing to add is that 2020 was the Year of the Coronavirus. I started writing this novel in March 2020, just as the coronavirus began its rampage across Japan, and finished it nearly three years later. In the interim I rarely set foot outside my home, and avoided any lengthy trips, and in that weird and tension-inducing situation (with a fairly long pause or cooling-off period in between) I worked steadily, day after day, on this novel (like the Dream Reader reading old dreams in the library). Those circumstance might be significant. Or maybe not. But I think they must mean something. I feel it in my bones.

I finished Part One first, and felt I'd completed the task I'd set out to accomplish. To make sure, though, I let the manuscript ferment for half a year, during which I realized this wasn't enough, that the story needed to go on, so I started writing Parts Two and Three. That's why it took an unexpectedly long time to complete.

In any case, I've rewritten (or perhaps completed) *The City and Its Uncertain Walls* in a fresh form, and honestly, I feel relieved. For so long this work had felt like a small fish bone caught in my throat, something that bothered me.

For me—both as a writer and as a person—this little bone was very significant. Rewriting the work for the first time in some forty years, and stopping by *that town* again, made me acutely aware of this.

As Jorge Luis Borges put it, there are basically a limited number of stories one writer can seriously relate in his lifetime. All we do— I think it's fair to say—is take that limited palette of motifs, change the approach and methods as we go, and rewrite them in all sorts of ways.

Truth is not found in fixed stillness, but in ceaseless change and movement. Isn't this the quintessential core of what stories are all about? At least that's how I see it.

Haruki Murakami
December 2022

A Note About the Author

Haruki Murakami was born in Kyoto in 1949 and now lives near Tokyo. His work has been translated into more than fifty languages, and the most recent of his many international honors is the Hans Christian Andersen Literature Award, whose other recipients include Karl Ove Knausgård, Isabel Allende, and Salman Rushdie.

A NOTE ON THE TYPE

This book was set in Monotype Dante, a typeface designed by Giovanni Mardersteig (1892–1977). Conceived as a private type for the Officina Bodoni in Verona, Italy, Dante was originally cut for hand composition by Charles Malin, the famous Parisian punch cutter, between 1946 and 1952. Its first use was in an edition of Boccaccio's *Trattatello in laude di Dante* that appeared in 1954. The Monotype Corporation's version of Dante followed in 1957. Although modeled on the Aldine type used for Pietro Cardinal Bembo's treatise *De Aetna* in 1495, Dante is a thoroughly modern interpretation of the venerable face.

Composed by North Market Street Graphics
Lancaster, Pennsylvania

Printed and bound by Berryville Graphics
Berryville, Virginia

Designed by Anna B. Knighton and Chip Kidd